DUNGEONS JUST WANNA HAVE FUN

DUNGEONS JUST WANNA HAVE FUN

BOOK 1

Christopher Hall
aka Maxlex

Podium

To the guys at SAGA, who taught me everything about being a murderhobo.

Copyright © 2024 by Christopher Hall

Cover design by Andrew Clark

ISBN: 978-1-0394-6518-3

Published in 2024 by Podium Publishing
www.podiumaudio.com

Podium

DUNGEONS JUST WANNA HAVE FUN

CHAPTER ONE

Somebody Got Murdered

Anton was having a bad day. The worst, perhaps, in his relatively short life so far. Now he was injured and running for his life. Arguably, things were looking up.

If I can just make it to the cave, he thought desperately. He could faintly hear the sound of clashing blades ahead of him. With luck, the laughter and jeers from the men following him would prevent them from hearing the same.

He almost blacked out before reaching the threshold. His vision wasn't working properly, and the cave opening wasn't lit. He stumbled as he entered the first room.

Tall for a natural cave, the ceiling was about twenty feet high, dimly lit by a glow that came from the walls. A large smooth platform was revealed by the light, raised about two feet from the ground. Behind it was his goal, a dark entrance farther into the dungeon.

On the platform were two animated skeletons fighting frenziedly with sword and shield. They did not react to his entrance, continuing their eternal fight. For his part, he ignored them as well, stumbling around the platform to get to the entrance. However, the rough ground betrayed him, and he fell with a grunt.

Scrabbling at the ground trying to get up, he heard to his horror the sound of voices behind him.

"So 'dis is where ya got ta," sneered an unfamiliar voice in a thick accent. Anton managed to turn himself over. At least he'd see the ones who killed him.

The courl who had spoken was distracted, though, looking at the skeletons. He said something to the others in their own language, and they laughed. The other two were human, with lighter skin than Anton's own.

Is this a chance? Anton wondered. He might as well try. If he could get farther into the dungeon, they might get caught in a trap that he could evade with his knowledge of the place. The skeletons were of no use, he knew. They were just level one, and decorations besides. They never left their platform or ceased their continuous combat.

The courl leapt up on the platform in a single bound, to the hoots and jeers of his fellows. Anton started crawling towards the exit, so he didn't see what happened next, but he heard a strangled gurgle that made him turn to take a look.

Gurgle? he thought. *Skeletons don't gurgle.*

Behind him, everything had frozen for a moment. The skeleton's rusty blade was somehow stuck in the cat-man's throat, and everyone's eyes were on it. Then the skeleton stepped back and withdrew his weapon, allowing the corpse to fall to the ground.

Recovering from their surprise, the other two soldiers leapt to the attack. Anton was still frozen.

That couldn't have happened! Those men are level twenty at least!

The rumor was that the Elitran Empire required its soldiers to have reached level twenty before they could join a raiding party, and there had been enough people with a long-range Identify skill to confirm it. And yet, as Anton watched, the skeletons calmly dodged the wild swings of the humans and thrust their swords with unerring accuracy into the narrow gaps between the raiders' partial plate mail.

Anton gaped at the sight for a moment more, frozen as the skeletons turned to him. Something about the smooth deliberateness of their movement made their fixed grins all the more terrifying.

Well, I guess I'll die to the dungeon after all, he thought, feeling consciousness slipping away from him. *Better that than being killed by a raider* was his last thought as he slipped into the gentle darkness.

"Hey! Wake up, asshole!"

It was the incongruity of the voice that woke him as much as anything else. Why was he hearing a woman's voice? He pried his eyes open to see something else that defied explanation.

Standing over him was a beautiful young woman, dressed in a strange garment. Something like a silk doublet, but *not*. The material was shiny like silk, but Anton had never seen a doublet like that. It was paired with loose pants made of the same material, and Anton's first thought was that it was entirely inappropriate gear for a dungeon.

The girl herself had shockingly white skin and brilliant blue eyes, contrasting with her midnight black hair. She was short and looked quite frail, with a delicate face that looked as if it might have been molded out of porcelain. There was nothing delicate about her expression, though, as she was sneering with disdain.

"Come on! You don't have to go home, but you can't stay here," she said.

"What? Who?" he managed to croak out. Looking around, he saw that the skeletons were still there, having taken a seat on the edge of the platform. Eyeless faces grinned down at him.

"I'm the landlord, that's who!" the girl exclaimed. "I'm kicking you out!"

Anton shook his head and immediately regretted it. "You can't own a dungeon, everyone knows that."

"I *am* the dungeon, fool! Who else would I be?" Despite her disdainful words, Anton was getting the feeling that she was enjoying this.

"I think that you're a very confused young woman," he said firmly. "Dungeons can't talk, and they aren't cute girls."

At that, the girl smiled, then she looked to the side into empty space. "No, I'm not going to kick him." There was a pause, and then she continued. "I think I'm above petty violence." Another pause. "Yes, but I have people to do that. Speaking of which."

She glanced over at the skeletons. "Lazybones, get over here and show this guy who he's talking to."

With a shrug—*A shrug?* Anton thought in disbelief—the skeletons slid off the platform and stood behind the girl as she faced Anton. Flanking her on each side, they fell into an unusual pose, tilting their shoulders and raising their elbows high. Their hands—hand bones—pointed at the girl from each side, as she crossed her arms and tilted her head.

"The name's Kelsey, asshole. I'm the dungeon of these here parts."

"Anton," he replied automatically, before shaking his head again. "The dungeon *can't* be called Kelsey."

"Why not? You know a lot of dungeons?"

"Uh . . ." There *was* a name for this dungeon, but with only one local dungeon, they'd always just called it "the dungeon." Anton racked his failing brain for the name but came up blank. Well, not entirely blank. "I think there's a dungeon down south that's called the *Ravening Dark*."

The girl scowled. "Well you can call me the *Hungering Abyss* if you really want, but Kelsey rolls off the tongue a lot better, let me tell you."

"Fine," he sighed. "You're Kelsey." He glanced again at the skeletons, still in their pose. If she could really control them, didn't she have to be the dungeon? Or a necromancer? He'd never heard of one outside of stories, but magic did exist . . .

"Great, pleased to meetcha. Now that we've got that out of the way, how about you get out."

"I can't even get up! And even if I could, if I go outside, I'm sure to get slaughtered."

"Oh, yeah, I was going to ask you about that. No delvers for three days, and then you start killing each other on my doorstep? What's up with that?"

Anton goggled at the woman before realizing that if she *was* the dungeon, or even if she had just been squatting in it for a few days, she would have no idea of what was going on.

"It's . . . it's a raid," he finally said. "Or an invasion. The Empire's raided us before, but never with the sort of numbers that could breach our walls."

"An invasion, huh? All new management, same as the old lot? How does this Empire treat dungeons?"

"I don't know?" he answered, but she wasn't listening to him.

"Ugh, sounds gross. We should do something about it." There was another pause.

"Um, who are you talking to?" he asked. Kelsey held up one finger.

"That's Mel," she said, after a pause. "She's my dungeon fairy, so I guess only I can see or hear her."

"What's . . . a dungeon fairy?"

"Why shouldn't I tell him?" Another pause. "Well, it's not *my* sacred charge. I bet you could unlock something that would let him see you, and then you could tell him that yourself."

Kelsey's eyes tracked something invisible moving away. "Yeah, that's what I thought." She returned her gaze to Anton. "I don't think she likes humans very much."

"Why not?"

"If I had to guess, it's because humans killed all her friends?"

"We did?"

Kelsey shrugged. "When a dungeon dies, its fairy lives on, to guide the next dungeon to get created. She won't say how long she's been doing this, but I get the impression that she had a long list of dungeons that she helped before me."

"Oh." Anton had never thought of a dungeon as something that *could* be a friend, but now he was feeling bad on behalf of his race. No one he knew had killed a dungeon, but he knew that humans did destroy them when they were inconveniently placed or got too dangerous to be near human settlements. "I'm sorry."

Kelsey snorted. "Apologize for your own crimes, worry about your own life. Speaking of which . . ."

She crouched down over him, looking directly down at his face. "You seem to be having a bit of a dying problem."

"Yeah," Anton admitted. He wasn't sure how bad his wounds were, but now that he'd stopped moving, tiredness was crashing over him.

She winked and waved a bottle in front of his face. A healing potion. A potion that had just appeared out of nowhere. He tried to reach for it, but his arms were too weak.

"Uh-uh, nothing in this world comes for free."

"You're not going to help out of common human decency?" he asked weakly.

"Not a human, remember?"

"What do you want then? It's not like I've got gold to tempt a dungeon."

"It's pretty simple, really. I want to go out and see what's going on, maybe do something about it."

"You'll help us?" Even as he said it, his hope faded. She'd *just* said that she didn't help for free.

"Helping is more of Mel's thing," Kelsey said, giving a little chuckle. "It's never been one of my core competencies."

Anton decided to save his strength and not respond. Kelsey frowned and started speaking more seriously.

"I need a guide," she said. "So here's my deal. You'll take me where I want to go, advise me on what I need to know. And I'll save you."

"Not like I have much of a choice," Anton sighed.

"One thing you should know, though. I count as an otherworldly entity, like a demon or fae. So bargains made with me are *enforced*, on both sides of the deal."

That made him pause. "You're a demon?" He would have reacted more strongly at the revelation, but moving was far too difficult at the moment.

"No. No! We just share a few similarities. Just that one, as far as I'm aware."

Anton sighed. "I still don't have a choice."

"There's always a choice, kid." The phrase sounded incongruous coming from that face, but for the first time, Anton started to think that she actually might be the dungeon that had stood outside of town for longer than he'd been alive. "If all the other choices suck, blame your life decisions, not me."

"I guess. But I still agree. Do we shake hands or something?" Then he groaned, as something took hold of him, an immaterial force that bound his entire body for just a moment.

Kelsey snorted and started feeding him the potion. "You feel it that way too, huh? Yeah, the bargain is struck. Enjoy your recovery."

She said it without laughing, but Anton was pretty sure it was a joke. He was aware of the pain that forced healing caused, but he'd never recovered from such grievous wounds before. He hissed between clenched teeth as the pain started to build.

"Well, no need for you to stay on the floor," Kelsey said. Somehow pulling a stretcher out of nowhere, she called over to her minions. "Get this guy on the stretcher and take him down to the fifth level."

Once again the eerily grinning skeletons approached. Anton would have flinched, but the pain was all-encompassing and it was all he could do to lie still as they manhandled him onto the canvas and started lugging him farther back into the dungeon.

The really bad thing about potions was that they kept the patient fully alert and aware as part of the full healing process. Anton would have given anything to fall back into blissful unconsciousness, but it was denied to him by the same magic that was knitting his flesh back together.

"You're not screaming," Kelsey said, walking alongside him. "I appreciate that. There should be an hour's worth of healing in that. When you're done, we'll get some food into you and then you can get some rest. We'll leave in the morning."

Anton wanted to glare at her, but this really was helping him. An hour-long potion was as powerful as Anton had ever heard a potion of being. It should restore him completely, no matter how bad his injuries had been. Eventually.

CHAPTER TWO

A New Day

W hat is this stuff? It looks like food but . . ." Anton trailed off, at a loss to describe what he was tasting.

Kelsey grimaced at her own, mostly untouched, bowl of what was supposed to be stew. "It's reprocessed mushrooms, basically. We don't have a lot of use for food around here."

Anton supposed that was true. The skeletons on this level certainly didn't need any. "Does 'reprocessed' mean take all the taste out? Because I've eaten mushrooms before."

"Not dungeon ones, you haven't." Anton blanched and started to gag. Kelsey waved reassuringly in response. "Don't worry, it's perfectly safe. Reprocessing in this case means, first, taking out the poison. After that, it means making them look like food."

She paused, considering. "I suspect the taste was removed along with the poison, but the rest of it didn't help. Eat up anyway. It's filling and healthy, and even hot."

Anton looked at her suspiciously but continued with his meal. He was hungry—healing demanded a lot from a person's reserves. Dungeon fungi—in this dungeon anyway—were renowned for their quick-acting and painful poisons. If he had taken one of them, he'd be dead already.

"Um," he said after a few mouthfuls, another question in mind. "I've been to level five before, but . . ."

"It wasn't like this?" Kelsey asked. He nodded and looked around again. Level five was skeletons, but not *maid* skeletons. He'd just been waited on by a pair of them. They curtsied, they had maid uniforms—right down to the little bonnets tied to their creepily grinning skulls. He'd caught glimpses of cook skeletons working in the kitchen as the meals came out. He'd seen other uniforms on his way in, but he'd been too distracted by the pain to identify them.

Skeletons didn't normally come with clothes. There were some that had armor, which made for a nasty fight but a good loot drop. He'd never heard of ordinary clothes being worn.

Kelsey shrugged. "Don't assume that you've seen all of a level just because you've found the way down."

"I thought the guild had mapped out all the secret doors, at least down to level twelve."

"They found most of the secret doors," Kelsey said with a grin. "They haven't found *any* of the *super* secret doors."

"I see," Anton lied.

"This area is for hospitality," Kelsey explained. "I thought I might have a use for it, and eventually I was right, even if it did take forty years."

"Is that why they're not attacking me?"

"Well, partly that. Also, you're with me, and also also you're bonded to me. I doubt the monsters see you as an outsider anymore."

Turning away from him, she addressed the empty air. "No we're not going now, he needs to rest first. We'll go in the morning."

She paused and listened to the air again.

"I know I said it was important."

She paused once more.

"Well, we got the important details of what was going on, right?" She glanced at Anton again. "If it's a raid, they'll have gone by morning, and if it's something more serious, we can address it during daylight hours."

Anton slumped, suddenly remembering that this meal hadn't been the worst part of his day. *Going back? I guess I have to, don't I?* he thought to himself.

Kelsey seemed to notice his sudden melancholy. "Girls, I think Anton's eaten all that he's going to. Can you get him to bed?"

Anton's strength seemed to have left him, so the skeleton maids assisted him to his feet, one of them supporting him as he left.

"Oh, don't let them get into bed with you," Kelsey called as she left. "They can't actually have sex, but they find the idea that someone might try *hilarious*."

Anton looked over his shoulder and then incredulously at the maids. The one in front waggled her hips suggestively. The motion made him realize that skeleton bones wouldn't support a dress that way, so she must have some sort of rigid frame underneath . . . just to let the dress hang properly.

Too weak to run away screaming, he let them lead him to his room. This part of the level, in contrast to the dusty stone halls that he remembered from level five, was lined with wooden floorboards and panels. The maids led him to a room with a bed, and just as Kelsey had predicted, they tried to get into it with him. After he pushed them away, they left. Like all skeletons, they were incapable of speaking, but he had the impression they were giggling.

Who knew this dungeon was so strange? was his last thought before slipping into sleep.

The next morning found Anton, after a breakfast that *looked* like bacon and eggs but *tasted* like a saltier version of last night's stew, headed back to town. Kelsey accompanied him, of course, still dressed in that impractical costume. She had added a pair of equally improbable short red boots to the ensemble—Anton wasn't sure, but he thought that she'd been barefoot last night.

"I'm not sure this is a good idea," he protested as they headed down the path. "You don't look like a Zamarran."

"That's fine, isn't it? I can be a traveler from the north," Kelsey replied. "It's not like anyone is going to mistake me for an Elitran."

That was true enough, Anton supposed. Elitran's humans had a lighter skin color than the darker brown shades of Zamarrans, but Kelsey's skin was so pale it looked as if the color had been drained out of her.

"Do you know any countries to the north? You'll need to give a name when people ask."

"Mel probably does." There was a pause before she said, "Chela. That should do."

Anton shrugged. He hadn't heard of it, but travelers from the north were rare. "Is Mel coming with us?" he asked instead.

"Nah, she has to stay in the dungeon," Kelsey said.

"Then how are you talking to her?"

Kelsey smiled. "I *am* the dungeon, remember? I'm in two places at once, so—whoa!"

The reason for Kelsey's exclamation was that they had moved out the copse of trees that shielded the dungeon's entrance from sight. Or from their perspective, the trees that had concealed the town that lay a short distance down the steep slope.

"It's so big!" Kelsey exclaimed. "It was just a village fifty years ago!"

"You visited back then?"

"No, the trees weren't here back then, I could see it from my entrance. Wow, things sure have changed."

"That they have," Anton said grimly. He was noting the breaks in the wall, the razed buildings and the fires that were still going. "Things can change a lot in a day."

"I guess," Kelsey said, watching him closely. "You've got friends, family down there?"

He sighed. "My family was on the wall. So was I, but I . . ." His voice trailed off, but he completed the sentence in his head. *Ran.*

"You survived," Kelsey said softly. "Something good is sure to come of that."

Rather than respond to that, Anton chose to change the subject. "So, you never explained about the skeletons."

"The skeletons? Which ones?"

"I think you called them the Lazybones?" he clarified.

"Oh, right." Kelsey paused for a bit as they walked downslope. "This is actually a bit embarrassing. Back when I was just a level one dungeon, those guys were my first monsters, guarding my first room. But . . . it took a while before anyone found me, so I went a long time before my first encounter. Those guys . . . they were supposed to be patrolling around the room, but they kept skiving off, finding ways out of my orders or outright ignoring them."

"Monsters can do that?"

"In the early days, I didn't have quite so tight a hold on things," Kelsey admitted. "It's easy enough to order monsters around when you're watching them, but making sure they stick, and that they get interpreted in the right way when you're not watching, is something you have to learn."

"I see."

"So eventually I got fed up with them. I told them to fight each other and not stop under any circumstances." She kicked at a small pebble on the path, avoiding looking at Anton, who was looking at her in disbelief.

"A while after *that*, we got our first invader. The first I knew about it was when they entered, of course, but that meant I couldn't change the orders while they were on that level. They were pretty surprised when they came in and got ignored. They poked at the monsters a bit, but then just left them alone and walked straight into the dungeon.

"I guess they passed the word around, because the next group just gawked at them and walked on by. I'd adjusted the orders by then so that they'd stop if attacked, but no one ever did."

"They were a bit of a talking point," Anton said. "People thought that it made our dungeon a bit unique." There had been a lot of speculation that they weren't monsters at all but some kind of animated feature.

"But wait," he said. "That wasn't what I meant. How did the skeletons kill those level twenty soldiers? They would have been elites, and the skeletons were level one!"

"Oh, that," Kelsey said dismissively. "Stats aren't everything." At his confused look, she explained further. "Levels are based on kills, but skills are based on actual practice."

"Wait, monsters can get experience, too?"

"Oh yeah, it just doesn't come up much since they lose it when they respawn. It's easier to just pay the cost for the base level you want."

"I'm still lost," Anton admitted.

Kelsey shrugged. "So those guys never got killed! They've been fighting against an evenly matched opponent, nonstop, for close on fifty years."

"Fifty years . . ." Anton said, trying to get his head around it.

"Humans get tired and need food and sleep. I doubt they average more than four hours a day of training. Those boys are as good as a human that's been training for three hundred years. Those 'elites' never stood a chance."

"I . . . skeletons . . . that's—" Anton stuttered, trying to get his thoughts under control. Another thought occurred to him, something he should have remarked on at the time. "They weren't in their usual spot when we came out."

"No," Kelsey pouted. "I can't have them do that just now. Since there were three soldiers, the experience was divided unevenly. Now one is level three, and the other is level four. They're not matched."

You could always respawn them, came the involuntary thought. He didn't waste breath speaking, though. Kelsey was odd in many ways, for a person and for a dungeon, but he doubted she'd throw away such a terrifying pair of monsters.

"After we left, I spawned some new skeletons and set them fighting," Kelsey continued. "They're pretty crap, though. I didn't want you looking at them. Hopefully, they'll get better before somebody actually looks at them."

"You can still do things in the dungeon when you're not . . . there?" Anton asked.

"I *am* there," Kelsey explained. "And I'm here as well. Don't worry too much about it, I get that it's hard for humans to grasp."

Anton wanted to object, but they had reached the gate to the city, which meant that they were in earshot of the guards. The gate was open. Yesterday, it had been opened by townsfolk fleeing, so it hadn't been destroyed like the gate to the west.

"Hey, Anton," one of the guards said. He knew them, of course, Jasper and Gerald. "You're looking . . . well?" Jasper continued.

Anton opened his mouth to speak, but the words wouldn't come. He knew these two had seen fighting yesterday. Given that they weren't heavily injured, they'd probably been on the inner walls, but still. They hadn't run.

"Healing potion," he eventually managed to mumble. It wasn't just that, though. He had been given new clothes this morning, replacing his blood-soaked rags, and his leathers had been patched up with methodical and precise stitching.

"Lucky," Jasper said. "Who's your friend?"

"I'm Kelsey!" Kelsey said brightly. "I'm a traveler from Chela, and I'm afraid I've found myself in your mess! Anton here was good enough to help me escape some raiders."

The guards looked surprised. "You picked a bad time to come south, ma'am. Were you travelling on foot all this way?"

"I *wasn't*, but . . . raiders," Kelsey said with a shrug. "They spoiled everyone's day yesterday."

"That they did." Jasper looked embarrassed. "Uh, Anton's a resident, so he's good to enter, but it's a silver to enter for travelers on foot."

"No problem, I have funds," Kelsey said, displaying a silver coin. Jasper took it and examined it curiously

"Local currency?" he asked. "Did you get that off Anton?"

"No, it's quite common in . . . that town just north of here."

"Cataca," Anton supplied, finally finding his tongue. Kelsey smiled at him.

"That's the one," she said. "I hear that they're made by a dungeon around here somewhere."

"You can talk to Anton about that, he knows it as well as anybody," the guard observed. "Well, welcome to Kirido. Sorry it's not looking its best."

CHAPTER THREE

Homeless

E ntering the town, they could see that the cleanup efforts had already begun. There was no sign of bodies in the streets, though cries coming from some ruined buildings suggested that the grisly task was not completed. The smell of smoke was still everywhere, but there weren't any fires visible.

"Where to first?" Kelsey asked. "Should we try to find your family?"

"What?" Anton exclaimed, startled. He'd been staring at the burned build-ings. "No . . . I know . . . my family are adventurers, so we were all on the wall. I—know what happened to them."

Kelsey gave him a long look. "All right," she said. "We can leave that until later. You'll want to check out your house then?"

"I thought I was taking you to places you want to see," he replied with some bitterness.

"Well, it's going to be a while before this place is ready for me to eat croissants on the boardwalk, so let's hold off on the tourist experience for now, okay? Show me your home."

"Sure." Anton started walking.

"Oh! Wait, there is something we need to do first." At her words, Anton turned around and looked at her expectantly. "We need to test out how the geas is going to function."

"Huh? What geas?" Anton said.

"Don't worry, it will be really simple," Kelsey said reassuringly. "You just stay here, and I'll go . . ." She looked around. "To that shop that still has a sign. Do you see it? I'll go there, stop for a moment, and then come back. You just need to stay here. Understand?"

"Yeah . . . but what's this going to test?"

"You'll see. Just remember, I'm going to come back. You just stay here." She patted him on the shoulder and started walking off.

Anton watched her go, puzzled. When she'd gotten about ten yards away, the thought bubbled up.

Is she going to leave me?

The idea was ridiculous in more than one way. Why would he care if she did? And hadn't she said that she would be right back? Nevertheless, as she continued to walk away, the feeling grew.

I'm going to be left all alone.

To die.

I'll die.

Before he knew it, he was running after her, catching up just as she reached the sign. "I'm here!" he gasped breathlessly. As soon as he caught up to her, he felt the fear fade away, to be replaced with embarrassment.

"What was that?" he asked, still gasping from his sprint. To her credit, Kelsey didn't laugh at him. A few passersby were looking at him curiously, and he flushed.

"It's hard to explain," Kelsey said, "And I wasn't sure it would work that way anyway. But now you've experienced it. You agreed to stay with me, right? That's how the agreement is *enforced*."

"I can't go more than ten yards from you?"

"Now that you know about it, you'll be able to resist it, to an extent."

Anton didn't know that he would. The geas had tapped into his fear, sending him back to last night . . . "How long?" he asked.

"Having trouble remembering what you agreed to?" Kelsey asked.

"I—no. I don't." While a lot of last night was blurred, their agreement was absolutely clear in his memory. Probably part of the *enforcement*.

"You'll take me where I want to go, advise me on what I need to know. And I'll save you."

"But that doesn't tell me how long the deal lasts."

"Yeah, it does." Kelsey grinned sheepishly. "Let's get moving, I want to be off the main street when you figure it out."

Anton started walking, mulling it over in his head.

"It doesn't say when it ends . . . so it doesn't end? Is that it?"

"That's about the size of it."

Anton's hand went for his sword before he remembered he'd lost it last night. "I made a deal that put me in *eternal slavery*?"

"Whoa there, kid! Let's have this discussion somewhere a bit more private."

She dragged him into an empty building that had been gutted by fire. Anton let her; he didn't want people to see him beat up what was apparently a young girl. Once they had some privacy, she turned and poked him in the chest.

"First of all. I can see you thinking that the deal ends if you kill me. And it does . . . but this body *isn't all of me*. If you kill me, all that will happen is you'll go running back to dungeon-me in a panic. Assuming I don't kill you because you pissed me off, you'll never get to leave."

Anton grimaced. That was probably correct. He wasn't going to get out of this that easily. Killing the dungeon . . . wasn't feasible, not without another forty levels. Or an army.

"Second. You're still free to do what you want, just restricted in a few significant ways. This deal could have been a *lot* worse for you."

"Why didn't you trick more out of me, then?" Anton asked. The rage was fading, replaced by a now familiar feeling of despair.

"I dealt for what I wanted," Kelsey said firmly. "And thirdly, part of the *enforcement* is that the deal has to be *fair*. Or it doesn't get made."

"How is eternal servitude *fair*?" Anton exclaimed.

"What did you trade it for?" Kelsey asked with a wry grin.

"My . . ." Anton groaned. "My life."

"Exactly. Now show me your home."

Anton's home still stood, but it wasn't habitable. The door had been smashed in and the place ransacked. The upper floor was a complete ruin, as the roof had caught fire. Like most of the houses in this district, the house had been brick and tile, but the roof timbers were still flammable. Collapsing the roof seemed to have put out the fire, so the house wasn't completely burned down, but it was ruined.

Anton picked through the rubble for a bit before giving up and collapsing against a wall. Kelsey let him mope.

"If it's all right with you," she said, "I can store all this stuff away somewhere safe, give it back to you when there's somewhere for you to put it."

Anton didn't object, so she started going through the house. Everything she touched disappeared. Burned beams, busted furniture, and all his remaining possessions. Anton watched them go and wondered if he would ever ask for them back.

"Whoops! Company." Kelsey stopped what she was doing and turned around, just as a familiar face came through the doorway.

"Anton?" Aris said when she saw him. "Anton! You're alive!"

She started to run towards him but stopped when she saw Kelsey. "Um, who . . . ?"

"Hi, I'm Kelsey," Kelsey said, sticking out her hand. Aris looked confused but held out her own in response. Kelsey grabbed it and started shaking it up and down.

"I'm very pleased to meet you! Are you a friend of Anton's?"

"Uh," Anton interrupted. "Sorry, Aris, she's used to . . . northern customs."

He turned to Kelsey and said, "Here, we hold our hands palm out to greet someone."

"Oh?" Kelsey said, letting go of Aris's hand.

"Yeah, like this." He held out his hand, and Aris matched the gesture. "If you know them, you can touch the palms; otherwise, you just want to hold them apart." They touched palms, and he smiled involuntarily at the contact. "Are you all right, Aris?" he asked.

Her face fell. "My parents came through all right, but . . . they took my little sister."

"Oh no, not Cheia." He reached out and pulled her into an embrace. She put her face against his chest and started sobbing.

Kelsey didn't interrupt, but she did take a few steps to put herself in his line of sight and gave him a quizzical look.

"Slavery," he said flatly. "They take the younger women as slaves."

Kelsey pursed her lips and frowned. She didn't say anything as she watched Aris cry for a while. The young woman was taller and carried significantly more curves than Kelsey. Her hair was shoulder length and quite richly curled. Like most of the locals, she had dark brown skin, but her eyes were a brilliant green.

"So . . ." Kelsey eventually said, once Aris had quieted. "Are you two together or . . ."

The two jumped apart, Aris apparently remembering that Kelsey was there. Anton was the one to answer while Aris stayed silent.

"Uh, well, we have an understanding," he said, embarrassed. "I'm still paying off my parents' loan for my adventuring equipment and getting money saved up for a home . . ." He trailed off, realizing that his plans had been overturned by recent events.

Aris spoke up suddenly. "Your parents! I was looking for you because of . . ." She stopped, choking up, and tried again. "Your family is in the temple. They . . . recovered them, and they're waiting for you before doing the final rites."

Anton staggered back from her. "No . . . I'm not ready, I'm not . . ."

"They can't wait forever," Aris said reproachfully. "There are so many waiting."

"I think we're going to have to drag him," Kelsey said thoughtfully. "C'mon, Anton, you know you'll regret it if you don't say goodbye."

She grabbed him by the arm. He tried to pull away, but what seemed like a casual grip was surprisingly strong. Aris grabbed his other arm, clinging on to him as she had before.

"Show me your family, Anton," Kelsey said, and he felt his resistance fade away.

CHAPTER FOUR

Material Girl

N ow this is more like it," Kelsey said, sinking her teeth into a leg of cold roasted chicken. "Better than breakfast, right?"

Anton agreed but picked at his own meal without much enthusiasm. They were eating in Kirido's best inn. Anton's family had been fairly well off, but this inn catered to the rich merchants that passed through. Few locals could afford to eat here except on very special occasions.

Stout walls and hired help had kept the inn relatively intact. There was damage to the exterior, but inside the biggest difference was the lack of customers. According to the innkeeper, the merchants that had been trapped there during the raid had left with haste as soon as they were able. Many of them had lost their cargo, but as long as they had their lives, they could start again when they got back to their hometowns.

Kelsey had dragged him away from Aris after the funeral rites were done. She'd said that she needed him as a guide for some errands she had in town.

"So what do you think, should we stay here for the time being?" she asked. "I don't think your house is going to be habitable soon."

Anton suppressed the pang he felt when she said "his house" and focused on the real issue. He looked around and lowered his voice.

"We're . . . going to have to sleep in the same room, aren't we?" he asked. They had experimented with the geas while waiting for things in the temple. It wasn't *just* distance that triggered his anxiety. Walls, doors, anything that separated them would cause the fear to build.

"I guess so, unless you've got a better idea." Kelsey dug into her meal, far more concerned with flavors than the conversation.

"It's just . . . a man and a woman, sharing the same room . . . it gives a certain impression."

Kelsey shrugged. "If it's sex that you're talking about, sure, we can do that. It's on my to-do list."

"That's not—" Anton checked himself before he attracted everyone's attention by yelling. He could feel his cheeks getting warm as he continued, more quietly.

"I already have . . . someone special. What am I supposed to tell Aris?"

Kelsey looked at him calmly. "Well, you're going to have to decide that for yourself." She held up a hand to forestall a response and continued. "I'm not about telling you how to live your life. So far, you've decided to keep my nature to yourself. I guess you figure spilling the beans would end badly for everyone— and you'd end up back in the dungeon."

Anton nodded glumly. Starting a fight between Kelsey and . . . everyone else probably ended with Kelsey's body dead. The other possibility was worse.

"Well, that's convenient for me," Kelsey said, "and I appreciate it. But . . . you have to tell Aris something, and it may as well be the truth. You can probably convince her of the necessity to keep quiet."

Anton nodded slowly. He thought Aris would probably understand why they needed to keep quiet.

"Plus, this way, you can also explain why I have to be there when you have sex," Kelsey continued blithely.

Anton groaned and shrank back into his chair. "Why . . . why would you even say things like that?"

"Hey, who knows? Maybe she's into it." Kelsey gave him a speculative look. "Maybe you are."

"How do you even know about sex?" Anton complained.

"Oh, adventurers do it in the dungeon all the time," Kelsey said with amusement. "There are a few alcoves where the monsters don't wander, so they find one of those and . . ."

"Stop! I don't want to hear it." Anton exclaimed.

"Fine, fine," Kelsey conceded. "Can you do me a favor and get us a room?"

"Why me?" Anton asked suspiciously. He was still resisting the obvious necessity of them rooming together.

"Because if I do it, he'll be bound to the contract. Which wouldn't be *bad*, exactly, but he'd feel it, and I don't want to get a reputation." She slid three coins across the table. Gold coins.

"Are you crazy?" Anton whispered urgently. "That's three hundred silver . . . even the best room here wouldn't cost more than three!"

"That's actually useful information," Kelsey said thoughtfully. "I thought it'd be, like, thirty. But I want you to establish a tab with the guy."

"Why? And why so much?"

"Look. Times are tough for you guys right now. The innkeeper has lost patrons and staff, and the place has gotten damaged. How is he going to provide a good experience to me if he's worried about his cash flow?"

"This is about . . . you getting a good meal?"

"Lots of *great* meals, hopefully. I haven't had a body to experience life with since—since forever, basically, so I want to get as much good stuff in as possible."

"This much, though . . . it could take you a year to run through this much of an advance."

"Wanna bet?" Kelsey asked, grinning. "I've got a lot of extravagant demands to make."

Anton followed Kelsey glumly towards the docks. The room key he'd just received was occupying his thoughts, or more accurately the look the innkeeper had given him. A local boy, rooming with a mysterious, rich stranger. Anton could have dealt with a judging look, but instead, the innkeeper's eyes had been approving. And more than a little jealous.

It wasn't the first such look he got as they went around town. Kelsey had him deal with the merchants they interacted with. Even without the enforcement to worry about, it was probably for the best. With exotic skin and flamboyant clothes, Kelsey would have been given short shrift in most of the businesses around town. They much preferred dealing with him and ignoring the bizarre foreigner.

Kelsey's errands seemed trade related, as she started throwing more money around than Anton had ever seen in one day before. First, she had leased an empty warehouse from a recently widowed owner. Makasa had been glad for the money. She was in the position of having to take over the business or sell it, and the income would help her out either way.

Anton was glad he could help someone he knew, but he was suspicious. "Why did you pay so much?" he asked as they moved on to the next errand.

"It's not like I'm short of funds." Kelsey shrugged. "I don't have *unlimited* gold, but I have enough that my main worry is setting off inflation."

"What's inflation?"

Kelsey stopped and turned to look him dead in the eyes. "There are some secrets held by dungeons, young man, that are too terrible for you to know." Then she smirked and went back to walking.

Their next stop was an actual ship. The raiders had come by ship but had actually landed down the coast and attacked on foot. The ships in the harbor had pulled out of the docks but stayed in the safety of the harbor. Now that the raiders had left, it should be safe for them to sail out, but there was still a lot of fear of piracy. At least that was how Captain Baker had explained it.

"No one wants to lose good money when they think we're going to be sunk!" the Kabiman exclaimed.

"That's a shame; the town is in need of a lot of things," Kelsey said sympathetically.

"And we have a need to sail!" Baker agreed. "But we have no money to be buying cargo."

Kelsey nodded thoughtfully. "We're actually looking to ship some things in . . . do you think you could get some of the things on this list—fairly quickly?"

She produced a sheet of paper, which the captain carefully clasped in his tripartite claw and brought up to his face.

"Most of this, maybe all of this, three or four days," he replied. "Expensive, though." He looked at Anton. "We?"

Kelsey smiled. "We're partners. Let's talk details."

Anton wanted to tune out the resulting discussion, but Kelsey kept him as part of it, maintaining the fiction that he was part of the deal. Fortunately, smiling and nodding were all that was required from him.

"I'm surprised you could read a Kabiman's colors," Anton said as they walked back into the town. "I thought it was a local skill." With their exoskeletons, Kabimen couldn't make facial expressions, but if you knew what to look for, the color of their shell changed to match their emotions.

"Kabimen came to the dungeon, like anyone else," Kelsey replied. "Though one thing I didn't see was people like that." She pointed at another Kabiman.

It took Anton a second to see what she was talking about. The person she was pointing at seemed normal to him. "Oh, right. There's a variation they call the war form, which is probably what you're used to seeing. Like the captain, their shell is reinforced with ridges, and one claw gets bigger. They tend to take warrior-type paths."

"Huh," Kelsey said thoughtfully. "So anyway, Kabimen came to the dungeon, so learning their colors came at around the same time that I learned your language."

Something about that statement seemed wrong to Anton, but before he could articulate why, Kelsey looked around and decided on a new destination.

"Let's check out the Adventurers Guild. I want to see how they've been managing the local dungeon."

"Sure thing," Anton said and started leading them in the right direction. "Are you sure, though? Aren't adventurers . . . your natural enemy?"

"Mm, maybe. It's a risk. What does your Identify skill say about me?"

"My skill?" Anton asked, taken aback. It was a bit rude to use Identify on someone you knew . . . but he had to admit to being curious.

"Kelsey" (Level ??)
Class: Necropolis (Rare)

That was surprisingly normal, all things considered. Not being able to see her level meant that she was at least twice his. So Tier Three or more. He'd never heard of her class before, but that was probably to be expected. He passed on what he saw.

"I guess the jig is up if they Identify me, then," Kelsey said, scowling. "My understanding, though, is that only adventurers get an Identify that works on everything."

"*Delver's Discernment* isn't the only such trait, but it's the most common," Anton agreed. "Maybe it's different for other classes, but adventurers tend not to use *Discernment* on other people."

Anton paused. "But . . . I have used it on a few people, and I've never seen anyone's name in quotes like that before."

Kelsey's eyes narrowed. "Someone's being an asshole," she said flatly. "I have an idea who, but there's not much we can do about it."

Anton stared at her for a few moments. Was she talking about a god? It was generally supposed that the gods were responsible, in some way, for how traits worked . . . and for dungeons as well.

CHAPTER FIVE

Bizarre Love Triangle

S o did you still want to go to the guild?" Anton asked. They had rounded a
corner and the building was right in front of them. The big "Adventurers
Guild" sign was a big giveaway.

"Sure, why not? Let's live dangerously," Kelsey said and entered the building.

Anton explained the main areas as Kelsey paused at the entryway to look
around.

"The main counter is on the right," he said, pointing. "That's for registration, banking, and general guild business. Right in front of us is the guild store."

The store was separated from the main open area by a large, wide counter
and a half-height gate. Sellers went to the counter, while buyers could go through
and browse the merchandise under the watchful eye of the on-duty shopkeeper.

"They buy dungeon stuff and they sell equipment," he said. Kelsey grinned
at him.

"I'm familiar with the stuff," she said brightly.

"Right," he said awkwardly. "Over on the left is the job board and the bar."

It was a little early in the afternoon for drinking, especially with how the
town was right now, but there were a few determined drinkers sitting at tables.
Kelsey glanced at them but turned her attention to the other side.

"You can introduce us, right?" she asked Anton, indicating the woman
behind the registration desk.

"Sure," Anton said warily, and they made their way over. "Ms. Mal, this is
Kelsey. She's . . . a traveler from the north."

The woman smiled at Anton. She looked to be in her late thirties and had dark hair bound in a tight bun. "Come on, Anton, you're not a kid anymore. It's just Liat."

"Uh, sure," Anton said. "Kelsey, this is Liat Mal, the administrator who runs this place."

"Pleased to meetcha," Kelsey said, remembering to hold out her hand properly.

Liat returned the greeting and then said, "You picked an interesting time to visit our town, Kelsey. Will you be staying long?"

"Oh, a few weeks at least, I think," Kelsey replied. "I had some questions about how your guild operates."

"Were you thinking of signing up?" As she spoke, Liat pulled some papers from below the desk and placed them on the desk.

"Maybe. What would be involved with that?"

"There are no real requirements for signing, but if you want access to the dungeon, you'll need to be tested to make sure you're capable."

"Oh, you control access to the dungeon? I didn't think it was fenced off."

Liat grimaced. "Well, perhaps 'control' is a bit strong. Under the laws of the Kingdom, dungeons belong to the crown, and while they can be administrated by the local nobility, they can't be owned by anyone. If we were to build something to control access, it would be seen as encroaching on the King's privileges."

"Ah, I see," Kelsey said, nodding.

"Nevertheless, since the guild exists to manage the risks posed by the dungeon, the Baron has granted us certain rights with regard to it. The gate guards on that side won't let you out if they think you're going to the dungeon without a pass, and under normal circumstances, there are patrols that pick up people trying to sneak in."

She frowned at Anton. "Anton should have been able to tell you all this," she said.

"Well, I wanted a second source," Kelsey explained. "I mean, he didn't even know the name of the dungeon."

"I know it!" Anton protested. "It just slipped my memory at the time,"

"We call it the *Dungeon of the Endless Battle*, after the fighting skeletons at the entrance," Liat said. She looked at Anton. "I hope you'll forgive his lapse; he's had a hard time recently. We all have."

"Of course," Kelsey said. "So you test people for competence?"

"We evaluate applicants based on their path and level and test their skill in fighting, evasion, and trap detection."

"I see," Kelsey said evenly. "And are there any other benefits to joining?"

"The dungeon is the main one," Liat admitted. "There's the shop and the bar, which are only available to members. We try to make the prices a bit better than what you'd get on the street."

"Oh yeah! Mind if I check out what dungeon loot sells for?"

"Be my guest," Liat said, gesturing towards the shop counter. "Oh, Anton?" she called, as he was about to follow Kelsey. "We've actually got something to discuss."

"Yes, ma'am," Anton said, glancing over his shoulder at Kelsey.

"Your parents," Liat said heavily. Anton looked stricken and turned back to face her. "They had an account here with us. Naturally, you were listed as one of the beneficiaries. The only beneficiary, now."

"Right. I . . . uh . . . I should . . ." Anton looked lost.

"You don't have to do anything now," Liat reassured him. "It's all been handled, the money has been transferred to your account already. You'll have inherited the house as well."

"What's left of it . . ." Anton muttered.

"Well, there's plenty of funds now to get it repaired. You and Aris can—" She broke off, as Anton just looked more upset. She glanced over at Kelsey, who was carefully examining a sheet of prices across the room. "Whatever you decide. I know your parents would have wanted this to be the start of something new for you."

"Thanks," Anton said. "Really, I—I just can't . . . Thanks." He turned away and went over to Kelsey.

"I can't believe this! They're buying bones at five copper for ten pounds!"

"Makes good fertilizer," the shopkeeper said, unamused by Kelsey's antics. "Already dried out and cleaned."

"Can we go now?" Anton asked wearily. Kelsey looked at him closely.

"Yeah, sure. Can I keep this?" she asked the shopkeeper, who nodded dourly. "C'mon, let's go."

The rest of the afternoon was spent wandering around the few shops that were open for business. Kelsey bought a few things, each of which disappeared into nothingness as soon as they found a place where they were unobserved.

"Buying things is fine," she explained. "After the deal is done, I've got the thing, they've got the money, there's nothing to be *enforced*. It's only when there's a continuing obligation that I need to worry."

"Is that the reason I'm here? You need me to make deals for you?"

Kelsey stopped him and put both hands on his shoulders so he was forced to look down at her. "You've been a big help today, Anton, I don't want you to think any differently. Everyone treats me better because you're around."

She looked down. "I'm sorry about your family. I'd change that if I could. But I'm really glad it was you that staggered into my cave last night. I'm glad you chose to live."

"I . . ." Anton didn't know what to say. At that moment, he *had* wanted to live. Just for an hour or even a minute more. Saying he regretted it now seemed churlish.

"And now," Kelsey said, "I think we should invite your girlfriend to dinner at the inn."

Anton definitely regretted it.

Dinner was in their private room. Anton hadn't known that the White Selkie *had* private dining rooms, but rich merchants apparently liked to conduct some of their business in private. Kelsey—technically *Anton*—had asked for the best suite, so it came with the additional room.

Kelsey had expressed a preference for the common area—she liked to people watch, she said—but for this meal, she had opted for the private room.

"This is going to get ugly," she said, just before Aris was due to arrive.

"This was your idea," Anton said glumly.

"Leaving it until later would just make it worse. We'll give her a good meal, good wine—not too much wine—and put her in a good mood before you drop the—before you tell her."

"Right," Anton said. Was this what it felt like before the execution?

The first part did go well. The food and wine were as excellent as advertised. Neither Kelsey nor Anton could really detect any sign of Aris's mood improving, though. Finally, Aris took the initiative to say something.

"So is this where you tell me you're leaving me for some rich outlander?" she asked challengingly.

"No! Well . . ." Anton trailed off. Despite rehearsing for this, he couldn't find the words he needed.

Kelsey saw him struggling and decided to step in. "Let's start with this. I'm a dungeon."

Aris blinked. "What?"

"*The* dungeon, in fact, the one up the hill. Circumstances aligned, and I was able to form a dungeon avatar, which is a body that I can wander around with while still remaining a dungeon."

Aris blinked again, and then looked at Anton. "What is she talking about?"

Anton waved vaguely at Kelsey. "It's . . . true."

"I've never heard of our dungeon . . . or any dungeon having an avatar thing," Aris said suspiciously.

"Well, it's not easy to do, let me tell you. You need to be at a fairly high level, and you need to convince . . . well, let's just say it's hard. I didn't have one until last night."

"And Anton had something to do with it," Aris said. It wasn't a question.

"Not directly, but he was involved in the circumstances. What he needs to tell you is that I saved his life."

"What? But he's fine!" She looked at Anton for confirmation, but he just sighed.

"I got injured on the wall. Lost my sword, saw my parents . . . I ran. The Elitrans . . . that damned courl . . . they found me. Chased me through the town, out into the hills. I thought I might lose them in the dungeon, but . . ."

"He'd lost a lot of blood," Kelsey continued for him. "Stopped moving and they caught him up."

"But you saved him," Aris said. "A dungeon, saving people."

"Oh, well, killing the Elitrans, that was all in a day's work," Kelsey said lightly. "But then I was left with this guy. He might have been dying, but there was no telling how long that was going to take. He wasn't going to be wandering into any traps, and I couldn't give orders to my monsters as long as there was someone alive on the floor."

"Wait, but you—" Anton said, remembering her orders to the Lazybones.

"An avatar is an exception," Kelsey said, grinning. "I can give orders to any monsters my avatar can see, regardless of whether the level is locked or they're outside of the dungeon."

Kelsey's grin grew wider. "And there was a mystery going on! No delvers for a while, and then these guys . . . *someone* wanted to know what was going on. Someone with the key that let me unlock this little feature that would solve the problem!"

"So why didn't you kill him?" Aris asked. "Isn't that what a dungeon would do?"

"I needed a guide." Kelsey shrugged. "So I healed him, but not for free."

"When I agreed," Anton said slowly, "it put a geas on me. I have to stay with her, take her where she wants to go." He'd planned to leave it at that, but to his surprise, the rest of his contract forced its way out of his mouth. "Advise her on what she needs to know."

"I don't understand," Aris said.

Kelsey started to speak, but Anton stopped her. He owed it to Aris to explain. "The geas means that I can't stay for more than a minute in a different room from Kelsey. I'm going to be following her around for the rest of my life."

"No," Aris breathed, horrified. "This can't be happening." She turned to Kelsey. "Why did you do this to us?"

"Would you prefer him to be dead? Because that was his other choice."

"You could have saved him! You didn't have to take him!"

She got up and took a swing at Kelsey, who took the clumsy blow without flinching.

"And why should I?" Kelsey replied coldly, standing as well. "I'm a dungeon. Killing people is what I do every day."

"I . . . you . . ." Aris fought for words. Then she glanced at Anton and burst into tears. "Why don't you kill me, then?" she cried and started to run from the room.

Kelsey was in the way, suddenly. Moving quickly, she intercepted Aris before she got to the door, gripping her by the shoulders.

"Is that it, then?" Kelsey asked, keeping her voice quiet, but speaking with intensity. "You're just going to give up on him?"

"No! I can't . . . I—" Aris struggled, but Kelsey's grip was unbreakable.

"You kids . . ." she said, half exasperated, half amused. "You love him, don't you? I know he loves you."

Aris just broke down into unintelligible sobs. "Here," Kelsey said. Without apparent effort, she moved Aris over to Anton. "Give your girlfriend a hug."

Anton did as instructed and enfolded Aris in his arms. She clung to him, still crying. He gave Kelsey a frustrated glare from over his girlfriend's head.

"Here's what we're going to do," Kelsey stated firmly. "You two are going to sleep in that bed tonight. You're *just* going to sleep, because you're such shy prudes, but that's a start."

"But—"

"Don't even start. Aris's parents aren't going to be expecting her back tonight, and I've seen *far* more intimate moments than two people hugging."

Anton tried to come up with an argument, but all he could find was "Where are you going to sleep?"

"Oh, I don't sleep. I'll just sit this body and focus on my other projects until morning. Now get on that bed before I put you there."

"Aris?" He looked down at her. She'd stopped sobbing and had moved on to looking embarrassed. "Is this all right?" he asked.

"My parents *did* say something about us being almost married already," she admitted.

"I *knew* this whole country couldn't be as uptight as you two," Kelsey muttered, loud enough to be clearly heard. "Place would have died out."

Aris turned around to glare at Kelsey again. "And you're just going to stare at us all night?" she asked.

"Not *at* you. I can't turn off the perceptions of this body, but I can focus on other things. Work on my projects."

"Projects? What sort of projects?" Anton asked. "A better kind of trap?"

"Right now, I'm mostly working on semiconductors," Kelsey replied airily. Aris and Anton looked at each other.

"What's a semiconductor?" Anton asked.

"That is the question, isn't it?" Kelsey said, suddenly more animated. "I mean, knowing it's silicon doped with impurities is all very well. But what impurities? How do you dope it? The whole thing has been a right pain, let me tell you."

"I didn't understand anything you just said," Anton said cautiously.

Kelsey waved in dismissal. "Yeah, it would take too long to explain. Years. You two focus on your own problems."

"All right," Anton said. "Good night, then."

"Good night."

CHAPTER SIX

Lessons in Love

As a baker's daughter, Aris woke before dawn. Her movements awoke the man beside her, despite her best efforts to untangle herself discreetly. Kelsey, of course, had been awake all along, and simply produced a lit lantern as Aris put her feet on the floor.

"Up early?" she asked brightly.

Aris looked at her warily, still not awake. "I've got to go," she said. "There's baking to do."

"Sure, sure." Kelsey held up the lantern. "You want this?"

Aris nodded. "Thank you," she said, looking for her shoes. They were, unfortunately in Kelsey's opinion, the only items she had taken off to go to sleep.

"So, you're feeling better?" Kelsey asked. "Less upset, more certain about how you want to be?"

Aris looked back at Anton. They *had* talked last night, in whispers, hoping that Kelsey wouldn't hear them. They hadn't figured anything out, but some things had been determined.

"I'm not giving up," she stated firmly. "I don't know what I'm going to do, but . . . I'm not giving up."

"Great!" Kelsey said, still chipper. "So as to *how*, there's something I want you to think about today."

"How?"

"How this is going to work," Kelsey explained. "So there are two options before you. Well, two categories of options. Given that I'm not going to go away, the pair of you can either get used to *ignoring* me or figure out how to *incorporate* me into your relationship."

"What? I don't . . . understand," Aris stammered. Anton was also looking confused and embarrassed.

"Look, I get that you're used to thinking of relationships as being between a man and a woman. But there are actually lots of combinations that are possible. Woman and a woman. Man and a man. And . . . combinations with more than two partners."

Aris just stared blankly at her. Kelsey sighed.

"Well, it's a process. Just think about it, okay?"

From the disturbed look on Aris's face, she *was* thinking about it. She didn't say anything as she took the lantern and left the room, pausing only to wave goodbye to Anton.

"All things considered, I thought that went fairly well," Kelsey said to Anton, now sitting up in bed.

"What . . . are you trying to do with all this—with Aris, I mean?" he asked.

Kelsey rolled her eyes. "I'm *trying* to help you two. If I'd known you were engaged, Anton, I'd—well, I probably would have still bound you. But I might have made the effort to reword the geas so you could get some distance."

Anton narrowed his eyes as his anger rose. "You could have made the effort anyway."

"Simple is best." Kelsey shrugged. "I didn't think it would matter. To be perfectly honest, I thought at the time that we'd be having sex by now."

"You—what—" Anton stuttered.

"Yeah, yeah, things didn't work out that way—but I thought it was a sure thing, you know? You're a twenty-year-old virgin, chained by fate to your more experienced savior, who happens to be occupying a"—she looked down at herself—"smoking hot body, if I do say so myself."

She looked amused at Anton's shocked face. "Don't try and tell me you hadn't had some thoughts in that direction," she said, smirking. "Now get your clothes off, it's time for a bath."

"What?" Anton had to admit that he did need a bath. However . . . "There are a few problems with that!"

"Oh? And what would they be?" Kelsey asked. Carefully selecting a spot, she caused a large washtub to appear from nowhere. "My facilities may be somewhat lacking, but I can manage a barrel and hot water. And we bought soap yesterday."

She placed her hand in the barrel and sloshing sounds emerged, along with some steam.

She's just going to call me a prude again, Anton thought, desperately trying to find a way out of this. "Shouldn't you go first?" he asked.

"Don't need to," Kelsey said nonchalantly. "Dungeon Inventory. Clothes go back in—and new ones come out." For just a second, she was naked in front of him. Before he could react, a different set of her strange garb was back on her body.

She had deliberately chosen a moment when he was looking at her, he thought. He glared at her, while he tried to suppress the part of him that wished she'd taken more time.

She grinned at him. "Dirt goes the same way, possibly the smallest and most useless Inventory item I've collected. Now . . ."

"Promise you won't look." Anton braced himself for the teasing.

"Sure," Kelsey replied. Anton looked up at her suspiciously. "What? It's not like you've got anything I haven't seen before. It does mean I can't wash your back, though."

"I can wash my own back, thanks."

"Fine," she said and sat down on a chair with her back to the bath. "Wash away, I won't look."

Anton watched her back for a moment but eventually decided to take her at her word. He got up and started to undress. It felt strange to do so with her in the room but he figured it was something he was going to have to get used to.

Kelsey had indeed provided soap, a washcloth, and a towel as well, so he got to work cleaning himself.

"Oh, I almost forgot," Kelsey said. He tensed, but she stayed facing away, tossing back some clothes. "I figure you'll want to keep your armor, but here's some fresh underclothes."

"Are those spider silk?" Anton asked, looking at the garments.

"Yeah."

"That's expensive."

"Not for me."

Anton supposed not. The spiders it came from were living in her after all. "Can you tell me about your Dungeon Inventory? Does it just make things out of nothing?"

"No? What gave you that idea? It's just a storage space that exists . . . outside."

"Outside of what?" Anton asked. This made for a nice distraction.

"Outside of everything. I can access it from anywhere within myself, and from this body. I can put things into it and take them out again later."

Anton had never understood where the bodies went; this must be the answer. But . . . "Where did you get a tub from?"

"I made it! Or, my skeletons did. Banging on planks and such."

"Why?"

Kelsey laughed. "Well, I happened to bind myself to a stinky boy, so I knew there would be some things I'd need. My skellies can whip up things pretty quickly."

"Do you magic up the wood, or does it come from the Haunted Forest?"

"You've heard about that? You never went that deep yourself. But yeah, while I'm limited to growing what seeds happen to fall in my cave, I can accelerate the growth and harvest the trees when no one is inside."

Anton grunted in reply. He had finished washing, so he got out and started drying himself. He picked up the boxers. They weren't dyed, but aside from that, they seemed like something a noble would wear. He pulled them on—a perfect fit. He tried not to think about why that would be so . . . but Kelsey had said that she had seen it all before. Was she speaking literally? Dungeons didn't have eyes, but she seemed aware of everything that went on inside her.

Deciding not to ask a question he didn't want the answer to, he pulled on the undershirt.

"Thank you for the clothes," he said, now pulling up his leather trousers. They were Tier Two gear, the most expensive thing he owned—though his new underclothes might beat that now.

"You are welcome! Now for today, I thought we'd finish cleaning up your home. Have you decided if you want to keep it?"

"I . . . still don't know." Anton sighed.

"That's fine, we still want to clean it up either way." She got up and went to the window. Dawn's first light was just breaking.

"Let's go, we've got a long day ahead."

By lunchtime, they had cleared out pretty much everything in Anton's house. Well, Kelsey had. Anton's contribution had been mainly playing lookout, as neither wanted anyone seeing Kelsey disposing of everything.

Before she was done, she came up to him. "Here," she said, holding out a scabbarded sword. "I noticed that you were missing yours."

Anton reached out hesitantly. "I lost mine on the wall . . . it was Tier Two with a sharpness enhancement. This is Dad's spare sword."

"Yours now," Kelsey said softly.

"I'm not sure if I should even bother," Anton said sadly. "I had a sword so I could delve . . . I doubt I'll be doing much of that in the future."

"Oh, I wouldn't be so sure. You still need to get levels, and what better way than killing skeletons?"

Anton gave her a puzzled look. "You'd be fine with that?"

"Fighting is what they do." Kelsey shrugged. "And they respawn. I used to really dislike adventurers when I still thought that they could kill me, but no one's gotten past the Dead Sea so far."

"You call it that, too?"

"I hear people talking . . . I know most of the names you have for things."

They finished up and went for lunch. Kelsey had apparently been making a list of all the foods she wanted to try and was going through it methodically.

Anton still didn't have much of an appetite. Afterwards, they visited the guild and spoke again with Administrator Liat.

"So I had some questions about the dungeon . . ."

"That's what I'm here for . . . but are you sure Anton can't answer them?"

"He's never been past level five, so it would all be secondhand."

Liat raised an eyebrow. "You don't think I've been down there, do you? My class is administrator, not adventurer."

"Well, sure, but you've been involved with collating all the information as it comes in, right? So you should be able to give a more organized impression. Anton's not great with details."

Anton took this slander with an expressionless face. Kelsey hadn't asked him about the dungeon, and he would have found it ludicrous if she did. It made no sense that she should be asking Liat about it, but all she'd told him was "I want to know what your guild knows about me."

Liat looked at the both of them and then sighed. "The first three levels of the dungeon are meant to imitate a crypt. The first level appears to be mostly natural, with sarcophagi in niches along natural tunnels. The sarcophagi contain zombies. Either opening the tomb or making too much noise will cause them to come out and hunt."

"So you can sneak through without fighting any of them?"

"To an extent. The treasure for the level lies in the coins left in the sarcophagi, so there's no profit to be made if you don't open them. And the passage to the next level is concealed in one of them. That's true for the next two levels as well—the passages are quite a tight fit, and are the reason why delvers here prefer flexible leather armor rather than steel."

"Anything useful from the corpses?" Kelsey asked.

"The zombies on this level don't leave anything behind when killed, except for the occasional core. The floor boss is a flesh golem—three corpses combined into one abomination."

Kelsey nodded along as Liat went through the entire dungeon, at least the levels that the guild had explored. Anton had to admit that after level five, his knowledge was somewhat sketchy. Liat described the skeleton levels, the spider caves, the revenant hive, and the Haunted Forest. Finally, she got to the twelfth level.

"So no one's actually beaten the Vampire Queen, and no one has found the boss of the thirteenth level—or if they have, they haven't come back."

Kelsey raised an eyebrow. "How did they get to the thirteenth if they didn't beat the boss?"

"The Vampire Queen can be bribed," Liat admitted, looking guilty. "The top-rated party made a deal with our lord to get two condemned criminals put in their custody. Somehow, they got them down to the twelfth level alive."

"They fed her?" Kelsey exclaimed, somehow managing to look shocked.

Liat nodded, looking a little sick. "The guild didn't authorize it, but they told us about it afterwards. She allowed them to pass once for each of their 'gifts.'"

"So what's the thirteenth level?" Kelsey asked.

"The Dead Sea," Liat said flatly. "The whole level is submerged and dark, and the passage to it is a slick-walled well about fifty feet deep. The Wyvern Scales did a quick scouting trip the first time and told us it was filled with undead fish and some kind of underwater zombies. You need to be able to breathe underwater and see in the dark to get anywhere—if you had a light source that worked underwater, it would attract too many monsters."

"Nasty," Kelsey said. "But not impossible for a top Tier Three party, I should think."

"They weren't discouraged," Liat admitted. "But they never came back from their second trip."

Kelsey cocked her head to one side. "What's that sound?" she asked.

Anton hadn't heard anything, but then it came again. Horns.

"Troops…" Liat said. "They sound like ours. Could those be the reinforcements?"

"Too late to do any good," Anton muttered.

"Let's go and see," Kelsey said, leading Anton out onto the main street. Liat stayed behind, left manning the counter, although many of her potential customers were also going outside to see what the commotion was about.

Taking advantage of the hubbub of the gathering crowd, Anton moved closer to ask Kelsey a question.

"Did you know about the Vampire Queen being bribed?" he asked quietly.

"Sure. Well, not about them being criminals," Kelsey said, speaking normally.

"Is that allowed? I thought everyone had to follow your orders?"

"Well, I do allow the intelligent ones a certain amount of discretion," Kelsey said. They were out on the main street now, and more horns were sounding from the gate. This was the gate that they had come through, not the hastily propped up remains on the other side of town.

"In Cheryl's case, I allowed it because I felt a bit sorry for her."

"Sorry for her? Wait—Cheryl?" Anton's parents had fought the Queen before they retired, and they'd told him that she was a sadistic predator. Once her superiority had been demonstrated, she would toy with a party, eventually separating one from the group and allowing the others to escape.

"She doesn't get visitors often, you know?" Kelsey continued on, oblivious to Anton's shock. "And she's *made* to want to drink blood. My mana can sustain her, but I can't relieve the craving."

"Why'd you make her, then?" Anton managed to ask. He'd let himself forget, he told himself. The cute girl in front of him was more than just a murderer; she *created* monsters designed to murder as many people as possible.

"Someone to talk to, mainly. Most undead are fairly limited conversationalists."

The troops had entered the town now, and Anton stood in silence watching them go by. There were some that cheered to see the cavalry unit trotting down the street, all bright colors and shining steel. But most of the crowd was like Anton. Not angry—they knew how long it took to ride from Bures, and these troops must have been riding hard. And for however long they stayed, they'd be an important protection against the raiders coming back. But the fact that they had been too late burned a hole in Anton's stomach as he watched them.

Kelsey watched them go by without any kind of emotion that Anton could see.

"No Tier Fours . . . but the leaders were pretty high. I don't think I've seen a level thirty-one here."

Anton twitched. She was using an Identify trait? As offenses against decency went, it rated rather lower than murder, but so far she hadn't done that in front of him.

"There aren't more than a handful of Tier Fours in the country," he told her. "We're a pretty small and out-of-the-way kingdom."

Kelsey nodded thoughtfully. "Hopefully they won't complicate matters too much. Do you think they'll stay long?"

"Probably until the walls are fixed?"

She grimaced. "Can't have everything, I guess."

CHAPTER SEVEN

Let's Make Lots of Money

O ver the next few days, Kelsey traded. She bought a wide variety of goods, all of which she had delivered to the warehouse. Some of the goods disappeared into her Inventory, while some were left lying around the warehouse. Then Kelsey started *producing* goods. Cut stone, lumber, and manufactured items all materialized out of nowhere.

She didn't start selling it until the first ship arrived back, only a few days after it left. Anton wasn't a merchant, but he had thought that most trade routes were longer.

"It's not about profit, Anton," Kelsey told him. "It's about maintaining cover."

"I don't know what that means."

"It's simple. People know that we're getting goods in and buying stuff here. They can assume that we're shipping it out to trade at a profit."

"Right . . ." Anton wasn't clear on how moving something to another town made it more valuable. His best guess was that it was a *Merchant Trait*.

"But they don't know *what* we're shipping out. So this can disguise the fact that some of this stuff is disappearing."

"I guess I can understand why you don't want people to know that," Anton admitted. "But why do you need all this stuff in the first place? Don't you just magic up what you need?"

"Monsters, I can make out of mana, once I unlock the patterns," Kelsey said. "But it's cheaper if I have the materials. Other stuff . . . like plants, I have to grow from seeds, and I'm limited to the seeds that enter the dungeon. Making stuff out of materials requires me to have stocks of that material."

"So all this stuff . . ."

"Seeds for more plant variety, foods so that everything doesn't have to be made of mushrooms, soaps, dyes that I don't know how to make. It's great stuff!"

Anton also talked with Aris. Not about their future. Kelsey advised him to leave that be until Aris was ready to talk about it. They chatted about inconsequential things, spending time together and, according to Kelsey, allowing Aris to get used to the "idea" of Kelsey.

Time passed, and Anton settled into a merchant's routine. He heard from the guild that delves were starting again. Kelsey managed this without any apparent effort from her avatar, other than to comment when one of the parties did something particularly amusing.

After her second shipment of goods came in, Kelsey gave Anton a satisfied look and said, "I think it's time. How do we get an audience with the Baron?"

Anton looked at her for a long moment before sighing. "My parents knew the castle chamberlain. I know where he drinks."

"Great!"

"He won't just give you an audience, though; you'll need to convince him. Why would you want an audience, anyway?"

"Anton, Anton, Anton," Kelsey said condescendingly. "Do you think I've been establishing myself as a merchant for nothing? I've got something to sell him."

"Ah, it's young Anton." Syon Osvor was a short bald man, with skin a shade darker than most of the town. If that wasn't a clue to his status, his richly embroidered clothes should have given it away. "What brings you here, with . . ." He looked at Kelsey in puzzlement. "I thought you and Aris had an understanding?"

Anton flushed. "This is Kelsey, my *business* partner," he said, stressing the word.

"You're forming a delving party? I didn't think they were opening the dungeon yet."

"They haven't, yet!" Kelsey said brightly. "That might be happening in the future, but right now we're partners in an actual business!"

Syon frowned. "Young lady, Anton doesn't know anything about trade. If you're taking advantage of him . . ."

"It's all right," Anton interjected. "It's not Dad's money that she's after, Mr. Osvor. She—we have got something that we want to sell to the Baron."

"You're a grown man now, lad; call me Syon," the chamberlain corrected absently. His attention was on Kelsey now. "And what is it that you have to sell?"

Kelsey leaned forward with a grin. "Weapons," she said. "Weapons that can turn the tide against Elitra."

The demonstration was held outside, in the castle's marshalling yard. A small gathering of the local notables was huddled at one end, while the three dummies were set up at the other. Anton had helped set up the dummies, the manual labor being his only real contribution to this demonstration. The wooden forms, he assumed, had been carved by Kelsey's skeletons. He tried not to think about where she had gotten the armor from.

Trudging across the yard to stand next to Kelsey, he took note of who was there. The Baron and his family, of course. His wife and his daughter, Suliel, were well known in the town, at least by reputation. Few had actually spoken to them, but Suliel was the unattainable dream of many of the locals of Anton's age.

Widely regarded as the most beautiful unmarried girl in town, marriage to Suliel was often claimed by Anton's peers as their ultimate goal. Everyone knew, though, that she was destined to marry some noble from out of town. If her skin had been darker instead of a shade lighter than both her parents, she would surely have been engaged already.

Anton had Aris, of course, but now that Suliel was just a short distance away, he had to admit that she was beautiful. Her long black hair was unusually straight, eschewing the curls that most Zamarrans either loved or lived with. Realizing that he was staring, Anton broke off his gaze before he could get called on it and trudged up to Kelsey's side.

Of the others in the crowd, Anton knew some of them. Syon was there, of course. Since this gathering was to see some weapons, Captain Rynmos was present as well. He was injured, which meant that the inner wall had seen some heavy fighting at least, even if it hadn't fallen.

The main reason the inner keep hadn't fallen was also there, Magister Tikin. Kelsey had fixated on him the moment he'd entered the courtyard. It was hardly surprising, given where magic came from. Anton had been worried that she might do something aggressive, but she managed to conceal her intent.

Looking at the mage, Anton had some mixed feelings as well. If Tikin had been manning the *outer* wall, his parents might still be alive. The Baron's decision to not risk his biggest asset might be understandable, but it still stung.

There were four more people that Anton didn't know the names of. Two of them were relatives of the Baron who didn't actually have titles. They managed estates outside of the town and had brought their soldiers in, both to protect them from the raiders and to contribute to the common defense. Anton didn't know them, but he could see their resemblance to his lord.

The other two, based on their uniforms, would be the leaders of the cavalry unit that had arrived too late to help. Kelsey had grimaced when she saw them. Earlier, she'd expressed the hope that they would be gone before they gave this presentation, but that was clearly not the case.

When it came to the presentation, Kelsey had wanted *him* to do all the talking, but in their rehearsals, she had proved completely unable to stop herself from jumping in. It had been amusing and relieving to learn that there was something she couldn't do. It wasn't that he was bad at giving the spiel, at least when it was just the two of them, but she was just so eager to show off her new weapons.

With relief on his part and frustration on hers, they'd agreed that she would do the talking.

"Gentle noble-folk," she called out, once Anton had indicated that the dummies were ready. "You have a problem."

The crowd all turned their attention to her, but the Baron wasn't willing to let her start.

"First of all," he interrupted, "I like to know who I'm speaking to."

Kelsey cocked her head, a picture of puzzlement. "I'm Kelsey."

The Baron shook his head impatiently. "I *mean*, remove your blocking device so that I can Identify you."

"Oh, I see. However, it's not an item that's blocking you. You might say it's an unfortunate magical condition." Despite her words, Kelsey didn't sound at all sorry.

"Liem?" the Baron asked his mage.

"There's magic about her, but it's not coming from any item," Tikin confirmed. "I'm not sure how or where it's coming from, though. I'd assume she was a mage casting a spell, but she's not wearing a core."

Anton kept his mouth very firmly shut. Kelsey had been certain that things would go this way, that everyone would assume that she was a human who was blocking their identification traits, rather than a dungeon that didn't fall into the skill's parameters.

"We do things a little differently up north," she said. "As you'll soon see. Any other complaints?" She looked around, but no one seemed willing to make a further issue of it.

"Right, then! You have a problem. Elitran raiders have a block skill that negates your archers and enough of them have *Leaping Attack*, which makes your wall . . . less than perfectly effective. Is that right?"

Anton had been with Kelsey as she gathered stories about how the town had been taken, and he knew it wasn't *that* simple. The Elitrans had dragged ramps up, shielded by the blockers, which let them get over the ditch and gave the leapers enough height to reach the walls. Ten feet had seemed high enough to Anton, who actually *had Leaping Attack*, but it had proved inadequate against the raiders' determination, ferocity, and numbers.

"So, I'm sure you're thinking that you need to build the wall higher," Kelsey went on, "but I have a better solution."

She lifted the long metal tube from where it had been resting on her shoulder. Uncharacteristically of her, she had carried the thing all the way up here from the warehouse. When he'd first seen it, Anton had thought it was some sort of reversed axe, with a metal shaft and a wooden blade. No doubt the nobles were thinking the same right now. However, the blade was actually thick, with rounded edges. It was the handle—and the metal tube, while not a blade, was the dangerous part.

"This," Kelsey said brightly, "is a rifle. Breech-loading, paper cartridges." She put the wooden part against her shoulder and took aim. There was a click, followed quickly by an enormous boom.

Everyone's attention had been drawn to the rifle's firing. No one noticed that one of the dummies had fallen over until Kelsey pointed it out. "Do we want to go over and see what happened, or do you want another chance to see how it was done?" she asked.

The crowd murmured among themselves, but eventually they all looked to the Baron. "Show us again," he commanded.

Kelsey grinned and did something to make the rifle open up in the middle.

"I went for smokeless powder," she said as she took out a paper packet and carefully placed it in the barrel. "Which, if you'd seen how much smoke black powder makes, you'd be more thankful for."

She brought the rifle back together and took aim at another dummy. This time, everyone paid close attention to the dummies and the space between them and the rifle. Kelsey fired again and one of the dummies toppled in an instant reaction.

More murmurs from the crowd.

"I might have seen something," the cavalry captain said uncertainly. "But it was so fast . . ."

"Shall we go look?" Kelsey suggested. They all trooped down to the other end to look at the fallen mannequins. At first, there wasn't much to see, but then Kelsey pointed out the small hole in the breastplate of one of them. When she removed the armor, they could all see that the projectile had carried on through and buried itself deeply in the mannequin's body.

"Too fast to see. Too fast to block, and if they hide behind their shields, it will go right through them. The rate of fire isn't quite as fast as archers, but you can fit more riflemen on the same amount of wall. You can train them for staggered fire, or you can do massed volleys, to *devastating* effect. What do you say, gentle nobles?"

"How many of these can you provide, and at what price?" the Baron asked.

"Well . . . I brought twenty rifles with me and two thousand cartridges," Kelsey lied. "But that isn't going to take you very far. You'll use that much on training alone." She smiled slyly. "You're going to need to be able to manufacture these locally."

She hefted the rifle and started pointing out the details. "I'm sure your smiths could figure out the firing mechanism easily enough," she said. "Making the grooves on the inside of the barrel without compromising the structural integrity is a bit trickier, but doable. The real problem is the ammunition."

"Alchemy, yes? We have some in town—"

"No, my lord," Tikin interrupted. "That's not alchemy. I can detect no magic from it whatsoever."

"Then how?" The Baron looked at Kelsey.

"It's of dungeon manufacture," she said smugly. "In the north, we have techniques to make dungeons produce what we want, instead of random items. I hear you have a dungeon nearby?"

The crowd went silent, and the Baron scowled. He looked over at the cavalry captain, who had put on a studiously blank face.

"Just what is your proposal," he said, spitting out the words.

"Well, if you just want what I've got here, we can negotiate a fair price," Kelsey said. "And if you want me to import more, well, maybe that can be arranged. I should warn you that it might take a while. Years, even. Aside from the travel difficulties, my country does *not* want these weapons getting out."

Kelsey sounded so concerned about possible delays that Anton almost forgot that her country in the north, and its mythical weapons, were entirely a fabrication. Watching her lie to his leaders stirred a number of emotions, which he tried to keep off his face. Unconcerned, Kelsey continued.

"On the other hand, if you allow me exclusive access to the dungeon, I can produce as many as you want and sell them at cost. Say five gold for each rifle, and one hundred cartridges for a silver."

"That's . . . not something I can promise," the Baron said, looking again at the King's officers. "Dungeons belong to the King."

Kelsey shrugged. "Ownership, who cares? I just need to be able to control *who* goes *in*, and you can leave what comes out to me. My understanding was that you were in charge of that little detail, but if you need to get the King's permission, I can wait."

She looked slyly over at the officers. "I'm sure the King will see the utility of his border towns having access to my weapons. I'm sure he'll agree to my terms."

The Baron glared at her but managed to keep his temper in check. "Give me a few days . . . to consult," he managed to say.

"Take all the time you need," Kelsey said. "Your man, Syon, knows where to find us."

CHAPTER EIGHT

I'm Just an Old Chunk of Coal

S o, did it not work?" Anton asked when they were back in the privacy of
the inn.

Kelsey made an ambiguous noise from around the delicacy she was eating.
Today it was bacon wrapped around pastries which themselves contained . . .
different things. They were quite tasty, but Anton was too nervous to eat. It
wasn't as if he was invested in Kelsey's scheme, but if it fell through, he was sure
to feel some of the blowback.

"Too soon to tell," Kelsey said, having swallowed her bacon pastry. "Ask me
again after tonight's meeting."

"Who are we meeting tonight?"

"I don't know," Kelsey said thoughtfully. "It might be the Baron, or it might
be Captain Whatsisname, whom we never got introduced to. Depends on who
is the most unscrupulous."

"Why—" Anton started, but Kelsey grabbed another pastry and pointed over
his shoulder. Looking around, he saw that Aris had entered the inn.

"Aris!" He stood up as she approached. Kelsey stayed where she was but
gestured to a chair and to a stack of pastries on the table. Her mouth was fully
occupied chewing.

"Hello," Aris said to them both, taking a seat.

"You've got to try one of these," Kelsey said. "I don't know if it's disloyal for
you, eating someone else's baked goods, but these are worth being a traitor for."

Aris giggled. "Actually, Dad made these," she said. "A special order that came in this morning." She did take one, nibbling on it daintily, as opposed to Kelsey who had popped the whole thing in her mouth.

There was silence around the table as the two of them worked on their food. Finally, Aris spoke up.

"I've been thinking about what I want, as you suggested," she said. Anton sat up a little straighter, bracing himself. Kelsey didn't show any obvious reaction but made an encouraging noise.

Aris took a deep breath. "I want my sister back."

"What? Aris, you—Cheia's not—" Anton couldn't finish the thought, looking at his girlfriend. But everything he couldn't say, she already knew. He looked over at Kelsey, who'd gotten a serious look on her face. She was still chewing, though.

"When the raiders came, I couldn't do anything," Aris said. "I hid, just like Cheia and the rest of my family. But she got caught, and I . . . I want to save her."

Kelsey chewed slowly, waiting until every bit of the pastry was gone before speaking. When she spoke, it was in a much more serious tone than her normal manner.

"I'm not exactly up on how things work out here, but I take it there's a *reason* that no one's organizing a rescue mission." She looked at Anton.

"It's not impossible," he admitted. "But there isn't any person or group here that could manage it."

"Your parents managed it," Aris said.

"Yeah . . . but they were level twenty at the time? Early Tier Three, at least."

"There are Tier Threes in town," Kelsey pointed out. "At least one delving team, those soldiers that came in. And the Baron's people."

"Rathuan's group doesn't stick their necks out for anybody," Anton replied. "They fought on the wall—" *For longer than you did,* came the thought, unbidden. "But that was fighting for their own lives. The Baron's men will stay here, with the Baron, and the King's men . . . well, I don't really know, but I don't think they'll abandon their mounts to go sailing after . . . regular folk."

Kelsey nodded slowly and then looked over to Aris.

"You could do it," Aris said to her.

Kelsey reached out for another pastry. She took a small deliberate bite, her eyes never leaving Aris.

"I've got a lot on my plate right here, in this town. I'm not in a position to go touring."

"But you could—if you wanted to," Aris said. "You killed those raiders, you saved Anton. From what Anton said, you're more dangerous than anyone in this town."

"Maybe, but I'm not part of this town. This isn't my problem."

"If you want—if you want me to think you're a good person, then you can't let this happen to my sister."

"Hey, that's not fair," Kelsey protested. "It wasn't like I was there at the time to stop it. This isn't my fault."

"It's my fault," Aris said miserably. "I should have found a way to stop them. So I'll make a bargain with you. What Anton did, or something else if you like. Help my sister and we can both be your slaves. Together."

Kelsey said some words in a language that the two of them weren't familiar with and then continued as they looked at each other in confusion. "What kind of show do you think I'm running here? Didn't I already tell you that Anton wasn't a slave? And what would I do with a baker's daughter, anyway?"

"I thought . . . some kind of sex thing," Aris muttered into the table.

Kelsey said some strange words again. "I try to expand your emotional and sexual horizons, so Anton can keep you as his girlfriend, and you think I want to turn you into a sex slave?"

"That's what happens to slaves," Aris muttered, thoroughly embarrassed now. "That's what's happening to Cheia."

"That's not the *only* thing you have slaves for," Kelsey told her. "Or . . . is it? I guess I don't know the local customs."

"Mom told me that they have all sorts of slaves in Elitria," Anton said. "But when they come here, raiders only take young girls . . . they're more valuable than anyone else."

"Charming. But to get back on track—"

"I know I'm just a scullion," Aris interrupted. "But I'm level five. I'm ready to take any Tier Two class you want—if I can qualify for it."

"Do you qualify for anything good?" Kelsey asked.

"Nothing that isn't common," Aris admitted. "But Anton could take me into the dungeon so I qualify for Delver. And . . . it gets harder if you don't go now, but the slave markets will keep records . . . we can find out where she was sold if it takes longer." She looked down again. "I don't want her to wait longer than she has to, but better we come late than not at all."

"Hmmm. I notice you said 'we.'"

"Well, she's not going to want to come with you. She knows Anton, I suppose, but it would be better if—well, whatever you decide."

"Hmmm. Go back to the bit about qualifying for the Delver class. That's a Tier One class, right?"

"Yes, but it's good for fighting and stuff. You get it . . ." she looked at Anton.

"You qualify by making it to the second level of a dungeon," Anton told them. "My parents took me."

"That's what they were doing back then . . ." Kelsey mused. "What else can you qualify for?"

"I'm not sure," Anton admitted. "To qualify for Tier One warrior-type classes, you need to kill something with a weapon—different weapons for different classes. There are supposed to be more stringent tasks to qualify for the higher-tier classes, but most simply follow the path."

"Which is Delver, Adventurer . . . Hero? That's what your parents were."

"Yeah." Anton got a little sad at the mention of his parents. "There's a Tier Four class on the path, but they said I should focus on getting the first three."

"Interesting. Why don't we take this upstairs?" Kelsey grabbed the last two pastries and led them up to her room.

"Now," she said as she sat them down at the meeting table, "I'm not going to make a bargain with you, Aris. That's dumb, and you don't have anything I want . . . at least right now."

"But!" she added as Aris started to protest. "If you want to improve yourself, either to go after Cheia yourself *or* make yourself useful enough that I change my mind, I don't mind helping you out a bit for free."

"I shouldn't object," Anton said despite himself. "But how come she gets free help?"

Kelsey raised an eyebrow. "Because she's *your* girlfriend, and since you're *not a slave*, it does behoove me to make sure you stay happy. Also, that potion was *really expensive*."

"Right, sorry," Anton said, embarrassed. "Thank you."

"You are welcome." Kelsey looked at Aris. "Well? I suppose I should warn you that it won't be *easy*, but you already knew that, right?"

"I—" Aris looked over at Anton's worried expression. "I want to become stronger, strong enough to help Cheia. What do I have to do?"

"You want to start right away, am I right?" Kelsey said thoughtfully.

Aris nodded. "Every day I delay . . . it gets worse for Cheia."

"Okay . . . unfortunately, Anton and I are stuck here for the time being. We're expecting company tonight." She paused a bit longer in thought and then said, "Can you sneak out of town once it gets dark and enter the dungeon?"

"What? Enter the dungeon alone?" Anton protested. "She can't!"

"Relax, I'll take it easy on her," Kelsey replied. "Can you do it?" she asked Aris.

Aris nodded firmly. "Anton and I used to sneak out all the time when we were kids. It will be even easier now."

"Aris . . ." Anton whined. "It's really dangerous in there."

"Don't worry, kid. She'll be fine. I'm not going to send her in empty-handed." Kelsey looked Aris up and down. "To start with . . . you don't have any weapon skills, do you?"

When Aris shook her head, Kelsey produced a sword out of the air. "This should do as a starter weapon then. A short sword. It's got an edge, which is always useful, but it's thick enough to just bludgeon things if you need to."

She demonstrated a number of ways to use the weapon, thrusting, chopping, and swinging before handing it over to Aris.

"Try it out," Kelsey told the girl. "Don't worry, you'll be getting plenty of practice."

While Aris took a few practice swings, Kelsey began muttering to herself and staring at nothing. "I've got nothing that will fit that chest . . . something over-sized? Too small . . . too long . . ."

Eventually, she found something that satisfied her and started pulling out armor pieces.

"Good boots, very important, see if these fit," she said, handing a pair to Aris. She then added some leather pants and some metal vambraces. "These strap on, so they're one size fits all, pretty much. Try out the rest." She shooed Aris into the bedroom to try everything on.

"Are you sure about this?" Anton asked once they were alone. "She'll die in there!"

"Relax, I'm not going to give her the full package. I'll tone things down for her and give her an escort."

Anton frowned suspiciously. Kelsey had thus far demonstrated a callous dis-regard for human life, masked by her desire to stay "undercover." Was it different when he or his friends were involved? Or was this more of the mask? Before he could put his doubts into words, though, Aris returned. She looked like a real adventurer now.

He quickly cast *Delver's Discernment* over her gear. It was pretty good, all Tier Two. Not enchanted, but a cut above what a delver would normally start with.

"It fits?" she said doubtfully. Kelsey nodded in satisfaction and handed Aris a scabbard that went with her new sword.

"Okay," she said. "You're going to want to bring some food and water. Tell your parents that you'll be away for a few days."

"Should I tell them why?"

"Up to you. You can tell them you're staying here, if you like."

Aris looked down, embarrassed. Anton imagined her ears were burning. His certainly were. Kelsey ignored their reaction and kept on with her lecture.

"Now, I'll be able to see and hear everything you do there—but I can't issue new orders to the floor you're on. So if you run into problems, go up or down a floor, and I should be able to sort it out there."

"So I can talk to you?" Aris asked.

"Yes, but I can't reply," Kelsey told her. "I guess, if this body isn't too busy, I can write out a note and leave it for you, but not on the floor you're on."

"I see," Aris said. Anton could tell that it was starting to sink in. This was going to be something really dangerous. He wished that he could go with her, but he already knew Kelsey wasn't going to be budged from whatever encounter she thought was coming. He may not have been a slave, but he was still chained to Kelsey.

"You probably want to change before you leave," Kelsey advised. "Get some rest—I'll be ready for you whenever, but it should be easier to sneak past the patrols at night." She pushed Aris back into the bedroom to change out of her adventurer garb.

"One final thing," she added when Aris was ready to leave. "Don't just grab the first new class that becomes available. We'll try a few things when I get down there, see if we can't find something good."

Aris nodded again and then left, clutching her armor and weapon.

"Stop looking at me like that," Kelsey said to Anton. "She'll be fine."

CHAPTER NINE

Late in the Evening

Anton hadn't actually expected Kelsey to be right about something happening that night. But when the two guards came into the common room, they were clearly looking for her. It was after sundown, but the common room was still full of drinkers and diners. No one looked twice at the guards when they came in and looked around, but Kelsey poked Anton and got out of her seat.

"Look alive," she said quietly. "We're up." The two of them headed towards the guards. They were quickly noticed—Kelsey was easy to recognize. If the guards were surprised to see their target headed towards them, they hid it well.

"Where are we going, boys?" she asked when they were close enough.

"Uh, this way, ma'am," one of the guards said and led them out of the building. To Anton's continued surprise, they did not head up to the castle but turned down a side street towards the merchant sector of the town.

"I thought we were going to meet someone from the castle?" he whispered to Kelsey.

"It wouldn't be much of a secret meeting if we held it there, would it?" she answered, and he could somehow hear her eyes rolling.

They walked on for a little while before she spoke up again. "Aris has reached . . . where she was going," she said softly, keeping her eyes on the guards. Anton didn't have anything to reply to that, but his heart clenched up in worry.

They walked a little farther before coming to a nondescript merchant's house, tucked away in a little cul-de-sac. Two more guards stood outside the entrance and opened the door for them as they approached. Nobody said anything; their escort just indicated that they should go first, and Kelsey walked straight inside.

Something about the door caught Anton's eye as they went in. It hadn't been apparent from the outside, but the inside of the door had been bound with iron. On an impulse, he used *Delver's Discernment* and noted that both the wood and the iron were Tier Three.

Not so nondescript then, he thought. Tier Three materials needed a higher-Tier craftsman to be worked without losing a Tier. Anton wasn't aware of any Tier Four craftsmen in the town, so this must have been ordered from the capital.

Ignoring all this, Kelsey just walked straight in. Anton followed, more cautiously. They found themselves in an undecorated room, furnished with only three leather-covered chairs with high armrests, and a table supporting a lantern. The Baron occupied one of the chairs.

"Baron Anat," Kelsey said, bowing. She took one of the remaining seats. "You know, if you leave your guards outside, it's pretty obvious to anyone that there's something going on inside."

Anton slunk into his seat as the Baron glared at Kelsey. He must have been considering her words, though, because he gestured at one of the guards.

"Bring them in," he said and returned his attention to the woman before him. Anton had never been so glad to be ignored.

"Sooooo," Kelsey said, drawing out the word. "It's been too soon for you to contact the King, but you've ditched his officers. Shall I assume that you want to make a deal behind the King's back?"

"Why would he want to do that?" Anton blurted out. He immediately regretted it as the Baron's attention was turned on him. Only briefly, though, as Kelsey kept talking.

"He must have realized that rifles aren't just good for defense, they're great for attacking as well." She gave the Baron a big grin. "Your lord is looking for a promotion. To Count . . . or Duke . . . or dare I say it . . . King."

Baron Anat scowled. "If you realized this, then why have this demonstration while Oldaw was here? He's already sent a message back, which I've had to . . . take care of. It's only a matter of time before he realizes that his man hasn't made it back."

Kelsey shrugged. "It's not like I care who I do business with, or what you do with the product afterwards. You, the King, or Captain Oldaw . . . as long as I get my dungeon, I'm happy."

"How mercenary of you," the Baron sneered. "But your antics have put me on a schedule. How long before our dungeon can produce a meaningful supply of these . . . cartridges?"

"Oh, it's very quick," Kelsey said. "I should be able to have replacements ready before you've gone through the initial supply."

Anton stared at Kelsey in horror. Was she really starting a rebellion? That was what they were talking about, weren't they? It felt as though he should take action, but even if he was willing to go against his lord, the four guards in the room would easily stop him. Not to mention that the Baron was of a higher level than him.

"You're very confident," the Baron said. "Is she right to be?" He turned the question on Anton, and Anton felt the pressure as the Baron turned some sort of leadership trait on him, forcing him to answer the question.

"She . . . knows what she's doing," he said. He wasn't trying to lie, and he wasn't exactly being forced to tell the truth either. "She . . . can control the dungeon."

The pressure let up, and Anton gasped for breath. The Baron returned his attention to Kelsey.

"There's just one problem," he said. "There's no way that I, or the King for that matter, will hand over a dungeon to a foreigner."

"Give it to Anton, then," Kelsey said, unconcerned. "He's my partner and I trust him to do what's right for me."

Somehow, even knowing everything that he knew about Kelsey, her unconditional expression of trust in him stirred a warm feeling in Anton's heart. *What are you thinking, you idiot! Of course she trusts you; she's got you tied to her.*

The Baron was less impressed. He snorted and said, "I don't know how you managed to get the town's favorite son doing your bidding, but I'm not fooled. No, you'll get your money, but it will be in exchange for whatever secrets you know that let you control a dungeon."

For the first time that evening, Kelsey's smile dropped. "That won't be happening," she said flatly.

"Oh, but it will," the Baron said. He gestured, and two of the guards came over to stand behind their chairs. The one behind Anton put his hand on Anton's shoulder. He was strong, and Anton was forced back into the seat.

Anton flicked *Delver's Discernment* across the room. All of the guards were more than twice his level.

"This cottage is one end of a secret tunnel that leads to my castle's dungeons," the Baron continued. "If I can't convince you to sell your secrets, I'll simply take them from you."

"So I take it negotiations are at an end, then?" Kelsey asked. She made as if to get up, but the guard forced her down. She didn't go down as easily as Anton had, but leverage was against her. Trapped in her chair like that, she seemed weak, unarmed, and helpless, but Anton knew she was anything but.

"It seems so," the Baron replied, sighing.

"No, wait—" Anton said, but it was too late. Kelsey had put her hands up and to the sides in what looked like a helpless gesture. It didn't look so helpless when the two skeletons appeared.

Each skeleton held one of Kelsey's hands. Their other hands each held a rusty sword, which they quickly brought into action. Before Anton could even finish his sentence, the swords had swung, and the guards behind both Anton and Kelsey had been decapitated.

Blood started spraying everywhere as the guards' bodies fell to the ground. The skeletons were unbothered, moving quickly to attack the remaining guards. The Baron had pushed himself back away from the fight, falling over his chair in his haste to get away. He scrambled to get up while pulling out his rapier.

Kelsey ignored the fight behind her, getting up from her chair and keeping an eye on the Baron as he got himself together. Glancing back at the skeletons, Anton judged that she was right to be unconcerned. While the guards were stronger and faster than the skeletons, the difference in skill was easily seen.

Faster strikes were predicted and parried. Greater strength was countered by properly applying the leverage that a sword granted. It was beautiful to watch, but this wasn't a demonstration match. Each clash added a line of blood to some part of the guards' bodies, as the Lazybones took their opponents apart, one slash at a time. Still, it was slow going, and Anton thought that once the guards got over their shock and triggered their higher-tier traits, the fight might turn.

Before that happened, the Baron entered the fray. He might not have been a combat specialist, but he was a Tier Three. Forgetting himself in his panic and rage, he lunged at Kelsey. If his strike had connected, he would surely have killed her and sent her secrets to the grave. If she'd been human, of course.

Since she wasn't, she just stood her ground and held out her hand. A metal device appeared in it, and there was a sound, unlike anything Anton had heard before. Sort of a loud *phutt*. The device jerked in Kelsey's hand, and a small hole appeared in the middle of the Baron's forehead.

Already moving forward, he seemed to trip as he slumped to the ground, dead at Kelsey's feet. His death proved fatal for his guards as well, distracting them when they could least afford it. The Lazybones took advantage of the openings, and just like that, the fight was over. Anton had not even had time to get up.

"Well," Kelsey said thoughtfully, "this is not how I hoped it would go."

"This is terrible!" Anton screeched. "You killed the Baron! We're going to be hung! What—"

He paused, as his thoughts caught up with him. "What was that thing that you used?" he asked in a still high-pitched but slightly more normal tone. A delver's curiosity about new items and weapons was a powerful thing.

"Oh, this?" Kelsey asked, waving the L-shaped device at him. "This is a gun, like the rifles."

"It's nothing like the rifles!" he said. "It's shorter, and less . . . tubey, and it doesn't make a booming sound."

"It's a more advanced version," she told him. "It holds nine bullets, and it can fire them as fast as I can pull the trigger. And it has a silencer, which I integrated since bulk isn't an issue when you can pull your weapon out of thin air."

Most of what she said went right past him, but one thing caught his attention. "Bullets are the same as cartridges? And it carries nine of them? That's . . . terrifying."

"They serve the same purpose, yeah, but they're different. Oh, that reminds me." Kelsey started casing around the room. She quickly found what she was looking for, a small brass object.

"Wouldn't do to leave evidence about," she said, passing it over to him. It was a tiny brass cup, strangely warm and smelling much like the smoke from the rifles.

"And yes, you guys can evolve," she said over his shoulder to the two skeletons covered in blood. Anton whirled around to see the Lazybones engulfed in a golden glow that seemed to emanate from their very bones. As he watched, transfixed, they grew a little, or perhaps just stood a little straighter. Their swords lengthened, and the rust and nicks that they carried were somehow erased. Armor—a breastplate and greaves—formed around them.

When the glow was finished, Anton recognized them as a pair of Skeleton Champions from level five.

"Monsters have something similar to your classes, but for them, it's a race, and it's much more all-encompassing," Kelsey said. She'd been cleaning up while he stared at them and had disappeared most of the corpses by now. The blood splatters on her were also gone—she'd changed clothes again, Anton realized.

"Back in the box with you," she said to the two skeletons, gesturing for them to come over to her. She held out her hands for them to take, then disappeared them. Now Anton was the only blood-soaked object left in the room—apart from the floor and bits of the walls.

"I thought you couldn't put living things in your Inventory," he said, still processing what had happened.

"Undead monsters aren't living!" Kelsey said gleefully. "Hell of a loophole, right?"

She looked him over speculatively. "But we can't have you wandering the streets like that. Do you just want to change your clothes, or do you want a bath?"

Anton stared at her blankly, before realizing she could just summon the bathtub again. "Just the clothes, please," he said. He did want a bath, but he couldn't imagine cleaning himself in the middle of this murder scene—even if it was missing the victims. Kelsey nodded and handed over a bundle of clothes.

"Go upstairs to change. I'll try and do something about . . . all this." She looked around. "Wait!" Summoning a wet cloth to her hand, she wiped down his face while he stood, unresisting. "You had a little . . . it's gone now."

Anton nodded and went upstairs, changing clothes methodically. What was going to happen to them? They had killed the Baron! Should they turn themselves in? Somehow, Anton doubted that that was Kelsey's plan. He'd never done anything worse than steal apples from his neighbor's tree, and now he was the worst kind of criminal.

Kelsey seemed entirely at ease with that, Anton realized. Of course, she killed people all the time; it was . . . normal, for dungeons. His only option was to hope that she knew what she was doing when it came to crimes committed as a human.

When he got back down, Kelsey had managed to clean a lot of the blood. The room still had a metallic smell, and the walls and floor were wet, but there was no sign of the red pools that had been there before.

"This place has pretty good drainage," Kelsey said. "Hopefully it isn't all going into their secret tunnel."

"What are we going to do?" Anton asked.

"About the Baron, you mean? It's not as bad as you're thinking." Kelsey said. "For one thing, he didn't want anyone to know that we were meeting, so there's a good chance the only people that knew were the ones he took with him. All of whom are dead."

"But people saw us with his guards. And what if he told his wife something?"

"Then things get interesting," Kelsey said, grinning. "But let's leave tomorrow's trouble until then. Right now, we've got to sneak out of town."

"Aris! We've got to get to the dungeon!" Anton couldn't believe that he'd forgotten about her, even under the current circumstances.

"Relax, she's fine. Well, fine-ish." Kelsey paused for thought. "Actually, before we get there, we should make a detour."

"What for?" Anton asked suspiciously.

"We need to stage a crime scene."

CHAPTER 10

Going Underground

ARIS

While Aris had been telling the truth about sneaking out of the town, there were a few things that she'd glossed over. For one, Anton had been with her on all of those occasions. She'd been the instigator, but she never would have been brave enough to go outside of the walls without Anton there to protect her.

For another, it had always been in daylight, and they'd never gone far. Just out to the fields to play, or up to the cliffs to look down at the harbor from above. They'd known the path to the dungeon, of course; their parents had made sure they'd known where it was so that they could stay away from it.

Tonight was nothing like those old times, but she was older now, equipped for adventure, and determined. She avoided the breaches in the wall—they were crawling with guards and lanterns—and made her way to their old climbing spot.

Someone—as kids, they'd never dared to find out who it belonged to—had left their apple tree to grow too high. While it was behind a wall, its branches stuck out over into the street, a tempting target for hungry young children.

Aris scaled the low wall easily and reached the lower branches. It was difficult, but the moonlight was bright enough for her to see what she was doing, as she climbed up and over. Moving to the other side of the tree, she saw that the higher branches still rested near the top of the wall.

Perhaps the reason that the tree had been left in place was that the soldiers appreciated the occasional free apple. Aris carefully repeated the climb that she'd done many times in daylight. Once on the wall, climbing down was pretty easy, and she let herself drop the last few feet.

Only then did the thought occur to her that getting back in this way was impossible. As kids, they'd just wandered back in through the gate, crying for their parents if the guards gave them trouble. That wasn't an option this time, but Aris had other, more immediate problems to think about.

Kelsey had made it sound as though it would be easy to get to the dungeon in the dark, but Aris was almost caught twice as she made her way up the hill. Outside patrols had been taken over by the late-arriving cavalry unit, which made the experience more frightening. She knew most of the town's soldiers; they'd give her a lecture if she got caught, but she'd be fine. These men, she didn't know. They might just ride her down if they saw her, or put a spear in her back.

Fortunately, being strangers meant that they didn't know the area well. Aris was able to slip by them on paths too thin for horses. It wasn't long before she found herself by the cave where the dungeon started. Light was coming out of it, and she could hear the clash of swords, just like the stories said.

Aris took a deep breath and entered the cave. She crept forward until she could see the two skeletons fighting on the dais. She stepped forward, and they stopped.

That wasn't like in the stories, but Aris had been told that her trip would be different. She froze as the skeletons looked directly at her, but she didn't run. After the fear faded, she took another step forward.

One of the skeletons picked up a lantern that had been sitting next to them and stepped off the dais. Holding the lantern high, it moved to the back of the room and then stopped, looking back at her. The other skeleton just stood there, holding its sword.

Aris moved towards the lantern-holding skeleton, keeping an eye on the other one. It stayed still, but her guide shone its light on a wide crack in the wall that led further back. She gritted her teeth and entered the dungeon.

The first level looked something like a natural formation. A narrow, twisting tunnel that led deeper into the darkness. It wasn't long before it opened out, though, and Aris saw her first sarcophagus.

Here, the tunnel was at least a yard across, and it looked as if someone had carved out a coffin-sized niche in the wall for the sarcophagus to lie in. Aris looked at it warily, but it was the skeleton that moved past her to approach it. Looking back at her, it waved its sword back and forth. Not threatening her, but . . . Aris felt herself blushing, as she realized she hadn't drawn her sword. Pulling it out, she nodded at the skeleton.

At her nod, the skeleton rapped three times on the lid of the coffin before moving back. For a moment, nothing happened, and then the lid began to slowly creak open.

Aris tightened the grip on her sword as the stench of rotting flesh hit her like a blow. As the lid rose, the living corpse that was pushing it open came into view. Aris swallowed as the lid fell back, allowing the zombie to clamber out.

Wait, I don't have to wait for it, do I? Aris thought to herself and took a hesitant swing. The blade sank into the creature's arm, clearly injuring it, but it was not even close to a disabling blow. The zombie hissed at her, in pain or anger, Aris couldn't tell. She ignored the sound and sliced at it again.

This time, there was a crunch of bone from the arm it had blocked with. It snarled at her and tried to grab her with its other arm, but she screamed and backed away. It was slow, too slow to catch her, but it lunged forward anyway.

Still screaming, Aris brought the short sword down against its head, causing it to crash against the floor. She struck it again and again until finally, it stopped moving. Gasping for air, she stood over the corpse of her first kill and tried to keep her stomach under control. As she watched, the corpse started dissolving into the dungeon floor, leaving nothing behind. She stared at the spot where it had been, wondering what had happened.

The change in the light broke her out of her funk. It was getting darker. She looked around to see that the skeleton had moved on, taking the light with it.

"Wait!" she called, but the skeleton only looked back and grinned, never stopping moving forward. Cursing, she hurried after it.

She hadn't quite caught up when it stopped of its own accord by the side of the next sarcophagus. Grinning at her, it slammed its sword hilt on the lid of the coffin three times.

Aris killed zombies. It was what she did, now. Killing them didn't actually gain her any experience—Scullions got experience from helping in the kitchen, not from killing—but she was getting better with the sword. She was still a novice, but her movements had gotten less clumsy, and her sword strikes were stronger and more accurate.

She'd also started to remember to collect her loot. Her guide gave her just enough time to collect what was left behind in the coffins, and one of the zombies had left behind some sort of crystal. She was thirty-three coppers richer thus far. Not bad for a night's work, and she had the feeling there was more to come.

This time, when she collected her coppers, she noticed that there was a metal ring, about three inches in diameter, affixed to the bottom of the coffin. Unsure of what it meant, she looked at her guide. It moved forward and put its lantern and sword down, and then pulled at the ring. A section of the coffin floor was pulled up, revealing a deep hole.

"I have to go down there?" Aris asked.

The skeleton didn't respond, but picked up its tools again and shone the lantern's light down into the hole. Aris could see that there were handholds for climbing down, but she couldn't see the bottom. Putting her sword back in its scabbard, she started climbing down.

It wasn't too far and she was soon standing on what felt like sand. The drop had been short enough that she thought she could have just jumped down without too much trouble, and once she'd gotten out of the way, that was exactly what her guide did. It landed with a thump, and Aris now had enough light to look around.

She was at the edge of a large cave. Above her, the roof sloped gently up from the wall, forming a dome about twenty feet high. The far wall of the cave was too far away for the lantern to illuminate, but the part she could see looked circular. Aris was just taking a step forward to see better when there was a tremendous boom from the darkness on the other side of the cave.

Swallowing, she drew her sword again.

The figure that emerged from the darkness was monstrous in every sense that Aris could think of. Taller and larger than a human could be, it shuffled forward on legs that were misshapen and of different lengths. Its arms were too long, its head too wide. Its torso seemed somehow twisted. And the smell . . . Aris had gotten used to the stench of death, and this was all of that, and more.

As it came close, Aris could see that it had been constructed somehow out of other bodies, flesh pressed together and merged into a horrible imitation of a human form. Its head was actually two heads combined into one nightmarish construction. Naked and hairless—but fortunately without genitals—it staggered forward with a terrible hunger in all four of its eyes.

Out of the corner of her eye, Aris saw her guide carefully put down the lantern and face the horror, raising its sword. It didn't move forward, though, waiting for her to make the first move.

Am I really going to do this? Aris wondered. By now, though, she was used to the weight of her sword, and the stench of her enemies. There was nowhere else to go but forward. *I hope he is as slow as he looks* was her last thought before she charged forward.

Ducking clumsily under a swinging arm, she came in close enough to try a slash against its torso. The blade cut in, but it was only a superficial slash. She kept moving, trying to get out of range before it could bring its arm around.

Reaching what she hoped was far enough, she heard a bellow from behind her and spun around. Her guide had stepped in and thrust its sword into the horror's leg. The wound looked deep and the creature had cried out in pain, but the leg still seemed to be working.

None of the earlier corpses had gone down with just one blow—or three— so Aris was not discouraged. She charged in again, managing another slicing wound, but this time she was not as successful in getting away. The arm came down faster this time and she was struck by a glancing blow.

It knocked the wind out of her and sent her sprawling. Gasping, she tried to recover, to at least roll out of the way of the follow-up strike that she knew was coming. A gust of fetid air came towards her, and she knew she was too late, but . . . something happened?

Finally managing to roll over—*too slow, too late*—she saw that the skeleton had blocked the horror's strike with its sword. It hadn't gone well for the skeleton—one of its arms seemed to have shattered from the power of the blow. The corpse golem hadn't fared too well either. The sword had sheared through the bones of the arm, and now its hand was hanging on by a thin rope of flesh and skin.

Only forward. Aris rose to her feet, sword in hand. This time she didn't get in as close, slicing at the other arm as the monster howled in pain. Her companion didn't seem to feel the loss of its arm, as it simply picked up its sword and renewed its attack.

The fight was long and bloody, at least for everyone who wasn't a skeleton. Aris took some cuts and bruises, but she managed to avoid a full-on blow as she hacked her way through the monster. It seemed as though it took forever, but she managed it.

When it finally slumped to the floor, there was a grinding of stone from the other side of the room. Aris had to carry the lantern now, as her skeleton companion only had one arm. The grinding had come from some doors slowly opening to reveal an exit and a chest.

Hurt, tired, and overly emotional, Aris approached the chest with caution and opened it. Inside it were twelve copper coins, a leather vest, and a note.

Congratulations on making it to level two! If you go on past here, you should qualify for the Delver class, but I'm curious to see if you can get something better if you go deeper! The next level is more of the same, but the corpses are faster. While you've been having fun, I've had time to make this vest in your size. You're welcome. If you can make it to level three, I can open up the hospitality area so you can have a rest. Good luck! – Kelsey

CHAPTER ELEVEN

Another One Bites the Dust

ARIS

Aris stared at the note in disbelief.

"Another level?" she cried out. Until now, she'd avoided speaking into the air. Even though Kelsey had said that she would be able to hear what was said, it felt wrong just talking to nothing. This was her breaking point, though.

"You bitch! You're just stranding me here, and I need to go down *another* level before I can take a break?" She screamed in frustration at her lack of things to call Kelsey. Anton knew better swear words, she was sure. She'd have to get him to teach her some afterwards.

If Kelsey heard her, there was no sign. Her one-armed skeleton guard just stood there waiting for her to move on. With a sigh, she took out the vest and tried it on. It fit perfectly, and Aris had to admit that she did feel more secure.

Grumbling to herself, she swept up the twelve coins and looked back at the corpse behind her. It had dissolved into nothing, leaving a crystal behind. It was a little bigger than the one she had picked up so far. Sighing, she picked it up, wincing as she bent down. Her injuries were mostly scratches and bruises. Nothing that would stop her, but they were painful.

Walking back, she glared at the skeleton. "Well?" she asked, "Aren't you going first?"

The skeleton just pointed the way with its sword. With an unladylike grunt, Aris stomped past it. As she entered the next room, she was confronted by another grinning skeleton. Confused, she took a step back, but the skeleton didn't attack. Its sword was drawn, but it wasn't like it had a scabbard to keep it in. It just stood there, and then held out its free hand.

Warily, Aris moved forward and tentatively held out the lantern. It took the lamp and then turned to lead the way down the corridor.

"Wait!" Aris called, but it didn't respond, moving away with her light source. Aris quickly hurried after it, cursing.

She tried to access her status while walking to the next monster. Sure enough, she now had access to the Tier One class, Delver.

Should I take it? she wondered. Kelsey had said that she shouldn't, but there were good reasons to take the class. For one, she'd get an immediate boost to her stats. For another, she would start getting experience for killing monsters. She'd be getting something for all this, she was sure, but it didn't compare to the experience gained from killing that Delvers got. There was a reason that Anton was three levels past her, in a *Tier Two class* to boot.

On the other hand, if she did qualify for a Tier Two class from further delving, she would have to finish all five levels of the Delver class before taking it . . . or would she?

No, she realized. Common wisdom said that you had to finish your class to qualify for the next one, but if she qualified for a *better* Tier Two class, then she qualified. She didn't have to finish Delver. If she didn't qualify for better classes, she could finish Delver and qualify for Adventurer.

Unless . . . taking Delver meant that she wouldn't qualify? Anton hadn't gotten any extra options from coming down further when *he* was a delver.

Aris's rumination was brought to an abrupt end as her guide reached the first of the crypts. This level was much like the first, but instead of a natural-looking tunnel, this one appeared to have been carved with tools. The corridors were slightly wider, and straighter, and Aris could see that there was a branching ahead.

Right in front of her, though, was a familiar-looking stone coffin. Just like before, her guide rapped on the lid.

Unlike all the other times, though, the zombie practically exploded out of its home. On the last level, the zombies had moved slowly enough that Aris had generally managed to get a blow in before they made it free. This time, though, Aris barely had time to make a startled squeal before desperately trying to get her blade between it and her.

She managed to disrupt its charge, but it kept up the attack, pressing her with clawed fingers and yellowed teeth. Aris used her vambrace to block as much as she could, but it grabbed on to her arm and started gnawing on her closed fist.

Screaming with pain and outrage, Aris brought her sword down on the monster's head. It didn't let go, so she swung it again and again until finally, the zombie dropped.

Wincing, Aris examined the damage. It wasn't too bad; the rotten teeth of the zombie didn't make for deep bites. It was bleeding, though, and her guide didn't leave her much time to recover. She barely had enough time to grab the five copper coins before it was moving again.

The second level went much faster than the first. Instead of a single, twisting passage, this level featured a confusing maze of carved passageways. In addition to disarming the traps, Kelsey had provided her with a guide that led her unerringly through the puzzle.

It was not all smooth sailing, though. The zombies here were too fast for her to easily dodge, and she picked up a number of bites and cuts before she found herself before the boss.

"Oh, gods . . ." she mumbled, as she stared at the hole at the bottom of the sarcophagus. "Am I really going to be able to do this?"

Her skeleton companion only grinned, holding the light steady on the passage down.

Aris ate the last of her food and drank the last of her water. She made sure her armor was all tightly fastened, and then she started the climb down.

Aris was expecting a faster abomination this time, and she wasn't disappointed. It charged at her before her guide made it down. A waft of its stench and a wet gurgling sound was all the warning she got before it came out of the darkness.

She dived out of the way, letting it smash itself into the cave wall. She recovered too slowly to slash it from behind, but she got another chance as her skeleton guide jumped down and distracted it. Both of their swords cut into it, the skeleton's into its fist and hers into its side.

From there, it was a desperate, brutal slog. The monster moved the same way as the boss from level one, but the added speed made it so much more dangerous. Just as she thought that she had its measure, a limb came out of nowhere to strike at her with full force.

She blocked it with the vambrace, but while the metal held, her arm did not. She felt as much as heard the crack of bone as her arm went limp from the pain. But even as she cried out, the skeleton was landing blow after blow on the creature's back. It cried out and slumped to the floor, but then whirled and engulfed the skeleton in a bear hug. They both crashed down, the abomination on top, skeleton bones cracking like twigs underfoot.

It wasn't her sword arm that was broken, and Aris knew that this was her last chance, so she ran over to the pair and started chopping at the thing's neck. It howled and tried to get away, but the skeleton held on to it, even as its bones were being crushed one by one.

Finally, it died. The bones underneath it made a few more rattles, but then the light in the eyes of the skeleton died out. Aris looked at the scene for a few moments, and then glanced over to where the doors were opening. She limped over. Every step caused her to wince as it jogged her broken arm. Carefully, she slid her sword back into its scabbard and then slowly released her death grip on the hilt.

Flexing her fingers to make sure they were still working, she picked up the lantern and headed to the exit. This time, the chest contained two silver coins and a small vial.

Aris looked at the vial warily. She thought it might be a healing potion. She *needed* it to be a healing potion, but taking it now would be a mistake. She knew that potions caused pain as they healed, and she didn't think she could remain conscious if she took it. There was supposed to be a rest area ahead, so she'd take it there. Shuffling forward, she went on to level three.

This time, she was met by two skeletons. In maid costumes. She remembered that Anton had mentioned non-standard skeletons, but she stared anyway.

"Are you my guides for this level? Please, I need to rest," she said.

The skeletons just grinned and then curtsied deeply, holding their skirts out to the side. Then they rose and started leading Aris along a corridor. Hopeful, but without much of a choice, she followed.

They went through a door and then passed by several more. This level consisted of corridors lined with blocks of stone, giving it the feel of a castle or a military fort. Only the lack of windows gave it away. After what felt like forever, they finally reached a room that held a bed.

"Thank you . . ." Aris mumbled. She stumbled into the room and sat down on the bed. Without a word, the two maids moved forward and started unstrapping her vambraces. Aris hissed with pain as they unbuckled her left arm, but the bony fingers were surprisingly deft, and gentle.

With her armor off, Aris could see that her arm was still straight. That was . . . good? She recalled fuzzily that it was worse if an arm was broken and bent. It shouldn't really matter to the healing potion, though.

There was no point in putting it off any longer, so she pulled out the vial and uncorked it. Wincing in anticipation, she downed the whole thing.

Pain bloomed throughout her, starting with her skin and then touching each and every wound that she had. When it reached her arm, it blossomed and Aris screamed into the empty room. It seemed to take forever, but eventually, it faded, leaving Aris an exhausted wreck lying on the bed. Sleep was a blessing, and Aris let it take her away.

CHAPTER TWELVE

Hit Me with Your Best Shot

Hey, you awake?" The voice came out of the darkness. Aris groaned and then yelped as she tried to move her arm.

"My arm still hurts," she complained, opening her eyes to see Kelsey staring down at her.

"It was only a five-minute potion," Kelsey said. "The bone has reset itself, and partially knitted, but it's not fully healed."

"Has it only been five minutes?" Aris asked.

"No . . . you've been out for hours. Anton and I got back about two hours ago. He wanted to see you, but I convinced him you both needed to rest. It's about two hours from dawn now."

"If I needed my rest, why are you waking me now?"

"Well . . ." A shifty look flicked across Kelsey's face. "It's probably best if Anton and I get back inside before dawn. I wanted to talk to you before we left, see if you want to come, or if you want to stay longer."

"Why would I want to . . ." Aris said before she remembered. "The classes!" she exclaimed.

"So, what did you get?" Kelsey asked.

"I did get Delver," Aris said, opening her status and scanning her available options. "Nothing new for level three, though," she said, disappointed. "I did get a Tier Two combat class, though—Swordswoman. It's only common, though."

"Does it say how you qualified for it?"

"I killed ten entities with a sword, without a combat class," Aris said, reading the description.

"So the same is probably true for other weapons," Kelsey said thoughtfully.

"Probably, but they're probably all common as well. Unless there are rarer weapons?"

"Mmnn. I've got a few ideas." Kelsey looked at Aris speculatively for a bit. "Let's go for a walk."

Aris sat up on the bed, only realizing then that most of her armor and clothes had been removed. She looked accusingly at Kelsey, who just pointed at the table beside the bed. They had all been cleaned and neatly folded.

"If the arm still hurts, we should get a splint and a sling," she commented and stepped outside. Aris had just about finished dressing when Kelsey returned with two skeletons, one in a short white dress and the other in a white coat. Aris stiffened as they approached, but they didn't have any weapons.

"Relax, they're just going to take a look at your arm," Kelsey said.

And indeed, the one in the coat approached and reached out to take hold of her arm. Bemused, Aris let it. It gently felt along the break, and then deftly started splinting the arm with materials handed to it by the other one.

"Couldn't I just drink another potion?" Aris asked, wincing as her arm was bound up.

"Potions are expensive," Kelsey replied disapprovingly. "They cost me mana, which is the only thing I really need to budget. Well, that and organics, I can never get enough of those."

Aris ignored the strange term, focusing on another peculiarity of the skeletons treating her. "Why are they . . . shiny?"

"They're coated," Kelsey said offhandedly as if that was meant to mean something to Aris. When Aris still looked confused, she elaborated. "Bone fingers are surprisingly good for a lot of tasks, but it wears out easily, and it picks up germs and stuff way too easily. So I found a coating that forms a nice smooth surface."

At Kelsey's direction, the skeleton held out a hand for Aris to feel. Sure enough, the bone was smooth under her touch, more like glass or pottery.

"It's very strange," Aris said. "Does it make them tougher?"

"Probably not." Kelsey shrugged. "But these guys aren't for fighting."

As she spoke, Aris's arm was safely tucked away in a cloth sling, and the skeletons withdrew.

"Let's go," Kelsey said and led Aris out of the room. She led Aris down a hallway that looked as though it belonged in a normal stone building, but it ended in a dead end, a solid wall of stone that made the passageway look unfinished.

Kelsey winked at Aris, and a humming sound made itself heard. Without fuss, the stone wall raised itself up slowly, revealing the passageway behind.

"Adventurers," Kelsey sighed. "They've got all sorts of ways of finding secret doors and stuff, so I came up with this."

"Isn't this a secret door?" Aris asked, confused. She noticed as they passed under it that the block of stone was massive, almost a yard thick. She didn't want to think about how much it weighed.

"The trick of it—or rather, tricks—is that it's too thick for them to sense the passage on the other side. It's not moved by mana, so they can't sense *that*, and it's just too heavy for any of their door-opening traits to do anything with.

"Door-opening traits?"

"Yeah, some of them can just touch a door, or a mechanism, and make it work. It's *such* a pain."

The humming noise sounded again as the stone was lowered back into place.

"But how do you move it, if not with magic?"

"Oh, I have my ways." Kelsey grinned. "But now, welcome to the working part of the dungeon."

The corridor here was much more utilitarian. The walls were perfectly smoothed, flat stone, not shaped to resemble cave walls or blocks. As Kelsey led Aris down the corridor, Aris could hear faint sounds that swelled and faded as they moved along the passageway.

Aris recognized some of the sounds. The hammering of nails into wood, the rhythmic crashing of steel from a blacksmith's hammer. But others were foreign to her. More of that strange humming, something that sounded like a metallic scream, and others too strange to describe.

Kelsey ignored all of that and led Aris to a small room, barely two paces square.

"You make things here?" Aris said, stepping warily into the room. "I thought dungeons just . . . made things out of magic."

"I *can* do that," Kelsey said. She touched a spot on the wall, one of many that were lit up, with symbols written on them. Most of them were numbers, and Kelsey had touched the one that was marked with a 10.

"But it costs mana . . . which is expensive," she continued. "For most things, it's better to spend the mana on skeletons and use them to build the things. There are some other limitations on the mana method as well."

Suddenly, the floor dropped out from under Aris. Or so it seemed because nothing changed in the room. Aris looked around, panicked by the sensation, but Kelsey seemed unperturbed.

"Oh, you'll get used to that," she said. "The room is moving down; we're on our way to the lower floors."

Aris stared. "How?" she asked.

"The same way as the stone," Kelsey said, smirking.

"Why—if you could have just brought me down, why did you make me go alone?"

Kelsey got a serious look on her face. "Listen," she said. "If I just walked you through everything, it wouldn't have been an achievement. I doubt you would have gotten the Delver class, and if you had, you wouldn't have earned it."

She clasped a hand onto Aris's shoulder. "Tonight you learned what it means to fight for your life. That's worth something, all on its own."

The room lurched to a stop, and the doors slid open. Aris could feel something like pressure bearing down on her.

"What—what am I feeling?" she asked.

"Increased mana density," Kelsey replied. "I need it for the more powerful monsters. This side of things, though, it's just skeletons, so don't worry."

"Why do you have so many skeletons?" Aris wondered.

"They're cheap and useful," Kelsey replied. "Better than humans for some things. And they're mostly made out of calcium, which I can extract from rocks, so they don't cost much mana. Anyway, we're pretty deep now," Kelsey said. "See if it's got you anything."

Aris checked her status. "Nothing's changed," she said, disappointed.

"I thought as much, but it was worth trying." Kelsey shrugged and pressed another lighted square. "Where we actually want to go is three floors up."

This time the room rose, making Aris feel heavy. Kelsey was right, though, and she had quickly gotten used to the strange sensation. When the doors opened again, Kelsey led her out, into what seemed like identical corridors to the ones on level three.

The identical corridors formed a maze, and Aris was quickly lost as Kelsey led her unerringly through them. After a number of turns, they reached their destination, a door, identical to all the others that they had passed by.

Kelsey opened it and led Aris through. Behind the door was a large room, with a table close by and a small crowd of skeletons standing at the other end.

Lying on the table was a small metal device.

"Here's your rare weapon," Kelsey said with satisfaction.

"What do you normally use this room for?" Aris asked in confusion.

"Oh, I set this all up while we were walking here," Kelsey explained. "Now what you're going to do is use this pistol to kill ten skeletons and see what that gets you.

"Is that all right? To kill your monsters?"

Kelsey raised an eyebrow. "Bit late to be asking that, don't you think?"

"I mean—those zombies were attacking *me*. These guys are just standing there waiting."

Kelsey sighed. "They're not real, Aris. The skeletons *act* like they have emotions, but they don't really feel them."

"But you talk to them . . ."

"I've had *very limited* conversational options for a very long time. Pretending that they were real helped me get through that, but don't mistake pretense for reality."

"I see," Aris said doubtfully. She turned her attention to the pistol. "How do I . . .?"

"You hold it like this," Kelsey said, demonstrating. "Use the other hand to brace it—it will make a loud noise and jerk back when you fire it, so get ready for that. This bit here is the safety. When it's like this, the gun can't fire; when it's like this, it can. Your finger comes in here and pulls the trigger to fire, but before that, make sure that you're pointing it at something you want to die."

Aris followed the quick stream of instructions as best she could, finding herself corrected, and then moved into the correct stance and position. Kelsey remembered at the last minute to stuff some cloth in Aris's ears—for protection, she said. Finally, Aris found herself with the pistol held in both hands, one eye sighting along the barrel.

"Okay, now pull the trigger," Kelsey said. Everything happened at once. The pistol kicked in her hand, there was a loud noise and a brief burst of fire and smoke, and one of the skeleton's heads exploded.

"Nice," Kelsey said. "Now do that nine more times."

Aris stared at her in shock. She'd almost dropped the pistol from the surprise of firing it. Now Kelsey wanted her to do it again?

"Come on," Kelsey encouraged. "You'll get something good from this, I'm pretty sure."

Gritting her teeth, Aris got to work. At least it wasn't as bad as hacking at zombies.

When she was done, with only a pile of bones remaining at the other end of the room, she checked her status.

"Oh! It's . . . a unique class?" she exclaimed.

Original Gunslinger (Tier 2, Unique)
Requisites: Complete Tier 1 Class. Kill 10 entities with Gunpowder-based
    weapons. No previous Combat Class. No previous Gunslingers.
Ability Improvement: 7 points per level. TADPW (2 Free).

"Interesting," Kelsey said, once Aris had read out the description. "There's probably a few others that you could get, but that sounds pretty good. You going to take it?

"I'm not sure..." Aris said. "You're the only one who can make these guns, right?"

"It's not magic or anything," Kelsey said dismissively. "I can keep you supplied, no problem."

"It makes me . . . truly dependent on you, though, doesn't it?" Aris objected. "I won't be able to do *anything* without the bullets."

"Plus seven to your abilities each level. Even if you never fire a gun again, that's almost twice the growth you'd get from a common class. Trust me, girl, we're going to go a long way together."

Aris looked at the strange woman doubtfully. But Kelsey was right. If Aris wanted to save Cheia, then she needed to take this opportunity.

"All right," she said and took the class.

Gunslinger Class selected.
Applying Benefits for Level 1:
Toughness + 1
Agility + 1
Dexterity + 1
Perception + 1
Willpower + 1
Assign free points:

The Scullion class hadn't ever offered a choice about ability points, but Aris didn't have to think hard about it. She would need strength if she was going to become a warrior.

Two points assigned to Strength.

Aris sighed again and called up her status.

Aris Lucina, Gunslinger (Level 1)
Overall Level: 6
Paths: Scullion (broken), Gunslinger
Strength: 7
Toughness: 4
Agility: 6
Dexterity: 4
Perception: 14
Willpower: 12
Charisma: 6
Traits:
Eye for Freshness
Heat Resistance

It wasn't very impressive—yet. She wouldn't get a new trait until she reached level two in Gunslinger, and ability improvement took time. She'd been born with a high Willpower and Perception, but the rest of her stats were decidedly average or below.

"Congratulations on making Tier Two!" Kelsey said happily. "We should wake Anton up and tell him the good news. But first . . ."

She sniffed the air. "You probably shouldn't see him smelling of blood and gun smoke. How about a bath?"

CHAPTER THIRTEEN

Slow Hand

ARIS

Aris had never seen so much hot water in her life. "This is a bath?" she exclaimed incredulously. "All of it?"

"Yeah, it must suck when you can't just carve out architecture with your mind," Kelsey replied. "Or just pipe and heat water as easy as thinking about it."

She stepped towards the pool and caused her clothes to disappear. Then she turned back, because Aris wasn't doing the same.

"Don't worry, the water's all recycled, and filtered and stuff. You don't have to worry about getting it dirty."

"That's not what I . . ." Aris said, swallowing the rest of the words.

"You're not worried about *that*, are you? We're all girls here," Kelsey said with a grin.

"You said . . . that sometimes girls can *like* other girls. Like boys do," Aris said.

"You've been thinking about that, have you? Come to any conclusions?" Kelsey stepped in closer—too close. Despite being shorter, and naked, she seemed incredibly intimidating to Aris.

"Do you—are you that way?" she managed to ask.

Kelsey smiled mysteriously. "I'm not human," she said. She started untying Aris's sling. "I don't have the same desires or needs that humans do."

She started working on gently removing the splint.

"We don't want to get this wet," she said. "It will cause the bindings to tighten more than they should."

As she worked, she continued with her original topic.

"But I do want to . . . experience all the good sensations that this body can feel, and that includes sex. From my perspective, the differences between men and women are purely superficial."

She started removing Aris's vest, undoing the lacing up the front.

"But this is just a bath, so relax and enjoy it. Do you need help with your arm?"

"No," Aris admitted. "I can move it."

"Then get undressed and join me."

The bath was amazing. Aris had never been immersed so deeply, never had a bath that was this hot, that could last for so long without the water getting cold and filthy. The soap was soft and creamy, lathering up without any stinging and anointing her with a slight scent of apples.

True to Kelsey's word, the water carried away all the dirt and suds, replacing them with endless fresh, hot water that melted the stiffness out of Aris's sore muscles.

Kelsey was annoyingly smug about it, once Aris had admitted that the bath was delightful. She insisted on washing Aris's back. It was . . . pleasant, if a little strange, Aris supposed.

"Are you imagining Anton doing this?" Kelsey teased, as she ran her hands down Aris's back.

"Don't be—" Aris started, but stopped herself. "Vulgar" was what she'd wanted to say, what she'd been taught to say, but it didn't feel right. The way Kelsey treated her body, the idea of sex, didn't allow for the word. She'd take it as a challenge, Aris knew.

Not that Kelsey needed a challenge. "Anton wouldn't be able to resist doing this," she chuckled, and her hands snaked around to caress Aris's breasts.

Aris let out a stifled shriek, but Kelsey ignored it, as she did Aris's sudden struggle to get herself free. Kelsey's flesh was warm and soft, but it was wrapped around bones with not the slightest bit of give.

I'm helpless, Aris thought. *Not just now, but since I entered this place, this place that is her. She can do whatever she wants; I can do nothing.*

Then Kelsey giggled and released her. "They're pretty big, aren't they?" she said. "I bet all the boys in town were after you."

Aris glared at the woman who was both her tormentor and patron. She covered her breasts with her arms. Well, one arm. Her broken arm was feeling a little sore. "Anton was always . . . there," she said. "The other boys knew . . . that."

"Childhood sweethearts, hey? Do you remember what brought you together?"

"He wasn't always as handsome as he is now," Aris confessed. "But he was always brave, and he saved me."

"You can fix ugly with levels," Kelsey said thoughtfully, "But bravery has to come from within. I'd say you made a good choice."

"Like I want to hear that from the one who stole him," Aris said petulantly. Kelsey only laughed.

"Good point! Well, it's my turn now." She turned her back to Aris.

"You want me to . . ." Of course she wanted her to. Scowling, she found the washcloth and started scrubbing Kelsey's back.

"Mmmm, that feels good," Kelsey sighed. "Are you curious?"

"No." Aris didn't have to ask about what.

"Liar. Have you ever felt another woman before?"

" . . . No," Aris admitted. She'd washed her sister, but that was before she'd grown and gotten as self-conscious about such things as Aris was.

"Then why not? Turnabout is fair play, after all."

"It's not the same thing," Aris insisted. "You want me to, I didn't."

"I guess. But it's all sensation, you know? It's not like it was unpleasant."

Kelsey's hands, softly caressing, *had* felt pretty good, but Aris wasn't going to admit that. "You scared me. I didn't want to feel that."

"Was it just fear . . . or was there some excitement in there?"

Aris felt her heart start to thud. "Just fear," she said hastily. Hoping to end the conversation, she thrust her hand forward and grabbed hold of Kelsey's chest. Just her good hand. It was . . . different from her own breast. Firmer, yet still soft, the nipple hard against her palm.

Aris snatched her hand back. "Happy?"

Kelsey giggled. "Very," she confirmed. "Let's get out of here and I'll make up for frightening you with a massage."

"What's a massage?" Aris asked suspiciously.

"You'll see. It's something that's good for sore muscles."

Leaving the bath was just a matter of walking up the provided steps. Kelsey offered to dry Aris, "because of her arm," but Aris insisted, and managed to dry herself. Before she could get dressed, though, Kelsey stopped her.

"This way," she said, leading Aris to an adjoining room that contained a table. "Lie face down on this," she told Aris.

"Why? And why can't I put on any clothes?"

"Because you have a beautiful body and I want to look at it," Kelsey said with a grin. She continued on, interrupting Aris's protest. "Also—I'm going to rub oil into your muscles, which I can't do if clothes are in the way."

"That's what a massage is? It doesn't sound like much," Aris said, ignoring the heat that came to her cheeks when Kelsey said she was beautiful. *Why do I care about that?*

"Eh, it's more than that, but you'll have to feel it to understand. Now get on the table."

Grudgingly, Aris complied, trying to expose as little of herself as possible. Kelsey ignored her efforts, summoning a bottle of what Aris guessed would be the oil.

"I don't think the nobles that buy this use it for massages," she said thoughtfully, "Just to smell nice. Should work nicely, though."

She started spreading oil on Aris's back, and Aris learned just what a massage was. She felt pleasure and pain in equal measure as Kelsey found Aris's sore spots with unerring accuracy and mercilessly destroyed them. Aris gasped as steel fingers found the knots in her muscles and released the tension that she hadn't even realized was there.

Kelsey mostly worked on Aris's neck and back, with some attention to the upper arms. By the time she worked her way down to the legs, Aris was too relaxed to protest when Kelsey started to tease her sensitive areas. Only a brief touch before moving on, but it made Aris aware of how exposed she was, and how helpless she was to do anything about it.

Finally, it was over.

"Roll towards me," Kelsey commanded, and Aris complied. She rolled onto the outstretched arms of Kelsey, who lifted her up easily and re-centered her on the table.

Belatedly, Aris realized that she was, once again, fully exposed to a grinning Kelsey. *Is she going to do all that to my front?* she wondered, half aghast at the thought. The other half was still purring with the release that she had already received.

"You've kissed Anton before, right?" Kelsey asked, leaning over.

"What?" Kelsey didn't repeat the question, just waited expectantly for the answer. "Yes," Aris reluctantly admitted.

Kelsey leaned in closer. "So if we were to kiss, it wouldn't be like I was stealing your first kiss or something," she whispered.

Aris just barely shook her head. Kelsey put her hand on Aris's shoulder, and then slowly moved it down to the breast. *I've gotten used to her touch*, Aris realized. *And I'm just as helpless against her as I always was.*

"It's just a kiss, after all," Kelsey whispered. "Just sensation. Are you curious?"

"Ye—" was all she had time for, before Kelsey's lips were pressing her down.

The sensation of soft lips against hers, softer and more delicate than Anton's, was soon disrupted by Kelsey's tongue forcing its way between her lips. Aris gasped, or tried to, but her mouth was covered, and Kelsey's tongue had just found her own. Aris lost herself in the feeling as her mouth was explored and exploited. Kelsey took her time enjoying Aris's mouth, only breaking off when they ran out of air.

"Was that unpleasant?" Kelsey asked mischievously.

Aris's breath had deepened, and her heart was beating like a jackhammer. Something was stirring in her, a warmth between her legs.

"No," she admitted. She wanted Kelsey to press her down again, to feel like she wasn't in control.

"Well, it's time to wake Anton."

Aris was already flushed, but somehow the heat in her cheeks became even more intense. *I don't want Anton to see me like this!* Just as quickly came the thought that maybe she *did*.

"Not for *that*, silly," Kelsey admonished her. "Put your clothes on first."

"What? But—" Aris managed to say. Her emotions were too confused to get a coherent thought out.

"Dawn's coming," Kelsey said. "We're going to need to get going soon if we want to get back into town without being noticed."

Aris's clothes, discarded near the bath, disappeared. Then they reappeared in Kelsey's hands.

"Here. I've got a feeling that today isn't going to be a good day to be missing from town."

CHAPTER FOURTEEN

Cold Cold Ground

SULIEL

Embarrassingly, the morning patrols had found her father's body before they knew he was missing. He'd been *missed*, certainly. He hadn't come back to Mother's bed that night, but these past few days it hadn't been at all unusual for him to nap in his study, or borrow a cot in the barracks. Or just work through the night. Things had calmed down enough that it shouldn't have been needed, but something might have come up.

So they had been *wondering* where he was, but not yet *concerned*, when word came that men from the Glimmered Lancers had found his body. Then they blew past concerned, and moved all the way to panicked.

Or perhaps *panicked* should be reserved for times like the night of the raid. Suliel had been kept as safely as possible that night, but she'd smelled the smoke and heard the screams. Felt the fear. Today was worse than that night in some ways, but today she wasn't feeling afraid of an unknown future that might include rape or death. Today, she felt her future settling down on her with grim inevitability.

Her father was dead. She was the Baroness now.

Technically, her mother was regent until Suliel reached Tier Two. But her mother had not been trained in such things, as Suliel had been, and was consumed by grief besides. Most of her vassals had tacitly accepted her new role, and Suliel could feel the experience swelling within her as they accepted her rule.

People on the path got experience for ruling, which made it hard for the young. No one wanted to accept leadership from a child. That was why Suliel was only level three, when most of the people her age in the village were level five, and on the brink of choosing their first adult class.

Thanks to her unfortunate circumstances, she would be joining them before too long. Idly, she wondered if she'd just qualify for Noble or a rarer variant like Embattled Noble, or Vengeful Noble. Those classes didn't have the best reputations, but they had better ability improvement, which wasn't to be refused. And she was feeling more than a little vengeful.

"His head is *missing*?" she asked the tracker. She was pretty sure his name was Empol. She'd wanted one of her men to look at the scene after the Lancers had brought her father back.

"Yes, my lady," the man said miserably. "The Lancers searched around for it when they found the body, but there was no sign, and I wasn't able to find it either."

Mother was going to die when she heard this news. The body had been brought back, but neither of them had seen it yet. She would have to notify the Church of Humanity that—

"My lady . . ." The tracker interrupted her planning. "There were a number of irregularities at the place where we found the bodies."

"Bodies?" Suliel asked. She'd only been told about her father, but it made sense that he hadn't been found alone. He would have had guards with him, after all.

"What irregularities?" Captain Oldaw spoke for the first time, speaking over her. It was his men who had found the body and were currently searching for the killers, so he'd invited himself to this meeting.

Empol looked nervously at the man and bowed his head, but he turned back to his liege to answer her question.

"The bodies are one of the irregularities, my lady. There were three guards found with his lordship: Anshy, Ruzute, and Iaim."

Suliel felt a physical pang of pain. Those had been some of her father's most trusted guards; she knew them well. Empol wasn't finished, though.

"Those might have been expected, but there were also three raiders."

"Raiders!" She looked over at Captain Oldaw in confusion. "But it's been days since they left!"

Oldaw nodded grimly. "That's what my men reported, too. There's no doubt about it—aside from the uniforms, one of them was a courl. We're scouring the area in case there's a force out there. These might have just been left behind. What other irregularities were there?" he asked the tracker.

Empol glanced at her but answered the captain's question. "My lady, none of the bodies left any tracks."

Captain Oldaw's eyes narrowed. "My men told me it looked like there was a fight."

"Aye, my lord, but it doesn't hold up if you look closely. I've got *See the Trail*, and there's not the tracks that there'd be if there had been a fight. There's some blood, but not enough, and it's not been sprayed, just . . . dribbled out of the wounds."

"But no tracks?" Suliel asked.

"Just two sets that weren't mine or your Lancers', sir," Empol said, nodding at the captain. "Leading in and leading out, joining up with the dungeon path. I couldn't follow 'em past that."

"But what . . . what does that even mean?" Suliel asked. "Two people couldn't have carried seven corpses all that way—at night—it's impossible."

"No horses? Or wheel tracks?" Oldaw asked the tracker, who shook his head. "It *might* be possible," he sighed. "A high Tier Three, or higher, with a strength-gain path . . . could maybe find a way to carry four bodies without leaving tracks."

He cocked his head in thought. "Or they could just have a storage item."

"Is there even a storage item in the country?" Suliel asked in disbelief. "Those are legends."

"They do exist," the captain pointed out. "And if we're dealing with a Tier Four, those sorts of legends become much more likely."

Suliel stared at the captain. "Are you saying that our most probable explanation is that a wandering Tier Four has *stolen my father's head* for some mysterious reason?"

Oldaw grimaced and didn't answer, but it wasn't as if Suliel had a better explanation. She turned to her seneschal.

"Get Mayn to look at the bodies, see if there is anything unusual," she said, naming the physician that attended her house. "Magister Tikin as well, have him check the bodies and the scene for magic."

The seneschal bowed and turned to leave, but she stopped him. "Have Captain Rynmos put together a squad of his best—" she choked for a second, the pang hitting her again, "—his best remaining men, to canvas the town and interview the castle staff. We need to figure out how my father got from this castle to that field."

Captain Oldaw was going to be a problem. She'd noticed that he hadn't accepted her authority, but she hadn't been able to call him on it because technically he wasn't subordinate to her. His men reported to him, and he reported to the King.

But these were *her* lands. Oldaw had consulted with her father before taking any actions—and he wasn't doing the same for her. The investigation into her father's murder was a civil matter, but he'd insisted that the dead raiders turned it into at least a partial military concern.

Was it just military pigheadedness, or was there more to it, she wondered. She was, she reminded herself, much more valuable as a bride than she had been yesterday. Before, someone who married her might expect to be a Baron in twenty or thirty years—as long as Father didn't sire a son. Now, though, whoever married her would become the Baron immediately. If the marriage happened before she reached level five, she might even lose access to the Noble class and have to take Lady like her mother.

The captain was still fairly young, unmarried, and presumably ambitious. He was of noble blood, but not titled. Younger sons often found their way into the military with hopes of earning a title, through either valor or marriage. Had he decided to settle for the relatively lowly title of Baron?

Mother would insist that she gave the idea *some* consideration. He was handsome enough, she supposed, with broad shoulders and wavy hair . . . but she already had eyes on someone her own age. He'd never been a *realistic* prospect, but once she was Baroness in her own right, Mother wouldn't be able to stop her.

Right now, Oldaw was giving a report on what his men had found outside of the town, at her insistence. She'd made it the price of him attending the meeting where she heard the reports from *her* men. He'd tried to barge through anyway, but she'd prepared her guards to keep him from the room until he agreed. This was, she'd had to remind him, *her* castle.

". . . so the whole area has been thoroughly searched, but nothing further has come up. The only place we haven't checked yet is the dungeon, so I've placed a guard on the entrance and sent a search party down to see if anyone is hiding down there."

Suliel frowned. "You should speak with the Adventurers Guild before you do that—I believe they were about ready to start sending delvers down there again."

He waved a hand dismissively. "It's already done. I expect a report back by sundown, and we'll be out of their way by tomorrow."

Suliel swallowed her anger at him, once again, taking action without consulting her. "Are you sure you want to do that? Your men aren't trained to delve, and the danger for this dungeon ramps up quickly . . ."

"It will be fine," he said carelessly. "My men train for harder things than this—and if there is someone down there, they will have to have cleared out the level they're on."

"Fine then," Suliel said coldly. They were his men to risk, after all. Moving on, she turned to her physician who was nodding slowly. "Did you find out anything from the bodies, Master Mayn?"

"Just one thing of note, my lady," her physician said, tugging nervously on his grey beard. He seemed to have noticed Oldaw's rudeness as well. "The, ah, wounds, yes. They were all made by the same kind, if not the same weapon."

"All the wounds?" Oldaw pressed.

"Yes, on our people as well as the raiders," the old man confirmed, "as well as the Baron's . . . neck wound. The cuts are distinctive, having a certain . . . ragged nature."

"Ragged . . . like a saw?" The Captain asked, then glanced at Suliel as if realizing he had gone too far. Her eyes had gone wide, and her skin was clammy.

Did they saw *my father's head off?*

"Nothing so extreme!" Master Mayn assured her quickly. "But something of that nature. A sword that had taken a great amount of damage, perhaps."

"Or perhaps one that was made damaged," Captain Rynmos said slowly. All of the locals exchanged a look, and her captain turned to Oldaw. "You might not be aware, sir, but one of the common monsters in the dungeon here are the skeleton warriors that carry rusty longswords."

"I see," Oldaw said.

"Skeleton warriors couldn't have killed the Baron, though," Rynmos cautioned. "By the time they get to Tier Three, their swords are almost perfectly made."

"And they would have left tracks, and they never leave the dungeon in the first place," Suliel pointed out. "We're still missing something. Rynmos?"

"My lady?" he asked, and then realized it was his turn to report. "Ah, I've got people asking around town if anyone caught sight of the Baron last night. I've confirmed that he was assigned those three guards. The last that anyone saw him was when one of the maids delivered his dinner to his study, as he'd requested. He wasn't there when she came back to collect the dishes."

He looked up from his notes. "None of the gate guards for the castle or the town wall reported seeing him. No one in town saw him. Is there anything else I should be asking about?"

Suliel considered the matter. "Have them ask about anyone seeing *anything* suspicious that night. Get me a report about the movements of anyone who was acting suspiciously, or is new to the town.

"And start with that strange northern merchant. She's suspicious, she's new, and she's linked to dungeons somehow. Find out what she was doing last night—what she's been doing all week. Then get her up here so I can speak with her myself."

CHAPTER FIFTEEN

It's Like That

Anton didn't normally sleep late—delving was a daytime activity. At least, that was the rule his parents had enforced. Underground, it didn't really matter what time of day it was, but you did want to be well rested.

Last night had been an exception. He'd only gotten a few hours of sleep in the Dungeon before Kelsey was waking him and dragging him back to the inn. He'd been too groggy to register how Kelsey had gotten them back inside. They'd climbed a dark wall at some point—Kelsey going ahead and dropping a rope ladder that looked suspiciously like the one from the standard guild pack.

He'd barely been awake enough to notice the presence of Aris, but they did exchange a few quiet words before climbing into bed.

This is the second time we've slept together but we still haven't—was his first thought on awakening. His second thought, hard on the heels of the first, was simply panic as he registered that Kelsey wasn't in the room.

He gasped and sat up straight on the bed, fumbling with the sheets as he made to race outside. Aris stirred beside him at the disturbance, making a noise he noted as being cute.

"What's going on?" she mumbled. Anton wished that he had time to answer, but he had to get to Kelsey. He was still wearing his clothes from last night, so he could—

At that point, his heart eased as he heard Kelsey's voice, just outside. She was close. And talking with another voice that he recognized.

"I will see him!" It was Liat, yelling angrily, which wasn't something that Anton had ever heard before.

"I told you, he's still sleeping—Oh, good morning, Anton. Sleep well?"

Anton had wrenched the door open. His panic didn't fully ease until he caught sight of Kelsey. For a second he just stood there, gasping for breath as the fear left him, taking in the sight before him.

Kelsey was standing in the middle of the corridor. In one hand, she held a large tray heaped high with fried eggs, toasted bread, and cooked ham. In her other hand, she held Liat's lower arm. Kelsey had twisted Liat's arm behind her back, effortlessly controlling both her and the plate of breakfast.

Liat's mobility may have been restricted, but her voice was not. "Anton, I— ow ow ow!"

"Don't interrupt," Kelsey admonished her.

"Please don't hurt her," Anton pleaded.

"She's fine," Kelsey assured him with a smile. "She's got something she wants to talk with us about, so if you and Aris are ready, we can have a chat in the meeting room over breakfast."

She glanced back at Liat. "Like civilized people, right?"

"Yes! All right! Just please—"

"Great!" She looked back at Anton. "We'll just be in there when you're ready, all right?"

Anton nodded, blankly. It hurt to watch her walk away to the next door down, but it was just the geas; he could resist it—for this long at least. Kelsey had Liat open the door for her and then walked through, leaving Anton with only a short window before he panicked again.

He went back into the bedroom. Aris was sitting up in bed, looking at him. She'd probably heard all of that, but he felt the need to fill her in anyway.

"Breakfast is served, next door?" he said helplessly.

Aris nodded. "I guess we should join them, then?" she asked. Checking under the sheets that she still had clothes on, she got out of bed and joined him.

"Anton," she said excitedly, "I got a new class! It's Unique!"

Anton ignored the pang of jealousy that he felt at the words. His own class was only Rare, though his path did lead to a *Unique Tier Three* class.

"That's great!" he said. He mostly meant it, though he did have some doubts that anything Kelsey had provided was without a nasty drawback. "Let's talk about it later, though, Liat's here."

"Should we keep it a secret?"

"Just for a little bit. Kelsey's . . . doing something, and we need to be careful until we know how it's going to turn out."

Aris looked at him questioningly, but he just shook his head. He couldn't bring himself to say that Kelsey had killed the Baron and was still trying to sell her weapons to anyone that would buy them. Instead, he led her through to the meeting room, where Kelsey and Liat were waiting.

Liat was sitting at the table with a sour look on her face. She didn't say anything as they entered, just glared at Kelsey. Kelsey had found additional plates and cutlery and was serving up three plates of the food. Anton had to admit that it did smell delicious, and he was very hungry.

"Eat up!" Kelsey said, taking her own advice and stacking a piece of bread high with ham and egg and taking a big bite out of it. Anton and Aris got started on their own meals, while Kelsey just chewed with a look of bliss on her face. Finally, she swallowed and started talking again.

"Liat has *agreed*," she said, glancing over at the now more subdued guild official, "that her business can wait until you're not starved."

"Did you want some of this?" Aris asked Liat, but the woman just shook her head.

"I've already eaten, thank you," she said coldly.

The food was delicious, like every meal at the inn so far, but the tension soured the taste. While Kelsey seemed entirely unaffected, Anton was done after only a few mouthfuls.

"Why don't you tell us what you're here for," he said to Liat.

Liat looked nervously at Kelsey who ignored her, preferring to focus on breakfast. Electing to continue, she spoke in a low, urgent tone.

"Anton. This woman is deceiving you. She wants to destroy the guild, the guild that you're a part of—that your parents were part of—"

"Not true," Kelsey mumbled around a mouthful of ham. "I don't want to destroy the guild."

"I heard all about your *deal*, you hussy," Liat sneered. "You want to take over the dungeon!"

Kelsey finished her mouthful and carefully swallowed. "First of all, I only offered that deal because of concerns that Kirido couldn't defend itself against the Elitrans. Concerns that I would have thought you shared."

She looked questioningly at Liat. Liat didn't respond, but she looked less certain of herself.

"If the Baron"—Anton couldn't help but flinch at the reminder, but Liat wasn't looking at him—"doesn't want the weapons, then that's fine. If he does, I'm going to need the dungeon to fill his order. And I'm going to need you guys to help me with that."

"The guild . . . helping you?"

"We're just two people, after all." Kelsey smiled. "I haven't brought anything to you guys because the whole deal could easily fall through. Using dungeons like this . . . it's normal to *me*, but I can see it's a big departure from how you people do things. I have no idea if the Baron is able to, or even *wants* to make the legal exceptions that would be required."

"How . . . are you going to do this?" Liat asked. "No one has made it to the bottom of this dungeon."

"You only need to do that if you're enslaving the dungeon," Kelsey said easily, not showing a flicker of emotion. "My methods are different—and will remain my own."

"I don't think that the guild—or the Baron—would go along with this if you were enslaving it," Liat admitted. "I'm not sure about working with you . . ."

"It would be more like working *for* me," Kelsey informed her. "I'd be in charge of the dungeon, and I'd pass the tasks that I have, both in and around the dungeon, to your Guild Master, and he can assign them as he likes."

Liat couldn't conceal her dismay over the thought of her guild being relegated to a subordinate role, but she focused on another aspect of what Kelsey had said.

"Around the dungeon?"

"Mostly guard duty, unless you guys have hidden construction talents," Kelsey clarified. "I'm going to need access to be much more controlled."

"There's never been a need for that before," Liat protested. "The dungeons belong to the Kingdom."

"Yeah, well that's going to change for this dungeon," Kelsey said, a hard edge suddenly appearing in her voice.

"I don't think the guild can support this proposal," Liat said, her own voice going cold as well.

"Well, it's not really up to you, is it?" Kelsey said. "You'll go along with what the Baron decides."

"That's true, but he does value our advice," Liat countered. "I'm sure he'll see the wisdom of keeping to tradition."

"I don't really mind either way," Kelsey said. She spoke lightly and easily, but Anton was fairly sure she was lying.

Wait—of course she's lying; the Baron's dead! He's not going to approve anything!

Anton grimaced at how Kelsey had already made him forget about her latest crime, but she continued talking to Liat.

"If he doesn't want the guns, if he wants to put tradition over saving the lives of his people . . ." Kelsey shrugged. "It's not my problem. I can move on."

"And sell these weapons to the Elitrans?" Liat accused.

"I don't need to." Kelsey shrugged. "They're already winning; they don't need them."

Liat struggled to find a response, but before she did there was a knock at the door of the bedroom.

"Just a moment," Kelsey said and went to the other door of the suite. Opening it, she called down the corridor. "Are you looking for me?" she said.

With the door open, the tramp of the guards' heavy boots could be clearly heard long before the pair appeared in the doorway.

"Ma'am, you've been summoned to the castle."

"Well, it's about time the Baron decided to talk with me," Kelsey said with a grin. By now, Anton was numb to mentions of the Baron, but he noticed that the guards flinched when he was mentioned. They didn't correct her, though.

"Anton, you're with me," Kelsey continued. "Aris, you can stay here or go see your parents, whatever you want. Liat, I'd invite you to join . . ."

"I'll go back to the guild," Liat replied stiffly. "The Guild Master will speak with the Baron."

"Fine, fine," Kelsey said. "Let's go."

The guards didn't seem to be happy with Anton accompanying Kelsey, but they seemed a bit nervous of the deceptively harmless-looking young woman. Anton wasn't sure if they had a danger sense, or if they'd heard that the Baron couldn't determine her level. Either way, they seemed satisfied that Kelsey was coming voluntarily—eagerly, even—and chose not to make a fuss about the extra person.

As they moved through the town, Anton noticed that there were several guards out and about. Not patrolling in pairs, but individually out among the townsfolk, speaking to people.

Something prompted him to mention it to Kelsey. "That's unusual," he said, pointing out one of the guards talking with a blacksmith.

"Is it?" she asked. Her eyes flicked about, noting the others. "Is something going on?" she asked their escort.

"I can't talk about that, ma'am," was the reply, telling in its own way. Kelsey pursed her lips in thought and kept on walking.

Instead of the courtyard where they gave their presentation, or the audience hall, the guards led them deeper into the castle. When they came to a door with a guard in front of it, they stopped.

The new guard frowned. "It was only supposed to be her," he said.

"Anton stays with me," Kelsey said firmly. Anton could only nod.

The guard frowned again. "Wait here," he said and entered the room he was guarding. There was a brief pause, and then a different man emerged. He didn't meet anyone's eyes but scuttled off awkwardly. A few moments later, the guard also emerged.

"Can we go in?" Kelsey asked.

"Not yet," the guard replied gruffly. It wasn't long before the awkward man returned, this time carrying a chair. The guard let him in, while Kelsey and Anton shared a look.

"Now you can go in," the guard said.

Anton and Kelsey entered cautiously, their escort just behind them. The room was sparsely decorated and held just four chairs. Two of the chairs were behind a small table and occupied. The two empty chairs sat in the middle of the room and were clearly for the pair of them.

As if she didn't have a concern in the world, Kelsey strode forward and sat in one of the chairs. "Hey kiddo!" she said brightly. "Is your dad letting you sit in on this meeting?"

One of the chairs was occupied by the awkward man. Judging by the papers and quills in front of him, he was some sort of scribe. The other chair was occupied by a beautiful girl with long dark hair.

"My father died last night," Suliel Anat said quietly. "I'm the Baroness now."

CHAPTER SIXTEEN

Something Just Ain't Right

SULIEL

The woman had brought Anton! Suliel didn't know if she was happy or angry. She reminded herself that she was the ruler here, and went with unemotional.

"Why did you bring Anton?" she asked coldly. Knowing that it would be useless, she ran Nobility's Privilege over the pair of them. As expected, it came up entirely blank on Kelsey. On Anton . . .

Anton Nos (Level ??)
Living Relatives: None
Citizenship: Zamarran
Primary Loyalty: "Kelsey"

The question marks had been there since he had reached Tier Two, an annoying reminder of just how far he was ahead of her. Living relatives was a somber reminder that almost the entire Nos family had been wiped out in defense of her town. Primary loyalty was just infuriating. Not least because Suliel was sure that the quotation marks meant that "Kelsey" had managed to find some way to insert faked details into other people's dossiers.

"Anton's my partner, he stays with me," Kelsey said with unnecessary smugness. Suliel stiffened, trying to hide her reaction. She must have failed because Kelsey quickly corrected herself. "My *business* partner," she clarified, watching Suliel carefully.

Suliel was mortified that she was apparently an open book to this woman, but Kelsey wasn't done. "I don't know if you're aware, but he's actually engaged to this girl in town? She—"

"Kelsey!" Anton interrupted. "Please don't . . . talk about that."

The damage was done, though. *Engaged? Commoners do arrange these things hastily, but still.* She had thought she'd have more time. At least Anton didn't seem to have noticed her reaction.

Fully aware of the emotional chaos she'd caused, Kelsey just smiled and leaned back on her chair. "So what can we do for you, Baroness?"

Suliel's glare was interrupted by a knock on the door. It opened slightly as she glanced at it.

"Ma'am—" her guard managed to say before he was interrupted and shoved farther into the room.

"Out of my way, soldier!" Captain Oldaw growled, forcing his way in.

"What is the meaning of this, Captain!" Suliel protested. Her two guests turned to look at his entry. Anton shrank back in his chair, but Kelsey was entirely unconcerned, looking back at the powerful man with clear amusement.

"I heard that you were interrogating suspects," Oldaw said.

"A suspect? Me?" Kelsey said with obviously false dismay. Suliel noticed in passing that Anton glanced worriedly at Kelsey, but Suliel's attention was on the captain.

"If this woman is an Elitran spy, then the defense of the realm is threatened!" Oldaw insisted. "Which is a matter for the King's officers."

"Really, Captain, do I look like an Elitran spy?" Kelsey said, chuckling. "Would an Elitran spy be selling you weapons that the Elitrans don't have?"

"No one is an Elitran spy, Captain," Suliel said in exasperation. "No one is even a suspect—yet. This woman is merely *suspicious*." She glared at the offensive merchant woman.

"I must insist on attending this interrogation," Oldaw stated firmly. Suliel was glaring at Kelsey when he said it, so she was able to notice that in response, Kelsey met her gaze and gave a tiny shake of her head.

Is she frightened of him? But that didn't match the rest of her demeanor. Strange as that might be, it seemed as if Kelsey was sending her a message.

"That won't be necessary," she snapped out as decisively as she could. "Please leave us."

"But I—"

"If anything comes up that is relevant to your duties, you will be informed. Now leave—or do I need to inform the King that one of his officers is overstepping his authority?"

For a long, tense, moment Captain Oldaw considered his options. Suliel's words were a bluff, and they both knew it. Any word that Suliel sent to the King would be entirely dependent on the Captain's good graces to get through. Under normal circumstances, it would be his man that delivered it!

That would not be the case for long, though. Sooner or later, he would be moved on to check another attack or return to the capital. Unless he did something . . . final, her words would eventually make their way to the King.

Suliel let out a slow breath, as Oldaw decided not to take that step . . . today.

"As you say, milady. I shall take my leave then." He turned and left without another word.

You have reached Level 4.
Please select a new trait.

Suliel ignored the message, even as it made her heart sing. Instead, she turned Nobility's Privilege on Anton again.

Anton Nos (Level ??)
Living Relatives: None
Citizenship: Zamarran
Primary Loyalty: "Kelsey"

Still over twice my level! It should have been infuriating, but giddy with both her level increase and her still fresh victory, she couldn't bring herself to care. Instead, she turned back to Kelsey.

"What was it you wanted to tell me?" she asked.

Kelsey just smiled and nodded towards the scribe who was writing down everything that was said. Suliel glanced at him. The implication was obvious, but she was new to this kind of game.

You're the Baroness now, get used to it.

"Belze . . ." she said slowly.

"Yes ma'am?"

"Stop writing."

Her scribe looked at her in surprise, but obeyed her instruction, wiping off his quill and bowing his head.

"I suppose you're going to say that you trust all these people?" Kelsey said, gesturing at the guards.

"Of course." She couldn't help but feel doubt when questioned like that, but she kept it off her face, and out of her voice.

"Well, that's your decision, I guess," Kelsey said philosophically. "Let me make one thing clear. I don't know who killed your father. But I do know that he had a secret meeting last night. With me."

"About the rifles," Suliel said woodenly.

"Of course. He wanted to make a deal that the good Captain Oldaw wouldn't know about."

"Why?" Her father didn't have the same problem with Oldaw that she did. Well, actually, it was possible that Oldaw had been asking her father for her hand, but even so, it wasn't the same sort of pressure. He was secure in his position, in a way that Suliel definitely was not.

"He didn't say, and I'm not really in a position to speculate," Kelsey replied. "I'm an outsider here." Suliel glanced at Anton, who seemed lost trying to follow the conversation. As a commoner, he could hardly be expected to know much about the goings-on of the nobility.

"What deal did he want, then?"

"He wanted me to spin out negotiations, make it seem like we hadn't concluded the deal," Kelsey said. "But in reality, I sold him my stock for two hundred gold."

Two hundred! "My father gave you two hundred gold last night?"

"Oh, no, I sold them on credit." Kelsey smiled. "Since you're the Baroness, I guess that means you owe me two hundred gold."

Suliel gave Kelsey an icy glare. "There was no sign of the weapons anywhere near the place my father was killed. I'm not going to give you two hundred gold on your say-so."

"Of course! But the weapons will turn up," Kelsey said, still without any sign of concern. "Once they do, I'm sure you'll either help me regain my stolen property or claim them for yourself. In which case, I'd expect you to honor your father's deal.

"As long as the money isn't missing from the treasury . . . I'll think about it."

"Sooooo . . . .," Kelsey said, dragging the word out. "Now that we're all up to date, I can think of one person who might have killed your father and stolen my rifles. Can you?"

Suliel glanced involuntarily at the door. The implication was obvious, but . . . "It can't be him. He's loyal to the King."

"Is he? Do you know that for sure?" Kelsey asked. "And even if he is . . . it's not unknown for there to be tension between the crown and the lesser nobles . . . any chance of that here?"

Suliel frowned. "I don't know," she admitted. She had been mostly kept away from such matters. Her mother might know if she was in a fit state to be talked to.

"It's tough to be in charge," Kelsey said sympathetically. "I wish I could help—but even if I could, you probably wouldn't let me. There is some good news, though it's rolled all through with bad."

"What's that, then?"

"You won't need to wait for long," Kelsey said. "Whoever's behind this, they're going to want to use those rifles. They're the only ones in the country, so once they do, you'll have your murderer."

"How is that bad news?"

"Chances are, they're going to be using them on you." Kelsey leaned forward and patted Suliel's hand lying numbly on the table. "I'm rooting for you, though!"

Suliel stared up at the woman, her mind whirling with suspicions and speculation.

"Was there anything else, or can I go?" Kelsey said brightly.

"I . . . no, you can go," Suliel said, giving up. Kelsey grinned at her.

"Just keep in mind, the deal with the dungeon for ammunition is still open," she said. "For as long as I'm in town—and yeah, I guess you don't want me to leave? For the foreseeable future then."

Suliel sank her face into her hands as the woman left with Anton.

"Uh, ma'am?" Belze asked cautiously. "What should I write down as happening here?"

Suliel thought about it. "Can you . . . can you write down some questions with boring answers?" she asked. "Nothing about what was said here."

"Of course," Belze said. "Leave it to me."

"That goes for all of you," she said to the guards. "No one hears of what was said here." They both nodded.

Suliel sighed. "I need to go talk with my mother," she said. But first . . . she accepted her new level.

Please allocate 1 free Ability point.

So far, she'd always put the extra point in Charisma, but . . . she was a Baroness now. Her father wasn't going to be able to protect her. *My low Agility could get me killed*, she thought and allocated the point there.

Status
Level: 4
Class: Scion
Path: Scion
Strength: 2
Toughness: 9
Agility: 2
Dexterity: 9
Perception: 13
Willpower: 11
Charisma: 10

Traits:
Nobility's Privilege

Available Traits:
Desperate Defense | Flair for Administration | Aura of Nobility | Bind
    Servant | Chance of the Moment

All of the available traits were ones that had been known for a long time. The
benefits and drawbacks of each had been part of her education.

Desperate Defense was one of the rarer combat traits to be made available for a
noble, but if her current problems resulted in combat, she was sure to lose. *Flair
for Administration* was what she would have taken if her father was still alive. It
gave a supernatural skill with numbers and bookkeeping. If she'd taken it, Father
would surely have given her greater responsibilities, increasing her rate of experience gain.

Chance of the Moment was a trait from level two . . . they were sometimes
offered again. She'd passed it over in favor of *Nobility's Privilege*, which was a must-
have for any noble. *Chance of the Moment* let you see the significant moments in
your life as they came about. The momentous decisions, the moment the tide
turned, the moment it was too late to turn back. Chance didn't tell you what to
do, but it let you know when a moment was important.

Bind Servant allowed you to take a person who felt some loyalty to you and
turn them into a servant who would be loyal forever. Hated by some, but it was
something that was needed by the ruling class. In her case, though, she had a
castle full of loyal servants. She could make one of them more loyal, but the gain
would be minimal.

Or she could use it on Anton. Make him forget Kelsey and that other girl.

That . . . wasn't what she wanted. A servant wasn't a lover, even if she ordered
him into bed. With reluctance, she turned to the one she was going to take.

Select Aura of Nobility.

This would make everyone see her as someone who *should* be obeyed. Only
people of her Tier and below, but she wouldn't be Tier One for long. It didn't
compel obedience, only gave an impression, but there was only so much a Tier
One trait could do.

Soon. Soon I'll be a noble.

CHAPTER SEVENTEEN

Sixteen Shells from a Thirty-Ought Six

MEL

There are people coming inside, and they're not adventurers!"

Kelsey grunted in acknowledgement. "Yeah, I know," she said, stating the obvious. She would have known the moment they entered inside her. She didn't seem to care, though, which was what had Mel agitated.

"Only adventurers are supposed to come in! Isn't that the rule?" she asked. It had been the case for at least fifteen years, and Mel had been very pleased to learn that it was an enforced rule for the local area and not random happenstance.

Kelsey sighed and turned away from the sight of her skeletons carefully distilling the oil that she'd brought in from the outside. Her original avatar looked exactly the same as the new one that was out in the city, but this one was purely a mental construct. It helped focus her attention and gave Mel something to talk at. By mutual agreement, Kelsey pretended she didn't notice anything that Mel did out of sight of her avatar.

"These guys are the cavalry that showed up too late to help," she said dismissively. "There's a bit of a power play going on. I think they're just camping outside to show that they don't answer to the locals. That, and they might be looking for whoever killed the Baron."

"Do they know we did it?" Mel asked nervously. Dungeons weren't *supposed* to go out and kill people. Sure, dungeon breaks *happened*, but they were shameful incidents that fairies didn't like to talk about. Fortunately, for all her strange ideas, Kelsey agreed with her about that. She disdained sending out her monsters to randomly kill, on the grounds that it was inefficient.

"Nah, and even if they suspected, it's not like they're going to find evidence lying around. Don't worry, I've got all the traps and stuff set up."

Mel had protested Kelsey disabling almost all their protective measures on the first two levels for the last run, but only a little bit. In truth, she found the idea of a run being carefully calibrated to threaten, but not outright murder, an exciting one. It harked back to the original purpose of dungeons. She just wished it was feasible for anything other than a very special occasion.

"Can we watch, just to make sure?" she asked nervously. She didn't actually need Kelsey's permission to flit upstairs, nor did Kelsey need her avatar to sense what was going on. But she wanted to talk while she watched, which required Kelsey's presence.

Kelsey sighed, but it was an indulgent one, so Mel flitted upstairs, passing through the ceilings and walls as if they didn't exist. Kelsey didn't follow her. Instead, she re-manifested herself when Mel had stopped moving.

"There they are," she said, entirely unnecessarily. "Metal armor," she added with disapproval.

Kelsey snorted. "I'm surprised they didn't try taking their horses in."

"Oooh, horses?" Mel asked. "You still haven't brought in any big animals from outside."

"I brought in some chickens," Kelsey replied. "Most of the livestock was killed or taken by the raiders. What's left is needed for breeding or food, so it wasn't for sale."

"Horses would be nice, though," Mel said. "We could have Skeleton Riders."

"It's on the list," Kelsey said, amused. They continued to watch, completely undetectable, as the party of ten men made their way through the crypt of the first level.

"They're not avoiding the mushrooms," Mel noted with some glee. The invaders weren't dumb enough to *eat* the mushrooms, no one had fallen for that in thirty years, but disturbing the mushrooms had its own dangers. The spores had various deleterious effects.

Kelsey hadn't been warned about the spores at the guild, but adventurers knew to be careful about such things. Despite how carefully she had placed them, adventurers rarely disturbed them enough to trigger the spores.

Rarely wasn't *never*, though, so they had been surprised that no one had figured out the effects. Mana levels being what they were on the top floor, they hadn't managed anything spectacular, but still.

The first kind of spores had only a mild disorienting effect, which took some time to take hold. Unlucky adventurers probably assumed it was an effect of the third floor. The other main kind was even more subtle. The spores, too small to see, were sticky and slightly corrosive to metal. Arms and armor exposed to them would corrode at two or three times the normal weight until the spores were carefully washed off.

It was one of the ways that Kelsey discouraged metal armor. Coming up was another one.

"Bet the first one gets stuck," Mel said.

"No bet; they *always* get stuck," Kelsey replied. The invaders had found no real challenge to killing low-level zombies, so they had reached the entrance to the first boss chamber quite quickly. As Aris had discovered, this was a narrow shaft leading into darkness. She hadn't had any problem getting down, but she was fairly small and hadn't been wearing partial plate. Unlike these guys.

"See?" Kelsey said as the first man started shouting and struggling. "At least his buddies can pull him out."

In the early days, there had been some tragic (or amusing, depending on who you were rooting for) cases of lone delvers, fully armored, getting stuck with no one to help them. They'd died eventually, which had allowed Kelsey to collect the corpses and clear the passage.

Back in the present, Mel and Kelsey watched as the men argued for a bit and then started stripping off their armor. Belatedly, Kelsey thought to read out her Identification results.

"The one in charge is a knight, level eighteen," she said, pointing. "There's a scout, level fifteen, two horsemen, and eight lancers, all low teens."

"How far do you think they'll get?" Mel asked.

"I dunno. They're not going to be challenged by any monster fights until they get to level five, so it will probably be environmental effects that stop them. They've got the scout to point out the traps, but that might not help when they get to the places where the traps can't be avoided."

"Anything against poison, you think?"

One by one, the soldiers dropped down the hole. The two watchers didn't bother descending to watch the boss fight, preferring to watch the remaining man bundle up armor and toss it down.

"No, so the spiders should take out a few . . . they might stop there to get the wounded back out."

Kelsey hissed to herself, drawing in breath as she thought. The final man made his way down to find the fight already over. The two drifted down, watching with amusement as the men all put on their armor again. They'd have to remove it at the end of this level as well.

"I think it might . . . be the best idea if these guys didn't make it," she said thoughtfully.

"A total wipe? Why?"

"Well, I said this was a power play, right? I'm not clear on the details, but there's a daughter that's set to inherit from the Baron. I'll bet I can get a better deal from her than I could from a Tier Three knight with ambitions."

"Right . . ." Mel said, not really understanding.

"So I should do something to bolster her political position, right? If knight-guy loses these men, not only is he down in numbers, he looks stupid for sending them down there."

"Well, killing intruders is what we're here for," Mel allowed. "But won't that stir up resentment? And how are you going to kill them *all*, anyway? You said yourself that they'll pull back when things start going bad."

"I might have to cheat, just a little." Kelsey looked both guilty and gleeful at the thought.

"You're not thinking of using *those*, are you? You agreed it was a bad idea!"

"Against adventurers, yeah," Kelsey agreed, "But these are soldiers; they don't have all the tricks that adventurers do. If someone gets away, yeah, it would be bad. But as long as I get them all . . ."

"Didn't you say these men were needed for the defense of the town?" Mel tried. "This Baroness won't thank you for reducing their military strength."

"Like I care about that," Kelsey snorted. "Just makes *my* deal more attractive, you know?"

"What deal is this?"

"Oh . . . just that I provide them the means of protection, while they let me control the dungeon."

"Means of . . . you're going to give them guns?" Mel asked in disbelief.

"Just muskets," Kelsey replied.

"Even so, you don't want to make the invaders *stronger*!" Mel protested.

"They won't be invaders. They'll be allies keeping everyone else away from us."

"That doesn't sound like a lasting arrangement. Eventually, they'll lose a battle and get their muskets taken away from them. And with your example, who's to say they won't develop better guns?"

"Oh, they will, guaranteed," Kelsey said. "Progress is inevitable. That's why we need to get on the side of someone up there, so they can get stronger and look after our interests topside."

"But that's . . . crazy!" Mel exclaimed. "You can't ally with those people! They're the enemy!"

"Right now they are," Kelsey countered. "But if we can play our cards right, they'll see the advantage of either working with us—or *for* us."

Mel was starting to understand. "This was the real reason you wanted the avatar form, wasn't it? You wanted to *talk* with these people!"

"And you were fine with that, when *talk* meant gather information," Kelsey replied.

"I thought you meant interrogate! But you made a deal with Anton, and then you went outside . . ." She trailed off as a sudden thought struck her. "What did you mean when you said they'd let you control the dungeon?"

"Ah well, they don't actually know I'm an avatar," Kelsey confessed.

"They don't? How?"

"They just haven't worked it out yet. You told me there were ways that people controlled dungeons, so I just told them I was one of those."

Mel giggled despite herself. "They're so dumb."

Kelsey shrugged. "Seems like dungeon avatars are pretty rare," she said. It certainly hadn't been easy to persuade Mel to unlock the option. "Hopefully, I'll have some deals in place before they work it out."

"Oh, I get it. Once they've made some deals, they won't be able to break them," Mel said. "They'll be stuck." *Just like you were*, she carefully didn't say.

"Something like that," Kelsey agreed. The look on her face suggested that Mel hadn't avoided the topic as well as she should have. Then she smiled again and changed the subject.

"So, back to the party wipe," she said.

"I still think it's a bad idea. Is it really necessary to reduce this knight?"

"I don't know, that's the thing. If I don't do it, I might regret not taking this chance, but killing people—"

"Is never a waste, I know. I suppose I'm on board. How are you going to do it?"

"I'm reconfiguring level three right now," Kelsey told her. "I doubt these guys are going to spot a secret passage."

"They do have that scout; he'll have some sort of detect ambush trait."

Kelsey snickered. "It must have been going off nonstop since he came down here."

Mel laughed, and they kept watching the party as they methodically swept through the level two zombies. It took them a little longer to find their way through the maze, and the noise of their armor managed to wake a wave of zombies, but even en masse the low-level monsters couldn't do much to the soldiers.

The complaints when they got to the end of the level and found another narrow shaft were vociferous and caustic, but Kelsey just laughed. The second-level boss was just as easily taken down.

It was at this point that Kelsey started getting tense. The argument over whether they should put their armor on again was amusing, but eventually, discipline won out. As expected, they went right past the newly constructed secret door and came to the entrance of the first chamber.

It was here that the scout called a halt.

"Ambush!" he called out. The troops halted and clutched their weapons more firmly.

"Ahead?" the knight asked.

"Don't know, sir. No direction, just . . . soon."

The troops peered nervously in both directions, but they didn't have any choice but to proceed. So they did, slowly and carefully.

When they saw the skeleton warriors ahead, they were so relieved, they almost dropped their guard.

"Stay sharp!" the knight called. "This isn't the ambush."

He was soon proved right because as the soldier's front line cautiously engaged the warriors ahead, they heard the clatter of bones from behind.

"Rearguard, stand ready for assault," he called, but the soldiers there had already faced the rear with shields raised. It was just a small group of six skeletons that emerged. That meant they were outnumbered, but they should still have the levels to see them through this fight. Although the weapons that they were carrying seemed odd . . .

Before the rearguard could even step forward, the skeletons raised their weapons. A rapid clattering, echoing louder than anything the knight had ever heard, was the last sound to enter his ears.

"See?" Kelsey said, having been in the room the entire time. "Total party wipe."

"I suppose," Mel said dubiously. "It all seemed so easy. Is this the efficiency you love so much?"

"Sure is," Kelsey said cheerfully. With a wave of her hand, the corpses and equipment were removed for storage and processing. "You're dismissed," she said to the ambushing skeletons.

The six skeleton commandos, berets affixed at a jaunty angle on their bare skulls, saluted the thin air. As one, they turned and marched back the way they came.

CHAPTER EIGHTEEN

Pride and Joy

I can't believe that actually worked!"

Anton and Kelsey had rejoined Aris back at the inn and were having an early lunch. Roasted ham, cheese, and greens, served with a loaf of bread that Kelsey declared as delicious. Rather than eat it properly, Kelsey had wrapped a bit of everything in a thick cut of the bread and was munching on it with obvious enjoyment.

"Are you sure you should be talking like that?" Anton asked nervously, and quietly.

"It's fine," Kelsey said, waving her free hand at the room. "No one's near enough to hear if we keep our voices down, and I'm keeping an eye out for anyone paying too much attention."

Anton looked around nervously, but she was probably right. The common room wasn't full by any means, and the few guests they had were involved in their own animated discussions.

"What is it that we're talking about?" Aris asked. "Is it about the latest word? The Baron being dead?"

More guards had visited while the two had been attending the Baron, asking questions about last night, and passing on the news. Not being able to say that she'd been in the dungeon last night, Aris had claimed to be asleep in her home.

Anton looked stricken at his girlfriend's innocent question, prompting a look from Kelsey.

"Why—oh right, we never got the chance to fill you in, did we? Let's see . . ."

"You're going to tell her?" Anton asked with dismay.

"Sure, it'll be fine, Aris is part of the team now, right?"

Aris ignored the question, looking at Anton with concern. "Anton, you're worrying me. We've always shared—what do you want to keep from me?"

"He wants to protect you," Kelsey said lightly. "That sort of thing never works out—loss of trust, poisons the relationship, blah blah blah. The instinct isn't a bad one, though."

She cocked her head to one side, thinking. "It *is* a bit surprising, though, and we *are* in a public space . . . how about you hold your breath?"

"What?"

"If you're holding your breath, you can't yell about how mad you are, which would be *very bad*," Kelsey said in a reasonable tone.

Aris narrowed her eyes, as the pieces finally came together for her. "Are you telling me that you *killed the Baron?*" she whispered intensely.

"It . . . it was self-defense," Anton muttered miserably. "He was going to take her in, torture her for her secrets. He *said* he was going to do that."

"And I obviously couldn't allow that, so he had to go," Kelsey said with an easy smile, as if she'd been asking for another slice of bread.

"Oh no . . . we're going to be hanged . . . my family . . ." Aris was slowly starting to panic as she considered the possible consequences of Kelsey's hasty action. "We're going to be caught . . ." she whispered. Even as the fear consumed her, she still recognized the need to panic *quietly*.

"It'll be fine, don't worry," Kelsey said reassuringly. "I've got this."

"But they're looking for you . . . for us!" she said plaintively, looking at Anton.

"I'm going to get Captain Oldaw to take the blame,"

"Who? From the Glimmered Lancers?" Aris said, distracted. "Why would they believe that?"

"All part of my plan," Kelsey assured her. "I'll explain it in a bit. But first, didn't you want to tell Anton about your new class?"

"Oh!" For the briefest of moments, her fears were overcome by the excitement of telling Anton. Only for a moment, and then they crashed back down on her. She looked at Kelsey reproachfully.

"Go on," Kelsey said. "Tell him. Let me worry about the Baron."

Reluctantly at first, but with her excitement increasing as she went on, she spilled the beans. "Anton, it's a Unique Tier Two class! It's called Original Gunslinger!"

"It's a weapon-based class?" Anton asked. He had to smile at her growing enthusiasm. Unlike the Adventurer class, which got experience for "adventuring," weapon-based classes only grew from fighting with the appropriate weapon.

"Uh-huh! I think the Original part comes from the fact that I'm the first person to get a class for guns!"

"Monsters and dungeons don't count," Kelsey said wryly.

"What are the stats like?" Anton asked.

"Almost balanced—everything except Strength and Charisma, and there are two free stats! Anton, no one in the family has ever had a class with free stats."

"It's good, isn't it?" he said. He might not have made the most optimal use of his free ability raise, but he didn't regret it one bit.

"Actually, Anton gained a level last night as well," Kelsey drawled. "Still hasn't spent his free point."

"How could you forget a level?" Aris asked incredulously.

"I had . . . a lot on my mind," Evidently, running around in the woods at night, placing corpses, and avoiding capture by guards, counted as adventuring. That, or he'd gotten a share from standing idly by while his allies killed the Baron. He hoped it was the former.

"That's true. But you might want to spend it now."

"Oh, and your next level was going to be a trait level, wasn't it?" Aris asked excitedly.

"Yeah." Anton brought up his status.

Ability increases for Level 9 applied.
Anton Vos, Adventurer (Level 4)
Overall Level: 9
Path: Delver/Adventurer
Strength: 12
Toughness: 16
Agility: 12
Dexterity: 8
Perception: 9
Willpower: 12
Charisma: 9
Traits:
Delver's Discernment
Leaping Attack
Stone Skin

Assign 1 free point.

Anton thought about getting something other than his only pick for the last three years. Things were getting out of hand, and he might need one of the combat-oriented abilities more than before. On the other hand, he hadn't quite reached the goal he'd set for himself when he'd gotten his first class.

Ten Charisma. He'd overshot all of the kids who had teased him about his low score. Charisma was a fairly rare increase outside of merchants or nobility, and he had more levels than anyone else his age. But it wasn't enough to beat them; he wanted to achieve something that they never thought he could.

Maybe once I reach it, I'll be able to put my childhood behind me. Gods know that there's not much left of it.

Charisma.

Please select a new trait:
Ferocious Attack | Uncanny Evasion | Quick Attack | Impossible Block |
**   Pain Resistance**

"All of the options for level four are combat options—I'm going to take *Uncanny Evasion*, does that sound right?" He wasn't sure why he ran it past the others. For all his other choices, he'd talked it over with his parents first, so perhaps this was just—

"Ooo, that one is so annoying," Kelsey said, ignoring the sudden catch in his breath. "Just when you think you've got an adventurer pinned down, he slips out from under the blow."

"I'll take that as approval," Anton said and selected it.

"So, Aris," Kelsey said, as an inexplicable sense of how to *properly* dodge came over Anton, "What have you told your parents?"

"Nothing, yet," Aris replied. "I'm not sure how to tell them that I'm going after Cheia. Normally, this would . . ." She broke off and looked down, fighting off the tears.

"Hey, why so sad?" Kelsey asked.

"Getting your Tier Two," Anton said slowly, realizing he would have to explain. "It's when you come of age. There's a party and . . . stuff. Aris was going to be a baker, like her parents, but they put it off because of the attack."

"We had it all planned," Aris said, her voice becoming choked. "We were going to have a party, and Anton and his parents were going to be there, and we were going to get properly engaged. But then the raid, and Anton's parents . . ."

Anton wanted to say something comforting, but he was choked up as well. *I failed them. I ran,* was all that he could think. That left Kelsey, staring at them both with concern at the rapid deterioration in mood.

"Hey, don't cry! Look, we can still have a party."

"What?" Aris asked.

"A party! To celebrate your adulthood. We can have it here—I'll cover the costs, and you can invite whoever you want."

"A party . . ." Aris said, not quite believing what she was hearing.

"Tonight! It's not like anyone has anything else going on in this town. You and Anton haven't changed how you feel—so why not get engaged as well?"

"Could we?" Aris asked hopefully. "I mean . . . your parents . . ."

Anton took Aris by the hand. "I know my parents would have loved to have you as a daughter," he said. "They said it many times. If you'll still have me, with my"—he glanced at Kelsey—"additional burdens, then I'd be more than happy to marry you."

"*There's* that ten Charisma," Kelsey chortled, interrupting Aris's reply. "*Finally*, you're putting it to work."

Aris giggled at the look on Anton's face. "You really got there? Were you twelve when you made that promise?"

"Something like that," Anton admitted.

"Well, it looks like everyone has achievements to celebrate!" Kelsey exclaimed. She leapt up and dragged Aris out of her chair.

"Innkeep!" she called out. "We'd like to book the common room for a celebration! Your finest food and wines! Your—" She halted, looking over at the front door, where two guards had just entered.

"Actually, Aris, can you handle it all? The invitations and all . . . just tell this guy what you need." To the innkeeper, she said, "Anything she wants, on my tab, you understand?"

As the two of them both gaped at her, the guards approached, clearly looking for her. "Ma'am," one of them said, "we've been tasked to search your warehouse for the stolen goods. You—"

"That's fine, it's only to be expected. Anton!" she called, waving him over. "Aris, work it out—it doesn't have to be tonight, but better sooner than later, no?"

"I guess . . . I can?" Aris ventured. Kelsey gave her a smile, and then turned back to the guards.

"Well, come on, I'll take you to the warehouse." She headed out, Anton and the guards in tow.

"Don't you ever slow down?" Anton asked as they made their way over to the docks.

"Anton, I spent—"she looked over at the guards—"way too long sitting on my metaphorical ass to sit around and do nothing now. And since keeping you two busy keeps you distracted from being sad, bet on being overworked from now on."

Despite the late notice, and the rushed preparations, the party was a success. The White Selkie Inn opened its cellars and let the provisions flow freely. They didn't exactly have a surplus of fine foods and wine, but they *did* have a shortage of customers willing to pay.

Kelsey's offhand comment about no one having anything else to do was also true. Everyone was working from dawn to dusk repairing the town, or repairing their fortunes. Dropping into bed after eating was the norm.

The promise of fine food and wine, though, tempted many. The town needed a celebration, and word spread quickly among friends of the pair. That wasn't to say it was easy. Aris was rushed off her feet organizing things with the help of her parents. Anton and Kelsey came back after a few hours, having taken care of the searchers, but by then most of the work had been done.

"By the way," Kelsey said, just before the party was due to start. "When you announce your new tier, it might be a good idea not to mention the name."

"What?" Aris asked, the sudden stipulation derailing her. She'd been so busy that she'd forgotten to decide what she was going to tell her parents.

"It's just that no one knows what guns are. When they find out, it will be because Captain Oldaw gets caught with a crate of them—incriminating him in the murder of the Baron. Having someone with a class based on them could . . . spoil that narrative."

"What am I supposed to say then? That I took Baker after all?"

"Hmmm. Maybe that Anton helped you qualify for Adventurer? I bet it's possible; we didn't really try hard enough."

"Oh gods," Aris moaned. "I have to tell my parents that I'm leaving to find Cheia."

"Not tonight," Kelsey suggested. "Let's make tonight about you and Anton."

CHAPTER NINETEEN

I'm an Adult Now

Why aren't you drunk?" Aris giggled. "You kept stealing my drinks!"

"One of us has a superhuman constitution," Kelsey said reasonably, "And one of us had to stay conscious until all the guests had gone."

"It was a fun party," Aris sighed. "Wait, which one of us is con-conscious?"

"That'd be Anton," Kelsey said, looking over at him. "Though in his case, it would be self-conscious."

They were all standing in the luxurious bedroom that Kelsey's money had paid for. Anton, expecting the Baroness's men to come crashing through the door at any minute, had been too nervous to drink. He was still nervous.

"Kelsey, I—"

"Shh," Kelsey interrupted gently. "Let me worry about our problems. Tonight is about making Aris—and you—happier. It was a great party, right?"

"Right," Anton admitted.

"Aris told her parents about her new class . . . you both reconnected with your friends . . . had a chance to relax. You needed that." Kelsey walked forward as she spoke, taking Aris along with her. "And now . . ."

She looked back at Aris. "Remember what I said about a choice you have to make?"

Aris frowned, trying to think of what Kelsey was going on about.

"Ignore . . . or involve," Kelsey reminded her.

"Oh. Oh!" Aris felt the blood rush to her face as she looked at Anton, clearing away the light fog of alcohol. "Um. Involve?" she said hesitantly. "It would feel really weird if—"

"You don't have to justify it," Kelsey assured her. "They're your feelings, and this isn't a permanent decision," Moving closer, Kelsey started undoing the buttons on Aris's party dress. "You can change your mind at any time."

"Do . . . I get a say in this?" Anton asked. He couldn't take his eyes off the dark flesh of his girlfriend that was being slowly revealed.

"You're a guy, Anton," Kelsey said. "When your girlfriend wants to have a threesome, your enthusiastic approval is assumed."

As she said that, she made her clothes disappear. This time, new ones did not immediately replace them. Aris stepped out of her dress, and the two women stood before him. Aris had only her underclothes remaining, while Kelsey was entirely naked. She grinned at him and looked down.

"And it seems that assumption was right."

Anton was embarrassed, but he couldn't deny that he was aroused by the contrasting sight of the two women. He took a step towards Aris.

"I—" He looked at Kelsey, "I don't want to hurt her."

"You won't," Kelsey said. "She wants you to take the lead. Just kiss your girlfriend."

Anton did as commanded, stooping down a little to press his lips against Aris's. To his surprise, her mouth opened, and her tongue came out to tease him.

"What was . . . where did you learn that?" he exclaimed, breaking the kiss.

Aris giggled. "Did you like it?"

"It's just the start," Kelsey said. She moved her naked body up against him. It was surprisingly warm, despite its paleness. "Why don't you try it this time?"

Anton and Aris kissed again. This time, their tongues met and Anton lost himself in the sensation. This time, he only broke it off because he felt Kelsey tugging at his clothes.

The girls giggled as they relieved him of his clothing and he removed Aris's remaining garments. He cupped his hands over her full breasts, marveling at the sensation. Then he gasped, as Kelsey's hand wrapped around his member, pulling the skin back.

"What do you say we take this to the bed?" she breathed. She didn't let go of him as they moved over, grinning at his embarrassment at being led by his manhood. She only let go once they were all on the bed, arranged according to her directions.

Aris lay in the middle, on her back, with her partners sitting up on each side of her.

"This is a little embarrassing," she said, half-heartedly trying to cover herself with her hands.

"Just relax," Kelsey crooned. "Anton needs to get to know your body. Spread your legs a bit."

"But it's—" Aris protested.

"It's not ugly at all. See? Anton can't take his eyes off you."

Sure enough, Anton had his gaze fixed on Aris's sex.

"It's—you're beautiful," he breathed. "Can I?"

"Let me show you," Kelsey said. From Aris's other side, she reached out and gently caressed between her legs. Aris gasped at the feel of Kelsey's fingers as they expertly ran along the folds of her vulva.

"You see how sensitive she is?" Kelsey said as Aris moaned. "As you touch her, she starts getting moist; getting ready for you." She gave Aris an assessing look, and then slightly increased the speed of her fingers.

"Everyone is different down here," she said. "You need to learn what a girl likes, where she likes it. See?" She changed from long slow strokes to a fast flicking motion, watching as Aris's moans turned into gasps.

"And then there's this," she said, her finger lightly brushing Aris's clitoris. Aris held back a scream, but her back arched at the contact.

"Wait, I'm not ready—" she protested, but Kelsey was merciless.

"You don't start with this," she cautioned Anton. "But once she's started . . . here, you take over." She moved her hand out of the way, pushing Aris's thighs further apart to give his hand better access. He was clumsy at first, but he soon learned to take Aris's moans as his guide to better performance.

"Good, now start rubbing the clitoris . . . gently!" Kelsey told him. He did as commanded and was rewarded by a mewling yelp as Aris lost herself to his attention. Kelsey shifted her position to move closer to Aris's face and breasts. She started fondling them, looking Aris deep in the eyes as she did.

"Do you like what he's doing to you? Do you like being fingered by your man?" she asked.

"Mnnnn," Aris gasped, unable to form words.

"Are you ready for him to make you a woman?" Kelsey asked. "Do you want to feel him inside you?"

"Yes! Yes!" Aris said.

"All right, then spread your legs a little more and raise your knees up slightly."

Aris complied with Kelsey's instructions, as she moved Anton into position over Aris. Despite focusing on Aris, his erection hadn't gone away and was made even harder by Kelsey squeezing it gently.

"When I say, give one thrust forward," she commanded, "and then hold it until Aris says you can move."

She guided Anton into position, resting his tip right on Aris's entrance.

"It's hot," Aris gasped.

"Now!" Kelsey ordered, and Anton thrust forward. The sensation was like nothing he'd felt before. Under him, Aris cried out.

"Ahhh!"

"What's wrong?"

"It's fine, this is all normal," Kelsey assured them both. "Just keep on holding."

"It's—it's all right!" Aris gasped. Her body tightened around his erection. "It just hurt for a bit, but . . . you can move now." Her arms came up and pulled him in for a kiss, and Anton threw away restraint. He withdrew slightly and then pushed in deeper, delighting in the way that her sex gripped him and the way she shuddered at his penetration.

The sensation must have been much greater than before, as Aris cried out with every thrust. Her back arched, and her arms and legs tried to pull him closer.

"That's the way, Anton," Kelsey urged him on. Her hands were on his back, caressing him. "Keep going until she comes."

Anton didn't need encouragement. He thrust into Aris, again and again, going wild as his motions propelled her to greater flights of ecstasy. He kept going, losing himself. Kelsey's words became meaningless and all that mattered was the girl underneath him. When she finally shuddered in a spasm of delight, he felt something give inside of him. His own muscles spasmed and he felt a warm, wet sensation surround him.

His strength flowed out of him, and he collapsed on the bed, rolling on his side to avoid crushing Aris.

"Typical male," Kelsey said with amusement. She lay down next to him, fitting her curves into his side. "Did you enjoy your first time?"

"It was . . . amazing . . ." Anton panted. "Did I do all right?"

"Ask your girlfriend," Kelsey suggested. Aris rolled onto her side, facing Anton, and snuggled up to him, mimicking Kelsey's position. Somehow, he found the strength to move his arms, putting one around each woman to hold them closer.

"It was amazing," Aris agreed. She rested her head on his chest.

"Tired out?" Kelsey asked.

"It's been a long day," she replied. "And I feel so good right now."

"I just want to stay like this forever," Anton agreed. A delicious lassitude was creeping over him, but he remembered one thing he had to say.

"Thank you for . . . guiding us," he said, struggling to find the words.

"I had entirely selfish reasons, I assure you," Kelsey replied. "I didn't want to see you two mess things up." She moved languorously against him, letting him feel the curves of her breasts and belly. "Next time, maybe I can have a little fun as well?"

Anton was enjoying the feel of her body so much that it felt entirely natural when she moved up and gave him a slow, sensual kiss. For a moment he forgot about the murders, about his deal. Even about his parents.

"Rest now," she whispered. "You've had a long day. Get some sleep."

Aris murmured something in response, but she was already drifting off. He felt himself relax further, letting himself go. He was safe, and warm with his two women by his side. He could . . .

Kelsey watched the two of them as they fell deeper into sleep. Once she was sure they weren't going to wake up, she carefully untangled herself from Anton's grasp. Pulling a soft rag out of nowhere, she carefully wiped the two of them clean of all the bodily fluids that had been spilled. There were still some blood-stains on the sheets, but the inn staff would take care of that.

Slowly, cautiously, she moved Aris back into Anton's arms. They both made contented noises and pulled each other closer. Rolling her eyes, she pulled up the sheets and covered them with a blanket. Finally satisfied with the condition of her charges, she returned her clothes to her body.

Moving silently around the room, she picked up the discarded clothes and vanished them. They would be cleaned and dried by her skeleton laundry service and returned neatly folded before morning.

Finally, she sat down and took a book out of her Inventory. She glanced at the lantern, and then at the bed. Shrugging, she brought out her own light source. A desktop electric lamp, with a big heavy base to store the battery. She turned it on and then blew out the lantern. She hadn't managed LEDs or lithium batteries as yet, but this was far better for reading.

She opened the book and started to read. This was one of her purchases that she hadn't had time to go over. Books were expensive in this world, but money was no object when it came to what she wanted.

The subject of the book was an overview of the many gods that this world had on offer. Despite the long length of time that Kelsey had been here, there were still large gaps in her knowledge. Very few delvers cared to discuss religion while in a dungeon—except in the most basic of senses. Kelsey had seen a dozen gods called on for aid, but not once had one responded.

Given her background, Kelsey might have taken this as evidence that none of the gods existed, but she knew that they did. One of them was responsible for her being here, after all.

CHAPTER TWENTY

The Message

SULIEL

May I have a word with you in private, my lady?"

Liem spoke softly, but with urgency. Suliel gave the mage an irritated look. She was busy right now, with reports both verbal and written, giving orders regarding the reconstruction and trying to figure out who had killed her father.

Right now, she was reading the latest report about the northern merchant. Apparently, she'd hosted a gathering last night, at which Anton had become *officially* engaged. Suliel carefully refrained from grinding her teeth. She'd always known that her chances of marrying Anton were remote, but this just drove it in. *I was too late, even though I was so close!*

If she'd gained her second tier, she wouldn't be at her mother's mercy for marriage partners, and she could at least *try* to get to know him. It had always been a long shot, but now he was getting further away. This engagement, and his mysterious business partner . . .

Liem coughed, reminding her that he'd made a request.

"Why?" she asked brusquely. He only glanced significantly at the other servants who filled the room.

"Fine. Clear the room, please." She watched him waiting impatiently as her people filed out. He didn't seem alarmed, just agitated. When the last person had left, he carefully checked the window. Suliel didn't know what he was looking for, magical eavesdroppers perhaps. He did the same for the door, asking the guards to move away and not let anyone approach.

Suliel waited patiently for this interruption to her workday to end. Finally, he stood before her and bowed.

"My lady, have you heard of the Rose Circle?"

"I have heard rumors," Suliel said carefully. She had no idea if they were true or not, but she had heard things when visiting her relatives and other nobles.

"Your father was a member of it," Liem said bluntly.

My father was a traitor? She couldn't believe it. Anticipating her objections, Liem held up a hand.

"Wait. It's not what you think. The Rose Circle . . . do you know of the King's sister . . . his older sister?"

"I've heard that he had one. Didn't she die before the succession?" It was before her time. It wasn't a good look to have your siblings die before you ascended the throne, but the King had reigned since before she was born. If there was something fishy about her death, it had been kept well hidden.

Liem sighed. "The truth is, she was alive when the old King died. As the eldest, she was in a position to inherit, so she took the King class."

"And King Kidar killed her?" Suliel had read enough history to make the connection.

"No, she is still alive, in hiding," Liem told her.

"But that . . . wouldn't that prevent his Majesty from taking the class?" King was a unique class. Only Tier Two, but that was necessary to make it available for anyone who met the stringent criteria. Namely, *being* the king of a country.

Liem shook his head. "He was forced to take *False King*."

Suliel's eyes widened at the scandal. It wasn't that the class was *required* to rule, but if you didn't take it, it told everyone that you were not the rightful ruler.

"How have the nobility stood for a False King standing over them?" she asked incredulously.

"The class has some traits that let his Majesty conceal his true class," Liem said bitterly. "Those that know are in the minority and are forced to keep silent for fear of execution. Or side with him for personal gain."

For just a moment, Suliel was lost in the excitement and the romance of it all. Bringing down the False King! Then reality reasserted itself. Just knowing this could get her killed. Either by the King or by the Rose Circle, if they thought she was going to spill their secrets.

"Why are you telling me this now?" She didn't have time for palace intrigue; she had a town to protect! A town with a suspect captain . . . now that she thought of it, this threw the tension between Captain Oldaw and her father into a new perspective.

"For two reasons, my lady," Liem said, interrupting her train of thought. "For one, as your father's heir, you are entitled to membership in the organization."

Do I want that? she wondered. Now that she knew about it, she didn't have much choice.

"Membership is not automatic," Liem cautioned. "You must make a contribution to the cause in some way, to prove both your loyalty and your prowess."

Suliel's eyes narrowed. She didn't like the position she was being put in. Either she went to the King, sullying her father's name, or she had to contribute to these people? Liem carried on, unaware of her concerns.

"The second reason is that your father saw these guns as a way of breaking the tyrant's hold on this country," he said. "He sent a message to the Circle. I don't know what was in it, but it must have informed them about the weapons."

"You don't know what he said?" Suliel asked. "Didn't he trust you?"

Liem bowed again. "I'm not a member of the Circle; only the nobility can be," he explained. "And so I can't be privy to Circle communications."

"You're not a member? Then how do you know all this?"

"Each member has a number of trusted servants," Liem told her. "I served in that role for your father."

And now? Suliel thought, but she didn't voice the question. If she didn't join the circle, Liem would be cut off. Either another member would take him from her (because a mage was a rare and valuable subordinate) or he would have to be silenced.

"As I was saying," Liem resumed. "Your father sent a message. This morning, a response came."

From who? Suliel wondered, but Liem wouldn't be able to answer that. He took a small golden device out of his robes and set it on her desk.

It was a bird, constructed of ornately sculpted brass and steel. Its eyes were of some red rock—possibly ruby—and they shone as if there was daylight behind them.

Suliel didn't exclaim in shock at the sight of an enchanted item. She'd seen them before, and she was aware her father owned some. It *was* more complicated than any others that she'd seen, though.

"Press your finger to the tip of the beak," Liem instructed, and she did what he said.

"Ow!" she exclaimed. It was sharper than it looked, and she had felt a pin-prick of pain. When she swiftly withdrew her hand, there was a small drop of blood on the beak. As she watched, it disappeared, drawn into the mechanism.

The bird sang a brief three-note tune and then a hatch in its chest opened up, allowing a small cylinder to fall to the desk below.

"The reply," Liem said. His eyes were fixed on it, but he made no move to take it. Wary of further bites, Suliel reached out carefully and took the cylinder.

It turned out to open with a simple twist, allowing Suliel to read the message inside.

Secure the weapons at all costs. Arriving in three days to collect. —Kinn

"How long ago was this message sent?" she asked.

"It would have left yesterday," he replied. "Assuming it came from some-where in the Kingdom."

She nodded and scrunched up the tiny slip of paper. "Can you dispose of this?" she asked, handing it to him.

He nodded, and his hand was suddenly engulfed in flames, instantly burning the paper to ash. Suliel smiled at seeing a party trick that had been repeated many times in front of her.

"My lady?" Liem asked.

"Uncle Riadan will be here in two days," she said. "Please have everything made ready for him."

"As you say, my lady." Liem bowed and left the room. It wasn't long before her servants came filing back in, and she could get back to work. One thought stuck in her mind, though, preventing her from fully concentrating on the tasks before her.

So my uncle is a traitor, too . . .

He wasn't really her uncle, Suliel was well aware. Part of being a noble was know-ing in exquisite detail just how closely related every person in the relatively small group of noble families was to one another. Uncle Riadan was just a close friend of her father's who had been there throughout her childhood. If he'd had a son, she might have been engaged already.

He would, once he got over the news of her father's death, be expecting her to agree with whatever he said and join this conspiracy of his. Suliel's mother would almost certainly go along with whatever plan he came up with.

Suliel wasn't so sure that she wanted to. She was an adult now, or almost. She wasn't going to be jollied into treason by some sweets or a ride around the courtyard on Uncle's shoulders.

I have to find those guns. Possession of those would give her options. With the weapons, the Rose Circle would surely let her join on her own terms. Or she could take them to the King to be rewarded . . . she would have to give him Uncle, but her father's name could be kept out of it.

Finding them was the problem, though. She had her men searching the town. The first place they looked was that woman's warehouse, but she had apparently been telling the truth. There were no weapons in there. So the search had expanded, but it was slow going. Still, something as large as a crate couldn't stay hidden forever, could it?

The flaw in that reasoning was easy to find. Her father had been found outside the walls, so the goods he had purchased might well be outside as well. Suliel couldn't believe that the killer—or killers—would leave a crate worth *far more* than two hundred gold just out in a clearing somewhere. Something—any-thing—might happen to it.

However, there just weren't that many structures nearby that could act as shelter. Most of them had been checked out already . . . admittedly by the Lancers. Suliel felt the worm of paranoia that Kelsey had planted twist a little deeper into her heart. She wouldn't have expected Oldaw to go against the King, but what if the King's interests and her father's diverged?

I should lodge a quest for the guild to search the woods for that damned crate, she resolved. It's not like they're doing anything with the dungeon entrance occupied.

That was yet another annoyance. For Captain Oldaw to take it upon himself to occupy the dungeon, just because he thought someone might be hiding in there . . . she would have to take that up with him later. Maybe bring the Guild Master in for support. She sent out a messenger asking for him to attend to her.

Then Suliel heard an unexpected sound. Her mother's voice. It was from too far away to make out what she was saying, but Suliel would know that voice anywhere. Excited at the thought that her mother had come out of seclusion, she dashed out of her office, leaving the scribes to continue as best they could.

Led by her ears, she found herself heading towards her mother's chambers. Disappointing, but it was to be expected that her mother hadn't gone far. When she rounded the corner, she caught a glimpse of her mother going back into her rooms. With Liem Tikin.

Suliel stopped short at the sight of the mage in animated conversation with her mother. In the brief second that it took her to recover, the pair entered the room and closed the door behind them.

That's odd, what does Liem want with my mother? she wondered. She was about to knock on the door and find out when a servant arrived with an urgent message.

"My lady, my lady—thank the gods I've found you!" he exclaimed, short on breath. "There are zombies in the town!"

CHAPTER TWENTY-ONE

Rise Up

We needed a distraction," Kelsey said as if it was obvious.

Anton's sword sliced through the zombie's neck, decapitating it in one blow. There was a trick to doing that and not getting splattered zombie flesh on you, but he had had plenty of practice.

"You call this a distraction?" he asked. Despite the urgency of his question, he kept his voice low. Not that there was anyone listening to them. Those not fighting zombies were running for their lives.

"Yeah, and if you keep killing them at that rate, it will be wasted. Come on, this way."

Anton had no choice but to follow, but he diverged as much as he could to take out scattered, shambling, walking corpses. The zombies had spread out randomly, chasing people when they could. Most of them had started ineffectually pawing at doors, trying to get at the living that they smelled inside. "Why should I help you?"

"Well, if this doesn't work, I might have to try it again," Kelsey said carelessly. She walked easily down the street as if she had no reason to fear the living dead. Which, of course, she didn't. "Ah, here we are."

They had arrived at the back entrance to the barracks for the town guard. Or close to it, at any rate. Kelsey was hanging back, looking for guards or witnesses. None were visible.

"Do you want to wait here?" Kelsey asked. Anton just glared. "No, seriously, the more you push it, the more distance you'll be able to get. I've just got to dash in there and find a good place. It shouldn't take a minute."

"Fine," Anton growled. He was just glad that they'd left Aris behind the stout walls of the inn. Kelsey had said something about it being too dangerous for her, but he'd assumed that she was talking about some specific action that they would be taking. Not that the streets would be filled with corpses.

Kelsey grinned at him and dashed off. He started feeling anxiety about her the moment she reached the door, but he distracted himself with his *very real,* not manufactured by some damned geas, concern about wandering zombies.

It worked, but only just, and only because she was as quick as her word. "Okay!" she said brightly. "Let's go kill zombies!"

"Are you going to explain what's going on?" he asked, but he was already moving. It was only a matter of time before a zombie caught up with a defenseless civilian.

"Sure! You remember that we set the new girl looking for the guns?"

"Baroness Suliel," he corrected. "Of course. You said that there was no danger of her finding them because they were in your Inventory."

"Right. And everyone knows that the Shimmering Lancers are being quartered in those barracks, right?"

"*Glimmered* Lancers," he said, not sure why he was bothering. Another zombie came into his reach and was cut down.

"Well, now the guns are in the barracks, so all we have to do is wait until someone finds them!"

"What does that have to do with zombies?" he exclaimed. He would have sworn, but his parents had raised him better. Another zombie fell to his blade.

Kelsey frowned. She wasn't having any problems keeping up with Anton, even as he ran at full tilt. "I thought I already explained this bit," she said. "The Lancers have people in the building, so I needed a distraction that would get every fighting man out in the street!"

Anton looked at her, aghast. "So you flooded the town with zombies?"

"Relax, these are all level ones," Kelsey said. "They can *barely* gnaw a kid's skull open. You see, I snuck out last night while you were asleep—"

Anton felt an intense feeling of outrage that *she* could separate from *him* while he was asleep, but he couldn't do the same. Not that she ever slept.

"—did you know that we were being watched by the city guard?" Kelsey continued. She held up a finger near his face, which Anton jerked back as a spider appeared on it.

"Sleeping poison," she explained. "He was standing right out there in plain view." The spider disappeared, much to Antón's relief. He'd heard stories about the undead spiders.

"So, I just wandered around until I found an abandoned house that had a cellar with a stout door, and then I filled it up with zombies! Then it was just a matter of time before someone started wondering about the noise."

Anton shook his head. *How many people had died this morning?* Kelsey clearly didn't care. Weakening the zombies may have minimized casualties, but Anton was pretty sure that was more to do with lowering mana costs than it was about saving lives.

"Didn't this waste a whole lot of mana?" he asked.

"Oh yeah, and everything that dies out here is a complete waste for me," Kelsey complained. "But . . . I did come into a bit of windfall recently, so it's all good."

Anton decided that he didn't want to know. He focused on saving people.

"But why couldn't I have come?" Aris asked when they returned to the inn. "I'm a gunslinger now!"

"And where are your guns?" Kelsey asked, amused.

"You *said* you were going to provide them," Aris grouched.

"And I will. Just . . . not yet. We need to wait until this whole business with the Baron is sorted out."

"And when will that be?"

"Who knows?" Kelsey said. "I'm sure they'll find the weapons fairly quickly, but depending on who found them, and what they do, it might take a while."

There was an urgent rapping on the door to their room.

"Or," Kelsey said with a grin, "It might all happen very quickly."

"We're being framed," Captain Oldaw protested. "It's so obvious, it's insulting."

"Are these your weapons?" Suliel asked Kelsey coldly, ignoring the captain.

"Well, let's see," Kelsey said. "Sure would be embarrassing if someone else had brought in a crate of these unique rifles!"

She took one out of the crate and made a show of examining it closely. "No, these are mine, all right!"

She grinned brightly at Suliel. "So efficient! I knew that I was right to put my trust in you."

Suliel scowled at her but didn't respond. Instead, she turned to Captain Oldaw. "And you have *no* explanation of how these got here?" she asked.

The captain managed to look embarrassed and angry at the same time. "They must have been brought in during the dungeon break," he said. "The killers must be—"

"In league with the dungeon?" Suliel asked coldly. "The dungeon that your men are guarding the entrance of?"

"There . . . there must be a second entrance," Oldaw protested. "Those zombies didn't get past my men."

"Nor did they climb the walls," Suliel sighed. "But the dungeon has *never* done anything like this before. I can only assume that it was provoked."

"By us?" Oldaw blurted.

"Who else? Just what have your men been up to, up there?"

"Nothing! They're just guarding the entrance and . . ." He looked away. "The party we sent down looking for the perpetrators didn't come back," he admitted.

"The entire party?" Anton asked in surprise. He managed to not look at Kelsey.

"What's that to you, boy?" The change in Captain Oldaw's voice, from desperate to contemptuous, couldn't have been more complete. To Anton's surprise, it was the Baroness who responded.

"He may be young, but he's an expert delver," she said, causing Oldaw to look back at her and wince. "The sort of expert adviser that might have saved the lives of your squad, had you been willing to listen."

She smiled warmly at Anton. "Was there something you wanted to say?"

"Uh, well . . . your ladyship," Anton stammered. "It's just that . . . were your men at around level twenty?"

"Fifteen and up," the captain said shortly.

"And . . . I don't know how it is, but they'd be trained in close combat, not just lances?"

"Of course," the captain sneered.

"Then . . . I don't see how they'd have problems with the monsters, at least at the early levels, but you don't have any trap-finding or poison antidotes, do you?" Anton glanced nervously at Kelsey, but she was just smiling innocently.

"We don't . . ." the captain admitted.

"There are some nasty traps starting on the third level," Anton explained. "There are earlier traps, but they get worse at that point. The thing is, I don't see the traps taking out the entire party—your men would turn back if they had a few injured or poisoned, right?"

"Of course." The captain had lost some of his arrogance now and was listening more seriously.

"So it does sound like they got ambushed by something down there. Unless they got as far as the Spider's Nest."

"Or they weren't killed at all, and you have a squad wandering about without supervision," Suliel interjected sourly.

"My lady, I would never . . ." Oldaw protested but stopped when she waved him to silence.

"Your missing squad is a distraction from the real matter here. My father . . . I can't overlook this. There is a credible accusation against you, Captain, and while the evidence is slim, you don't have a defense, do you?"

"I—" His posture slumped slightly. "Only my reputation."

"I don't have the standing to render judgment," Suliel admitted. "Even if I could claim to be impartial . . . Captain Oldaw, I must ask that you step down from leadership of your unit and submit to house arrest. I will write to the King and ask him to send someone qualified to rule on this matter. Will you submit to the law, Captain?"

There was a long, dangerous moment as the captain considered his next action. Finally, to the relief of everyone there, he nodded.

"I trust his Majesty to grant me a fair trial," he said. "Inform Verhon that he has command," he told one of his men. "I will be at the castle."

"This isn't over," Suliel promised him. "If any evidence comes up exonerating you, I'll make sure your lieutenant has access to it."

She looked over at Anton. "Can you let your guild know that I will be coming over to fund two quests."

"My lady?"

"One to find the second entrance of the dungeon. The other . . . I want to fund a deep delve. Their most experienced delvers, to go as deep as they can. If someone is hiding in the dungeon, we need to find them."

"Yes, my lady." Anton glanced at Kelsey, but she seemed entirely unconcerned.

"And shall I just get someone to move my property back to my warehouse?" she asked.

Suliel sighed. "The rifles must remain with me."

"No problem. You can have someone drop off the gold at the Selkie. No rush." She flashed Suliel a sly smile. "You've been so helpful recovering them, I know that you'll be just as diligent in paying your father's debt."

Suliel grimaced. She'd never agreed to the deal . . . but she was sure that she could get reimbursed by the Circle. Possibly she could get even more than two hundred gold for the things. Having clear and unopposed title was worth the money.

"I'll need you to stay in town until the trial is done," Suliel told the woman.

"I'm not going anywhere," Kelsey said agreeably. "If that's all, then I'll take my leave."

"This isn't going to work," Anton complained as the pair made their way to the guild. "You saw how suspicious the Baroness was."

"Don't let her get in your head," Kelsey advised. "That's what they want you to think. Oh, I'll never get away with it, so I won't even try."

She snorted. "If you never try, you definitely won't succeed. She's suspicious of me, but she's going down a bunch of false trails. People hiding out in the dungeon, as if!"

"She's not wrong about the dungeon colluding with the killers, though," Anton pointed out.

"I may have been a little too overt," Kelsey said. "Ultimately, it doesn't matter. Though this expedition is going to put a crimp on things. I wanted to get Aris a few more levels."

Anton didn't reply. While he was in favor of the idea in principle, he didn't trust Kelsey with any kind of approval from him. There was a brief pause that passed for companionable silence.

As they reached the guild, Kelsey spoke up again. "She did have one good idea, though."

Anton glanced at her as he reached for the front door. She was sporting a wicked grin. "A second entrance to the dungeon . . . has potential."

CHAPTER TWENTY-TWO

Our Lips Are Sealed

No. You absolutely can't!"

Anton didn't want to have this argument here. Despite Kelsey's apparent lack of concern about talk that might give away her nature, having this discussion in the middle of the Adventurers Guild was utter madness.

If he didn't say *something*, though, he had the sinking feeling that Kelsey would just go ahead and do it before they left the building. So he was doing his best to dissuade her while they stood in line to see Liat. Without saying anything incriminating.

"It's not as easy as I make it sound," Kelsey mused. "Because the town is at a lower elevation, it would make sense to connect the lower levels directly. But aside from the danger, there's mana pressure to consider."

Anton was sure that "danger" in this case meant danger to Kelsey, from having her lower levels directly accessible from the ground. Not the danger that Anton was worried about. But before he could say anything more, Liat dismissed the person at the counter and was ready for them.

"I'm sorry, we still don't have any word as to when the dungeon will be open again," she said automatically as they approached. Then she noticed who they were and the professional look on her face slipped off.

"Oh, it's you," she said, glaring at Kelsey. "What do you want."

Kelsey grinned. "We're passing on a message from the Baroness."

"It's not official," Anton interjected. "She just thought you'd appreciate a heads-up before the official requests arrive."

Liat sighed. "You'd better see the Guild Master then."

"We could just pass it on to you . . ." Anton tried.

"No, he wanted to meet Kelsey," Liat said resignedly.

"Aw, I want to meet him too!" Kelsey said.

"Sure. This way." Liat came out from behind the desk and led them up a stairway to the Guild Master's office. Master Nyer was doing paperwork when Liat led them in without knocking. He looked up and rose to his feet when he saw who it was.

"Anton, my boy!" he said, hobbling around the desk to greet them. He was of average height, with light brown skin that gave away his foreign parentage, much like Anton. His most obvious feature, though, was the stump of his truncated leg. A wooden foot strapped to the end of it let him walk, but even after long experience with it, he was still quite clumsy.

"Hi, Uncle Delir," Anton said, embarrassed. He could barely remember the incident that had caused his uncle's retirement from adventuring, but he was painfully aware of who had caused it.

"I hear congratulations are in order," Delir said, pulling the younger man in for a hug. "I'm sorry I couldn't make it to the party, but the paperwork has been killing me."

"That's all right. It was short notice, after all. Uh, this is Kelsey." Anton pulled himself out of the embrace. "Uh, Kelsey, this is Guild Master Delir Nyer. He was in a party with my parents about eight years ago."

"Until I lost my foot," Delir agreed easily.

"Pleased to meet you, sir," Kelsey said, holding out her hands. Looking down, she added, "Can't that be healed?"

Delir sighed as he led them over to the more comfortable chairs he used for meetings. "There are healers in the capital that can manage regeneration, but there's a complication. Some kind of unusual poison."

"Oh?" Kelsey said innocently.

"They never managed to identify it, but they called it fleshrot," he told her. "It stays in the wound, so any flesh you regenerate just dies on you. It spreads, too. I need regular healing just to keep the rest of the leg from dropping off."

"Uncle, the Baroness said that she was going to send you two quests," Anton interrupted before Kelsey could ask more questions. "She thinks the zombies came from a second entrance and she wants a quest to find it."

"Sounds like a good way to keep the lower ranks busy," Delir commented. "Offer it as a prize, so that she only has to pay the winners."

"I suppose. The other one . . . she wants to fund a deep delve."

"Fund?"

"She thinks that there are people hiding out in the dungeon," Anton explained. "So she wants a party to get as far down as possible and check."

Delir raised an eyebrow. "Pretty brave, hiding out in a dungeon." He leaned back on his chair and closed his eyes for a moment in thought. "Liat. You should go back and man the counter."

"But sir, she's . . ."

"She's got nothing to gain from harming me, and if she did, what would you do? I'm the one with Adventurer levels. I may have lost my foot, but I haven't lost my traits."

Liat nodded, and with one last glare at Kelsey, left the room.

Delir looked over at Kelsey. "You know, young woman, you probably noticed that Anton was raised to not use his *Discernment* on people."

"I had," Kelsey agreed. "It's not a habit shared by the nobility here."

"I suppose not," Delir chuckled. "I'd heard that *Nobility's Prerogative* doesn't work on you."

"Mmm. I can't say I'm broken up about that," Kelsey said.

"*Delver's Discernment* works perfectly well, though," Delir said.

"Ah." Kelsey got very still. "I suppose the jig is up then?"

"Kelsey . . ." Anton warned.

"It's really true then? I don't see how our dungeon can be walking around town, but that's the only thing that fits with a class of Necropolis."

Kelsey narrowed her eyes. "I'm my own dungeon, thank you very much."

"Oh, I didn't mean to imply ownership," Delir assured her. "Merely association."

"Fine then." She sat back and regarded him carefully. "You're taking this very calmly," she said.

"The fact that dungeons have the potential to become intelligent is one of the secrets of our guild. Watching for the signs has been one of my jobs . . . but this has been very sudden. How long have you been awake?"

Kelsey gave him a long look but eventually shrugged. "Since the beginning," she said. "I didn't want people to know I was different until I could get around the ban on talking to them."

"There's a ban on communicating? How fascinating."

"And isn't *that* annoying," Kelsey agreed. "No getting monsters to talk for me, no sign writing. You can only do the most roundabout things to try and talk to people."

"We had thought that new dungeons just had problems learning languages. But there is some kind of rule?" Delir leaned forward intently. "Enforced by the gods?"

"Hell if I know," Kelsey said bitterly. "But they seem involved in the whole process."

"Fascinating. Do you remember how I lost my leg?"

"Sure." Kelsey smiled, reminiscing. "Gut-ripper spider, one of the big ones. Got you with the cursed undead poison."

"We haven't seen it much since; is there a reason for that?"

Kelsey scowled. "Didn't really work out. The idea was to put it in the smaller spiders, let them get a bite in without getting noticed. Then a week later, your leg drops off."

Anton shuddered at the casual way Kelsey was talking about mutilating people. But Delir didn't seem to mind.

"What went wrong?" he asked.

"Problem is, in small doses, it gets cleaned up by your general healing spell, which adventurers are always getting as a matter of course," Kelsey explained. "You need a big dose to get it established enough to resist a cure, hence the big gut-ripper. But even then, it's not as effective as something like the acid-blood or the sleeping death."

She grinned slyly. "When you didn't come back, I thought I must have gotten you. Looks like my one casualty wasn't even that."

"So sorry to have inconvenienced you," Delir laughed. Anton looked at him in disbelief.

"How can you laugh about that?" Anton exclaimed. "She was trying to kill you!"

"Well, that's what dungeons do." Delir shrugged. "We're the ones intruding on them, after all."

Kelsey sat back, looking pleased. "So what do you do with this secret knowledge of yours?"

"Once we recognize the signs of a developing mind, we can start negotiations with it, of course!" Delir chuckled again. "It's a lot easier when you can just talk with the other side. The first thing we try to communicate is that under the Kingdom's law, dungeon cores are protected from would-be wizards."

Kelsey frowned. "That would be a lot easier to believe if you didn't have a wizard right here in town."

"Liem's core has been handed down for at least three generations—he didn't take it himself. It hasn't always been this way, but there hasn't been a core taken for a century at least—in this country." Delir paused. "You might know better, but to my knowledge, once a core has been . . . bonded for use, it's not able to go back to being a functioning dungeon."

Kelsey paused, holding up a finger to keep him from continuing. After a few moments, she sighed. "That's . . . probably correct," she said.

Delir nodded soberly. "We've found that if a dungeon is convinced of our good intentions, they reduce the lethality of the monsters and traps. It seems like they *want* people to delve. Given the right encouragement, they can be more generous with rewards."

"And you want me to do that . . . give out more rewards, kill fewer people," Kelsey said.

"Yes. But what do you want?"

"Safety is a big one . . . how many dungeons have you made this deal with?"

"There are only three other dungeons in Zamarra," Delir said. "One of them is too young to be communicated with. The other two we've been reasonably successful in . . . lowering their lethality."

"Just two?" Kelsey said doubtfully.

"The philosophy is common along this coast; there are other nations with similar laws," he told her. "I can't speak for how successful it has been."

Kelsey grimaced. "That's not exactly reassuring." She paused and then continued. "To start with, before we get to talking about each other's feelings, I want to make sure that this all stays between us."

"Naturally. I can respect the trust you've shown us," Delir said quickly. "Your existence is already a guild secret."

"I think we can do better than *that*," Kelsey muttered. "You know, there *is* an antidote for the undead curse."

"What?" Delir was suddenly sitting up straight, looking at Kelsey intently.

"The powdered scales of one of the fish in the Silent Sea," Kelsey explained.

Delir slumped. "No one's come back from the sea alive. It might as well be on the moon."

"That's not an issue for me," Kelsey told him. "I can get you some, in return for your silence on everything you learn about me."

"To everyone? Not even my colleagues in the guild?"

"Everyone," Kelsey stated firmly.

"Kelsey!" Anton interjected.

"I was getting to it! Jeez." Kelsey looked back at Delir. "If you take this deal, you won't be able to break it."

"A geas?" Delir asked, startled. "That isn't something that other dungeons have been able to do."

"I'm special," Kelsey said with a grimace, "In more than one way. If I make a deal, then both sides are bound to it."

"I—" Delir started, but stopped, lost in a struggle with himself.

"Kelsey, don't do this," Anton said urgently. "Didn't you say you didn't want to make deals?"

"I've got to protect myself, Anton," Kelsey said reasonably. "I don't want this knowledge getting out."

"He already said he'd keep your secrets! You don't need to bind him."

"But then he wouldn't get his antidote. Don't you want your uncle walking again?"

"It's fine, Anton," Delir said. "It goes against some guild principles, but in the interest of building trust between us, I can make some compromises."

"If you want to build trust, you should just give it to him, to make up for injuring him back then! Putting a geas on him isn't trust, it's control!"

"Give it to him?" Kelsey exclaimed. "That's—wait." She looked at him closely. "Are you telling me something I need to know?"

"Yes, I—what?" Anton replied, confused by her phrasing.

"Never mind." She sighed and looked back at Delir. A glass vial filled with a silvery powder appeared in her hand. "Looks like it's your lucky day. Please, accept this gift as a token of our friendship."

"My lady this gift . . ." Delir's voice shook as he accepted the vial. "I will do my best to repay the generosity you have shown me."

"Yeah, I'm a real peach," Kelsey said sourly. "I'm not sure how that's best applied. I'd take it to an alchemist or priest before you start rubbing it on."

"I shall. Thank you again, my lady."

CHAPTER TWENTY-THREE

Making It Work

F irst of all, I must know—how are you able to do this? Why have I never heard of another dungeon doing so?" Delir asked his question entreatingly, sitting on the edge of his chair. Kelsey looked back at him, considering her answer.

"It's the fairies, isn't it?" Anton said, causing both of them to look at him in surprise.

"Fairies?" Delir asked.

"Yeah," Kelsey said. Turning to Delir, she explained. "Dungeons have helpers that guide their development and keep them on track."

She scowled at the empty air. "In my case, thanks to a certain contract, I can't choose a development option unless Mel agrees."

"You said that it took you a long time to get Mel to allow you to take an avatar," Anton said.

"You have no idea," Kelsey agreed. "For other dungeons . . . if they've grown up with only their fairy for company, they'd probably stick to whatever options she said were a good idea."

"Why would these fairies be so against you having a body?" Delir asked.

"She wouldn't say, specifically," Kelsey mused, "But there's only one thing it could be. Orders from her god."

"The god of dungeons?" Delir asked excitedly. "Do you know their name?"

"Isn't that part of your guild's secrets?" Kelsey asked.

"Alas, no, we've never been able to find out which god was responsible for dungeons," Delir lamented. "Most gods of a terrain—forests, mountains, rivers, what have you, can be reached by a cleric in the appropriate domain. Nothing happens when you try that in a dungeon."

"Huh," Kelsey said. "Well, Mel's god is called Riadi."

Anton and Delir looked at each other. "I don't know that one," Delir said. "Anton, could you fetch me that book with the green spine?"

He pointed to the bookshelf, so Anton got up and found the book without difficulty. The title of the book was *Divine Classes and Paths.*

"I don't have much in the way of religious texts," Delir explained, paging through the book, "But the specialist clerical classes all name the god that is their patron, and they should mention something about the god."

He kept thumbing through the pages but eventually found what he was looking for. "Aha! Disciple of the Endless Wheel—A Unique Tier Three! Goddess is Riadi, the goddess of . . . reincarnation."

"That sounds about right," Kelsey said with a sour look on her face. "She must have absorbed the god of dungeons."

Anton didn't know what reincarnation meant, but Delir was not so ignorant. "Then . . . you weren't merely born with intelligence, but kept your memories of a previous life?"

"Quick on the uptake, aren't you?" Kelsey said. "And no, I don't want to talk about it. Can we move on to more current matters?"

"Some of these revelations, though . . . it would mean so much to the guild if some of them could be passed on . . . without revealing anything personal about yourself, of course, and kept behind our oaths of secrecy . . ."

"No," Kelsey said flatly. The Guild Master sighed.

"As you wish. Perhaps, in the future, you could agree to meet with some of my peers?"

"Maybe. We'll see once . . . things are settled."

"Very well." Delir sighed again, shifting his thoughts to less academic matters. "Knowing that you are a dungeon puts these quests into a different perspective. Did you wish for your second entrance to be found?"

"There is no second entrance—at least, not yet." Kelsey glanced slyly at Anton. "I just brought the zombies out of storage in an abandoned cellar."

"I'm sure that you had your reasons, but we would all appreciate it if you didn't do anything like that again," Delir said reprovingly. "I haven't heard that anyone died, but there were a few close calls."

"No promises," Kelsey muttered, but Delir had already moved on.

"And this party hiding in the dungeon . . . that's clearly not the case, which means . . . Oh no." Delir looked sadly at Kelsey. "You killed the Baron, didn't you?"

"I'm claiming self-defense," Kelsey said. "Is that going to be a problem?"

"It should be," Delir said slowly. "I counted Renn Anat as a friend, and his daughter is far too young to lose her father."

"Maybe I should do something nice to make it up to her," Kelsey muttered, glancing speculatively at Anton.

Ignoring her, Delir continued with his reasoning. "But . . . if I brought you to trial, would a judge be able to ascertain your guilt? His traits work on people, much like *Noble's Prerogative*."

Kelsey shrugged. "Hell if I know. No one's ever used them on me before."

"Normally, when a dungeon kills someone, it is taken as an act of nature, not a murder," Delir continued. "There is no precedent for a dungeon that can wander around the town."

"That can't make it all right for her to just murder people," Anton protested.

"And yet, you have not denounced her yourself," Delir pointed out.

"That would just . . . cause more deaths," Anton said miserably. "If the guard tried to capture or kill her . . . she'd release more monsters on the town. Even if they succeeded, they'd have just killed her body—the rest of her would still be up the hill."

"I'm a judicial anomaly!" Kelsey chuckled.

"But you were human once, were you not?" Delir asked.

Kelsey looked at him warily. "Once. A long time ago," she said.

"But you remember being a mortal. You must remember weakness and fear, and loss." Delir looked at her earnestly. "Can you not relate to us on that basis? Outside of your walls, can you not see us as more than food?"

"If I did," Kelsey said coldly, "it might make it harder to kill delvers when I need to."

"You're older than the guild," Delir said thoughtfully. "There must have been some incidents in the past. But it has been, what, twenty-five years since someone seriously sought after your core?"

"Twenty-five years is a drop in the bucket," Kelsey sneered. "And who knows what the future will bring? The Elitrans were just here—I know they harvest the dungeons of their neighbors if they can."

"They are a cruel people, I cannot deny it. But the answer is not more cruelty on your part. Not to the people here that don't deserve it."

"The Baron deserved it! He was going to torture me!"

"Anton *just* told me that nothing they did to this body would hurt the real you. Would you even have felt it?"

Kelsey looked away. "If I had dissolved the avatar, Anton would have been in real trouble. Same as if I'd let this body die."

"So there is *someone* here that you care about."

"Maybe." Kelsey shifted in her chair, carefully not looking at the other two. "Look. I've set events in motion. Things are going to happen now, whatever I do."

"The guns," Delir said.

"Yeah. I can't tell you what's going to happen, but I think there's a good chance I can swing it so that Kirido is strong, defended, with Suliel in charge. That's a good result, right?"

"Are you willing to let Suliel be in charge? Once she learns about her father, she'll want to come after you."

"I'm gonna frame that knight-captain for it," Kelsey explained. "Once she's killed someone for it, she'll feel better."

"That's . . . not how it works!" Delir said, raising his voice in exasperation. "And you're talking about executing our staunchest defender."

"*I'm* your staunchest defender, Delir," Kelsey stated firmly. "With what we can do with the guns, and . . . other stuff, there are going to be big changes around here."

"I don't want big changes," Anton said suddenly. "I want my old life back."

"I didn't take that life away," Kelsey said. "The Elitrans did. And you know they'll be back for more. There's no going back; there is only forward."

Delir looked a little sick as he slowly shook his head.

"I'm not going to denounce you either," he said. "As Anton says, doing so would cause more suffering. Just please, try to moderate things as much as you can."

"I always do," Kelsey assured him. She ignored the look on Anton's face. "It's not like I get pleasure from killing people—and I don't even get experience unless they're in my dungeon."

Delir sighed in defeat. "What should I do about the quests?" he asked.

"Fill them, of course. I don't mind if people run around town looking for something that doesn't exist, and people have delved into me before."

"If the Baroness is funding things, this party might be better equipped than previous ones have been," Delir warned her. "Even if they have potions, adventurers tend to be loathe to use them when they're paying for them out of their own pocket."

"I'll keep that in mind," Kelsey said slowly. "But as long as they don't go for my core, I don't have anything to worry about—right?"

"That would be against the law," Delir agreed. "As long as the Baroness doesn't have a reason to do anything foolish, you should be fine."

"She's already got a suspect in custody," Kelsey said. "It will be fine."

"Out of curiosity," Delir asked, "How are you going to fool the judge?"

"Do I need to? He won't be coming after me."

"But he will be judging Captain Oldaw," Delir pointed out. "He'll have truth-sense or some other way of judging guilt. When he interviews Oldaw, the captain will be found innocent.

Kelsey stared at Delir blankly for a long moment. Finally, she spoke.

"Well, crap."

* * *

Kelsey swore all the way back to the inn. To Anton's disappointment, Aris had left a note saying that she was going to go check on her family. Which left Anton to deal with a frustrated Kelsey.

"You didn't know about judges?" he asked.

"No, for some reason none of them ever came down to the dungeon," Kelsey snapped at him. "But it's okay, I can deal with this. All we have to do is make sure he doesn't testify."

"How?"

"Killing him would be the simplest way," Kelsey mused. "But I'd have to make it look like an accident if I don't want to compromise Suliel's position . . ."

"Please don't," Anton said, without much hope of being listened to. "No, wait, you're talking about killing a level twenty-something—"

"Twenty-six," Kelsey put in.

"A level twenty-six soldier, who is in a cell owned by a person you don't want to implicate, *and* you want to make it look like an accident? Even you're not so crazy as to think that can work."

"Shut up," Kelsey said irritably. Anton lay back on the bed and ignored Kelsey pacing. He thought about last night. He wanted to talk to Aris about last night, ideally without Kelsey being a part of the conversation.

"We could kill the judge . . . but then we'd just have another murder investigation on our hands. Suliel isn't going to trust us until her father's killer is put away, so that would just delay everything . . ."

"Didn't you used to plot silently?" Anton asked.

"I'm involving you in the process . . . there may be other aspects of this situation I've missed due to my having been living under a rock these last fifty years."

"If you want me to be *actually* involved, stop thinking up plans that kill people," Anton said waspishly.

Kelsey raised an eyebrow at him but then grinned. "Whaaaat?" She said with exaggerated disbelief. "Without killing *anybody*? How is that even *possible*?"

"Give it a try, you might like it," Anton said, his sour tone undercut by Kelsey's giggles.

"But you know what they say—you can't make an omelet without killing a few people."

"I don't know what an omelet is," Anton said stiffly, "and if it involves killing people, I don't want one."

Kelsey howled with laughter. "It's even funnier when you don't get the joke," she said. She suddenly stopped laughing. "Actually, I just had an idea."

"Please tell me it doesn't involve killing anybody."

"That would be pretty crazy," Kelsey said. "So crazy it just might work."

CHAPTER TWENTY-FOUR

The Tide Is High

I t's so simple," Kelsey said, her eyes shining with excitement. "We just have to break him out of prison!"

Anton buried his face in his hands. "That's not going to work—you were there when he surrendered himself! He's not going to cooperate; he knows the judge will clear him of guilt."

Kelsey waved her hand dismissively. "Details. Okay, *technically*, we'll be kidnapping him, but rescue sounds a lot better."

"Of course it sounds better when you lie about it," Anton retorted. "And even that's a—what are you going to do with him, if you manage to *kidnap* him?"

"Oh wow, kid, I appreciate the enthusiasm, but there's a lot of problems to overcome before we get to that stage. Focus on what's in front—"

"Don't avoid the question. What are you going to do with him?"

Kelsey gave him a long look and then sighed. "Quicker than I thought," she muttered under her breath. "I guess you've gotten tired of letting grief consume you?"

"I want to grieve," Anton said slowly. "But I can't. I don't have the time to because you're . . . threatening everyone."

"Little old me?" Kelsey asked with a disarming smile. "But *fine*, while it would be *easier* for the guy to just disappear, we can hold him until it's too late for him to do any damage, and then release him."

Anton gaped at her. "You're talking about one of the leading defenders of the kingdom!" he said. "You can't understand the damage just holding him would do—or how difficult it would be to hold him against his will!"

"I saw his level," Kelsey told him. "And as for defending the realm, it doesn't seem to me that he's doing much of that."

Anton winced. "It hurts that he didn't make it here on time," he admitted. "But the Lancers can't be everywhere, and no one knows where the raiders will strike."

"If you say so," Kelsey said without conviction. "But right now, he's standing in the way of my building up this town's defenses until it can take a raid without trouble."

Anton opened his mouth to speak, but Kelsey kept talking over him. "And he's *also* going to be the one that gets the Baroness after us if we don't frame him. Is that what you want?"

"No," Anton admitted sourly. "But how are you going to keep him?"

"Inside me, of course?"

"But you can't access your—oh no. You can't put an entrance in the town."

Kelsey grinned. "I think you mean that I *shouldn't*. There *are* technical challenges, to be sure, but nothing that's going to stop me."

She giggled. "It's funny—Oldaw thinks there are enemies hiding out inside of me when it's going to be him that is."

Anton felt the despair rise up within him again. Kirido was going to be destroyed, his friends all murdered by monsters, and there wasn't anything he could do to stop it. It must have shown on his face because Kelsey gave him an irritated look.

"Don't look so gloomy about it—it's going to be perfectly safe!" she said. "Kirido is going to be richer and safer than you can possibly imagine."

"Or it will be razed off the face of the earth," he said gloomily.

"Well, that's always a possibility," she agreed. "But I prefer to not dwell on the worst-case scenario."

Kelsey opened the door with a key she'd looted from either the dead Baron or one of his guards. Anton was standing next to her, feeling far too conspicuous.

"Why are we doing this in daylight?" he whispered. "I thought we were going in at midnight."

"It might take us some time to find the secret tunnel," Kelsey said easily, stepping inside. Anton followed and she closed the door behind him, removing one source of his anxiety.

"What makes you so sure there is a secret tunnel?" he asked. Hopefully, there *wasn't*, and Kelsey would have to give up this mad idea.

"If the Baron didn't have a place to meet us, conveniently accessible by a secret tunnel, he would have shown up at our inn, all hooded up and mysterious. There would be no point in him sneaking through the town and then having *us* sneak through the town as well. Twice as likely to get his secret meeting noticed."

Kelsey started scoping out the interior walls. From experience in her dungeon, Anton knew that she was checking to see if there were any walled-off areas.

"But since he did bring us here, then there must be such a tunnel," she finished. Completing her inspection of the walls, she started examining the flagstones. "We just have to find it. C'mon, don't adventurers have special senses for finding secret doors?"

"*I* don't," Anton said. Nevertheless, he started examining the floor as well. He did know what to look for, after all.

It didn't take them all day, but it did take over an hour before they found the release at the bottom of the kitchen wall which allowed one of the flagstones to be raised. A yawning pit containing a ladder beckoned them. Beckoned to Kelsey anyway, as she immediately started climbing down.

"It's not dark yet!" Anton protested.

"I just want to take a quick look," she told him. "We won't open any doors or anything, but I want to see how this tunnel runs."

Groaning to himself, Anton followed her down. She didn't seem bothered by the darkness, and Anton was used to using ladders without being able to see. It wasn't far to the bottom, and once they got there, Kelsey pulled out one of her strangely bright lanterns.

In the harsh, white light of the lantern, Anton could see that they were in a tunnel that headed in two directions. Kelsey looked both ways thoughtfully. Wide enough for two people, with a flat floor and an arched roof, the tunnel had clearly been carved by either magic or strong stoneworking traits.

"The castle would be that way," she said, pointing, "And in the other direction would be . . . the harbor?"

Anton tried to imagine the angles from his knowledge of the town. "I think . . . farther along the coast? On the other side of the bluff?" There were some cliffs there; it was possible the tunnel came out in some caves.

"*Outside* of the harbor . . ." Kelsey mused. "I wonder . . . is it possible that the Baron was smuggling contraband? How scandalous!"

"Maybe his ancestors?" Anton suggested weakly. He didn't see why the Baron would need to avoid his own tax, but he could see that the Baron would occasionally need to sneak things in and out of his town.

"We've got some time, let's check it out," Kelsey said. Anton didn't really see the point, but he wasn't eager to go in the *other* direction, so he agreed and they started walking. It wasn't long before the slight salty smell, ever present in Kirido, started to intensify. It was soon joined by the smell of rotting seaweed.

"We're getting close," Kelsey said, just before a gate became visible in the light she was carrying. It blocked the tunnel but impeded them not at all because a mechanism set into the wall opened it without issue. Beyond it was a natural cavern, poorly lit with a green light that came from around a bend.

Anton was too cautious to walk through a gate until he knew how it would close, so he stayed where he was while Kelsey investigated how to open it from the other side.

"It looks like it's only meant to be opened from the one side," she eventually reported. "Unless there's a hidden lever somewhere. It doesn't look like it closes on its own, though.

Anton nodded. There had been no sign of a timer mechanism, and it had stayed open in the five minutes that Kelsey had spent searching around the entrance. They moved forward to see the source of the light.

Turning the corner, they could see that the light came from a pool of water that must have been connected to the sea. They both stared at it for a bit.

"The cave must only be accessible during low tide," Anton eventually ventured.

"A real smuggler's cavern," Kelsey said thoughtfully. "I've heard of them, but..."

Anton frowned, trying to think of where Kelsey would have heard of *that*. She sometimes seemed to know the strangest things. He wasn't given time to ponder, as Kelsey soon shook off her thoughtful mood.

"Right!" she said. "Let's close this up again and get back to business!"

Reluctantly, Anton followed her back into the tunnel. This time, they continued on past the ladder leading to the safe house (another strange term of Kelsey's) until they found themselves at the tunnel's end and another ladder.

"This is great," Kelsey said, looking up. "This is gonna be just perfect."

She shone her light up the shaft, and Anton could see that it ended in a trapdoor. Much like the other shaft, there was another lever that probably unlatched it.

"Let's go back," he urged, in case Kelsey got inspired to go while the castle was still active.

Once they were back in the safe house, Kelsey sank into one of the comfortable chairs.

"We're really going to do this?" he asked her.

"Oh yeah—I mean the first time we should just check things out, and only steal him if we see a good opportunity. But unless you've got any other ideas of how we're going to get out of this . . . yeah."

"And you don't have a plan of . . . how?"

She shrugged. "We don't know what's there yet, so let's just sneak in without getting caught, and see what we find. Just like you adventurers do all the time."

"Undead aren't really that perceptive," he told her. "You'll find human guards are a lot more alert."

She nodded. "Still, we've got some advantages." She held up a finger. "Remember these?" she said, as a small undead spider appeared on it. "These guys can bite them and send them to sleep."

"You're just going to use sleeping spiders, right?" he said, eyeing the creature warily. A spider that small couldn't bite through his *Stone Skin*, but that didn't mean he was comfortable being in the same room as it.

"Yes, mother," Kelsey said. "No lethal attacks, no letting them run loose through the building out of my line of sight."

She brightened. "Still. These guards won't have *Poison Resistance* or *Stone Skin*. It's so annoying how you guys ignore a lot of my stuff."

"They're likely to have *Danger Sense* or *Alertness*, though," he warned her. "And a high enough Toughness ability can make you resistant to poisons all on its own."

"We'll be careful," Kelsey told him.

He sighed. "Have you still got the copper-bound chest from my parents' house?"

Kelsey raised an eyebrow. "Sure. You want it?"

At his nod, she summoned it to the room, placing it on the floor between them.

"What's in it?" she asked.

Anton knelt before the chest and opened it. It wasn't locked. "My parents' alchemical tool kit," he said. "They took most of the really good stuff to the wall, but . . . there should be something here that we can use."

Kelsey looked interested but let him continue on his own. The chest contained three deep trays, subdivided into compartments, and he lifted them out to peruse the contents.

"Oil of silence," he said, taking out a stoppered jar. "You put it on your shoes, it makes your footsteps silent."

"Is that what does it?" Kelsey asked, leaning forward. "I always thought that some of you were suspiciously quiet."

Anton pulled out a bag and emptied the contents into his hand. Four hollowed-out monster cores glowed slightly as he held them. "Translocation orbs," he said. "Only four of them, though."

"I hate those things," Kelsey complained. "Why do I even bother having doors?"

When crushed, a translocation orb would teleport its user forward one yard. They were expensive—a Tier Three item, but worth every silver under the right circumstances. Anton set them next to the oil and pulled out the next item.

"Sentry beads," he said, his voice echoing strangely. "Just one pair."

"I don't know that one," Kelsey said.

"Whatever sounds one bead hears, the other makes," he told her. "You can use them for communication, or as a way of listening out for things at a distance."

"I can see how that would be useful," Kelsey said. "I'm getting interested now; what else have you got?"

CHAPTER TWENTY-FIVE

Papa Don't Preach

Most of Anton's inherited stash proved less than useful for their expedition. There was an everlasting light stone in a ring setting that his mother had worn before she had gotten married, but it was too small for Anton to wear.

"I could resize this if you like?" Kelsey offered, toying with the mechanism that covered the stone when you didn't want it to shine. "Or have a skeleton do it, same thing."

"I don't think so . . . maybe Aris could wear it?" Belatedly, Anton realized that the wedding ring his mother had replaced this with hadn't been returned to him. That was probably because her body had been looted by the raiders. His breath caught in his throat, and he didn't hear Kelsey's reply.

"What?" he eventually managed to say.

"I said it's fine either way. We've got my torch and these dark-vision potions if we need to sneak around in the dark."

"Right." Weirdly, he found himself focusing on the least important part of what she had just said. "That's not a torch, though."

"What?" Kelsey said, taking another look at her magical light.

"A torch is a stick with fire on one end," he explained carefully. Explaining things carefully helped keep his thoughts under control. "That's a magical light."

Kelsey gaped at him for a moment and then grinned. "Oh, Anton," she said. "That's wrong on a couple of counts, but right now the only thing I can think about is that you've spent your entire life carrying around sticks on fire as if that was a useful activity."

DUNGEONS JUST WANNA HAVE FUN   137

"What are you talking about?" Anton asked.

She moved closer and placed her hand on his shoulders. She gazed up at his face, her expression filled with an emotion that Anton couldn't place.

"It's just that there are going to be a lot of changes in your life, Anton, changes that will hopefully be for the better. You won't have to care about sticks anymore, I promise."

Suddenly she froze and then relaxed. "Whew! Okay, that was careless. Only making a *metaphorical* promise there." She took a step forward and engulfed him in a hug.

"No more sticks, Anton. No more sticks."

"That's . . . uh.. great? I'm really pleased by that." Anton said, totally flummoxed by her behavior.

"It *is* great," she said, releasing him and returning to her more cheerful default. "You'll see. Sorry, I get a little emotional when I remember that you grew up without an mp3 player."

"I—" *don't know what that is,* Anton started to say but thought better of it. It might set her off again. "That's fine," he said instead. "Shall we finish going through this stuff?"

They did, but the good stuff had already gone. The healing potions, for example, had all been used up on the wall. There was a selection of antidotes, including a Tier Three universal antidote that would cure almost any Tier Two poison. That, along with the six Tier Two antidotes for *specific* poisons that were a requirement for delving past level five in Kelsey's dungeon.

That wouldn't do them much good for this . . . delve. Anton was a lot more comfortable thinking of it that way. Other terms, like "crime" and "treason," floated around in the back of his head, but he pushed them back.

Potions of water breathing, of free movement . . . Anton wondered if his parents had harbored ambitions of getting past the Vampire Queen and exploring the Silent Sea. Not useful now. Nor was the potion of warmth or the philter of lightness. Anton took the philter anyway. It combined well with his *Leaping Attack*, allowing him to attack someone over a hundred yards away. You never knew when something like that would prove useful.

That was about it, though. Anton resolved to see about getting more alchemicals soon. Not right now, though. Anything he used tonight might have questions asked the next morning about who had purchased them.

Since they still had time, Anton insisted that they go looking for Aris. They hadn't really talked about last night, and while a private conversation didn't seem possible, Anton was getting a little anxious to see her again.

They found her at the first place they looked. She was being kept busy at her parents' bakery, which delayed any heartfelt conversation but ended up with the two of them invited to a family dinner that night.

"I don't know about this . . . are you going to tell them about me?" Kelsey asked. The two of them were waiting for the sun to set at the cleaned-up shell of Anton's house. It was nearby, and Kelsey brought in some chairs for them to sit on.

"If I do, are you going to try and put a geas on them?" Anton asked.

Kelsey looked away. "Nah, it's fine. I got a little panicked when the head of the organization devoted to plundering me knew, but I'm over it."

"Do you think you might be willing to come clean then? Let everybody know what you are?"

"You think that's a good idea?" Kelsey asked, surprised. "That would mean letting Suliel know who killed her father. It may have given her a promotion, but I don't think she's going to be grateful."

"Probably not," Anton agreed. "It's just the deception and misdirection . . . it's getting to be a bit much."

"Deception is a part of any conflict," Kelsey replied. "Whether it's a duel or a war, you always have to keep your opponent in the dark about your next action."

Anton looked over at her. It was getting late in the day, and even though his place didn't have a roof, the shadows of the walls covered everything in near darkness. Kelsey had brought out an ordinary lantern to keep them from sitting in the dark, setting it on the ground. Lit from below, her pale face could have passed for a living corpse or a vampire.

"Are . . . are you at war with my town?" he asked carefully.

She considered the question carefully. "Not with your town," she finally said thoughtfully. "Though it could be said that they've been at war with me since the beginning."

"They—we—didn't know you were a person."

"Would that have made a difference? Will knowing make them less likely to attack—or more? If Suliel's father had died in the dungeon, she wouldn't hate me as much as she does right now—without even knowing who I am."

She picked up the lantern. "No, I'm not ready to come clean. Let's go meet your family."

Meals in the Lucina household might not be as fancy as the fare served at the inn, but they were cooked just as well. Kelsey brought out a ceramic jug of wine, claiming that it had been left over from the party. Wine of that quality was *not* a customary part of the family meal, but it was welcomed.

Anton felt himself relax in the warmth of the domesticity. His family had often eaten with Aris's, and he could almost imagine that they were there with him. The conversation flowed freely. Important topics—and Anton could tell that there were serious questions coming—were put off for a later time.

Kelsey proved to be quite knowledgeable about the characteristics of ovens, of all things, which turned out to be a popular conversation choice in a room full of bakers. Anton didn't understand half of it, but he preferred that to the vague lies that Kelsey told of the northern lands. She seemed to have an endless font of made-up stories to entertain her audience.

Eventually, though, the questions that had been waiting had to be asked. It started with her father.

"Aris tells us that you are going to take her to go after Cheia," he stated gravely. His name was Belan, but Anton had never called him anything other than "sir."

"It's more the other way around, but that's right," Anton replied.

"We've lost one daughter already, we can't lose another," Etase said.

"Mama, we haven't lost Cheia. We can get her back."

Etase just shook her head. "I know you have a strong class now, but Anton—you fought on the wall. You know just how strong the soldiers were. Aris is only level six, and you're . . ."

"Level nine," he supplied. Their eyes widened in shock. Last week, he'd been level six. "It's been . . . I tried to convince Aris, but she's determined to go. Not right away, but after a few levels—"

"And we have Kelsey to help," Aris pointed out. Her parents looked at their strange guest, who shrugged.

"I am Tier Three," she admitted. "And an experienced traveler to boot. I can help them get to where they're going. They're going to have to grow a lot on the way, though."

"We will," Aris said firmly. "I'm not going to let them take my sister. I'll get however many levels I need."

"In the dungeon, you mean," Etase said disapprovingly. "You know how dangerous that place is."

"Anton can keep me safe there, you know that," Aris said.

"Mum and Dad delved long enough to retire," Anton said. Etase and Belan looked at him, while Kelsey just smirked when they weren't looking.

"They knew—they taught me—about not pushing too far, about staying safe. I think we'll be a lot safer in the dungeon than most." He could see Kelsey's amusement at his words, but she kept it limited to a wry smile.

They wanted to disagree with him, but they had known his parents. Known that his parents had allowed him—even encouraged him—to delve. Under strict supervision at first, but eventually on his own. No matter how they grumbled, they trusted him to keep her safe there, and he felt warmed by their trust.

"We know that you will keep her safe here," Belan admitted. "But once you go out there . . ." He fixed his gaze on Kelsey. "Just who are you and why should we trust you with our children?"

Anton flushed at his sudden inclusion into the Lucina family. Kelsey just raised an eyebrow.

"I'm sure you've heard stories," she said.

"We've heard that you're sharing a room with Anton, which is hardly proper when he's engaged to Aris," Etase said disapprovingly.

"That's complicated . . ." Kelsey said. "Aris knows the full story, but ours is a business relationship. As much as I'd prefer otherwise, he only has eyes for your daughter."

"We asked Aris about it . . ." Etase said.

"She wouldn't speak of it," Belan added.

"I'm not going to either—it's none of your business," Aris stated. Anton felt his face burning and hoped his skin was dark enough to hide it.

That . . . wasn't the end of it, but it was the end of anything new being said. Etase and Belan clearly didn't like the idea, but the unspoken threat that Aris would go and stay at the inn hung over them. In the end, the Lucinas would rather spend more time with their daughter while she was here than drive her away trying to keep her safe.

So despite strong feelings, the dinner ended mostly amicably. Aris led them outside, and Kelsey courteously went on ahead, stopping far enough to let Anton believe she couldn't hear them, but close enough that her absence wasn't giving him a heart attack. He embraced Aris and held her close. For the obvious reasons, of course, but also because it let him whisper in her ear.

"I could go back with you," she said softly.

"We're . . . going to be doing something dangerous tonight," he replied. "It's best if you're not involved."

"More dangerous stuff? I could help!"

"It's sneaky . . . even if Kelsey let you have your weapons, they'd give us away. Please stay here?"

She tensed against him but then relaxed. "All right," she said. "But you owe me one."

"Whatever you want," he said. "Are . . . *we* all right?"

"What do you mean?" she asked curiously.

"Well, I mean . . ." he could feel his face burning, and his cheek was close enough to Aris's that he imagined she could feel it too. "We never got a chance to talk . . . about last night . . ."

"Idiot," she chuckled. "Give me a kiss."

He did so, and she locked her arms behind his head, pulling his face into hers. He let her, feeling the warmth of her lips, the surprise of her tongue . . .

How did she know how to do that? he wondered. *Do girls just get taught these things?*

He'd forgotten the question before they finished the kiss, though, forgotten everything except for the girl in his arms.

"There," she said. "Go do your stupid thing. I'll see you tomorrow."

CHAPTER TWENTY-SIX

This Charming Man

Anton wasn't sure if he was eager to get started on this insane endeavor, but he was definitely eager to get it over and done with.

"Before anything else," he pleaded, "can you *please* change into something less distinctive?"

Kelsey looked down at herself, dressed in a bright red shirt and loose gold—gold!—pants. Like everyone else in town, Anton had given up wondering how she made such things, and he thanked the gods that no one had yet asked her if they were available for sale.

"I suppose they are a bit conspicuous," she said. Wise to Kelsey's ways—or at least *wiser*—Anton had already looked away.

"Spoilsport," she said. "All right, it's safe to look now," she told him a moment later. Anton waited for another moment before turning back cautiously. Kelsey was now wearing heavier cloth pants. Still dyed, but this time a deep blue, and she was wearing a shirt with a slightly lighter shade of blue.

"Can you move in those?" he asked. "They look . . . scandalously tight."

"They're not that tight!" Kelsey replied indignantly. "Relaxed fit." She demonstrated by bending over and lifting one leg . . . and Anton had to look away again.

"If you say so," he muttered. "Can you get the oil out now?"

Kelsey snickered but acquiesced gracefully, pulling out the bottle with a flourish.

"Normally, we'd just put a drop on our boots," Anton explained, "but this time, I think we might be better with total coverage. There are going to be at least some people there with Perception in their class advancements, so they'll be able to hear if anything is amiss.

"Are soldier classes going to have Perception advances?" Kelsey asked curiously. "Wouldn't they focus on Strength, Toughness, and so on?"

"Soldiers have to keep watch," he pointed out. "That's enough for at least a partial. And there are scouts and things."

He took a deep breath. "And wizards are always strong in Perception and Intelligence. I would expect Magister Tikin to have more than thirty."

"More than me. Good to know," Kelsey said, the playful look leaving her face. "How do you know that?"

Anton felt his face warm. "Every kid wants to be a wizard when they grow up," he said. "And I had access to class books at the guild."

Kelsey frowned at him, but then shrugged. "Fair enough. Wizards *are* awesome. How does this work, then?"

"It spreads magically," Anton told her. "Hold your nose and mouth closed, or it will get inside you and prevent you from speaking."

Once she had pinched her nose shut, he reached out with the bottle and squeezed a few drops on her shoulder, taking careful note of the faint glow from the oil as it spread to gauge its progress. It started on the outside of her clothes and then slowed down as it spread to cover the inside of her garment, and her skin as well.

Anton kept adding drops each time the glow started to fade until finally, the oil had reached her shoes.

"Raise up one foot, and then the other," he said, adding another drop. Then they were done. "You can open your mouth now."

"Can I still talk? I can!" Kelsey said. She slapped the wall next to her to confirm that no sounds were being made.

"My turn," Anton said. He handed her the bottle and went through the same process.

"Are we ready to go then?" Kelsey asked. Anton nodded.

"Just remember to only talk when we need to," he reminded her.

"I might find that difficult," she admitted. "I'm used to snarking in front of delvers who can't hear or see me."

"Just . . . try," Anton said, unsure of what to do with that admission. It might explain a few things about her general behavior, though.

Sneaking through the town, travelling through the tunnel, and climbing up to the castle had all been accomplished as easily as Anton might have hoped. There was only one horrible moment, as they passed along the tunnel.

Kelsey had stopped to examine the wall, and Anton had felt a clench in his stomach when he noticed that the uninterrupted smooth stone had been replaced by cut stone blocks. It was just a small section, with the blocks defining an archway, still filled with the original smooth stone.

"Don't worry," Kelsey said with an impish grin. "It's not ready yet, I just wanted to make sure that it was lined up correctly."

Anton glared at her, but he didn't have anything to say that she hadn't already ignored.

"If things go bad," Kelsey said, "like *really* bad, I can make a breach here for us to escape into. If that happens, then there will be . . . sort of a mana explosion?"

"You want us to run *into* an explosion?" Anton asked.

"If I have to go that far, it will be a lot less dangerous than *not* running into it," Kelsey said. "And it won't be an explosion, exactly, just . . . really weird. I'm not sure what it will be like for humans, but it shouldn't be too dangerous."

Anton just shook his head, and they resumed their journey. Climbing up to the castle was a longer climb than Anton had expected, but the well-maintained ladder made it easy.

Now, they had come up through a trapdoor and found themselves in a cupboard. Or a room the *size* of a cupboard, perhaps. There was a noticeable lack of items being stored in it.

"This is intimate, isn't it?" Kelsey murmured to him as they tried to determine if it was safe to open the door. Anton flushed. The cupboard would be cramped for one person, and he was finding himself bumped up right against Kelsey's warm body. It was hard to tell in the darkness, but he thought that she was subtly making the problem worse, leaning into his inadvertent contact.

While he struggled to come up with a retort, Kelsey suddenly stiffened. "Wait," she whispered. "Footsteps."

Anton couldn't hear the steps, but he heard the door open in the room beyond.

"Perhaps, if a treatment is required, then this room will do for privacy?" a man's voice asked. Anton thought it sounded familiar, but he couldn't be sure.

"I would never have dared enter here when my husband was alive," a woman's voice replied. Anton heard her voice catch when she said "husband" and felt an immediate kinship. "Suliel hasn't yet made it her own, but she's been so busy . . ."

"Of course, she has been," the man agreed. "Just take a seat, and we'll begin."

Suddenly Kelsey's eyes started to glow. Not strongly—if they hadn't been in the dark, Anton probably wouldn't have noticed. Kelsey didn't seem to have noticed; she was staring fixedly at the room on the other side of the wooden door.

"Oh . . . Oh! That's so much better!" It was the woman—Lady Anat, Anton supposed. Her voice sounded so much happier now, it was almost unrecognizable.

"Of course it is. You know that you can come to me any time it becomes too much," the man said. Anton was pretty sure now that the man was Magister Liem Tikin.

Kelsey's eyes were still glowing as Tikin continued talking.

"I wanted to talk to you about Suliel," he said. "It's important that she get married soon."

"Oh, but she wants to wait until she achieves the second Tier," Lady Anat said. Her voice seemed detached to Anton as if she was in a daze.

"I don't think we can wait that long," Tikin said. "Events are proceeding too quickly, and Suliel doesn't seem inclined to continue her father's work."

"My husband's work?"

"The Rose Circle. She has not been as eager to join as she should be."

"Oh . . . I never really paid attention to what Renn did there . . ."

"It was very important to him. Suliel needs to marry someone who can continue your husband's work."

"I suppose . . . someone already in the Circle?"

"Or someone who already knows of them. Someone like your husband's loyal servant."

"You?" Lady Anat asked the question with more emotion, and it seemed as though she was going to break out of her trance. Kelsey's eyes glowed brighter.

"Me," Tikin said firmly.

"I suppose . . . that might be a good idea," Lady Anat softly agreed, as if she were drifting off to sleep.

"I think we're done for now, my lady," Tikin said. "Why don't you go back to your rooms and sleep. You should find things easier in the morning."

"Yes . . ." was all that she said. The door to the room was opened again, and closed, both people having left.

"What was that, with the glowing eyes?" Anton asked once he was sure they were gone.

"He was using magic on her," Kelsey said thoughtfully.

"You could tell that, from the other side of the door?"

"I'm made of mana, Anton," Kelsey said impatiently. "I can tell when someone's using it. It's interesting that my eyes glow when I see it, though . . ."

"What sort of magic?" Anton asked. "Was he controlling her?"

"There was some control, but it wasn't very strong," Kelsey replied. "I don't think his core is strong enough with Control Mana to do what he wants. He was mainly using *Destroy* and Mind Mana."

"He was destroying her mind?"

"Mind covers everything to *do* with the mind," Kelsey explained. "Thoughts, emotions, knowledge. I think he was destroying her *grief*, at least initially. Then, maybe, her suspicions?"

"So every time she got suspicious of something he said, he destroyed it?"

"Something like that," Kelsey agreed. "I'm sure he'd rather have controlled her, but he might be able to get what he wants that way. Eventually."

"He mostly does fire magic," Anton mused. "I didn't know he could do mental stuff."

"Well, the evidence is that he doesn't do mental stuff *well*," Kelsey said. "But given the prize of a barony, I guess he thought it was worth a few risks."

"Are we—are you going to do something about this?"

"Hmm. It does get in the way of *my* plans, it's true. I quite like Suliel, and I'd like to see her as Baroness in her own right. And I *do* hate wizards. But! Let's get back to our plan."

She snapped on her torch and quickly looked around the cupboard.

"Anton," she said, cocking her head. "That back wall, does it look . . . detachable . . . to you?"

"This is great!" Kelsey said, exuberantly but quietly. "Secret passages in the medieval castle! Very fantasy!"

"I'm glad you approve," Anton said dryly, ignoring her odd expression. He did agree that travelling through the admittedly tight passageway was a lot better than sneaking around where there were guards to be found. Or rather, guards to find *them*.

"Keep an eye out for spy holes," Kelsey told him. "We know that whatshisface is being held in one of the guest bedrooms, and if you're going to have a secret passage, it's a given that you'll be wanting to spy on your guests."

"Sure," Anton said. "Does that mean we should keep the torch off? If there's chinks for the light to shine through . . ."

Kelsey thought about it as they carefully moved along. "I think it would be okay," she said. "You're going to want them plugged up when you're not using them, or people might notice . . . like that one!"

She skipped half a step. Snapping off the torch, she pried out a triangular stone from the wall and stretched up to put her eye to the gap.

"Just an empty room," she sighed, disappointed. Then her eyes started to glow again, and she whipped her head around.

"That way," she declared. Pausing only to put the plug back in, she hurried on. Anton hurried after her as best he could in the darkness. It wasn't as if there was more than one way to go, after all.

The panic was beginning to start as he caught up with her, staring through another hole in the wall. She backed off as he approached, and let him take a look.

There was some light on the other side, but nothing to be actually seen. There were two voices, though, speaking out of the line of sight of the spy hole.

"You wake me up, and set my guard to napping, just to ask me about my matrimonial ambitions?" It was Captain Oldaw speaking, just as arrogant in a cell as he had been when Anton had spoken to him before. Anton drew back from the hole so that they both had equal access to listen to the conversation. He noted that Kelsey's eyes had stopped glowing.

"You are a man in need of friends, Captain Oldaw." It was Tikin again. "Lord Kinn will be arriving soon—he was a close friend of the Baron."

"I'm going to be cleared of those charges, as soon as Lady Suliel brings in a judge."

"Lord Kinn will arrive sooner, and he is not so reticent as our lady," Tikin countered. "Without someone to speak to him for you, it could easily go badly."

There was a long silence before Oldaw spoke. "While a barony is a tempting target to snatch up, I have my eye on grander prizes. Tier Four is within my grasp, and I don't plan on changing my path until I get it."

"I understand, my lord. What I would like in return, if you have felt my services to be useful in clearing your name, is your support towards my claiming the prize for myself."

Oldaw snorted with amusement. "Looking to rise to greater heights? I'd reconsider. She's a pretty girl, but she is her father's daughter. Take her Noble class away from her, and she's more likely to aim for Assassin than Lady."

"Let me worry about that, my lord."

"Fine, fine. Prove of value to me, and I'll offer my support to this thing of yours," Oldaw said. "If it works out, you'll have an ally in the capital—*if* it works out."

Kelsey went to put the stone back but stopped. Silently, she made the bottle of silencing oil appear and put a drop on the rock before easing it back into position. Then she pushed Anton back the way that they had come. It wasn't until they had moved almost all the way back to the escape shaft that she spoke.

"This wizard, he's a busy boy, isn't he?"

CHAPTER TWENTY-SEVEN

We Don't Need Another Hero

W hat?" Kelsey asked. Her voice stayed quiet, but she managed to convey a dangerous intensity. "What did you just say?"

Delir Nyer swallowed nervously and wiped some sweat from his brow. "I just got back from the castle, and I've already tried to talk her out of it, but she insisted, and she is the Baroness . . ."

Kelsey leaned back in her seat, her eyes still fixed on the Guild Master. "I'm starting to think that maybe I don't like Suliel as much as I thought."

"I don't understand," Aris said. She was the actual reason they were here. Aris needed to be registered with the guild and Kelsey had wanted that to be handled by the Guild Master personally. She wanted Aris's class kept under wraps for as long as possible.

The Guild Master had been out when they arrived, but when he got back in, he called them to his office and dropped his bombshell.

"Why is it so bad that Magister Tikin will be joining the expedition?" Aris continued.

Nyer glanced at Kelsey to see if she wanted to answer, but she was focused on her own thoughts, eyes narrowed. "Ah, well, Miss Lucina."

"Aris, please."

"As you wish . . . It's common knowledge among adventurers that dungeons *do not like* the presence of wizards."

Aris frowned. "I thought that knowing that dungeons were people was a guild secret."

"People have a tendency to see personality in all kinds of things, regardless of whether it is there," he said pompously. "Since even the least communicative of dungeons have their own wants and needs, most adventurers assume there is some sort of intelligence behind it."

"Why the secret then?" Aris asked.

"What *is* secret is that we have established communications with some dungeons. If the wider membership knew, we would face a lot more pressure to get the dungeons to 'cough up the treasure.' They might insist that instead of negotiating from a position of trust and friendship that we take a harder line."

"Can you even threaten a dungeon?" Aris wondered, looking at Kelsey speculatively.

"Some might say that that's what the Lady Suliel is doing," Nyer replied, glancing nervously at Kelsey.

"Tikin's core, where he gets his powers from, was made from the core of a dungeon," Anton cut in.

"Isn't that—I mean, he's the one person who doesn't need another one, right?"

"Wizards can upgrade their cores by absorbing another dungeon core," Kelsey said, breaking from her silence. "As far as I know it's the only way they can increase the power of their spells."

"It's not based on their level?" Anton asked, interested.

"Their level is part of it, but the actual magic comes from the core, so ultimately the magic they can do is limited by it." Kelsey rose to her feet and started pacing about the room. "I don't think this changes anything, except that I might have to take this expedition more seriously."

Nyer nodded. "Did you want these two—or even yourself—added to the roster?"

"How is that possible?" Aris asked. "We're not elite adventurers. Well, I'm not, and even Anton . . ."

"It's an expedition," Anton explained. "Instead of a single party, there will be a large group, with teams being left on each floor to prevent the dungeon . . . Kelsey, from respawning the monsters or resetting the traps."

"If they expect to reach level twelve then they need twenty to thirty adventurers in addition to the main group," Nyer said. "Before, we would have been hard-pressed to complete the roster. Now, we may need to recruit amongst the soldiers."

"Who's the main group?" Kelsey asked.

"Rathuan's team, with the magister accompanying," Nyer said in a studiously neutral voice.

"They're good," Kelsey admitted. "I don't . . . I don't think you guys should be a part of it. It might be nice to have you clear out and let me rig an ambush for these guys on the way out, but that would probably hurt your reputation later on."

"We wouldn't do it anyway," Anton said coldly. "Delvers on the way *out* can't possibly be a threat to you."

"They might be," Kelsey said thoughtfully. "If I had to reveal one of my secrets to drive them back, I would very much like the information to not get back. After all we've been through, you won't kill one little human for me?"

"No," Anton said, looking away from her batting her eyelashes at him. "Bad enough I have to be there when *you* kill people."

"Is that what happened to the soldiers?" Nyer asked suddenly. "They found out one of your secrets?"

"Who knows?" Kelsey said. "Are they even dead? It's mysterious!"

"Will it be a problem if we don't join up?" Aris asked.

"No, it's fine either way," Nyer assured her. "I'll just say that Anton didn't want to risk angering the dungeon with a mage in the party . . . there might be others who also refuse. If enough do, it might help convince the Baroness."

"Well, I'll keep an eye out on who does come down," Kelsey mused. She grinned wolfishly. "Maybe I'll play some favorites from now on."

"Really?" Nyer asked.

"Eh, there's a limit on what I can do there," Kelsey admitted. "I can give some special orders before they come down, and they can be something like 'focus on the guy with the axe,' but that sort of thing never works out as well as you'd like."

"I see. Should I keep you apprised of the final list?"

"No need." Kelsey waved him off languidly. "Unless there's a surprise inclusion over level twenty-five, it should be fine."

"Like Captain Oldaw?" Anton asked. Kelsey whirled to look at him.

"He wouldn't!" she said. "Would he? Would that be good or bad?"

"You said he was level twenty-six," Anton pointed out. "And he will want to know what happened to his men."

"He's under house arrest, though," Kelsey pointed out. "And you're not supposed to solve the case you're accused of. Very bad, conflict of interest and all that."

Turning slightly away from them, she muttered, "You're a loose cannon, Oldaw—turn in your badge!" Whatever the sentence meant, it seemed to amuse her.

"Okay," she said, turning back to them, "I'll keep him in mind as a possible entrant. If that's all, we should get back to registering Aris."

"Of course. Now, what did you say her class actually was?"

After the paperwork was done, they headed back to the inn, and Anton got nervous again. He thought that Kelsey might want to do . . . things. Not that he didn't want to—with Aris, he definitely did—but Kelsey made things so much more complicated.

Last night, he'd been exhausted after their illegal infiltration and had gone straight to sleep. It hadn't been the physical activity as much as the extended period of constant tension. They'd explored the secret passage and found that the only exit was the one in the study. There were spy holes to three more rooms, one of them the room where they had been interviewed, and two more guest bedrooms, currently empty.

Then Kelsey had decided to carefully search the Baron's study.

"I need more information," she had said. "About the situation here, about who Suliel answers to, what her connections are. Who is this Lord Kinn guy, and whose side is he going to take?"

Valid questions, Anton supposed, but he couldn't really help her with them. The desk was too small for two people to sit at, so he had the choice of looking over her shoulder or the slightly more useful activity of listening at the door for further interruptions. No one came as Kelsey flipped through books, ledgers, and correspondence, looking for something revealing. It had been hours before she had let them leave.

Now that they were back, she seemed to be evaluating something. She looked at the bedroom, then back at him. She made a slight grimace and led them over to the table, what she had called the "meeting room." So this was going to be a serious talk?

If so, Aris somewhat spoiled the mood by insisting on sitting in his lap. He didn't object, and Kelsey just rolled her eyes.

"Guys," she said. "I think we need to work on Suliel a bit more."

"What did you have in mind?" Anton asked curiously. He was cautiously optimistic that she'd chosen phrasing that didn't directly translate to "kill."

"Well . . . Suliel likes you," Kelsey said.

"So what?" Aris asked with a flat tone that Anton found confusing.

"More than she does you? Well, she hardly knows me, but that's not surprising. She owes you money and you're a mysterious stranger . . . that's . . ." Anton trailed off because of the looks the other two were giving him.

"I mean she likes you like Aris likes you," Kelsey said. "She wants you to kiss her, and then lift up her dress and bend her over and then pound her like—"

"Yes, fine, I get it, there's no need to be vulgar!" Anton exclaimed, his face burning.

"She's young, so she's probably not into the freaky shit that nobles get up to," Kelsey said thoughtfully. "Although you never know, they like to leave books lying around that detail all *sorts* of things so the kids can be properly educated before they get married."

"I said that was enough," Anton complained. "Was that what you found in the study?"

"No, I was speaking of nobles more . . . generally," Kelsey said with a shrug.

"So what?" Aris repeated. She half turned on Anton's lap and put her arm around his neck, pulling herself closer as she leaned against him. Anton responded by hugging her closer still. She was warm and soft and . . .

"Wait, you knew already?" he asked as he realized that she hadn't been surprised. *Anton* was certainly surprised.

"Not specifically," she confessed. "But all the girls have been noticing you since you got to Tier Two so quickly. Most of them know enough to keep their grubby hands off you."

"You've been keeping him all to yourself since you were kids, haven't you?" Kelsey said with amusement.

"Until recently," Aris said, glaring at Kelsey. "We had an *understanding.*"

"Right . . . so what I'm saying is, we'd get a lot better treatment if Suliel thought that Anton was interested in her—or at least receptive to her advances."

Anton felt Aris tense up. "You want him to lie to her?" she snarled.

"Doesn't have to be a lie," Kelsey replied calmly. "She's a very beautiful girl. Isn't she, Anton?"

Aris whipped her head around to look at him.

"*You're* beautiful," he said. The answer came easily to him, and it seemed to be the right one, as Aris relaxed and gave him a warm smile.

"But the answer to the actual question is . . .?" Kelsey pressed.

"Well . . . I've never gotten a good look at her, but she does seem kind of . . . pretty," Anton admitted.

"How is she generally described? You answer, Aris, I don't want to get your boyfriend in any more trouble than he needs to be."

Aris sighed but answered honestly. "They say she's the most beautiful girl in town, even before you consider her skin tone."

"And it's only going to get better, right? She's got a Noble class that's gotta have Charisma improvements."

"I've got free points! Two of them! I can get ahead of her with a few more levels—"

"That'd be dumb, and you know it," Kelsey chided. "You need those other stats if you're going to rescue your sister.

"But . . ."

"You don't need more Charisma," Anton said. "You were nice to me when I had just one . . . and I love you already."

Normally Anton would have stumbled over a line like that, but once again, the right words just seemed to find their way out. *Is this what ten Charisma does?* Anton wondered.

Aris ducked her head and looked away from him. She was probably blushing furiously. Kelsey wasn't finished, though.

"The same goes for you, Anton. Unless . . ."

"Unless what?" Anton asked, feeling the heat in his cheeks. Kelsey wasn't the first person to tell him that putting points in Charisma was holding him back.

"Unless you start *using* those points. Use your charm for more than just turning on your girlfriend."

"I don't know what you mean by that, but I'm not going to abandon Aris, just to help you out with your . . . our . . . problems with Suliel."

"First of all, who said anything about abandoning Aris? Just add Suliel to your harem."

"My . . . what?" This time it was Anton's turn to look away to hide his blush. His skin wasn't as dark as Aris's and he was sure it was clearly visible. Kelsey pressed on, regardless of his feelings.

"The other night you had two girls in bed with you . . . what do you think of three? What do you think about having another girl that looks at you the way Aris does?"

"I . . . Aris . . ." Anton stammered. Apparently, his Charisma didn't help him against Kelsey.

"*Second* of all, it doesn't have to be that serious," Kelsey said.

"What?" Anton said, confused at the sudden change of direction.

"She probably knows you're engaged; she'll probably be fine with just friendship, at least to start," Kelsey explained.

"If that's the case, then why did you say all the . . . other stuff?" Anton exclaimed.

"Because . . . a harem is your best option, and the more you think about it, the sooner you'll come to accept that. You *and* Aris."

"I just don't think it could ever happen. There's no way that Aris *or* Suliel would ever accept a situation like that."

"Oh, you'd be surprised. Now let's go over some things for the next time we meet with the Baroness, and then we can get down to the dungeon for some target practice."

CHAPTER TWENTY-EIGHT

Bad to the Bone

Despite Kelsey's strategy session, it wasn't the case that they could set up a meeting with Suliel by themselves. So the next order of business was a delve.

"We won't have much time before that expedition starts," Kelsey explained, "so if we want to get you two some experience, we should do it this afternoon."

"Does that mean . . ." Anton asked, not really wanting the answer that he knew was coming.

"Yes! The new entrance is ready," Kelsey confirmed enthusiastically. "I was working on it all night."

"A new entrance?" Aris asked, confused. "Why do you need another one?"

"Because those doofus troopers are *still* camped outside my entrance," Kelsey grumbled. "I ought to break, just to teach them a lesson."

"Is it well hidden?" Aris wondered. "I hear that adventurers have ways of detecting dungeons."

"Yeah, some of them can follow the mana," Kelsey said. "A second entrance should be masked by the mana coming from my main . . . but if they get close enough to it, they'll know what it is. As to how well hidden it is . . . well, judge for yourself."

"We should just move in here," Kelsey said, unlocking the door with her stolen key. "People are going to start thinking we own the place, the number of times we've been through. Is there some sort of registry about who owns what?"

"Of course there is," Anton said. "It's . . . handled by the mayor, I think."

"The entrance is in the middle of town? Isn't that dangerous?" Aris hissed softly. Unnecessarily, since they were now in the house and were unlikely to be overheard, but her nervousness was showing.

"A little, but I should have enough traps and monsters in to make it fairly safe," Kelsey said. "Oh, wait, you meant dangerous to the *town*."

"Now you're starting to see what I have to deal with," Anton complained. "I guess the answer is—it depends on her."

Kelsey winked at Aris. "So totally safe, as long as you keep me supplied with those bacon-wrapped pastries. Now let's get down to business."

She started unlocking the trapdoor, while Aris elbowed Anton. "Was she serious about the pastries?" she asked.

Anton sighed. "I wish it was that easy to keep her from being a danger."

They descended into the tunnel and made their way to the actual entrance. The flat stone that had filled the carved archway before had been replaced with a pair of intricately carved stone doors. They opened outward, something Anton could tell because they were slightly ajar.

"I can't keep them closed, unfortunately," Kelsey said. "Most of the mana leakage will head down the tunnel and out to sea, but some of it will find its way to the safe house, and some of it will go up to the castle. Should be fun if people go looking."

"The tunnel goes up to the castle?" Aris exclaimed, scandalized. Anton had a more thoughtful look.

"Can't Magister Tikin sense mana?" he asked.

"Maybe I'll get lucky and he'll come down to investigate on his own," Kelsey said with a grim smile. "Anyway!"

She pulled the doors open, revealing the crypt inside. Anton stepped forward cautiously as she waved them through. The room was lined with six intricately carved sarcophagi, and Anton could detect just the slightest smell of rotting meat.

"Zombies again?" he asked.

"This room is technically part of the first floor, so yeah, zombies," Kelsey said. Aris joined them in the room, looking warily at the coffins. "I think we're going to skip the easy levels, though, so these guys can stay down for now."

"Why have them at all, then?"

"Well, I don't want people having a shortcut, so there has to be something to stop them," Kelsey said. "And monsters help with mana absorption . . . it gets technical."

"So it will be zombies, then ghouls, and then ghasts, just like the main route?"

"Yeah, but instead of a maze of tunnels, there will just be these rooms, and you can fight them all at once."

Anton shrugged and made for the next door. Before he got there, he froze.

"And the traps?"

Kelsey smiled. "Of course there are traps." She went over to the wall and pulled on a piece of stone that was almost indistinguishable from the rest of the intricate carving. There was a clunk from the door. "All safe now!" she announced.

Anton frowned at her, and then cautiously moved up to and opened the door, carefully examining everything before he touched or stepped on it. When he got the door open, he paused at the threshold, looking back at Kelsey who held the torch.

"Let's get a move on," she said. Taking the lead, she led them past two more rooms of sarcophagi, disarming the traps as she went.

The last room she led them into had no sarcophagi. Instead, six armed and armored skeletons stood against the walls. Two in front of the door, and one in each corner. Anton warily stepped into the middle of the room, trying to keep an eye on each one.

"Now these look a lot more fun to fight!" Kelsey said, shining her light on each of the skeletons in turn. "Ready?"

"Wait, now?" Aris exclaimed, clumsily drawing her machete. "You haven't even given me my guns yet!"

Anton also drew his sword, slowly and carefully, while keeping an eye out in all directions, identifying his enemies.

Class: Skeleton Warrior
Level: 6

Higher than Aris, he noted. "Can I get my own torch?" he asked. The skeleton outpost on floor four was actually kept lit by torches maintained by the skeleton guards themselves, but Kelsey clearly wasn't giving any intruders that came this way an easy break.

"Sure," Kelsey said. She summoned an identical light and passed it to him.

"Thanks. Can you can keep Aris lit up?" he asked. Whatever skeletons used for eyes, they didn't require light, so fighting them in the dark was a significant disadvantage.

"Sure thing, boss. Let's start you on one each, eh?" As she spoke, two of the skeletons, from opposite corners, stepped forward.

Leaping Attack.

Before either of the warriors could come near Aris, he shot forward and landed a hit on the nearest one. His Tier Two blade—his father's Tier Two blade—glowed with magic as its enchantment empowered his strike even further.

With one stroke, he cleaved his way through the skeleton's shoulder, ribs, and spine. Not waiting for it to fall, he immediately moved on to the next target.

Leaping Attack.

He leapt again, not for the other moving skeleton, who was already preparing for his charge, but for one of the ones that hadn't moved yet. It was active, but it seemed that it was still under orders to stay where it was. It started to bring its blade up, but it was too slow to stop his vertical cut from coming down on its head.

"Cheater!" Kelsey called out, and the other skeletons all started to move towards him. There were four left, but one was still heading towards Aris, who was readying herself for its attack. That left three for him—the two closest that had been standing in front of the door, and the last one, on the other side of Kelsey and Aris, in the opposite corner.

Leaping Attack.

All of the skeletons were ready for him now, but he didn't go for any of them. *Leaping Attack* required that you make an attack, but it didn't say *what* you needed to strike. Anton's sword rang against the stone wall as he struck it a glancing blow, just as he intended. He'd jumped back to the entrance, avoiding Kelsey and Aris and confusing his intended target.

It had braced for a charge and was now off balance as he came in from the side. This time, he didn't have the supernatural skill that came with the trait. Nor did he have the extra momentum that the leap added to the blow. But he wasn't unskilled with the blade, and this was a Tier Two weapon, easily able to damage a monster of this level.

Their swords clashed three times, each time a blow from him matched by a block from the monster. Each time the block was weaker, more hastily reached for. His fourth strike sheared through the upper arm bones of the skeleton, and his final blow was unopposed.

He took a moment to take stock. Aris had engaged her target and was exchanging attacks for parries with it. The other two . . . he smiled at the sight. Kelsey had evidently ordered all the remaining skeletons to attack him, so the final pair had split up to avoid Aris in the center of the room and were making their way around to him.

The timing was about right, so . . .

Leaping Attack.

The downside of *Leaping Attack* was that it flung you directly at your target. If someone was expecting it—and these skeletons certainly were—then the target just needed to brace, take a step forward, and skewer you with your own momentum.

That was how it went if you just relied on your trait. If you were trained by the Nos family, you learned how to work around your weaknesses. Without hesitating for a moment, Anton attacked, not the skeleton, but its *foot*.

Diving under the blade that would surely have disemboweled him, Anton struck at the foot, easily cutting it in half. Unfortunately, that wasn't anywhere near as devastating a blow on a skeleton as it would have been on a human. Skeletons didn't feel pain, and while its footing was less secure now, it wasn't going to fall over that easily.

Leaping Attack also helped you land properly after your leap, so Anton tumbled with far more than his normal skill, rolling behind his target and springing to his feet. His opponent barely had time to swing around before his next blow was falling.

"Hey! You're not supposed to use me as terrain!" Kelsey called out. She took a few steps back, out of the way of the other skeleton that was chasing Anton. Anton had indeed been using her to block its approach, but she'd already given him all the time he needed. The monster he was fighting was off balance and injured. A high blow, a leg sweep on its good leg, and it was toppling, unable to block his final blow.

He backed away from the final remaining skeleton as he checked on Aris. She seemed fine. Kelsey, despite her protests at his behavior, was keeping her well-lit. She didn't seem to be damaging the monster, but she was holding her own at least. He could take his time with his own battle.

Out of tricks, he still out-leveled and out-skilled this monster. Their blades clashed—this was a fairer fight than the other engagements, but the outcome was never in doubt. After only a few blows, he was able to knock the other's sword out of line, exposing its vulnerable neck. His blade flared with magic again as he relieved the skeleton of its head.

"That was nowhere near as challenging for you as it used to be," Kelsey accused him. She kept an eye on Aris's fight, as did he. Now that he could look more closely, he saw that she was winning this fight. She was mostly blocking the skeleton's blows, and those that she didn't were wasted on her armor. Her own strikes were slightly more effective.

"Why did you give her a Tier One weapon?" Anton asked.

"I'm not made of magic," Kelsey replied. "She's Tier Two now; she doesn't need the help."

Indeed, even as they watched, Aris landed the final blow. She didn't shear through any bones, but the accumulation of light damage was finally enough to overcome her opponent. The lights in its eye sockets went out, and it clattered to the ground in pieces.

Aris looked around wildly, to see only Anton and Kelsey remaining.

"Where are the others?" she asked.

"Anton cheated," Kelsey said sourly. "I guess we're going to the next level."

"I just realized," Anton said, "there are no bosses at this entrance."

"Only one boss per level, those are the rules," Kelsey explained. "But enough of that."

She dragged the door open. There was only darkness beyond.

"We're back on the main line of the dungeon," she said. "Welcome to the Necropolis."

CHAPTER TWENTY-NINE

Ghost Town

When Anton shone his light into the archway, it revealed only some wooden panelling about three feet further in. He gave Kelsey an unimpressed glance.

"Well, come on, it's a secret entrance, after all," Kelsey said defensively. "If it opened out in plain view, everyone would see it."

"A secret entrance, or a super secret entrance?" Anton asked, recalling her words from when they had met.

"Just the first one," Kelsey replied. "But it's been a while since I made changes to the outer ring, so I think they've given up on searching it for secret doors."

Anton nodded. He knew what the outer ring was. "Before we go farther, aren't you forgetting something? Or did you mean for Aris to delve without her weapons?"

Kelsey looked blankly at him for a moment and then started. "Oh! Right. I meant to ask—Aris, did you feel like you were getting any experience from that skeleton you killed?"

Aris looked at them both and then frowned in thought. "I don't think so," she said slowly.

"I see . . ." Kelsey said. "I thought it might be the case, but I wanted to check. You only get experience when you kill something with a gun."

"Holding," Anton said.

"What?" Kelsey asked, looking back at him.

"A Swordsman gets experience when they are holding a sword. They don't have to actually *use* it, as long as they're holding it when doing something . . . exciting. Original Gunslinger is the same, only with guns, right?"

"I suppose," Kelsey said, her face falling. "I guess you guys have been studying this for a while, haven't you."

"The guild has lots of books about how different classes get experience and what traits they get," Anton explained. "You can borrow them and read them at night if you like."

He looked at her carefully. "Are you . . . disappointed by that?"

"No, it's fine." Kelsey shook herself. "There's no need to research stuff when it's already been done. That's—that's right, I was going to give you your guns, Aris!"

Kelsey held out her hands. What appeared was not a gun, but an entire table, loaded with gear.

"Step right up, folks!" Kelsey said brightly. "These are going to be your guns from now on, Aris."

She picked up and held one out to Aris. "These are what we call a revolver," she said. "I'd call them Smith and Wessons, but any resemblance is entirely coincidental."

She demonstrated how it worked to Aris, making her go through the same motions that Kelsey did for her own copy. Anton followed along, speaking up only when Kelsey was putting the bullets in.

"Only six bullets?" he asked. "So it's not as good as the ones you used?"

"Eh, there are a lot of very annoying people—somewhere—who would love to argue that with you," Kelsey said. "In this case, though, there are a few reasons why I went with revolvers. First of all, they're more reliable than automatics."

Kelsey held out her hand and made her gun appear. "If my gun jams—stops working—I can just disappear it and summon another one while a crew works on fixing it. Aris can't do that. Revolvers are a lot more forgiving and don't have complicated parts that need regular cleaning. They do need cleaning, and I'll be showing Aris how to do that after this delve."

She vanished the gun again and picked up a complicated leather harness. "The other main reason is thematic. The term gunslinger became known when people were using guns like these. I'm not sure if it makes a difference, but she should probably lean into the theme. Try these holsters on for size."

It was complicated, getting the harness on over Aris's armor. She ended up having to wear her scabbard on her back to keep it out of the way. Kelsey added a side pouch for ammunition, and further supplies went into Aris's backpack. When they were finally done, Anton and Kelsey walked around Aris, examining her closely.

"I think that's good?" Kelsey said. "It's not too heavy, is it?"

Aris shook her head, while Anton spoke up. "I don't think she can reload while wearing those gloves."

"Oooh, good point. Hand them over." Taking them, Kelsey made the gloves disappear. "I'll have the boys do something with these, but you should be okay without them for now."

"But . . ." Anton said.

"This isn't the level with the little spiders," Kelsey said, exasperated. "Or the touch poisons."

"I suppose. Try not to touch anything," he cautioned Aris.

"Finally. Can we go now?" Aris asked.

Anton was first into the entrance, reflexively checking it for traps. With none found, he detached the wooden panel. It looked exactly like the one in the Baron's cupboard, which he felt had to be deliberate. With the way clear, he shone the light around.

"It's just a room, from one of the houses in the outer ring," he called back.

"That's what I told you," Kelsey muttered waspishly. She had, but he hadn't been planning on trusting her. They moved forward, out of the house.

"It's so dark," Aris said. They stood in a quiet alleyway, looking out at what might have been a normal town street if it were not for all the skeletons.

"Skeletons can't see light," Anton explained. "They can hear, but they won't react to our voices unless they're hunting us."

"Why is that?" Aris asked, turning to Kelsey, who shrugged.

"In theory, these townsfolk should be chattering up a storm," she said. "In an early version, they did, but it wasn't . . . great. Just the constant clatter of teeth, it got annoying. *Then*, everything got so silent, it was too easy for them to hunt you all down."

"So our voices are drowned out by the silent chatter?" Anton mused. "In theory, we can sneak past them, but we are here to get experience. We want to make our way to the back of the ring . . . I think we're about halfway around?"

"Right," Kelsey confirmed. To Aris, she explained: "There are three streets that ring the city. You want to make your way to the center, and you can either follow the rings around—"

"That's the longest route," Anton interjected. "The other way is that you can find a route through the houses that separate the rings. It's a bit of a maze, though."

"Which way should we go?" Aris asked.

"Well, that depends," Anton mused. "Talking doesn't attract them, but those guns are loud. I bet firing one will bring in all the nearby ones?"

"Maaaaybeeee," Kelsey said. "I couldn't possibly comment."

"That's what I thought," Anton said. "So what we do is go . . . up. Let me give you a boost."

He easily boosted Aris high enough for her to scramble onto the roof of the one-story building. The alley was narrow enough that he could chain two *Leaping Attacks* to join her, his sword striking a glancing blow on the flat stone.

For whatever reason, the buildings in this city had flat roofs, edged with a low wall just high enough to stop you from stepping off accidentally.

"More cheating?" Kelsey protested. She easily leapt up to the roof in one bound.

"Why is there a roof?" Aris asked. "Aren't we underground?"

"It's a huge cavern," Anton told her. "Sometimes, teams come in and launch a light star potion up to the roof. Then you can see the whole thing. Each ring has taller buildings, until you get to the citadel, which reaches to the roof. It's pretty impressive—I'm surprised Kelsey hasn't lit it up to show it off."

"*I* can see it just fine," Kelsey groused, but she seemed pleased at the compliment. "Don't see why I should spend a lot of mana just to give you cheaters an advantage."

Choosing not to respond, Anton shone his light down at the street. A number of skeletons, dressed in a variety of costumes, were staring up at him. Instead of charging him, though, they were fixed in place.

"They've seen us, but . . . they can't get up here?" he speculated. "Try shooting one."

Aris looked at him doubtfully, but carefully aimed at one of the closer ones. When she pulled the trigger, there was a flash and a loud crack. Anton winced so hard at the sound that he almost didn't notice the skeleton fall.

"That's so loud!" Aris exclaimed. "Is that going to bring the entire town here?"

"It'd be even louder if you were in a building," Kelsey pointed out. "Out here is something like open air . . . and no, not the whole town. The shot echoed so much that most of them can't tell where it came from."

She pointed her torch down the street. At the very edge of the light, more skeletons were shuffling forward. Instead of being busy at some imagined task, they cast their gaze back and forth as they slowly moved forward. Hunting.

"Better get to shooting more of them," Anton told Aris. She nodded and took careful aim again. This time she missed the head, the bullet striking a rib bone. The skeleton seemed unhurt and started moving towards them.

"Sorry," Aris said.

"Keep shooting," Anton told her.

"Won't this mean I'm getting all the experience?" Aris asked, but she kept firing anyway. Skeletons were drawing closer, but thus far, they seemed unable to climb the walls. It made them easier targets for Aris.

"Nah, he's raking it in, I'll bet," Kelsey said sourly. "Coming up with sneaky plans that protect you."

"I can't have been the only one to have done this," Anton noted. "There's not many that want to get a bow past all those winding tunnels, but there are some."

"Most of them just use their meat shields to keep the bones at bay," Kelsey explained. "And when they *do* get on the roof, it's just temporary. They don't have a way to get half of an *entire ring* of skeletons to show up for target practice, so they shoot a few, and then move on."

As she spoke, Aris was carefully and methodically taking out skeletons. She didn't hit every time, but she had already reloaded once, leaving her second gun ready for an emergency.

"This is just embarrassing," Kelsey muttered. "*Climb*, you bastards!"

Anton swore as the milling crowd below began to do just that. They weren't good at it, and the stone walls of the house they were on offered few handholds. But it wasn't long before they worked out that they could climb each *other*.

"*That's* more like it!" Kelsey crowed.

"Anton!" Aris called out, worried that the horde was coming closer.

"Keep firing, I've got this!" he called back and started culling the undead that got too close. His sword slashed out, severing the neck of the first. Knowing he would have to make it last, he tried to minimize the duration of his sword's enchantment, pulsing it as his father would have. He only needed the effect for the brief time that it was slicing through his enemy.

"Behind you!" Kelsey called. He whipped around to see a skeleton clambering up over the back wall.

Leaping Attack. His sword smashed into the skeleton's chest and it fell back below, probably dead, but definitely gone. All the while he heard the steady *crack, crack, crack* of Aris's firing.

"I made a level!" she called.

"Don't take it now!" he yelled. He was pretty sure she wouldn't have wanted to distract herself in the middle of combat, but the temptation might have been irresistible. He could feel his own level getting closer, but he still had a way to go. These skeletons were still below him in level, so he wasn't gaining as much as Aris.

He lost himself in the rush, using *Leaping Attack* to go from one edge of the roof to another, and slashing at the head or grasping hands of another skeleton. Again and again he smashed his sword against them, sending them to the bottom in a clatter of bones.

And then . . . there weren't any more. He looked around wildly for the next attacker, but none showed themselves. He looked over at Aris, grimly reloading. She looked over the wall and raised her gun . . . but didn't fire.

"They're all gone," she said. "Just bones."

Anton stared at her until he was distracted by a sound. He jerked his gaze to the side, to find Kelsey clapping her hands.

"See! That was much more exciting than a boring old turkey shoot!"

CHAPTER THIRTY

Beat It

ARIS

Aris looked on as Anton and Kelsey squabbled. Despite her words, Kelsey didn't seem upset at their so-called cheating, and she could tell Anton was giddy with relief that she had made it through the fight unharmed. She would have joined in, but she had other things to consider. She accepted her level.

You have reached Level 2.
Applying Benefits for Level 2:
Toughness + 1
Agility + 1
Dexterity + 1
Perception + 1
Willpower + 1

Please select a new trait:
Stone Skin | Sonic Resistance | Ferocious Clean | Cold Resistance | Pain
    Resistance

Please allocate 2 free Ability points.

Where should my points go? she wondered, and called up her status.

Aris Lucina, Gunslinger (Level 2)
Overall Level: 7

Paths: Scullion/(broken), Gunslinger
Strength: 7
Toughness: 5
Agility: 7
Dexterity: 5
Perception: 15
Willpower: 13
Charisma: 6
Traits:
Eye for Freshness
Heat Resistance

Since her fight with the zombies, she had felt that her Strength was lacking, but her guns didn't really take that much Strength to use. It seemed like Dexterity would be more useful for using guns. Toughness was good, but so was Agility. Her Perception and Will were so high she thought that they didn't need any help—they would progress naturally with her class anyway. And of course, there was Charisma. It was vanity, but a look at her boyfriend reminded her that vanity got results.

"Um, a little help here? I'm trying to decide my level bonuses," she called over.

"What traits did you get?" Anton asked immediately.

"Stone Skin, Cold Resistance, Pain Resistance and . . . *Sonic Resistance?"*

She left off *Ferocious Clean*. That was left over from her Scullion class, and she was fairly sure it wasn't going to come in handy with her present occupation.

"Sonic refers to sound," Kelsey said. "So you'd be resistant to noises loud enough to cause damage."

"That's . . . pretty uncommon," Anton said skeptically. "*Stone Skin* is a good all-round defense."

"True, but she makes loud noises *all the time*," Kelsey pointed out. "Maybe her Toughness is high enough to keep her from going deaf, but immunity to that might not be bad. Plus, you squishy humans don't tend to have good defenses against the few things that *can* do sonic damage."

"I liked the idea of *Pain Resistance?*" Aris tried.

"Pain can be incapacitating," Anton replied. "But with your Willpower, you should be able to push through it."

"You certainly managed okay the first time," Kelsey put in.

Aris scowled. "It wasn't fun, though." She did think they might have a point, though. Better to not take damage than ignore it after the fact. "What about my free points?"

"Mmm, your weak points are Toughness and Dex, right? Best to put one in each."

"What about Charisma?" she asked. He smiled.

"I already told you that you're beautiful, right?"

She felt her cheeks heat up. "I suppose," she admitted. *But I don't want to be left behind*, she replied in her thoughts. She returned her attention to her status.

Just one point in Charisma can't hurt, she decided. The other point she put into Dexterity. She hadn't been as swift at reloading as she would have liked.

That just left her trait to choose, and she was somewhat torn. *Stone Skin* was a commonly desired defensive trait, she knew that. But they said that good things came from selecting the rarer traits. And her ears *did* hurt.

"I think I'm going to get Sonic Resistance," she said.

Anton shrugged. "It's your decision," he told her. "You're already wearing armor, after all."

Aris nodded and selected the option. She took one final look at her status.

Aris Lucina, Gunslinger (Level 2)
Overall Level: 7
Paths: Scullion/(broken), Gunslinger
Strength: 7
Toughness: 5
Agility: 7
Dexterity: 6
Perception: 15
Willpower: 13
Charisma: 7
Traits:
Eye for Freshness
Heat Resistance
Sonic Resistance

"All done," she said. "Did you get a level?"

"No," Anton replied. "I made progress, but these were all lower-level than me."

"That'll change as we progress," Kelsey promised. "Are we ready to move on then? How's your ammo supply?"

"Oh!" Reminded of the need, Aris broke open both her guns and started filling them up, along with the two fast-loaders that Kelsey had supplied. Aris's left-hand gun had only been fired a total of four times, Aris having saved it for the times when she hadn't had time to reload.

"You should swap them around," Kelsey told her. "Wouldn't do for one to get more worn than the other."

Aris followed her instructions and then checked her supplies. "I still have about two-thirds of the bullets you got me."

"You took out fifteen skeletons with thirty-some bullets then," Kelsey calculated. "Not bad, but we need to work on your aim."

"Level four will generally have some kind of attacking trait," Anton said.

"Let's get to it then, the skeletons aren't going to wait all night!" Kelsey said.

They got down off the roof. Anton hung off the edge, dropping down the remaining distance. He then caught Aris when she jumped, which she was both pleased and embarrassed by. Kelsey muttered something about putting in stairs next time, before stepping off the edge and falling without any visible discomfort.

Kelsey told them that they had "thinned out" the skeletons of the first ring, so Anton was willing to try a different tactic for the rest of the ring. Proceeding cautiously along the street, they engaged individual skeletons at the limit of torch range. Anton let Aris do the bulk of the work, only stepping in when the skeletons got too close.

At Kelsey's request, they didn't stop to pick up any bones.

"I've got that expedition coming down, probably tomorrow, and respawning will go quicker if I've got the raw materials to work with," she told them. She didn't have any objections to them taking the silver coins that appeared, nor the five mana cores that they found.

"What *are* these, anyway, and why do monsters have them?" Anton asked.

"Waste magic," Kelsey replied. "If there's ever more magic than I can use, it goes into the monsters and makes those. I can't do anything with them."

"They don't make the monsters stronger?" Aris asked.

"Did you notice those guys being noticeably stronger?" Kelsey asked. "No. Monsters can get levels and tier up like humans, but the stones don't have anything to do with that."

They proceeded around the ring, slowly killing skeletons. Once, Aris ran out of bullets and Anton had her duck into an alleyway to reload while he held off a group. That was the only really threatening moment, though. Aris felt that while this strategy had taken much longer, she had killed more in total.

"Twenty-three," Kelsey confirmed. "And I've been counting the shots this time—thirty-eight. So you're getting a little better."

Aris shrugged. She could *feel* that she was a better shot now. She was more comfortable with the gun, and her reloading was smoother too now. The new strategy meant that she had more time to aim, but she was also shooting from farther away, so it evened out.

She was pleased to note that her ears no longer hurt, even a little bit. "If I've killed more, why haven't I gotten another level?" she asked.

"You're not getting as much of a bonus from the difference in levels," Anton explained. "And you need more experience for level three than you do for level two. You must be getting close, though?"

"I think so," Aris agreed. "What's next, then?"

"Mini-boss!" Kelsey exclaimed. Anton nodded. He had mentioned that they could bypass the Skeleton Sergeant by finding the right way through the maze of alleys, but they were here for monster-fighting experience. They had actually passed the guardhouse and pointed it out to Aris, but they'd wanted to clear out every skeleton on this street first.

"Let me fight him," he told Aris. "He's not a good match for you, and he's the only thing on this ring I can get good experience from."

"Sure," Aris said. "You've fought him before, right?" she asked with a worried tone.

They returned to the guardhouse, a plain stone building much like all the rest. The only difference was that it was two stories, and instead of an ordinary door, it had a tall double gate that stood half open.

Anton looked at the darkness beyond and then looked at his torch.

"Normally, I'd throw the torch in first," he said. "This looks more fragile, though?"

"Yeah, don't *throw* it, you big lug," Kelsey said. "We can stand by the door and light it up."

"Sure," Anton agreed and passed the light over to Aris. With both hands full, she couldn't reload easily, but there should only be one monster left on this ring.

Illuminating the inside revealed nothing, only an empty room, perhaps twenty feet square. Anton took a deep breath, drew his sword, and then leapt inside.

The strike came while he was still in the air. Aris didn't know what Anton had been aiming for, but as the sergeant dashed out of hiding, Anton *twisted*, somehow moving out of the way of the blow.

"I hate *Uncanny Evasion*," Kelsey remarked, without heat. "Are you going to let him show his arse to you like that?" she called out. "Show some hustle, Sarge!"

"Are you . . . cheering for the monster?" Aris said, outraged.

Kelsey smirked. "Whose side do you think I'm on, kid? I may have taken it easy on you for your first run, but Anton doesn't need any training wheels."

Indeed, Anton seemed to be doing well. Having only a sword against the sergeant's sword and shield was a disadvantage but Anton's strength and speed made up for it. Aris gasped as one of the skeleton's blows landed, but it was only a glancing hit and seemed to be absorbed by Anton's armor.

Despite landing a few blows of his own, Anton didn't seem able to significantly damage his opponent. The sergeant had armor of his own, and while a few bones crumbled under Anton's strikes, that didn't seem to slow the skeleton down at all.

Aris didn't see the end coming, but she realized after the fact what had happened. Anton managed to jolt the monster off balance when he had lined himself up just *so*. He used that jumping attack of his, leaping to the wall and then right back again, slamming his sword into the sergeant's unprotected back.

"Foul!" Kelsey called, but the fight was over. The sergeant fell into pieces, the light fading from his eye sockets. Ten silver coins appeared from nowhere and fell to the ground.

Anton glared at Kelsey. "Could you *not* call out distracting things while I'm fighting?"

"Come on." Kelsey grinned unrepentantly. "You got angry. You fought a lot better than the other times you fought that guy."

Anton rolled his eyes. "That might have something to do with the levels, don't you think?"

"Maybe. But I think it was passion!" Kelsey declared.

Anton just shook his head. He picked up the sergeant's shield and slipped it onto his arm.

"I didn't think you used a shield?" Aris asked.

"It's too much trouble bringing one through the upper tunnels," Anton replied. "There are archers on the next ring, though, so I might as well use it."

"I could have carried one for you!" Kelsey said brightly. Anton gave her an unimpressed look.

"I'll keep that in mind for next time," he said. "Let's keep moving. The skeletons will be a little tougher in this ring, and I don't think the rooftop plan will work. The buildings are taller, and they have archers."

"So what do we do?" Aris asked.

"This time, I think we want to keep to the alleys. The archers won't go into them, so it will thin out the numbers that we have to deal with at any one time."

Kelsey nodded. "Good thinking. The echoes from your shots will be even more confusing in the alleyways, so that will help keep them from finding you."

Anton nodded. "Right. Let's go."

CHAPTER THIRTY-ONE

Dancing in the Dark

A nton finished off the last skeleton of the latest group. He quickly glanced over to make sure Aris was free and then paused to accept his new level.

You have reached Level 5.
Applying Benefits for Level 5:
Strength + 1
Toughness + 1
Agility + 1
Dexterity + 1
Perception + 1
Please allocate 1 free Ability point.

Dexterity, Anton thought. That would bring all his characteristics to at least ten. His parents had often drilled into him the importance of having no weak areas.

"Did you get your level yet?" he asked Aris, coming over to her so they could speak quietly. They were in the maze of buildings of the second ring, so sight lines were short. There could be skeletons just around the corner, listening out.

Aris nodded, half distracted by choosing her upgrades as she reloaded. "I'm ready," she said when she finished.

"All right, let's go back out to the street to get some archers," Anton said.

Their strategy for this ring had been to lure the normal skeletons into the maze, where they could be fought without support from the archers. The archers were pretty good shots, and they had no compunctions about firing into a melee.

They didn't like getting into close combat, though, so they stayed on the main street where they could keep their sight lines long. By ducking into the maze, Anton ensured that the only threats were close-in melees.

For ranged weapons, Aris's pistols were surprisingly effective in close combat. They had to be careful about attacking—they'd worked out that taking turns worked best. Aris took five shots and then reloaded while he fought. Then he stepped back and let her fire again.

The downside of this strategy was that he was a lot closer to her pistols when she fired. They were *loud*. They'd tried the oil of silence but it hadn't made a material difference, even when applied to the bullets.

"Problem is, it isn't the gun making the sound, it's the explosion," Kelsey explained. "Maybe if you put the stuff inside the bullet, but . . . let me try it in a more controlled environment."

It took her a little while, time that was spent by Anton and Aris hacking and shooting at more skeletons, but eventually, Kelsey reported back. She didn't go anywhere, of course, but she spoke up during a lull in the fighting.

"No dice," she said. "It's still just as loud, and it does . . . this to the bullet at the moment of firing."

She held up a hand with a splash of vivid green in it.

"It turns it green?" Anton asked stupidly.

"Among other things," Kelsey said sourly. "Whatever this stuff is, it's not the same metal that it started out as. Never mix alchemy with chemistry, kids."

They persevered, anyway. Anton's Toughness was high enough that he wasn't injured by the repetitive noise, and Aris had no trouble at all now that she'd taken *Sonic Resistance*. If Kelsey was affected, she showed no sign of it.

Taking out the archers was just a matter of getting close enough to light them up with a torch. That meant getting into arrow range, but Anton could hide them both behind his new shield until they got close enough for Aris to pick them off.

The guardian for the second ring—or mini-boss as Kelsey put it—was also an archer, tucked behind his own set of ramparts. Getting to him was a pain. Not impossible, especially with *Leaping Attack*, but a pain nonetheless.

This time, Aris just shot him, while Anton blocked incoming arrows. Then they could take their time climbing up the rampart to get to the gate.

"This seems like a good place to take a break?" Anton said.

"It's safe," Kelsey confirmed. They sat on the stone, and she started handing out food and drink from her Inventory.

"We're getting so much experience," Aris commented. "Or at least I am?"

"I was getting a fair bit until I made a level," Anton confirmed. "The difference between fighting monsters at your level and monsters just one level below isn't small."

"The next ring is mostly level tens," Kelsey commented. "So you'll be back to earning soon."

"Is that normal, though?" Aris asked. "I've made two levels already—I know delving is the fastest way to get levels, but it's not *that* fast, is it?"

"You're fighting monsters at least two levels higher than you," Anton explained. "You couldn't normally do that without those guns, and even your armor is better than normal."

"And the *way* that you're delving is a little different," Kelsey said. "You're killing *everything*."

"Isn't that normal?" Aris asked.

"Normally, you're delving for the money," Anton told her. "So you want to get to your target floor as quickly and as easily as possible. Then, you only kill enough monsters to get as much loot as you can carry."

"You don't *want* experience?"

"Experience will come on its own. You want money more, so you can buy the right equipment, weapons, alchemy . . . we've only been taking the coins and the cores, leaving a lot of loot behind."

"The clothes fade away, but the tools, the weapons, the bones can all be sold," Kelsey said, whipping out a copy of the guild's price list. "You could have made twice as much money as you have, but you'd have been loaded down too heavy to walk."

"Going as a group of two probably has something to do with it," Anton said. "Or . . . are we a group of three?"

"Two," Kelsey told him. "And you're right. Some of the experience is split between party members, and delving as a large group is less dangerous, which means less experience."

"So, if I hadn't reached my level cap, I would have gotten a lot of experience for my first delve?" Aris asked.

"Well . . . those guys were mostly below your level. Only the Corpse Abominations were at level five or higher. And delving isn't a core activity for the Scullion class . . . But bonus points for doing it alone, sure."

Kelsey grinned wickedly at Aris. "As it was though, you got nothing. Though Mel was pretty happy at seeing your run."

"She likes watching people get injured?" Aris asked sourly.

"Little bit," Kelsey admitted. "But, no, it was more about how you were getting closer to the original holy purpose of dungeons."

"You . . . know the original reason the gods had for creating dungeons?" Anton asked, perking up. "I thought you were only fifty years old?"

"Still older than both of you put together," Kelsey snipped at them. "And, well, I know what Mel's told me. I don't know if she was around at the *start*, but she *is* properly immortal."

"Uncle Delir would give his other foot for that story," Anton said. "Is it a secret?"

"I don't think so?" Kelsey said, looking thoughtful. "I certainly don't care. I don't see how it's relevant to anything anyway."

She picked up the torch. She had set it to shine against a wall for more general illumination, but now she held it under her face, shining upwards. The shadows it cast made her pale face even more unsettling.

"This is an old story," she said. "We have to go way, way back, before any of the races learned how to work metal, or how to build out of stone. Back then, your ancestors were wearing skins from animals that they'd managed to kill with sharpened sticks."

She cast her gaze over both of them, making sure she had their attention.

"There weren't nations back then. No barons or kings. There was family, and there was the *tribe*. And even back then, there were traditions, traditions that have been long lost."

She got a thoughtful look again. "I'm not sure if you had classes in those days. Nowadays, you stop being a child when you get your first level at fifteen, but back then . . . I don't think that had been implemented yet. Instead, there was a ceremony for a child to perform, before they could become an adult.

"Each tribe had their own ceremony but generally, they travelled to a sacred place. A hole in the earth, a cave, or a hidden grove in the forest. The child would go down into that hole."

She snapped her torch off. There was still some light from the other torch, left pointing at a wall, but the illumination was greatly reduced. Kelsey's pale skin reflected the dim light, making her look like a ghost in the darkness.

"It might be a tunnel just wide enough to crawl through, or a maze of twisting passages, or an underground cavern of unfathomable size. But there was always something else. A monster that the child had to avoid, evade, or even slay. And when they defeated it, by whatever method, they came out of the cave an adult."

Kelsey snapped her light on again, still pointed at her face from below. Aris gave a muffled squeak.

"Now, here," Kelsey said with a grin, "is where the horror story starts, at least as Mel tells it. Time passed, and the mortals advanced. They invented crafts, created weapons, and they brought them to the sacred places. The first time a sword was used to kill the monster, the child looked down at it in the light from his torch and wondered what he'd been so afraid of. He never felt the fear that his predecessors had felt, and had to find another way to become a man.

"The gods intervened and made the challenge harder. Deeper caves, more monsters, traps, and hidden dangers. But the mortals adapted. They had lost their sense of the sacred and now saw dungeons as something that could be exploited—an endless source of resources.

"And then they learned that a dungeon core could give them magic."

Kelsey spun the torch and let the beam point to the floor in the middle of the group. There was a long silence as everyone considered what she had told them. Finally, she spoke again.

"And that's the story! Kind of sad, but it's all in the past now. Shall we get going again?"

"I feel bad . . . like my ancestors shouldn't have done that?" Aris said uncertainly.

"You can't fight progress," Kelsey told her. "If all that stuff hadn't happened, you'd be sitting in dirt, chewing on raw meat."

"So were dungeons sentient, even that far back?" Anton asked.

"I'm not sure," Kelsey admitted. "I think, back when they were just one monster that respawned, they could have just been a spell cast by a god. Then as they got more complex, they had to be managed by a core . . . and at some point, that core became complex enough to become sentient."

Anton opened his mouth to say more, but Kelsey cut him off with a gesture. "Enough reminiscing," she said. "I think you kids have got another level in you today."

The final ring was a mix of archer, guard, and "noble" skeletons. They were all armed, which made for a significant upgrade from the largely civilian skeletons of the outer rings.

"There are four guard posts that block the road," Anton explained. "Whichever way we go, we'll have to get past two of them. We can use force, or we can go around, via the maze again."

The buildings on this ring were all three stories high, and they were joined at different levels, forming a tightly packed, three-dimensional maze.

"Actually, twenty-three different mazes," Kelsey explained, proud of her obstacle. "And of course, only four of them have entrances on both sides of the guardhouse. All the others are just there to waste your time."

"I'm guessing you're not going to guide us through the mazes," Anton said. A sniff was his only reply. "So I think we want to avoid them this time. Especially since there are . . ."

"Thieving Skeletons," Kelsey said with some relish.

"Yeah, those," Anton said, wincing. "They hide out in the maze, and they're really good at ambushes. My Perception has improved since then, but I think I'd rather rely on your guns in the street."

"Won't we get swarmed again?" Aris asked.

"We'll have to stay mobile to make sure that doesn't happen," Anton said, "but I think we can manage. The skeletons here are tougher, but there are fewer of them. If you focus on the archers and the nobles and let me handle the ones with armor, we should be able to take them down quickly.

"All right," Aris said nervously. "I'm ready."

"Okay then!" Kelsey said. She had a hold of the door to the next ring. "On your marks! Get set! . . .

"Go!"

CHAPTER THIRTY-TWO

It Takes Two

They smashed through the final ring. While the skeletons matched his level now, Anton was stronger and tougher than any of the skeletons here. He could feel his experience increasing as they went down under his blade.

Aris did as well, or better. She focused on the archers while he engaged the nobles. The boom of her guns seemed almost continuous until he realized that his ears were just ringing from the previous shots. They had to hole up in a house so that he could recover his hearing. Aris, of course, was entirely unaffected.

"We're not stopping for the loot?" Aris asked when he could hear again. Anton looked at Kelsey. The loot was better on this ring. While it was still all Tier One gear, the swords were fancier, and there were silver rings on some of the noble skeleton fingers.

"I haven't been worried about money since this started," he admitted. "Dad wanted me to earn my gear, but between my inheritance and Kelsey, that's been pretty much taken care of."

"Reduced to being a sugar mommy, and I'm not even getting the benefits," Kelsey mused idly. "How far I've fallen."

Anton glanced at her, but by now he knew when she was talking only to amuse herself, so he continued on.

"The experience is what we need right now, so we want to press on," he said.

Aris nodded. "It's exciting, isn't it?" she asked, grinning. "This has been so much better than my first time."

Anton groaned, recognizing the symptoms. "You've gotten a taste for it," he said. He glared over at Kelsey. "You've given her dungeon fever," he accused.

Kelsey shrugged. "No different from most of those that come down here," she said. "Adrenaline, danger, gaining levels. Not my fault that those are addictive."

"Aren't you the same?" Aris asked. "Why would you keep coming down here before, if you didn't feel this alive?"

"Yeah, I feel it," Anton admitted. "I guess we match better now, hey?"

"Believe it!" Aris exclaimed, jumping up to him and giving him a passionate kiss. Before he could respond, she had released him and moved over to the door. "Ready for another run?"

"Hang on, I've been working on something," Kelsey said. She handed Anton two small objects that felt . . . odd. They squished under his fingers and then sprang back.

"Stick those in your ears," Kelsey advised. "They'll muffle the sound somewhat. With your toughness, I doubt you're going to suffer permanent hearing damage, but let's not take risks, okay?"

Anton looked at the earplugs suspiciously but did as she said. He hadn't enjoyed his ears ringing.

"I'll take the lead," he told Aris. His voice sounded strange, but he could hear himself perfectly well. "Ladies first is only for when there aren't monsters."

"After you then, my champion," Aris said. Her voice was muffled, but he could hear her. It might prove different once they were in combat.

Champion, Anton thought, as he unbarred the door and looked outside. *I like the sound of that.*

Skeleton Lord (Level 13)

The second most powerful skeleton in the dungeon, Anton thought. *Only the Skeleton King is mightier.*

Of course, skeletons were by no means the most powerful monsters down here. But this was a milestone nonetheless.

"Remember," he whispered to Aris, "only aim for the head. If you knock any bones off, he can just reattach them."

Aris just nodded. Talking as quietly as they had to, he probably wouldn't be able to hear her anyway. He stepped forward and started the fight.

Instead of an arena, the lord held court. The floor was stone, but elaborately decorated in marquetry of differently colored marble. Around the room were twelve different doors where members of his court could enter to aid their lord. Aris's job was to keep an eye on them, while he fought the lord.

Anton had never actually fought the lord before. He'd been in a party that had, but it had been their leader who fought the lord while Anton helped with the court. The thought of fighting him with just two people was both terrifying and exhilarating.

He looked as if he was set to expect a leap, so Anton moved forward behind his shield as quickly as he could while maintaining his guard. At the last moment, he surged forward, aiming his blade at the lord's head.

The lord's sword came up to block. Unlike the rapiers that the skeleton nobles carried, this was a heavy blade, ornamented with gold on the hilt, and an inlay on the blade. The skeleton grinned as it met Anton's strike and pushed him back.

For the first time since reaching level ten, Anton was fighting an opponent stronger than him.

At that moment, the roar of Aris's gun echoed about the chamber as she shot at the skeleton courtier entering. Then again, as the first shot had missed.

The Skeleton Lord kept his grin, but he was distracted by the suddenness of the loss of his ally and glanced over. That was enough for Anton.

Leaping Attack.

The lord was fast, but not as fast as Anton. He couldn't get his sword up in time—but he did manage to block with his free arm. Anton cursed to himself but pulsed the enchantment anyway. Magic flowed through his sword and cut cleanly through the bones. It was a hit, but not a critical one. The hand fell to the ground. Anton leapt back, trying to keep an eye on both the lord and his arm.

Unlike skeletons of a lower level, the lord's bones remained animated when separated. Anton scowled as the hand flipped itself over and came crawling towards him. It would be mainly a distraction, but—

No, Anton realized. *It's stronger than me, so if it manages to get a good grip on my body, it can squeeze strongly enough to hurt, maybe even break my bones.*

"Aris!" he called, "Watch out for a hand on the ground!" It would be quite difficult for her to take out the hand—he wasn't sure that hitting any particular bone with a bullet would cause it to fail.

Her gun roared again, this time only once. Another courtier down. Anton had to take down the lord before the courtiers started to overwhelm them. *Leaping Attack* took him to the side, allowing him to avoid the hand, and he raced in to attack once more. This time, he let the lord start his blow and used *Uncanny Evasion* to get out of the way. Twisting under the lord's blade, he brought his own up. Glowing with magical power, it cut through the skeleton's costume and smashed into its ribs, shattering a number of them. He didn't reach its spine, though.

Anton cursed and backed away. Superficial damage only. He looked quickly for the hand—still a little distance away but still crawling towards him. He reversed course and charged in again, letting *Uncanny Evasion* take care of the skeleton's attack. He was still new to the trait and wasn't quite used to letting it move him, but it still worked for him. He swayed to the side to avoid the downward strike, and *this* time he was in a good position. He remembered to activate the enchantment in time, and his glowing blade traced a perfect curve that ended in the middle of the Skeleton Lord's skull.

In death—real death—the Skeleton Lord's only sound was a clatter of bones as he fell to the ground.

"Is that it?" Aris asked. Anton tore his gaze away from his opponent and looked around. There were *four* piles of bones covered in robes—apparently, he'd missed a few of Aris's shots. Kelsey came into the room, clapping slowly.

"Not bad," she said. "Though it's a lot easier when you can take potshots as they come out."

Anton wasn't really paying attention to her, though.

You have reached Level 6.
Applying Benefits for Level 6:
Strength + 1
Toughness + 1
Agility + 1
Dexterity + 1
Perception + 1

Please allocate 1 free Ability point.

Strength, Anton thought. He'd be stronger than the Skeleton Lord. Not, he thought, stronger than the Skeleton King.

Please select a new trait:
  Disarm Trap | Danger Sense | Sense Mana | Ferocious Attack | Detect Trap

It would be nice to have two attack traits, but Anton's parents had told him many times that an adventurer had to be more than a swordsman.

"Going where others cannot," his father had said. "Doing what others cannot."

Seeing what others cannot, Anton finished for himself and selected *Sense Mana.*

"Oh, I got another level!" Aris said. Anton ignored her for a moment, focusing on his new perception. His sword and pants had an aura about them now. Not glowing so much as having another color—one Anton had never seen before—laid over them. Kelsey looked surprisingly normal. Hadn't she said that she was made of mana? Around the room, the doors all also had another, different color.

They open and close on their own, Anton realized. *That must take mana.*

The other mana-colored thing was the lord's chair. As he glanced at it, it slid to the side, allowing a chest to rise up from the floor.

"Ta-da!" Kelsey said. "Your floor reward."

Anton frowned at her for a second and then remembered to remove his earplugs. "That's better," he said. "I can still hear you, but everything sounds weird."

"Does it help with the gunshots, though?" Aris asked, coming up to him.

He smiled at her. "Yeah. You picked Dex and Charisma again?"

"How'd you know?"

"Not much has changed since the last floor," he pointed out. "So not much reason for you to make a different decision. What traits did you get?"

"An attack one!" she replied excitedly. "*Sure Shot*."

"She's gonna be a monster," Kelsey said, joining them. "You want this as a souvenir or something?" She held up the lord's sword with incongruous ease. It wasn't as *long* as a great sword, but it was thicker and heavier than it needed to be, made for a monster that was stronger than the human norm.

"There's not much of it, but that *is* real gold," Kelsey said. 'And it's not that bad of a weapon."

Anton took it and gave it a swing, just to see. "There are a few people in the guild who have gotten theirs enchanted," he said. Despite the extra weight, it probably only did as much damage as his Tier Two longsword, *before* the enchantment was taken into account. "What does the writing say?"

"Oh, that? It's written in a language from far, far away, and it says: 'My wielder is a complete ass.'"

Anton rolled his eyes. "Yeah, I'll pass on that, thanks."

Aris giggled. "Does the Skeleton King have writing on his blade as well?"

"Yes," Kelsey said loftily. "But you'll need to beat him before I tell you what it says. Some things have to be earned. Speaking of which . . ."

She gestured at the chest. "Your reward."

Anton glowered suspiciously at the chest. "Stand back," he told Aris and gave the heavy sword in his hand a few practice swings. Approaching the chest from the side, he swung the sword down at full extension, slamming it into the locked clasp at the front of the chest.

The lock, the clasp, and part of the chest shattered and splintered under his blow, but Anton was already leaping backward. A grey mist billowed out of the broken chest, forming a small cloud about five feet across which quickly started to disperse.

"A trap? How did you know?" Aris asked.

"Floor reward chests are *always* trapped," Anton said.

"They weren't on my first delve."

"She disabled all the traps on those levels, remember?"

Kelsey clapped again, this time a little more enthusiastically. "I knew you'd remember. Don't worry, this wasn't going to be anything permanent—just agonizing."

"Why would you *do* that?" Aris asked. "Aren't you helping us?"

"This *is* helping you," Kelsey said. "I wouldn't be doing you any favors if I let Anton get soft, and this helps him train *you* to be more careful."

"Should have taken *Disarm Trap*," Anton muttered. He carefully levered the chest open with the end of the lord's sword. It was looking a little worse for wear. The trap must have been an acid cloud.

"You took *Sense Mana*, though, didn't you?" Kelsey said. "Adventurers always take the haxor trait."

Anton frowned at the unfamiliar word but decided to ignore it. The chest contained two minor healing potions, some coins, and a helmet. A magical helmet if his new sense was right.

"What's this?" he asked.

"A piece of Tier Two equipment is a normal reward for this floor," Kelsey said.

"Yes, but normally you recycle stuff from previous adventurers," Anton said, "This is new."

"You know, I clean things properly before I give them back! Some of them are as good *as* new. And I can't do that *all* the time. Sometimes I have to make something."

Anton took the helmet out of the chest. It was mostly leather but reinforced by a steel cap and a nose guard. It looked as though it would fit him exactly.

"What does it do?" he asked.

"Protection against sonic attacks," Kelsey said. "It should also *enhance* your hearing, when that wouldn't be causing damage."

Anton looked at her again, before slowly putting the helmet on. It fit perfectly.

"Thank you, Kelsey," he said. She looked embarrassed.

"Well," she said, "I *am* supposed to be helping you, after all."

CHAPTER THIRTY-THREE

Keeping the Dream Alive

L et's call it a day," Kelsey said. Aris looked at her in astonishment.

"What? But we've only just whoooaaa . . ." She suddenly slumped, almost falling, as the energy that had been animating her suddenly left. "What?"

"We've been running on excitement and level-ups," Anton said, coming to her side to support her.

"Adrenaline," Kelsey corrected him. "It feels good until you stop, and then you crash."

"If you say so," Anton said, frowning. "How long have we been at it?"

"Well, not a full day, but plenty long considering the work," Kelsey said. "You went right through lunch—about six hours all up."

"We missed lunch?" Aris exclaimed with dismay. "No wonder I feel so hungry!"

"Food in our bellies would have slowed us down when we were fighting like this," Anton explained. "As it was . . . that was pretty slow for clearing out the fifth level."

Kelsey shrugged. "It's not like I keep a speed run ranking table. There were only two of you, and you were actually trying to clear, not just pass through."

"Um, I think you forgot the important bit, where we missed lunch?" Aris said. "Do we have to go back to town to get some food?"

"No, I can feed you here," Kelsey laughed.

"Not processed mushrooms again?" Anton asked warily.

"I've stocked up," Kelsey promised him. "No more mushrooms. Though, fair warning, they're still new to cooking food for humans."

* * *

"This isn't bad," Anton admitted, swallowing another mouthful of stew.

"It's not *great*, though," Kelsey said. She was taking small spoonfuls from her own bowl, not eating out of hunger but evaluating the food. Anton and Aris had no such reservations and were barely taking the time to chew. "How's the bread, Aris?"

"It's pretty good, for home-cooked," Aris said. "You've at least got a proper oven."

"Good ingredients, good tools," Kelsey said. "I guess good skills will take a bit longer."

Aris shrugged. "My father says it takes good traits to bake really great bread. *Temperature Control, Infuse Flavor, Perfect Timing* . . . some others. Are your skeletons going to get that?"

"Probably not," Kelsey said, making a face. "Not unless I take them to Tier Three. They just get one trait that lets them mimic their human profession."

"You can always hire in," Aris said, giggling. "Though I guess you might have some problems with that."

Kelsey snickered. "I could just blindfold them until I get them in the kitchens—or kidnap them!"

Anton glared at her.

"I'm kidding, I'm kidding," Kelsey said, laughing. She watched with amusement as the two adventurers finished off their meal, taking a second before she finished with her first.

"I see what you mean now, about food slowing you down," Aris groaned. "I think I'm ready for bed."

"The sun's barely set," Kelsey informed her, "Are you sure you want to sleep so early?"

"I'm just so tired," Aris said.

"Not too tired for a bath?"

"Oh!" Aris said, excited and wary all at once. "I guess . . . I could go for a bath?"

Anton frowned, puzzled at her reaction. "What's the big deal?"

"Oh, you'll see!" Kelsey teased him. "Bath, then?"

Aris nodded, and Kelsey helped the two of them up and led them to the bathing complex.

"So, my recycling is good enough it doesn't really matter, but there's a washing area at the front where you use the soap," Kelsey explained as they went. "Then you rinse that off and step into the hot tub farther back for a nice soak."

"That's the best bit," Aris said. They got to the entrance, which turned out to be *entrances*.

"Boys through that one, girls through this one," Kelsey said. "There would be a sign, but I have *issues* with that."

"Are you joking?" Anton asked.

"No, really, I can't do signs." Kelsey looked at him innocently, and then smiled. "She'll be fine with me—and I would have thought you'd appreciate some time alone."

"We both know I won't *actually* be alone," Anton replied.

"You're never alone in a dungeon," Kelsey agreed. "I wonder if I should make that my advertising slogan?"

"What? I—"

"Just go, I promise. Aris is too tired to get into more trouble."

"I really am," Aris sighed.

With a frustrated mutter, Anton acquiesced and entered the bathhouse. He had to admit it was luxurious. Shelves for his clothes, thick towels, and the same soap that Kelsey had procured before. He quickly worked out that the lever on the wall made water fall from the ceiling, and soon after determined how it controlled the water's temperature.

Washed and rinsed, he approached the hot tub with trepidation. The bath Kelsey had made before had been large, but this was ridiculous. Large enough to seat eight people comfortably, and so deep that he couldn't see the bottom through the cloudy water. The steps to enter were quite obvious, but Anton hesitated, struck by the thought that it looked like nothing so much as a human-sized cooking pot.

Eventually, the knowledge that Kelsey was watching him and would tease him if he took too long spurred him into action. He took a step in. It was hot, *almost* too hot to bear, but not actually unpleasant. He walked down the steps. The pool proved to be waist deep, deeper than any bath he'd ever had. He moved to the edge and sat on the ledge there. It was . . . so relaxing.

Anton felt the small scrapes and aches of the day melt away, along with his stress.

There must be something in the water, making it feel so good. That's why it's cloudy, he thought to himself. Almost against his will, he felt his muscles relax. He slid forward on his seat, sinking deep enough that only his head was out of the water, resting on the edge.

So very nice . . .

"Gonna turn into a prune if you stay there too long." A familiar voice jerked him out of his reverie. Had he been asleep? He didn't think so, but somehow he'd failed to notice Kelsey's arrival. She was standing at the edge of the pool, completely naked. Anton quickly looked away, but the image was burned into his mind's eye. Little details, like how the skin on her torso was even paler than her face and arms. Or the fact that, unlike Aris, Kelsey had no hair between her legs.

"Don't be so shy, you deserve a look," Kelsey said. "Turnabout is fair play after all. It's not like I haven't seen what you've got."

There was a splash behind him, as Kelsey, disdaining the steps, simply stepped into the pool.

"Understand," she said, "turning away from me isn't hiding anything, it's just hindering your participation in this conversation. The water isn't hiding anything either—nor will your clothes."

That made him turn around. "You can see through my clothes?" he asked. She was standing, just out of arm's length, grinning at him, her pale breasts clearly visible above the waterline.

"Not *see*," she said thoughtfully. "It's a little difficult to describe to a human . . . I'm *aware* of every part of your body, regardless of whether it's clothed or not. When you're *in* me, my knowledge of you is far more complete than if I was looking at you naked."

She glanced down. "Not doing it for you, huh?"

Anton's face, already heated by the pool, got more so. "Of course not," he protested. "I'm in love with Aris!"

"Right, right," Kelsey sighed. "It's just sex, Anton, it doesn't have to have anything to do with love. Let's try something different, though—you're mad at me, right?"

"I—" Anton cut himself off. Mad didn't begin to describe all the things that he felt about her. "Not just—"

"Sure, sure, it's complex, but the anger is in there, right?"

Anton felt there were a thousand things he should say to that, but only one came to mind. "Yes."

"So we should work through that," Kelsey said. "You've been holding it in, it's not healthy. Get it out of there."

"What are you talking about?"

"There's stuff you want to say to me, right? Say it. I'm a big girl, I can take it."

"You—" Anton started. "It wouldn't make any difference."

"Can you really say that for sure? I've listened to you before. Come on, get it off your chest. Or even better . . . hit me."

"What?"

"You want to, right? But you've been scared. So take a free shot, as many as you like."

"I'm not going to hit a girl," Anton protested.

"I'm not a girl, though, I'm a monster." Kelsey stepped forward. "How many times have I seen that thought on your face? I'm a danger to your town. I need to be stopped."

"You're not—I'm not—" Anton felt trapped as she came closer. Despite what she had said, Anton still felt that getting out of the water would be exposing himself to her. So he was trapped. "It wouldn't—you wouldn't be stopped."

"Don't know unless you try," she said. She'd stopped approaching, too close for Anton's comfort but still far away enough that he could—no.

Anton didn't see the slap coming. He felt the pain on his face, felt his head turn. Afterwards, he would realize that it was done with just a fraction of her strength. Just enough to sting, just enough to provoke him. At the time, though, all he knew was that when his head turned back again, she was right in front of his face, *smirking* at him. The anger had always been there, in him. In a split second, it was *all* of him.

His return blow wasn't a slap; it was a full-throated punch. Thrown in haste, it was nonetheless as strong as he could make it. Her head rocked back with the blow, but she quickly returned it to an upright position. She looked at him and smiled. Was there the tiniest amount of swelling on her lip?

"Not bad," she said. "Harder."

"Damn you to the Hells," he said and hit her again.

He knew—*knew*—it was useless, but he had to try. She was stronger, tougher, and faster than him. If he'd had a weapon he might have been able to do real damage, but in hand-to-hand, it all came down to the difference in Tiers.

She didn't dodge, though, or block. His blows all landed as he swung at her in desperation, making him feel that maybe he could win. All he achieved, though, was to make her take tiny steps backward.

"Tell me what you're mad about!" she yelled as he pummeled her.

"You stole my life!" he yelled back.

"I *saved* your life," she countered.

"You took *everything* for that!"

"Did I? You've still got Aris. You've still got your town, your home."

She had her back now to the edge of the pool and couldn't retreat farther. Anton swung at her again.

"You took—"

"I didn't take your family."

Suddenly the anger was gone, and Anton was empty. "My—I miss them."

His strength disappeared, leaving him limp. He would have collapsed into the water, but Kelsey grabbed him, holding him up easily. He clung to her and started sobbing.

"Mom . . . Dad . . ." he mumbled into her breast.

"There, there," she said, patting his head. "Get it all out." Her sympathetic manner was entirely belied by the look of exasperation on her face.

Anton awoke to the feeling of someone kissing him. As sleep fell away, he remembered the previous night and instantly panicked.

"Kelsey!" he shouted, sitting bolt upright in the bed.

"No, sorry, just me," Aris pouted.

Anton looked wildly around. "Sorry," he said. "I panicked . . . I thought . . ."

"Did Kelsey try something last night?" Aris asked. "I was worried she would . . . but she just put me to bed after the bath."

Anton looked at his knuckles. They were red, but most of the swelling had gone down. He vaguely remembered Kelsey rubbing something into them. He could punch—well, not stone, but wood at least—as hard as he liked without injury, but he'd hurt himself on Kelsey's cheekbones.

"Yeah," he said. "She tried something, but we didn't do . . . anything."

Aris kissed him. It was a long kiss and gave him time to notice that they were both still naked. He was just starting to draw her closer when she broke it off.

"Good," she said. "At least that's what I want to say. I do want you all to myself."

"That sounds fantastic," Anton said, drawing her in for another kiss.

"But . . ." she said when they were done. "I don't think she's going to give up, and we're kind of stuck with her, aren't we?"

"Boy are my ears burning," Kelsey said, walking into the room before Anton could answer. "Ready to start the day?"

She was fully clothed. Aris made a yeep and pulled the sheets up to cover the two of them.

"More leveling?" Anton asked.

"I'd like to, but I've got other guests today. The expedition has started."

Kelsey gave them a speculative look.

"So unless you want to get dressed quickly and take a quick jog across the Necropolis before they get down here . . . you might as well stay in bed all day."

CHAPTER THIRTY-FOUR

Down in It

MEL

They're coming! They're coming!" Mel called, flitting down to the fifth floor.
Kelsey kept her sigh to herself. She had, of course, been aware of the delvers as soon as they'd entered the cave, but Mel did tend to get excited about every intrusion. The fact that this was an expedition, and that they'd had advance notice, had only added to her anticipation.

"I'll be done with this in a bit," Kelsey said with her physical body. She'd been working through the night on some minor modifications to Skeleton Town. Walking through with Anton and Aris had given her a new perspective showing her a few things that she wanted to change.

"Aren't you going to come and watch?" Mel asked anxiously. "You'll have to get out of here before they come, anyway!"

"Sure, sure," Kelsey replied. Splitting her perceptions was fairly easy for her now, but it felt . . . odd to do it when both points were inside her. Nevertheless, she started moving her physical body to the secret apartments where she'd stashed her guests. At the same time, she manifested an astral body and followed Mel up to the other levels.

"I haven't seen these ones before," Mel announced as they arrived.

"There wouldn't be much point in clearing the first level with veterans," Kelsey explained. "Might as well let the noobs get the experience."

She cast her gaze over the three young men and one woman determinedly chopping down zombies as fast as they could.

"Tier One warriors and one scout," she mused. "A few levels higher than their class level, so they probably abandoned their path when the raiders came and got a few levels during the battle."

"I'm surprised they survived!" Mel said. "Didn't Anton say the raiders were at least level twenty?"

"Someone's always lucky," Kelsey said dismissively. "They were probably on part of the wall that didn't fall, or next to a veteran or something. Look, they've noticed."

The fresh delvers *had* noticed something that didn't fit with what they had been told. After a brief discussion, one of them went back to the entrance and called out, while the others resumed zombie hunting.

"These levels are such a waste," Mel complained. "No one comes in here that isn't at least level five."

"Eh, there's not much I can do when I'm limited to level two monsters and below," Kelsey admitted. "Even the little spiders can only manage mild poison at that level. Grossing people out might turn *someone* back. Now, hush, I want to hear what they're saying."

The young warrior was now talking to an older and more familiar figure.

"Rathuan. A blademaster at level twenty-three," Kelsey said for Mel's benefit. Mel probably recognized him, but she was a bit iffy at remembering humans. Also, he'd gone up a level since he was last here.

"Sir, there's no copper appearing in the coffins," the youth said.

"Sarcophagi," Kelsey corrected automatically.

Rathuan scowled but changed it to a reassuring smile when the kid quailed. "Don't worry about the cash, we'll chip in a few silvers to make up for it," he said. He clapped the youth on the back and sent him back into the fight.

Rathuan himself retreated to the cave entrance. Kelsey and Mel followed him. A lot of delvers didn't realize that the cave actually counted as part of the first floor. The expedition seemed to be using it as a combination staging area and command post. Rathuan avoided the group of lesser delvers getting ready to go in and headed for a smaller group of his peers.

"Here we go," Kelsey said. "Risor. Twenty-one," she said, pointing to a shifty-looking guy playing with some daggers. "Inutan, a Tier Three cleric at level nineteen," she continued, indicating a woman with midnight skin and close-cropped curly hair. "And Buraia, a level twenty-four archer."

Finally, she looked over at the last member of the group. He was standing a little apart from them and had already attracted Mel's undivided attention.

"And of course, Liem Tikin, magister, level seventeen."

"Bad news," Rathuan said in a low voice. "The dungeon has stopped the rewards."

Kelsey smirked as the group started muttering mild curses.

"She's already pissed, *and* we're bringing a mage in?" Risor grumbled, casting a dark glance at the mage in question. Liem raised an eyebrow in response.

"Don't tell me you actually *believe* the superstition that dungeons are intelligent?" he asked scornfully.

"Call it a superstition if you like," Rathuan said, "But there's not a veteran of *this* dungeon that thinks *it* isn't."

"What nonsense," Liem replied. "And you've even assigned a gender to it."

"Too vindictive to be anything different," Risor muttered. Buraia kicked him.

"Think about what this means, though," Rathuan insisted. "The dungeon reacts. We're supposed to be looking for a group hiding out in it. Do you think that's the reason why we're not getting rewards?"

"The obvious reason to cut off the rewards is to discourage delvers," Inutan said thoughtfully. "But would a dungeon not expect us to dislodge its unwelcome guests?"

"Or they've been farming the upper floors and the dungeon wants to stop giving them coin," Risor said. "But wait—if it wanted that, it wouldn't give them anything. It'd just not repopulate the floor."

"You're reading too much into this," Liem said. "Perhaps it just ran out of copper deposits."

"The way I see it," Rathuan said, "is either it's warning us off—trying to stop us from confronting who's down there—"

"That would mean that she *likes* us," Risor pointed out. "Pretty sure that isn't the case."

"Don't let your personal experiences with women mislead you," Inutan said with a sweet smile. "She probably likes the rest of us just fine."

Kelsey snickered.

"The other possibility is that the dungeon is angry for the obvious reason."

"And what is that?" Liem asked, challengingly. Most of the group looked away, but Rathuan pressed on.

"Everyone knows that dungeons don't like wizards." Everybody (except Kelsey and Mel) carefully avoided looking at the reasons why, currently hanging from Liem's neck.

"What's especially worrying about that possibility," Rathuan continued, speaking over Liem's protests, "is that this is happening on the first floor."

"What's worrying about that?" Risor asked. Buraia gave him the answer as she came to the same realization.

"It had to change it before we arrived," she said. "It can't change a floor we're on, so . . ."

"It would have to already know we were bringing a mage," Rathuan finished.

"Ooops," Kelsey said, unrepentant. "Perhaps I gave a little too much away?"

The advance team had cleared the first floor in the time that the leaders spent talking. A second team, slightly more experienced, moved forward. One person from the first team went with them; the other three would remain on the first floor, preventing the dungeon from restocking that floor. The rest of the expedition followed at a leisurely pace. The leaders stayed near the front, in case they were needed, but the early levels were not a great challenge for the well prepared.

Progress was swift through the first four levels. It actually got a little easier as they went, as more people were being left behind, reducing the challenge of managing such a large and unwieldy expedition. It was only when they got to the fifth floor that they stopped, spooked by Kelsey's changes.

"What's wrong?" Liem asked when he caught up with the front line. With more space to work with, a larger number of expedition members had started fighting, hewing into the skeleton merchants and guards with enthusiasm. The leaders, though, were hanging back, examining the surfaces of the buildings with suspicion.

"It smells different," Risor said.

"And this," Rathuan said, pointing to the building. "I don't know what the purpose is."

"Why did you change it?" Mel asked. "I mean, it *is* freaking them out, which is reason enough, but . . ."

"I haven't been happy with the performance of the skeletons when they're tracking with sound," Kelsey said. "And listening to the kids yesterday, I think they're being confused by all the echoes."

"All right?" Mel said.

Kelsey sighed. "So, you get echoes from flat, hard surfaces," she said. "Breaking up the surfaces, even if it's just with a repeating texture, tends to break up the sound."

"And the lichen? I assume that's what they're smelling."

Kelsey nodded. "Plants would actually be better, but then I'd need to light this place up for them. Lichen will grow in the darkness and soften the surfaces."

"Is it working?"

"With this many people, nothing's going to really work," Kelsey said, shrugging. "We won't get a real test until a small group goes through again."

"Well, it's certainly started an argument," Mel said, pointing out the leadership group.

"Must you really attribute every random change to some malevolent intelligence?" Liem said with an exasperated tone.

"Only the ones that are," Risor shot back. "I can't believe you're so dumb not to see it. The dungeon only makes changes that make it a better killer."

"And how, exactly, does a smell and some patterns make it a better killer?"

"Well . . ." Risor looked uncertain. "I'm not sure. Maybe it's poison?"

Rathuan frowned, taking the idea seriously. "We have antidotes, but no one has reported symptoms of poisoning," he said. "If it is an airborne poison, can your magic do something about it?" he asked Liem.

"Air magic is not . . . one of my areas," Liem admitted. "I could try and burn it out of the air."

"That might cause more problems than it solves," Inutan put in urgently. "There is a limited amount of air down here; you don't want to set the whole cavern on fire."

Liem nodded. "I'm sure this is just a random change," he said.

The expedition continued, more cautiously, through the same maze of streets that Anton and Aris had challenged yesterday. They left six members behind this time, to account for skeletons that had stayed hidden.

There was one small detour before they left.

"What is this?" Liem asked when they showed him a blank wall.

"It's a secret door," Risor told him.

"It *might* be a secret door," Inutan said.

"Shut it. I know a door when I see one. *Hidden Secrets Revealed* is screaming at me right now."

"And yet, your *Allow Unwanted Passage*, which you have often told us can open any door with but a touch, does nothing."

Liem looked at the two bickering delvers and shrugged. "I have no answers for you. Stone is also not my expertise. I can see that it is infused with mana, but that is true of just about everything down here.

"Worth a shot to ask," Risor said.

When they moved on to the sixth level, Rathuan became a little more active. "I'll take the Skeleton King," he told the other expedition members.

Buraia snorted her amusement. "He hasn't been a challenge to you for years," she said.

"Still," Rathuan said. "He is a true swordsman. He deserves a good fight."

As Buraia had predicted, the fight was over very quickly.

"Oh I remember this guy now," Mel said. "He fought Cheryl, didn't he?"

"To a draw," Kelsey agreed. "Or at least . . . he delayed her long enough for his party to get out once she injured Risor. He's a level higher now, so . . ."

Mel looked at the blademaster uneasily. "Do you think he can beat her?"

"I don't think he plans to," Kelsey said. "Now that there are fewer people around, have you noticed that two of them are tied up?"

"What? Where?" Mel flitted around. It was pointless to compare her limited point of view to the total awareness that Kelsey enjoyed within her own volume, but she really was quite obtuse sometimes.

"There are people tied up! Cat-people!" Mel reported a few moments later.

"They must have been left behind by the raiders," Kelsey explained. "They must be planning on feeding them to Cheryl."

"Again? Are you going to allow that?"

"Eh, I don't see why not," Kelsey said. "Actually . . . I might have to jump in and take one for myself."

"You want to play with the cat-person? They do have nice fur."

"I'm just thinking that they speak a different language in Elitra," Kelsey said. "Zamarrans speak a trade-tongue, so we might get by, but it would be useful to have someone to learn the native language off."

She eyed the two prisoners speculatively. "I'll have a word with Cheryl."

Mel ignored her, already distracted by the delvers levering the King's throne from the floor. Despite counting as a separate floor, the King's Citadel was actually slightly above the town it ruled over. The next level, though, was a return to form. The Spider Warrens lay beneath the Citadel, and were accessed via a short shaft.

"Everyone got their antidote potions?" Rathuan called out, to various sounds of agreement."

"Actually, Captain, I think I can contribute here for the first time," Liem said, looking down the hole.

"Expedition Captain is a mouthful of a title and it only lasts for this delve," Rathuan said. "Just call me Rathuan. How can you help?"

"Spiderwebs are flammable, are they not? And fire *is* one of my areas of expertise."

"Uh, that's been tried," Rathuan said. "It's not just spiderwebbing down there, there's something else that burns. Everyone who's tried to burn them out has gotten caught in their own conflagration."

"They were not fire mages," Liem said haughtily. "Rest assured, I can clear out the next level from here *and* prevent any fire from making it back to us."

"Oh, can you now?" Kelsey said. "Bring it."

CHAPTER THIRTY-FIVE

Into the Fire

MEL

The throne room of the Skeleton King was big enough to hold the entire expedition, at least those that hadn't already been left behind to guard the previous floor. Now they all backed away from the hole that had been under the King's throne, giving the mage room to work.

Everyone, that is, except for Kelsey and Mel, but they weren't really there in any physical sense.

"I like it when they use fire on this level," Mel said. "But . . . is it going to work if they're not down there to be burned?"

"It won't work the same way," Kelsey told her. "But it will still be fun."

The fairy clapped her hands with excitement. Kelsey just smiled and opened the vents.

"Hurry up," she said to the mage, who couldn't hear her. "I'm wasting mana here."

"Really?" Mel asked in a concerned tone.

"Eh, not really. Just a small leakage."

The intangible barriers that kept Kelsey's mana contained worked a lot more efficiently if they were backed up by physical barriers. That was why each floor was separated as much as possible from each other and (until recently) had only one entrance and exit.

"Floor" was actually a misnomer at times. The Citadel was its own floor, despite being on the same level as the three rings of the town. That was why it was entirely sealed off, except for the entrance. While its towers appeared to have windows and arrow slits, they were just fake alcoves, not connected to the inside in any way.

It was the magical barriers that defined a floor, not the physical levels. Barriers that could, with some effort, be twisted and shaped the way she desired. The main consideration in their arrangement, aside from the necessity of them being nested within each other, was that no action could be taken on a floor that was occupied by sentients.

There were exceptions to that, though. Her avatar was one, allowing her to order any part of her that it was in line of sight of. Another exception was that electrical signals cared not for the magical delineation of floors. A wire could transmit a signal from floor ten to floor one, with no effort at all. Mel didn't understand how it worked, but she did appreciate the results.

"Did you hear that?" Liem asked.

"Hear what?" Rathuan asked. Perception wasn't on the Blademaster advancement path.

"A . . . thump. Like a rock falling to the ground? It sounded quite loud, but far away. From both below, and also on this level."

Kelsey scowled when he spoke, but Mel didn't think the wizard noticing the vents opening was going to change anything. Kelsey's dungeon didn't actually need vents. Strictly speaking, none of her monsters actually required *air*. She had done some experiments early on, thinking that asphyxiating all the intruders would be a much easier method of defending herself.

She had found, though, that the air mana she produced would naturally produce clean air over time. Mel had been surprised by her complaints, because what did she expect air mana to do? She could manage to sustain pockets of different gases in small volumes, but sadly, switching to an entire atmosphere of noxious air was not possible.

So while she didn't need vents under normal circumstances, there were times when they were useful, and she believed in being prepared. Keeping them open like this did cost mana, though, so they both hoped that the mage would get on with it.

It wasn't long before they got their wish. With a gesture, the mage sent a column of fire down the hole. There were some scattered cheers from the men at the sight, and then there was a muffled thump as the webs and spiders down there ignited.

"Poor spiders," Mel intoned, not at all concerned about the undead that were getting incinerated down there. More than any other of Kelsey's creations, the spiders were semi-biological killing machines, with not even an attempt at a personality.

Mel wanted to go down and see it start, but she also wanted to see what was going to happen up here, so she stayed where she was, listening.

"Time for the gas-o-line!" she giggled. Kelsey's strange version of oil was delivered by another one of her ingenious mechanisms. Pipes concealed in the ceiling were blocked off by a special alloy that melted with only a little extra heat. Once a fire started, the blockage was removed and the gas-o-line could flow freely.

"I told you, there's something else that burns down there," Rathuan said.

"Indeed," Liem said. He had a look of concentration on his face, one hand still pointing down the hole. "The shaft is acting like a chimney and drawing the flame up. I'm not sure if it would get high enough to be dangerous, but I'm keeping it back."

Much like a chimney, thick black smoke was now starting to billow out of the shaft, causing him to cough.

"Can't you do anything about the smoke?" Rathuan asked, stepping back from the choking cloud.

"Sadly no, but it should be fine," Liem said. "See, it's been drawn up."

Sure enough, a slight breeze was picking up the smoke and carrying it upwards. Rathuan stared at the ceiling, wondering where it went. Before he could say something about it, the sound started.

It started as a low moan, coming from below, making the intruders shiver and grasp their weapons. Even as they looked around for the source, it quickly grew, becoming louder and more high pitched, turning into a ghastly scream. At the same time, the smoke grew thicker and rose more swiftly to the ceiling.

"This is new?" Mel asked Kelsey. Since their communication was actually mental, she had no problem with being heard.

"It's the vents," Kelsey explained. "All that air moving through them makes a sound, and if you shape the pipe right, it sounds like a scream."

"It seems effective at scaring them, at least?" Mel suggested, looking at the effect it was having on the adventurers. She supposed it would also be heard out in Skeleton Town, scaring those left there as well.

"It's just a distraction," Kelsey said. "It takes time to get all the air moving right." She was looking at the nervous adventurers, but Mel knew that her attention was on the entire setup. The vents above, the fire below.

"Now," she said after a considered moment. At her will, the vents in the roof closed. The smoke stopped boiling upwards and recoiled back down on the adventurers, causing them to cough and choke. Kelsey gave them a moment to enjoy it and then shut off the lower vents. The howling stopped, but that was the least of the effects.

With no fresh air from below to feed it, the firestorm would quickly go out. But before that, it sucked all the air out of the spider level, desperately consuming it for a last gasp of life. The smoke and noxious air still fled upwards, pushed by heat and momentum, but now there was no way for it to escape from the Citadel.

Only the mage noticed when the fire went out, and he barely had time to consider the reasons why it did. He was too busy holding his sleeve to his face and coughing to really pay attention.

The adventurers, or at least some of them, were more prepared. Rathuan's hand went to his waist and pulled out the correct potion as if he practiced it every day. He downed it with equally well-practiced speed.

"Water-breathing potions!" he yelled as soon as the potion took hold. Water-breathing potions didn't actually allow you to breathe water, they just created air in your lungs. They had planned to save these for the water level, but they were useful for many emergencies.

He quickly checked on his party, who all seemed fine, having already realized the need for the potions. Next, he checked on the wizard. The smoke was still blinding, but then it suddenly seemed to clear.

What it revealed was anything but heartening. Magister Liem, blinded by smoke, choking for air and groping for a potion to let him breathe, had been unprepared for the next stage of Kelsey's trap. As the heat from the extinguished fire cooled, and the momentum of the air diminished, a volume of high pressure found itself connected to a volume of low pressure with nothing to hold it back.

The sudden wind that sprung up swept the struggling wizard off his feet and down into the shaft.

"Nice!" Kelsey exclaimed. "That went better than I thought it would."

Mel clapped delightedly at Rathuan's cursing. He went over to Inutan, who was carrying the spare potions.

"The mage fell down the shaft! Get down there and see if he's still alive," he shouted. She nodded, and he went to check on the rest of the expedition.

"Shall we go see?" Kelsey said to Mel, indicating Inutan as she grabbed Risor to help her down. Instead of climbing, he just grabbed her by the arm and used his trait. Mel didn't know what it was called, but it let them fall safely and silently to the next level.

Their invisible watchers were there first, of course, already observing the fallen mage with interest.

"Oh, he's still alive," Mel said, disappointed. They watched as Inutan fed him a potion for his breathing, then looked at the rest of him.

"Better if we set his leg while he's still unconscious," she told her companion. "Can you hold him, here?"

No strangers to emergency first aid, the two of them worked efficiently to straighten Liem's broken leg and checked him for other injuries before bringing out a five-minute healing potion.

"Hold him down," Inutan said. "I doubt he's ever had one of these before, and we don't want him thrashing around with that leg."

Risor grinned his agreement and pinned the unconscious mage to the ground. Bracing one hand on the mage's chest, he immobilized the wizard's leg with what would be a painful grip on his thigh. It looked awkward, but the difference in Strength was high enough that it would suffice.

Inutan sighed, but went ahead and fed Liem the potion. As soon as it entered his mouth, he started to stiffen.

"Calm down, mage," Inutan said, perhaps a little more harshly than she should have. "This is a healing potion. Move, and you'll waste its effects."

Liem made a grunt, possibly to tell her he understood, but the pain was more than enough to break his resolve. Before long he was thrashing and moaning beneath them. Both the adventurers had experienced this before, from either side, so they just continued to hold him impassively until the five minutes were up.

There was no need for a timer. The moment the potion ran out, Liem stopped fighting them and slumped to the floor with relief.

"That will do for now," Inutan told him. "Your leg should be knitted, but don't try standing on it yet. You've still got another thirty minutes on your breathing potion, so just wait there while we see what Rathuan wants to do."

She indicated to Risor that he should keep watch on the tunnels with his *Darkvision*, and then climbed up to get instructions. Rathuan was putting the expedition together again.

"We need to move quickly," he explained. "We don't have enough breathing potions to dose everyone again, so we need to get through the nest while they're in effect."

"Why'd they have so many breathing potions, anyway?" Mel asked. Now that it seemed that the wizard would live, they had drifted back up to the Citadel.

"Must have planned for an extended trip in the Silent Sea," Kelsey said. "But I guess that's off the table for now."

"What about the guards for the spiders?" Inutan asked, rudely talking over the people she couldn't hear. "Will they be able to stay on the level if the air is still bad?"

Mel snorted. She knew that the air would be replenished by the time the potions ran out. But a human couldn't be expected to know how dungeons worked, she supposed.

Unaware that his concern was unfounded, Rathuan sighed. "We have a few potions left," he said. "It will have to be enough . . . if they stay by the entrance and open it periodically . . ."

No exit from a level would open until the entrance was closed. All adventurers knew that, though they didn't know it was a deliberate safety measure on Kelsey's part. The low mana pressures on the upper levels let her get away with a narrow passage between levels, but at these depths, the mana barriers needed to be reinforced with doors.

"Well, that's about it for this level," Kelsey said. "The spiders are just about all cleared out, so their next big challenge is the Gloomy Woods."

"It was fun!" Mel exclaimed, "And a bit different from other times. It was very loud, though; I hope it didn't disturb your guests."

Kelsey raised an eyebrow. Mel had avoided Anton and Aris since they first arrived. Transparently fishing for information about them was unlike her.

"It's fine," she said, deciding to indulge her fairy's curiosity. "They didn't notice; they were too busy with their own affairs."

CHAPTER THIRTY-SIX

The House is Rockin'

C lean clothes," Kelsey announced, pulling a bundle out of thin air and setting it down on a small table next to the bed. "Freshly laundered by your friendly neighborhood skeleton maid service."

Anton looked at his clothes and thought about who had gotten him into bed without bothering to dress him. The smirk on Kelsey's face told him that he didn't need—didn't *want*—to mention it. Instead, he focused on the matter at hand.

"Do we . . . need to get into town today?" he asked.

"Nope!" Kelsey said brightly. "Not unless you have plans that I don't know about, in which case I'm shocked—shocked!—that you'd keep such things from me."

"So we could stay . . . right here?" Aris asked and giggled. The slight movement was enough to remind Anton that she was right next to him, naked, under the sheet.

"Sure! In fact, if it's like that . . ." Kelsey's smirk grew wider but somehow failed to transition to an honest grin. "How about I get out of your hair and give you two lovebirds some time alone, eh?"

"Sounds great!" Aris said. Anton was more suspicious.

"Why would you do that?"

"If that's an invitation for me to join in, it's a very clumsy one," Kelsey snarked. She continued over his spluttered response. "No, seriously, you guys could use a bit of a break, and opportunities to get some time alone—from me—won't happen often."

"Well yeah, but you've been . . ." *Insistent* was the word he wanted to use, but he couldn't bring himself to say it, or what came after it.

"Anton, Anton, Anton," Kelsey said, insincerely sad. "We're bound by that geas! It's not that I *want* to watch the sweat run down the curves of your muscles as you bring Aris to the heights of pleasure with—"

She leaned in, emphasizing and enjoying the effect that each word had on him. "Your. Rock. Hard . . ."

She trailed off, staying just close enough to make him uncomfortable, before backing off. "But we're stuck with each other! But if you don't want to take this chance . . ."

"Fine! Yes please, you're being very generous!" He quickly stuttered out the words, desperate for her to not say another thing.

"Excellent! Well, breakfast is ready next door, along with enough food and drink to keep you until tonight."

Kelsey cocked her head and touched her chin, the very picture of a thoughtful look. "I'm going to suggest that you don't leave these apartments—don't open any closed doors, basically. I'll leave a path open to the baths, if you're interested."

She gave an embarrassed shrug. "I'm just not one hundred percent sure about the orders on the skeletons. I *think* it will be fine, but with my avatar away, I won't be able to stop them if there's a problem."

"If this a setup for some sort of training scenario . . ." Anton said suspiciously.

"No, hand on heart, it's just a precaution," Kelsey said. "It's just easier to keep them out of here, and that way you don't have to interact."

"Wait, if your avatar isn't going to be *here*," Aris said, "where *are* you going to be?"

"Oh, I thought I might pop into town," Kelsey said. "Be seen without Anton for once. You know, I think they might be starting rumors about us! Anyway, Bye!"

And with that, she was gone.

"So, breakfast?" Aris said, turning around in his arms to kiss him. Anton savored the feeling of her skin sliding under his hands, the softness and the warmth of her lips on his. She smelled of the same soap he'd been using last night. Unheeded, the sheet she had been holding fell back to the bed.

"You know," he said reluctantly, "she's not really gone. She's still watching us."

"I know, but just pretend she isn't?" Aris said. "It *is* a lot easier when she's not . . . visible."

She kissed him again and he slid his hands down her back. He didn't want to take them off her. "I love you," he said. His stomach chose that moment to gurgle. Loudly.

She giggled. "I love you too," she said. "Breakfast?"

They got partially dressed to eat. Anton didn't feel comfortable eating hot food without pants, and he wouldn't have been able to focus on food at all if Aris wasn't wearing a top. Afterwards, he took a cursory glance at the rest of the food Kelsey had provided. Bread, cold cooked meats, cheese . . . plenty of wine.

Then Aris dragged him to the bath.

"I thought boys couldn't go into the girls' bath?" he said.

"Oh good point, we'll have to go into yours," she said, giggling again. She led him straight to the hot bath, pausing only to grab some soap from the cleaning area.

"Kelsey told me that this was a terrible sin," she said, "but also that her 'systems' could handle it, so don't worry about it."

She dropped the soap by the side of the bath and then wiggled out of her shirt. Anton couldn't help but stare, his own clothes forgotten until she winked at him.

"Are you just going to stand there, or get in?" She took her own words to heart and carefully stepped into the bath.

Anton goggled for a moment more and then worked his way out of his pants, his stiffening member already proving an impediment. When he got in, Aris was ready for him with the soap.

"Wash my back?" she said coyly, handing it to him. Then she turned most of the way around, enough to show her back while still looking at him with greedy eyes.

Anton stepped forward. *We already washed last night,* some part of him protested. *We don't need cleaning again.* He paid it absolutely no heed as he lathered his hands up and slid them across Aris's chocolate skin. She sighed and leaned into his touch.

He managed to make more than a token effort at cleaning her back before sliding his hands to where they really wanted to be. Aris made a startled yelp when he grasped her big, beautiful breasts, but didn't protest as he drew her closer and started giving her front a much more thorough washing. She rubbed her soapy back against his chest as he played with her breasts, drawing soft moans out of her as he brushed against her hardening nipples.

"You're poking me," she giggled, not talking about his hands. Anton thought for a second and then bent his knees to adjust for her shorter height. His member slid down her back and then moved between her legs.

"Ah! Wait, I'm not ready—" Anton couldn't wait, though, the feel of her skin against him driving him to urgency. He slid between her legs, not entering her, but rubbing against her sex as she gasped with the sensation. "Oh! That's good . . ." she moaned as he pressed against her.

She reached down and gently brushed against his tip as it poked out from between her legs. This time it was Anton's turn to yelp at the touch on his most sensitive spot.

"Is that all right?" Aris asked, rubbing her finger back and forth. "Does it feel good?"

Anton could only gasp in agreement. She slid her fingers underneath and pulled up on him, pushing him harder against her sex. Then she tilted her hips. She could only move a short distance, but she rubbed herself against his member, eliciting moans from both of them.

"I think . . ." she gasped, as Anton squeezed her nipples in retaliation, "I'm ready now."

Anton had to agree. He gently pushed her forward until she was leaning on the side of the bath. She keep her hips angled for him, giving him one final caress as he pulled back and then plunged back in.

Aris gasped as he entered her, and cried out when he made it all the way in. "Yes! More!"

He didn't need any encouragement. Somehow, she felt even hotter than the water they were in, her heat enfolding him. The feeling of her inner walls holding him as he withdrew was amazing, and he quickly forced himself back in. A guttural moan escaped him, and he stopped thinking.

He moved his hands down to her hips for better leverage and started to thrust. He barely noticed that she was thrusting back, pushing off the bath wall in time with him.

She was saying something, but he couldn't make it out. It wasn't important. The only thing that mattered was the link between them, the beat of their synchronized lust as he went in and out of her. As long as they kept up the rhythm, he thought, they could keep going, keep this feeling going forever.

It was Aris that reached her limit first. He felt the trembling start all through her body. Just the slightest twitch at first, but it quickly grew into a spasm that had her gripping him even more tightly. He wasn't sure if it was that, or the strangled moan of pleasure that she gave that set him off, but he groaned with the power of his own orgasm, as he shot his seed deep within her.

Aris spasmed again as she felt him go off inside her, and then went limp. She was not unconscious, but he had to support her as she drooped with exhaustion. Sliding out of her, he turned her around so they could kiss. She was so light in his arms.

He sat down on the underwater ledge and let her recover on his lap. She was pressed so closely against him that if he'd still been hard they would have been still making love. As it was, though, he just enjoyed the warm feeling of her body against his.

Eventually, she could speak again.

"That was . . . intense," she breathed softly. Then she giggled. "You're terrible at washing, I think that I'm dirtier than I was before."

Anton smiled. He felt something lift within him. "Give me another chance, I'll wash every part of you sparkling clean."

"Mhmnn, yes," Aris replied. "Take as many times as you like."

He did wash her then, gently exploring every part of her with his hands. He gave proper attention to her back this time, before moving on to her front, her legs, and other parts.

He brought her to another orgasm with just his fingers, more gently this time, letting her lie back against him while he "cleaned" her sex with vigorous movements of his fingers.

Then it was her turn to clean him, her soft hands running over his body while her lips found his in a passionate kiss. Anton wasn't sure what that had to do with cleaning, but he certainly enjoyed it. When he felt himself responding again, he decided he was clean enough.

Aris gave a squeal as he lifted her up, stepping out of the bath with her in his arms. He took some care as he climbed the steps with her unfamiliar weight. Slipping and falling would be embarrassing.

"What are you doing?" Aris asked. Despite her protest, she seemed perfectly happy to be held, wrapping her arms around his neck and relaxing against him.

"I thought it was time to get dried off, and move back to the bed," he said.

Aris's eyes glittered. "No need to dry off," she said.

Despite that, they did. Aris's impatience evaporated at the feel of the soft towels rubbed against her skin by her lover. They dried each other off quickly but thoroughly. Aris demanded to be carried again, and Anton was happy to comply.

When they got to the bedroom, Anton tossed Aris onto the bed and was on top of her before she finished bouncing. She pulled him down for a kiss, and he exulted in the feel of her softness beneath his weight. Her legs were spread invitingly, and he could feel himself getting hard again.

"Are we really going to stay here all day?" Aris asked when they finished the kiss.

"We can stay here forever, as far as I'm concerned," Anton replied and went down for another one.

At the back of his mind, though, one thought managed to intrude, before he drove it away. *What's Kelsey doing?*

CHAPTER THIRTY-SEVEN

She's No Lady

SULIEL

Suliel had just finished breakfast when her guards brought word that the "foreign merchant" was at her gate, looking to see her.

"She said it was about your debt, my lady," he told her, face expressionless.

That was quick, Suliel thought. She hadn't believed Kelsey when she'd said she was unconcerned about immediate payment, but she thought that the woman would wait a *little* longer before trying to turn the screws.

Suliel had the money in her treasury, but she planned on waiting to see if she could get Father's conspiracy to pay for them. Her uncle didn't arrive until tomorrow, but she could surely put this grasping merchant off for that long.

Still, it wouldn't do to *ignore* someone you owed a debt to, so Suliel instructed that the woman be shown into the nicer meeting room.

Suliel made the woman wait, of course. Not for long, as she didn't want the pale-skinned foreigner in her castle any longer than she had to. Long enough, though, to make the point that merchants waited on nobility, not the other way around.

Kelsey seemed unperturbed as Suliel swept into the room.

"Your ladyship," she said, rising to her feet and bowing. *Not* curtsying, but she no doubt followed strange northern customs. Suliel was more concerned with other matters.

One other matter in particular. "You didn't bring Freeman Nos with you," she said, keeping it formal. She wasn't sure if she'd ever *had* to speak formally of a commoner before, but the proper term was part of her education.

"Disappointed?" Kelsey asked neutrally, but just the word was a taunt. "I'm afraid that Anton has other affairs to take care of. It's just us girls today."

"That's fine," Suliel said, keeping her feelings off her face. She took a seat and gestured for Kelsey to do the same. "I must say, I didn't expect you to come after your money quite so quickly."

Kelsey waved her hand. "Oh, I just said that so you would speak with me," she said, giving Suliel a wide smile. "I came here to talk about something else."

Suliel smiled back, thinly. That was the problem with some lenders. They felt as though you were at their beck and call until you paid them off. Her father had warned her about the type. And told her how best to deal with them.

Unconcerned, Kelsey continued. "Now that we know each other better, I've been thinking that I should fill you in on a few things. Though . . ." She looked around. ". . . this conversation might be better held in your father's study."

"How do you know—" Suliel started, then stopped herself, feeling the heat in her cheeks. Of *course* the merchant could guess her father had a study. What Baron would not?

"I've been there," Kelsey replied. "So I can tell you that there's a painting in there—of Rale Anat, who I'm guessing is your great-grandfather."

"Did my father tell you that?" Suliel demanded. She hadn't been in her father's study often, but she knew the picture was there. She also knew it didn't have a nameplate. She'd had to ask her father who it was.

Kelsey just smiled. "We can talk about your family history if you really want, but there's something in the study far more important for me to show you."

Suliel stared, but only for a moment. She knew how this would go—demands for more information would only be refused, giving an opportunity for Kelsey to look mysterious while Suliel looked foolish. She could throw the woman out, but if she wanted to find out what Kelsey was talking about . . .

"Very well," she allowed. She had, of course, her father's key, so they went straight there.

"You really should have started using this room, you know," Kelsey said as Suliel turned the key. "I bet there's a lot of correspondence in that desk that you need to review,"

Suliel knew that Kelsey was correct, but she wasn't about to take her advice. To Suliel's surprise, Kelsey paid no attention to the writing desk, or to the painting on the wall. Instead, she strode over to the cupboard at the back of the room, opened it, and stepped inside.

"What are you doing!" Suliel cried and rushed over. She was quick enough to get a quick glimpse of Kelsey as she started climbing down a hole in the cupboard floor.

"Come on, what are you waiting for?" Kelsey asked with a wink as she disappeared into darkness.

Suliel froze, trying to think through the possibilities. There was a *secret passage* in her father's study, leading who knew where. This woman knew about it, knew about where it *went to*, which meant . . .

It goes outside, she's had access to the castle this entire time . . . and she's getting away!

Objectively, Suliel might have agreed that Kelsey's actions weren't those of someone trying to escape. If Suliel didn't follow, Kelsey would come back to taunt her more. But her instincts were crying out. Kelsey *knew* things that Suliel *needed* to know; she couldn't let Kelsey get away.

Cursing to herself, Suliel looked around the room. There were guards outside, and lanterns, but if she wanted to keep this all secret, she would have to leave them outside. The study was lit by a light-stone hanging over the writing desk. An extravagant expense, but it meant that her father could stay here overnight without having the servants come in to refill oil lanterns.

Now she thought it might have another purpose. She swiftly stepped over and removed it from its hook. The decorative worked silver that held it was designed to be hung from a hook . . . or a wrist.

Stepping out of the room, Suliel addressed the guards. "We will be in discussions for some time; see that we are not disturbed."

Going back inside, she headed to the cupboard and shone her light down, only to see that Kelsey had descended out of the light's range. She only saw a ladder, extending farther down. Having no choice, she put her foot on the first rung and started her own descent.

The light attached to her wrist was enough for her to find the next rung without groping around, though her dress did get in the way. She kept looking down, trying to see the bottom, and was eventually rewarded when a steady yellow light bloomed below her. It was too far to see much, but she was encouraged to climb on.

When she got to the bottom, Kelsey was there, holding her own magical light. She had ended up in a tunnel, far below the surface. The walls looked carved rather than natural and there was only one direction to travel.

"Need a quick rest?" Kelsey asked.

"I'm fine," Suliel replied, not eager to show any weakness. Kelsey didn't show any sign of being tired, but the report Suliel had read mentioned that Kelsey had claimed to be Tier Three.

"This way, then," Kelsey said, smiling, and led the way down the tunnel. They didn't have to go far before coming to an interruption in the smooth walls.

It was clearly carved by different hands, an arch of cut stone blocks framing stone doors kept invitingly open. Torches burned inside, spilling a warm flickering light into the tunnel.

There are people down here? she thought. Torches wouldn't burn for long without someone tending them. Kelsey didn't seem surprised and walked straight in. Suliel hesitated at the threshold, casting a glance down where the tunnel continued. Kelsey turned and looked back at her.

"It goes on and ends up in a cave in the cliffs," she said. "And there's a fork that leads into a building in town. Not *very* interesting, compared to this."

Grimacing, Suliel entered the room. She wasn't going to stop now. Looking around as she crossed the floor, she saw that it was bare except for sarcophagi lining the walls.

Is this my family's crypt? she wondered. *No, we don't have one of those . . . I think? Wait . . .*

"How is this possible? We're below the town, and the dungeon sits on a hill. There shouldn't be crypts *below* the town."

Kelsey clapped, drawing her attention. "Nice deduction! But this isn't those crypts. Same theme, different location."

"Does this mean—" She was interrupted by a soft thud. Whirling around, she saw that the doors had closed behind her.

"That's right," Kelsey said brightly. "You're in the dungeon. Come on in a bit farther, and we'll have a talk." She moved over to the door, and then paused again, as Suliel hadn't moved. "Unless you'd rather deal with what's in the box?"

"Dungeons," Suliel said slowly, "only get worse the farther you get in."

"True enough," Kelsey laughed. "But you're safe enough with me."

Suliel doubted that, but she stepped forward anyway. The next room was much the same as the first but with a pair of wooden chairs with a small table between them. Kelsey took one and gestured for Suliel to take the other.

"That's better," Kelsey said when they were both seated. "I imagine you have a lot of questions, so why don't we start with them?"

Suliel narrowed her eyes. "You killed my father, didn't you?"

"Whoa," Kelsey said, raising her eyebrows. "That's a hell of an accusation, considering you've already got a guy locked up for that upstairs. What makes you think I did it?"

"I arrested Captain Oldaw because I couldn't see how those guns could have ended up with him," Suliel said bitterly. She gestured around her as she continued. "But clearly, I don't have the faintest idea of what's going on, do I? Of what's possible or not. All this crazy talk about a team in the dungeon, it's all been your misdirection. *You're* in the dungeon, *you're* the one we've been looking for, right under our noses."

"You're seriously saying 'I don't know what's going on, so it must be you?'" Kelsey said, incredulously. "I've never felt so victimized."

"I never believed that Oldaw was capable of murder," Suliel spat. "And I've never trusted you, either. It was just the evidence I saw . . . but that wasn't evidence at all, was it? And I notice that you still haven't *denied* it."

"Fine, fine," Kelsey said, rolling her eyes. "I did it, I killed your father." She cocked her head slightly, seemingly unconcerned by Suliel's growing rage. "What do you think happens now? Going to kill me back?"

Suliel *wanted* to revenge her father, right then and there, but her upbringing and training were telling her to consider her options. She *had* a weapon, a Tier Two dagger—more of a small sword, really. That, in the hands of a Tier One like herself, against an unarmed Tier Three like Kelsey . . . could only end one way.

Kelsey might not even *be* Tier Three. They had suspected the involvement of a Tier *Four* from the start. If no one could read her status, she might well have lied about her level to fit in.

Part of her wanted to try it anyway, but even if it was a bluff and Suliel managed to get her revenge, she'd be left locked in a dungeon without whatever Kelsey was doing to hold the monsters back. There wasn't any way for victory.

Kelsey watched Suliel's struggle with interest, waiting for her to reply.

"I imagine," Suliel said carefully, still struggling with control, "that what happens next is whatever you brought me down here for."

"Well, I didn't bring you down here to accuse me of murder, that's for sure," Kelsey said, pouting. "Still, at least it's out of the way, and we can start to move past it."

Suliel gritted her teeth.

"Or maybe not," Kelsey conceded. "Look, I'm sorry about your dad. But it was self-defense! He was trying to capture me, take me away for torture. Lord only knows what he would have done to Anton."

"Anton?" Suliel said. She felt a quick pang of concern, fear, and . . . betrayal. "Anton was there, when you killed my father?"

"Hoo boy," Kelsey said. "This is going to be a long conversation."

CHAPTER THIRTY-EIGHT

Sweet Dreams Are Made of This

SULIEL

L et's start by addressing a misapprehension," Kelsey said, ignoring the hurt expression on Suliel's face. "I'm the dungeon."

"What." Suliel didn't, *couldn't* react to such an outrageous suggestion. It was as if Kelsey had said, "I am cheese," or some other meaningless statement.

Kelsey sighed and placed her hand on the stone table. It seemed to be attached to the floor as if it had grown out of it. Now, at Kelsey's direction, it grew higher, the central support extending and then contracting. All the while, the surface of the table remained in contact with Kelsey's hand as she raised and lowered it.

"So . . . you have a stone-shaping trait?" Suliel asked. "Is that supposed to convince me of something?"

Kelsey sighed and snapped her fingers. A pair of skeleton warriors suddenly came into being behind her. Suliel jerked back out of her chair, sending it flying. She drew out her dagger without thinking and assumed a fighting stance.

The skeletons, however, did not move to attack. Instead, they spread out their arms, each still holding a sword and a shield, and began to move up and down, kicking up with one leg at a time and bringing the other down. They stayed in one place, but their legs moved with a clatter that was almost . . . rhythmic?

"They've been working on it since I took them off gate duty," Kelsey said, "But I guess you're not in the mood to give a critique." She snapped her fingers again and the skeletons disappeared.

Suliel stayed in her fighting stance. Kelsey hadn't appeared surprised by the dagger concealed in her dress and didn't seem concerned by it now. Now that it was out, it seemed a shame not to try and stab her with it . . . but no. She was a noble, and she was not going to embarrass herself fighting an opponent she could not beat. Moving carefully, she sheathed her weapon and retrieved her chair, sitting down again in front of Kelsey.

"I don't . . . understand what you are saying," she said. *Or believe*, she added in her head.

Kelsey shrugged. "I am the dungeon," she repeated. "I'm all around you right now. The floor, the walls. You're breathing my air. This body that you see is a . . . tool, that lets me communicate. I've only recently gained the ability to make it."

"My father knew this?"

"No," Kelsey said. "You know, he's not the only relative of yours that I've killed. Delem, Prinit, Ablet . . . they were all Anats. Used to be that your family took its own risks."

Suliel did know those names, from her family tree. She hadn't known any of them. Her family hadn't lost someone to the dungeon since before she was born.

"So . . . if I were to stab you, would the dungeon die?" Suliel asked. She wasn't sure if she *believed*, not yet, but she was starting to come to terms with understanding.

Kelsey blinked. "Dream on, girl. But, if *someone of considerably higher level* were to stab me, no. This body might die, but I can just make another one."

"It doesn't matter," Suliel declared. "I still want justice for my father."

"You can't have it," Kelsey told her, flatly. "I'm not a subject of your king, or of any other state. I'm not human, and humans that go up against dungeons get what they deserve."

"You may not be human, but you *are* mortal. You're not a god, to lord it over the rest of us."

"Yes, *about* that," Kelsey said, eyes narrowing. "I hear that I've you to thank for a wizard being a part of the latest expedition."

"That's—" Suliel gulped, remembering what the Guild Master had said about wizards and dungeons. "That wasn't about killing you! And if it *had* been, it would have been nothing more than you deserved!"

"So this is how it's going to be from now on? Your barony, at war with me?"

"Well . . ." Suliel hesitated. She glanced back at the exit, remembering that it was sealed. She was entirely dependent on Kelsey's goodwill to leave. Not to mention that her barony *couldn't* go to war against the dungeon. They needed the steel and currency that came out of it . . . out of her. If they *were* able to kill her, they'd be just another fishing village.

"We can't do that," she admitted.

"We need each other," Kelsey pressed, leaning forward.

"What . . . do you need us for?"

"I need—I want your town to protect me from the rest of the world," Kelsey explained. "I give you the tools you need to be strong, and then you can defend me without the need for me to spend mana."

"That's why . . . the guns? You *made* them?"

"Of course—and they're just a taste. If we work together, Kirido will grow, and prosper. We just need to let bygones be bygones, and put them behind us."

"My father is not a bygone!" Suliel said bitterly. "You need to take responsibility!"

"And do *you* take responsibility for every adventurer that's come looking for my core in the last fifty years?" Kelsey countered. "Not every one of them has been trying to kill me, but enough have."

"The guild says that you want adventurers to delve you," Suliel replied. "That's why you give out rewards."

"Well, it is a bit of a catch-22," Kelsey admitted. "I need adventurers to delve so that I can get stronger to defend myself against . . . delving adventurers."

"Catch-22?"

"That's when you're caught by the nature of a situation," Kelsey explained. "You *need* to do something, but doing that something undermines the benefit you'd get from doing it. So maybe you *shouldn't* do it, but . . ."

"You need to," Suliel finished, recognizing the connection to Kelsey's adventurer problem. "So the solution is . . . us?"

"I can provide the goods you need, if you keep your delves shallow, and keep anyone else from intruding," Kelsey confirmed. "It'd be nice if you sent some criminals down occasionally to get executed, but that's an extra."

Suliel wanted to protest the thought of feeding a dungeon lives, but she *had* authorized the expedition to take two prisoners with them. Distasteful as it was, she would not be short of morsels to send.

"One more thing," Kelsey added. "If we do start working together, it will mean that a dungeon, at least partially, is acknowledging your authority. That's the sort of thing that can give a Noble class some experience, am I right?"

She was right. Suliel could feel her class squirm at the thought of it, a distinctly new and not entirely pleasant experience. It must have shown, because Kelsey smiled a wide grin.

"Yeah, you like that idea, don't you?"

"Did you offer my father this deal?" Suliel asked, not dignifying the question with an answer.

"I was gonna," Kelsey replied, "My approach was a little more cautious, though, which may have been a mistake. Just offering the guns without explaining where they came from made him greedy for more and . . . well, I already told you."

"Why . . ." Suliel took a deep breath. "Why did you take his head?"

"Ah, that . . ." Kelsey managed to look embarrassed. "You see, I needed to conceal the fact that he'd been killed by a gun. That's moot now so . . . you can have it back, if you want?"

"I . . . don't know," Suliel stammered. Her father had already gone through his funeral rites *without* a head, so would that mean she'd have to go through them again? "I'll . . . have to talk with the priests?"

"Sure, sure," Kelsey said. "It's being . . . preserved, let's say, so there's no rush. Take as long as you like, just tell me when you've made a decision."

They sat in silence for a little while longer. Eventually, Kelsey spoke again.

"So, if you're willing to work with me, you can consider the guns you have as . . . reparations?"

Suliel gave a snort. "You really didn't care about the gold at all, did you?"

"Well, no one wants to work for free. But . . ." Kelsey held one hand above the other and made a waterfall of gold coins run from one hand to the other. "I'm not exactly strapped for cash."

"I'm not sure about your proposal," Suliel admitted. "Do I have to agree before I can leave?"

"No, there's no point doing this under duress," Kelsey said. Suliel glared at her—what was this if *not* duress—but Kelsey continued on. "We actually have a lot more to talk about, though."

"What else—wait, Anton!" She remembered the stab of betrayal when she learned he'd been involved with her father's death. "How is he involved in all this?"

"Anton owed me his life. His repayment was to bond himself to me."

"He's bonded to you? Isn't he going to marry Aris?" Suliel felt a stab of envy as she said that. She tried to hide it, but from the look on Kelsey's face, the creature saw right through her.

"Not like that, or at least not right now. It's complicated. But *you* must have a marriage coming up, how's that going?"

Surprised at the sudden change of subject, Suliel reached for a non-answer. "As you said, it's complicated. I have some prospects, but nothing has been decided yet."

"Hmm, I heard that Liem, that mage, was one of the prospects."

"Where did you hear that?" Suliel asked, perturbed. Her mother had mentioned him, but he wasn't a serious prospect.

"Oh, it was when I was sneaking around the castle, watching him use mind magic on your mother."

"What!" Suliel exclaimed, "That's not true! You're just trying to distract me from asking about Anton!"

"I do lie whenever it's convenient," Kelsey admitted. "But I'm not lying now."

Suliel frowned. "Liem *is* treating Mother," she said. "But it's to ease her grief, not putting thoughts in her head like you're suggesting."

"Yeah, he must not have very strong mind magic, if all he can do is destroy," Kelsey said. "But destroy mind covers a lot of options. He can destroy her grief, sure, until it comes back again. He can destroy her suspicions, preventing her from properly analyzing his suggestion. And he can destroy the memory of him giving it to her, making her think it's her own idea."

Suliel shook her head. "I know you don't like him, but you can't think throwing wild accusations out there is going to turn me against him."

"Maybe not," Kelsey shrugged. "But at least you won't be surprised when it happens. I figure he joined the expedition to make himself look all heroic . . . too bad there's nobody here for him to find."

"Just you," Suliel replied. "The one behind it all *was* hiding in the dungeon, we had that right at least."

"Congratulations," Kelsey said wryly. "Now, I'm betting that Liem has—or can get—the backing of the Rose Circle. You know about that?"

"How do *you* know about that?" Suliel demanded.

"Your dad had a lot of correspondence in his desk," Kelsey told her. "So I know that Liem isn't exactly *in* the conspiracy, but he knows about it. Your dad was looking to get you a husband from within the Circle, but Liem might be the next best thing."

"The Circle doesn't get a say in who I marry," Suliel said. In her mind, though, she was thinking about Uncle Ria. If he arranged a match, would her mother say no? Could Suliel?

"They all want you married to control you," Kelsey murmured. "You're still a Scion . . . not the real Baron. Someone else can come in and take that role."

Suliel snorted. "You want to control me," she pointed out angrily, "Don't pretend otherwise."

Kelsey spread her hands wide, placatingly. "Only within strictly defined and agreed parameters," she said. "But isn't it true that if you want to defy your mother's choice, you'll need a candidate of your own?"

"That might make things easier . . . but you're going to suggest Anton, and that's clearly nonsense. Aside from him being pledged to Aris Lucina, he's apparently *bonded* to . . . you."

She cast Kelsey a doubtful look. "Or are you saying that your bond can make him forget about her, and marry me? That's . . . not something I want."

"Hesitated there a bit, didn't you?" Kelsey grinned. "No, sadly, I don't have that kind of control over him. But he *does* listen to reason, and more importantly, he doesn't have to forget about Aris. Having multiple wives *is* a thing right?"

"Amongst the nobility, perhaps," Suliel said slowly. "But even then, it's quite rare—and Anton is not a noble."

"But if he marries you, he will be, won't he?"

"That's—" Suliel stopped, appalled. "Technically, I suppose? But to use the ennoblement of marriage to marry twice would be scandalous."

"I don't give a damn about the scandal, and neither should you," Kelsey said with a wide smile. "Once we've got *power*, people can talk all they want. The gossipmongers, your family, the Rose Circle. . . They'll all fall in line."

CHAPTER THIRTY-NINE

Eyes of a Stranger

MEL

When they got to floor eight, they took the hoods off the prisoners.

"What for!" one of them, Kusec, demanded in broken Trade. Their captor just smiled and gestured around them.

"You know you're in a dungeon, right?" he asked them. They shifted uneasily. They were not unfamiliar with the practice of feeding prisoners to dungeons. However, there was no need for the sacrifices to be brought in farther than the first level. Dead was dead; the dungeon gained no extra benefit from the deaths happening at a lower level. Did these savages believe otherwise?

"This floor doesn't have nice little rooms where we can keep you safe until the next room is cleared," the man continued. "This floor, we can be attacked from anywhere. You might need to run, so you'll need to see where you're going."

The two courls glared at the man. "Can fight!" Kusec said, rattling the shackles that bound his hands behind his back. He spoke more Trade than the other Elitran soldier.

Their captor laughed. "Yeah, I'm sure you could. Even wounded, you fight pretty good, eh?" he said.

Mel watched the exchange in fascination. She'd never guided a dungeon in courl territory, and while this wasn't the first courl she'd seen, they were still new and exotic. She flitted around the newly revealed pair, taking in their bestial faces from different angles.

Unable to see her, the two cat warriors were taking in the sight around them. One of them spat a bloody gob on the ground. Their captors had kept them alive, but they hadn't been healed.

"They've let this dungeon get out of hand," Kusec said to his friend. He spoke in Elitran, but Mel could still understand him. She didn't actually notice that he'd changed languages.

Mel didn't *understand* languages, exactly. As a mental construct, she only understood meaning, taking it directly from the minds of the people speaking. It allowed her to tell Kelsey what intruders were saying, but it hadn't been very useful in helping Kelsey learn the local language. There were many ways to say the same thing, she had been told, but Mel still didn't really believe that the sounds that people made conveyed *anything*. Why would they do it that way, when hers was so much more convenient?

"Spatial manipulation," the courl muttered, looking around at the faraway walls and lack of a ceiling. "We can't be more than ten levels down—they're going to be eaten by it."

"It's not spatial manipulation," Mel said loftily. She wasn't going to let the fact that he couldn't hear her get in the way of demonstrating her superiority. A lecture was definitely in order.

"This cavern is all real, hollowed-out space," she explained. "It *looks* like one big span, but it's actually supported by lots of arches. And those arches are supported by pillars disguised as trees!"

Kelsey watched on, not interfering. Her mental avatar was actually out of Mel's earshot, but that didn't keep her from being aware of what she was saying. Mel had given this lecture so many times that she mostly got it correct nowadays.

Mel continued on. "The irregular ceiling is concealed by the way the ceiling lights diffuse through the mist and the leaves." Kelsey had been so mad when she learned that she could have permanent rain clouds, but *not* permanent poison gas clouds. She'd cursed up a storm.

Ha! She'd cursed up a *storm* when she'd discovered *storm* clouds. Mel would have to remember that one.

The expedition had gotten itself together and started to move out. Mel got distracted from her lecture as those new to the floor started pointing out the sights. She always enjoyed hearing what others thought of Kelsey's work.

There wasn't much to actually see, but after the closed-in caverns and dark city above, it made for a nice change. This floor looked almost exactly like a forest just before it rained. The first floor to be lit with anything more than torches, it wasn't bright, but it could easily be mistaken for sunlight on a very cloudy day.

The cavern walls stretched out on either side of the entrance, but once you lost sight of them, there was nothing but forest. The safe way through was to follow the walls, but there were enough veterans of the dungeon here that they felt safe cutting straight through, saving some time.

"I wonder . . . are they not going to clear the whole forest?" Kelsey wondered aloud.

"Does that make a difference?" Mel asked.

"Well, if they leave some wolves up here, I could bring my avatar up while they're farther down, reposition some packs for a nice surprise on the way back,"

"That would be nice!" Mel said, clapping. "But isn't your avatar busy with *her*?"

Mel not mentioning Suliel's name wasn't because she hated Suliel in particular. She hated all humans equally; she just hadn't learned Suliel's name yet. Anton was special, of course, and Aris had been here long enough for her to make a good guess, but Suliel was still new.

"There will be plenty of time before they start heading back," Kelsey said. "I can make a bit of time in there somewhere."

It was at this point that the first wolf howl was heard, shockingly close. Undead wolves didn't howl as loud as living ones, but they were just as unnerving. Everyone jumped and then looked out at the forest while clutching their weapons. Mel laughed at the irony, because the howling meant that the wolf *wasn't* going to attack. It was telling other members of its pack that prey had been found, but that there were too many for one wolf to take care of.

Kusec took advantage of the moment of inattention to make a break for it, running back to the entrance. He didn't get far. One of the leaders broke off from the tightly packed group to go after the escapee. Pushing too hard, Kusec tripped on the rough ground and fell, hard.

"Nice try, raider," Rathuan said, dragging the courl to his feet. The prisoner glared at him.

"What for, us here?" he demanded, struggling against his chains. He was probably stronger than this man, but the iron shackles did their work well.

"Couple of possibilities," Rathuan admitted. He started dragging Kusec back to the group. "Could be you've got some compatriots down here."

"Com . . .patrots?" the courl asked.

"Other Elitrans. Down here," Rathuan said, speaking simply to be understood. Kusec's eyes narrowed.

"No," he said. He'd been asked about that before and still had the brands from the asking. He had to admit he didn't *know* his leader's plans, but having a force hide out in the local dungeon seemed insane. It was a *raid*, after all. Maybe these fools didn't know what that meant.

"Worth a try," Rathuan muttered. "If they *are* here, then you are hostage. Aye, you know that word. Otherwise, we trade you."

"Trade . . . with dungeon?"

"Nah, with a monster." Kusec's eyes widened and he started struggling again. Rathuan easily kept him restrained, laughing.

"Relax, raider! You're lucky. I heard that dying to a vampire's kiss is the best way to die."

"You talk dead often?" Kusec replied. They had returned to the group, and Rathuan threw him back into the grip of his handler.

"More than I'd like," he said. "When we get past the haunted house, you'll probably get a chance to hear it from the horse's mouth."

With that, he left him to go back to leading the way

"Hmm," Kelsey said. "I bet Anton would object if Suliel started trading her prisoners to me for favors."

"I'm not sure *I'd* like that," Mel answered, not liking being on the same side, even hypothetically, as Anton. "Getting your victims delivered all bound up— that's not proper dungeon behavior."

"We could make it interesting," Kelsey mused. "Let 'em loose on, say, this level with no weapons or armor."

"And watch the wolves chase them?" Mel asked, getting more interested in the idea. "I bet a Tier Three could kill a wolf with their bare hands. Not two at once, though."

"I knew you'd come around," Kelsey gloated. "Suliel might go for it . . . especially if she has some high-level prisoners. They're hard to hold, you know."

"But Anton wouldn't like it," Mel said, flatly. She didn't like how Kelsey was listening to a human now. It was probably because Kelsey wanted to have sex with him—ever since she'd gotten a physical body, she had been acting strangely. Bodies were trouble.

The expedition continued on. Around them, wolves slowly gathered, staying out of sight but giving the occasional howl to let them know they hadn't been forgotten. A smaller party would have been attacked by now, but the size of the force had kept the wolves at bay.

Instead, the wolves' numbers slowly grew as the expedition kept crossing different pack territories. It might have been wiser to seek out the elusive hunters while their numbers were still small, but no one wanted to leave the shelter of the group.

This situation couldn't last forever, though, and eventually there was a shout as the expedition saw its first wolf, barring the path ahead. The path was too narrow for the group, of course. They had been travelling four and five abreast, trampling through the bushes and bracken without any regard for the ecosystem. Spreading out in single file would have made them feel far too vulnerable.

It had taken a while, and a lot of cursing, for Kelsey to instill something like wolf pack tactics into the orders that governed the undead wolves, but she had succeeded. So the actual attack did not come from the front, but from the sides while everyone was looking forward. Lithe, low-slung figures dashed out of the concealment of the forest and struck at the adventurers with tooth and claw.

At first glance, they might have been mistaken for normal wolves. If their eyes were redder, if their skin hung more loosely over their rotted flesh, it wasn't something that would be noticed in the first blush of combat. But as they closed with the expedition, one major difference became apparent. The smell.

The unique aroma of rotten meat, which the party had gotten used to in the upper levels, had now returned. Unlike those zombies, the wolves were peak Tier Two monsters. They could dash in with unearthly speed, and their pelts could turn aside even Tier Two weapons if they weren't handled with enough skill.

By this point, though, half of the expedition was Tier Three. Not all of them were professional adventurers, but a soldier could strike down a wolf, if his arm was strong enough. And they had a mage as well.

Magister Liem Tikin made up for his previous performance here, sending precise spears of fire that struck charging wolves unerringly. The flames seemed to pierce right through the wolves' leathery skin and set fire to their very bones. The undead didn't feel pain, but they quickly collapsed into smoldering piles of ash.

The fight was soon over. No deaths, but there were some injuries that needed to be attended to. None of the wounds that the wolves left were clean, and they needed to be treated with clerical magic as quickly as possible. Healing potions only accelerated normal healing, and these wounds would just rot if left alone.

The expedition had come prepared though, so they moved on.

"You should have moved the spider nests," Mel told Kelsey. "They avoided them again."

"It means they're available for the return trip," Kelsey pointed out.

Rathuan, meanwhile, had moved up next to Inutan, the cleric of his party. "We're getting close to the mansion," he said. "Better start rolling out the blessings."

She nodded, and the expedition reorganized once more, forming a double line so that they could approach Inutan and another cleric for the blessing of their gods.

The two clerics chanted softly. They spoke a language Kelsey didn't speak, and that Mel didn't understand. The meaning of those words was not for her but for their gods.

Kelsey looked on, sourly. "You're not allowed to complain about the gods," Mel told her. "They can choose to protect the humans if they want to."

"It's just irritating. Ghosts are great, but one little blessing, and they can barely even hurt mortals. No possession, no heart grasping . . . it makes me wonder why I even bother."

"Not every party can take a cleric down with them," Mel said, with some sympathy. "The blessings don't last long."

"Long enough," Kelsey groused. "I guess they're ready for the mansion now. I just hope that Barry gives them some trouble."

CHAPTER FORTY

You Sold the Cottage

SULIEL

Father, forgive me for even considering this.

Suliel walked behind Kelsey, through stone corridors far underground. She'd been told tales of the dungeon as a child. The putrid flesh of the zombies, the poisons, the unending clatter of skeleton attackers. This was . . . not like that.

She *had* gone through the City of the Dead, as her parents had called it. It had already been cleared, though, by the expedition that she had funded. It was occupied now only by a few adventurers that Kelsey helped her avoid.

"Wouldn't do for you to get caught by your own expedition!" she joked. "I'd have to kill them to make sure word didn't get out," she added, still with the same bright smile. Suliel shuddered now, thinking about it. She seemed so human, this *thing* that Suliel was trapped underground with. That Suliel was considering yoking herself to.

Now, though, they had left the known dungeon behind. There were still skeletons about, but they were unarmed, busy with various tasks that Suliel didn't understand, even when Kelsey explained them.

"This is something that your builders are going to love," Kelsey said, taking Suliel into yet another room. "Liquid stone."

Suliel frowned, looking at the table and the demonstration that had been prepared there. "I'm not sure why anyone would want such a thing . . . and the only liquid I see on this table is water."

"Well, it doesn't start liquid. It starts as a powder," Kelsey explained, holding up a handful of a pale grey powder. "You mix it with water, and then it becomes a liquid."

The skeleton behind the table demonstrated the process for them. Silently, with a smile.

"And why would I want *liquid* stone?" Suliel asked, as she watch the skeleton mix and pour the slurry into a flat, square tray.

"As a liquid, you can put it into any shape you like," Kelsey told her enthusiastically. "And then it *dries* into proper stone."

The skeleton handed Suliel some smooth grey rock, shaped into half of a sphere. She hefted it. It felt like rock in her hand and seemed as hard. She rapped it on the table, timidly. It felt solid.

"Depending on your exact needs, you can mix it with sand or gravel, making it stronger," Kelsey said. The skeleton held up slightly different rocks, with a coarser grain.

"Do you use this?" Suliel said. She didn't want to admit it, but she *could* see the use of this. Kirido's walls *were* being rebuilt—with stone supplied from this dungeon, she now knew—but with this, they could be built faster, stronger, and higher.

"Nah, all my stone is liquid—when I want it to be," Kelsey demurred.

"Then why do you have it?"

Kelsey grinned. "I've been thinking about things that you guys might need—or want. The great thing about this is that you don't need me to supply it. You get a limestone quarry going, and you should be able to make an unlimited supply."

"But *how* did you know about it?" Suliel pressed.

"I know a lot of things," Kelsey answered evasively. "With this—like a lot of things—I had an idea for it and then spent some time working out the details. Or had these guys work out the details." She pointed at the skeletons.

Suliel glared at Kelsey, but what had worked on her parents was utterly ineffective on the creature in front of her. Kelsey was clearly intent on keeping at least some of her secrets.

"Now," Kelsey said, putting an arm around Suliel. "Let's talk trade goods. You need to increase your population, and the best way to do that is to generate wealth."

She kept talking as she led Suliel away, but Suliel was barely paying attention. Kelsey wasn't a large woman, only a little taller than Suliel, but her strength completely overwhelmed Suliel. She could no more move Kelsey's arm than she could walk through a wall.

Friendly as it seemed, it was just another reminder of how helpless Suliel was. She would have cried and spat with frustration if it weren't for two things.

First, the deal—the deals—being offered were good ones. Kelsey wasn't much interested in trade, as Suliel understood it. Aside from prisoners, Kirido didn't have anything that Kelsey wanted, in large quantities at least. But she *was* prepared to provide significant raw materials and manufactured goods for *free*, if it would bolster Kirido's defenses.

Finding the dungeon fifty years ago had jumped Kirido from fishing village to barony. Gaining access to the resources Kelsey had offered would push them to greater heights. County or duchy status—or even higher. Reading between the lines, Kelsey expected them to defend her against incursions, even if they came from the King.

The thought of setting her town against the Kingdom sent a shiver down her spine, comprised equally of excitement and dread. Naturally, she'd do whatever she could to prevent that confrontation, but sooner or later, Kingdom officials would show up looking for the source of her newfound wealth. And if they didn't, the Rose Circle would surely come calling.

It was terrifying . . . but that was the sort of thing that gave you a good class. You couldn't normally tell what your class was going to be, but Suliel had been yearning for her second Tier for a long time. She had been reaching out to it in her dreams, trying to get the feel of it. And now it was changing.

How powerful did a class have to be for you to *feel* it? Suliel didn't know, but she knew that making this decision would change her life. Even rejecting the offer might make a new class available. Not that she could afford to reject it.

Forgive me, Father.

Kelsey kept on, showing her wonders. Perhaps "wonders" was the wrong word; they were all profoundly *ordinary* products. No mithril swords or bejeweled rings here, only machines for weaving cloth, liquid stone, and pottery.

Pottery, for Denem's sake. Kelsey had made a clay finer than anything Suliel had ever seen and had shown Suliel a molding process to churn out any number of plates and cups quickly. It burned Suliel's mind to be considering such an ordinary product under such extraordinary circumstances, but she had to admit that they would sell.

"Now this is something you're sure to like," Kelsey said. She opened the door and gestured for Suliel to walk through. Numb from all of Kelsey's sales effort, Suliel stepped through without a word and gaped in shock.

For a long moment, Suliel stood frozen, taking in the sight of Anton's naked body as he lay atop . . .

There was a shriek from the girl as she noticed the pair of them. Thought caught up with intention, and Suliel whirled around, her face hot. Kelsey had already closed the door behind her and was grinning at her discomfiture.

"Baroness! I'm sorry, we weren't expecting—" the girl, Aris, exclaimed. Rustling noises suggested they were getting dressed, or getting under the sheets. Suliel swallowed, mortified. She glared at Kelsey, willing her to step out of the way and allow Suliel to leave the room. Kelsey just grinned.

"Gods save me, Kelsey, from your idea of a joke," Anton said from behind her, and a little thrill went through Suliel at the sound. He was *naked* right now.

"How was I to know what you were doing? I was giving you your privacy,"

Kelsey said innocently. Then she spoiled the effect by giggling. "It was pretty funny, though."

There were more noises, and then Anton said, "You can turn around now, Baroness."

Suliel cautiously turned around. Anton and Aris were now dressed, sitting on the end of the bed, facing her. Aris was looking down, giving the impression that her face was just as flushed as Suliel's. Suliel was having trouble looking at Anton's face, but looking lower was also . . . problematic. She glanced to the side and took refuge in etiquette.

"As I'm not properly confirmed in my position, the title of Baroness is unneeded. I should be properly addressed simply as "my lady" . . . but since our parents were friends, I hope you'll be comfortable with a less formal appellation."

"Uh, what?" Anton asked with a confused look on his face.

You idiot, Suliel! He's not a noble of the court!

Castigating herself, Suliel tried again. "I mean, you can just call me Suliel. If you like."

"Oh, uh, sure," he said. He glanced at the woman by his side.

"Her—I mean, you too, Aris," Suliel said. "Please just call me Suliel."

Aris looked up nervously. "Are you sure that's all right?"

"Yes. "My lady" might be more appropriate if you're in the castle, but down here—we can assume that we have privacy."

"From *most* people," Anton growled. "B—Suliel, I'm sorry about what just happened. If you're not aware, Kelsey knew full well what she was doing and what you'd see when she led you in here."

"I realize that, yes," Suliel said, and gave the unrepentant Kelsey another glare. "Despite . . . everything, I'm seriously considering her offer of entering into a conspiracy with her. And she has intimated that you might be a part of that."

"Uh, I'm not sure what you mean," Anton said.

"What she means is that we've got a lot of things to discuss," Kelsey said. "And we shouldn't do so just standing around awkwardly. So let's all squeeze into the bed!"

Anton just glared. Suliel's face was still burning, so she couldn't become more flushed.

"No," Aris said. "We're not doing that."

"Fine," Kelsey said. "There's a sitting room nearby, I'll serve us some tea."

Suliel was officially beyond being surprised at what was down here, but a sitting room with couches, a small table and a skeleton maid came close to breaking her equanimity. She took her cup with bemusement, a part of her noticing that it was made of the same ceramic that she'd been offered. It had been elaborately decorated, with . . . middling skill, she supposed. Hardly suitable for court, but in the homes of commoners it would—she shook herself, focusing on the matter at hand.

"So, your parents were friends?" Kelsey asked, starting the conversation. "But you don't seem to know each other well."

"Suliel was always kept apart from the other children," Anton explained. "I saw her parents more often than I saw her."

"As a noble, I had a lot of lessons," Suliel said sadly, "There wasn't much time for play, and when there was, it had to be with visiting cousins, or other nobles."

"I'm kind of surprised you know who I am," Anton said.

"At festivals . . . I had to stay with my parents, but I could look out over the crowd. Once you got your second tier, people started to talk about you."

"About me?" Anton asked, startled.

"Yes, I—" Suliel stopped, unable to continue further.

If you don't say anything, you'll never get the chance to!

"Um," she started. "I—part of getting confirmed as Baroness . . . my marriage . . . it has to be considered."

What are you saying, you fool?

"Um . . ." Anton said.

"What I mean is," Suliel said, trying to calm down, "is that I'm under considerable pressure to marry before I take my second tier. That way my husband can be the Baron, leaving me to take the Lady class."

"Is that what you want?" Anton asked.

"No, I want—" *To marry you,* she didn't say. "I want to marry—someone— of my choice, after I take my tier and my title."

"But it's not as simple as that, I'm guessing," Anton said.

"My mother . . . until I get my title, she is the one that decides," Suliel admitted. "I'm not sure of what arrangements she's made, but she'll want a match that's best for the family." She glanced at Kelsey. "She'd not been herself since Father d—was killed."

She took another deep breath. With some effort, she looked directly at Anton.

"Kelsey said . . . that you might be interested in—a second—marriage, with me."

Anton looked back at her, his face unreadable.

CHAPTER FORTY-ONE

Freaky Tales

MEL

"Well that was a disappointment," Kelsey said. "The ghosts didn't even slow them down."

"You knew that the mage was pretty strong at Destroy Mind," Mel pointed out. "That's all that ghosts *are*, really."

"Yeah, but still . . ." Kelsey watched as the expedition's vanguard ransacked her boss room—the lich's study. "I can't say I'm a fan of his *Destroy Magic* skill, either."

Barry the Lich had been a caster monster. Not a true mage like Tikin, he had a few spells to cast against incoming adventurers. *Frost Hold*, *Lightning Bolt*, *Missile Shield*, and *Mana Bolt*. Those were normally enough to give adventurers pause, but Tikin had been able to disrupt the spells as quickly as Barry could cast them.

That had occupied the mage, and if he'd been alone, that might have been a problem. But without a barrage of magical destruction to hold the adventurers back, they could walk right up to the lich and smash it with melee damage.

"He was level twenty-one!" Kelsey complained. "And they beat him to death with sticks."

Mel shrugged, refraining from pointing out that it had actually been swords that were used—and that the adventurers were all that level or higher. Kelsey never took helpful details like that well when she was ranting.

"I think I'm done," one of the adventurers spoke up. "Anyone else find anything?"

There was a chorus of nos from the other members of the party. Given the cramped nature of the mansion, they had left the other expedition members outside.

The first adventurer swore. "Gods damn it, that's another level with no treasure." It was Risor who spoke, the occult rogue.

"Collect the bones and skin," Rathuan said evenly. "They're worth something at the guild."

Kelsey's eyes narrowed. She would have preferred if the invaders came back with nothing, and her recently acquired price list put lich's bones at a gold piece per pound. As a Tier Three magical monster, its ground up bones were apparently of great use as an alchemical reagent.

The adventurers grumbled as they collected the corpse, and Risor was sent back to get the rest of the expedition.

The eighth and tenth floors of the dungeon were two vast caverns at roughly the same level. The point where they would have touched was blocked off by the Haunted Mansion, so once the boss was defeated, you just had to open the next door to proceed.

The next two doors, actually. The first set of doors shared the same theme as the rest of the mansion, made of a dark, mana-reinforced wood. Right behind them were a pair of stone doors, much more suitable for mana containment.

Rathuan paused before opening the final doors. "What does everyone have to keep in mind?" he asked the adventurers following.

"The revenants aren't actually our lost ones," one of the younger delvers muttered, embarrassed.

"Everyone got that?" Rathuan asked. "Because, I swear, every time I bring a newbie down here, they get the idea that they can save someone, or make love to someone, and it never. Goes. Well."

"I miss the old days, before they figured it out," Kelsey said, ignoring the muttered agreements being forced out by Rathuan.

"It was fun, wasn't it?" Mel agreed. "I just wish I could have seen what happened to the ones they captured and brought back to town with them!"

The two of them smiled at the memory, as Rathuan carefully opened the door. The doors opened into a small cave, carefully concealed within a fold of the cavern wall. Many an adventurer had been caught out on the way back, unable to find the right cave, and gotten caught in one of the *trapped* ones.

"Is it just me, or is it brighter out there?" Risor asked. Rathuan nodded in reply.

"Hard to say, but I think so. Cave seems empty—everyone move out carefully."

The expedition did so, Risor taking the lead, checking for traps. It was rare for the entry cave to be trapped, but on this floor you couldn't take anything for granted.

"It's clear," Risor said, having made it to the cave entrance. He peeked out, swore, and then took a longer look. "You gotta see this, boss."

Rathuan moved forward cautiously. Haste got you killed here, so even if Risor had proclaimed it safe, it was still worth taking your time. He looked out over the tenth level.

The tenth level was a little smaller than the eighth, but its roof was a single span, not supported by hidden columns. The higher mana density allowed for better structural reinforcement. As it always had, the level was a creditable imitation of the rolling hills found nearby. Small, woody copses dotted the landscape, but for the most part, it was open terrain. The ceiling was painted blue, and an imitation sun, bright and hot, shone down from the middle of it.

Risor had been right. It was brighter, and Rathuan could see the reason for it right in front of him. The entry cave was elevated and provided a good view across the well-lit cavern. As always, he could see the village that formed the final challenge for the level. The hills separated the floor into areas that held their own challenges and treasure, but if you wanted, you could proceed straight across to the end village.

What was new was the fields. Rathuan couldn't identify the crops from here, but they were definitely sown fields.

"Why?" Inutan said from beside him. "Revenants don't need to eat."

"A trap?" Risor suggested. "Either hiding in the fields, or the grain itself is poison."

"We could—and will—check for that before we eat any." Inutan said. "But that . . . seems too easy. Perhaps the revenants want to trade?"

"No surprise that a cleric of the god of trade would think that," Buraia put in. The female Archer was scanning the hills ahead of them for targets.

Inutan flushed. "Maybe, but what else could it be? When you grow food that you don't need, you have to be thinking of trading it to someone who does, right?"

There was a pause as the group considered the situation in the town above their heads. Kirido had been ransacked by raiders, who had made off with a lot of their food supply. They weren't starving by any means, but things *were* tight.

"Mark!" Buraia said suddenly, stiffening and half-drawing her bow. "Someone's coming out of the trees."

"Looks like we get to find out if your theory is correct . . ." Rathuan said, taking in the approaching figure. He turned back to the others. "All right, settle yourselves in. We won't be moving from the cave until we have a parlay."

Magister Tikin raised an eyebrow. "How do you know they wish to talk? I see no raised flag."

Rathuan grimaced. "It's revenants—they always want to talk, the better to creep you out."

Mel giggled. "At least that part still works,"

Rathuan continued, unaware that Mel was talking over him. "Normally, I'd say just cut them down before they start talking, but they might have some answers for us."

By the time the revenant arrived, the expedition had sorted themselves out, with just Inutan, Rathuan, and Tikin waiting outside the cave. As the god of trade, Denem's blessings weren't *terribly* effective against the undead, but they were better than a sword in the hand of a Tier Two.

The revenant stopped well out melee range. He was being covered by Buraia from the cave, and he was in range of Tikin's spells. If he was aware of this, he didn't show it.

"Wrath," he greeted Rathuan.

"Fear," Rathuan returned. "You should know Inutan, and this is Magister Tikin. He's ready to blow your head off with a fireball if you look at him funny."

"Good to know," the revenant said easily.

"You know this creature?" Tikin said with a disdainful tone.

"Faerdan Alons," Rathuan said, without any emotion. "The original used to be my mentor, five years back."

"And now there's me," Faerdan agreed. "Just like the original, with only a few improvements. Fear's a bit of a stretch from Faer, but I needed something to match Wrath here."

"What do you want, Fear?" Rathuan asked bitterly. "It had better not be to rehash old times."

"Do you think this is going to work?" Mel asked Kelsey.

"I dunno." Kelsey was watching the exchange intensely. "I never know with these damn things. For soulless wretches they're so damned willful!"

"Why not let Cheryl make the deal then?"

"She's just as bad when there's a pulse in the room," Kelsey said glumly. "Plus, even when she obeys me, she gets so damn whiny when I don't let her have her snacks."

Unaware of their watchers, the negotiators continued.

"No, we are not going to join you for a party. It's been ten years since that trick worked."

"Now, don't be like that. You came to trade, didn't you? Better to do that in comfort than out of a cave."

Rathuan narrowed his eyes. "What makes you say that?"

Fear grinned. "Have you become a monk, to say comfort *isn't* better? Or did you mean the trade thing?"

"Answer the question, damn it. How did you know we were here to trade?"

"The Great Dungeon . . ." Fear raised his eyes to the ceiling and clasped his hands together as if to pray. " . . . sometimes vouchsafes us with information about incoming invaders. I know you've got questions about *other* intruders, and that you've brought two delicious treats as a bribe."

There was a protest and the sounds of a scuffle from the back of the cave, but Rathuan ignored it. "They're for the Vampire Queen, not you."

"But *I* can answer your questions just as well . . . and you won't have to go through the rat maze."

"What do *you* want them for?"

"We do love the taste of warm mortal flesh," the revenant said, grinning. Something changed, like an illusion fading away, and his teeth were now twice as long and pointed. "But it is the Great Dungeon that desires your prisoners. We will only be able to keep them for a while."

He looked back at the cave. "I am empowered to say . . . that the Great Dungeon's desires for you do not include your deaths, and that should you cooperate you will not be killed . . . by the dungeon."

"What about by you?" Rathuan asked. The revenant grinned still wider.

"We are under orders not to kill them," he admitted. "But, we have other orders. We can defend ourselves if attacked, so who knows what might happen?"

"Who knows," Rathuan agreed. He wouldn't have put a copper bit on the prisoners living another day. But he'd come down here *expecting* to sell them to their deaths. "But who knows if I can trust you to answer my questions?"

"These are the dungeon's answers, not mine. This is the deal that I propose. Ask your questions, and I will answer them, if I can. If you are satisfied with the answers, you can leave the prisoners behind. If you are not, you can leave with them, or push on through to ask your questions of the Vampire Queen."

"Wait," Tikin interjected. "I thought we were going to *physically* inspect all the levels."

Rathuan grunted. "That was never a real consideration. Our contract is to go as deep as we can—and no one has ever come back from the Silent Sea. If the infiltrators made it past the Vampire Queen, then they're Tier Four for sure."

"*Tch.* My magic can get us past the vampire, I'm sure."

"And then? We used up most of our water-breathing potions, remember? How's your magic with water?"

"Not . . . so good," Tikin admitted. "I can't destroy an entire ocean, or create air for us."

"So this deal." Rathuan paused, considering the angles. "If we don't like the answers we get, we can always butcher our way through these guys, and the rats—"

"Good luck doing *that*," the revenant interrupted.

"*—like we planned* originally." Rathuan glared at the monster. "Or if we *do* like his answers, we can leave the prisoners with him, job done."

"The logic is sound," Tikin allowed. "Something about it rubs me the wrong way, though."

"That's just your conscience," Rathuan told him. "It goes away eventually."
He turned back to the revenant, still grinning its wide, toothy grin.
"You have a deal."
"An excellent choice, old friend. Ask your questions."

CHAPTER FORTY-TWO

I Wanna Stand Over There

SULIEL

W hy would you want that?" Anton asked in confusion.

Aris slapped him on the back of his head. He barely felt it, even with her increased strength, but he flinched from the glare she gave him when he looked at her.

"Don't you say that! You're the most eligible boy in Kirido! You got your second tier faster than anyone, and you're handsome and brave and . . ."

Aris stopped herself, belatedly realizing what she was saying. There was an awkward pause as Anton tried to deal with what she said. Or there would have been if Kelsey hadn't filled it.

"Woo hoo! Welcome to team poly, Aris!"

Aris looked down, embarrassed. "I'm not—I don't know what that's supposed to mean. I just . . . don't want anyone saying bad things about my *fiancé*."

This last was delivered with a challenging glare at Suliel, as Aris remembered where she stood in this discussion. Suliel felt as if she was going to burn up. After her admission, her cheeks were so hot that she thought she might self-combust or melt through the stone floor. Either one would be preferable to continuing this conversation, but she persevered.

"But I'm a commoner!" Anton protested. "She can't marry me!"

"That's just a custom, not a law," Suliel said. "My mother would not . . . approve, but nobles sometimes go against custom and marry commoners. That elevates—you would *be* elevated—to nobility."

She looked away again. She didn't want to say this, admit to her girlish crush, but she needed to make her case. Her suspicion—no, certainty—that Kelsey had locked the doors, took away her only other option.

"As to—" she started. "We may not have interacted much, but I've always been aware of you. There's not much for me to do at festivals, so I've often . . . daydreamed . . . about what it would be like to marry someone of my choice."

Aris scowled. "You and a lot of the town girls," she said. "I saw them off, but . . ."

She hesitated and started to look doubtful. "Nobility, though . . ." She looked back at Anton.

He looked straight back. "I don't care about a title," he said.

"Naturally, you would remain the primary wife," Suliel said desperately. Was she really saying this? Wouldn't it be humiliating to her to be not only married to a commoner but the *secondary* wife at that? Her mother would have a fit if she degraded the family that thoroughly.

I'm getting a title of rulership, she told herself. *A rare one, maybe even unique! That makes up for any humiliation I might subject the family to, and . . . I'd rather be a second wife to Anton than be sold off to whoever made the best pitch to Mother.*

"*Primary* wife," Aris said sounding out the word. "What does that mean?"

"Nobles can have more than one wife," Suliel explained. "It's not commonly done, but if Anton marries me and becomes nobility, he can marry you as well."

"But he'd have to marry you first," Aris said slowly.

"That's how it works," Suliel agreed. "Even so, which wife ranks highest isn't based on the order of marriage, so . . . I do recognize that you'll always be first in his affections. Nonetheless, I am told that I am quite attractive—"

"You're gorgeous," Aris snorted, rolling her eyes. "The most beautiful girl in Kirido, and a hundred miles around it, to hear men talk."

"Not as beautiful as you," Anton said loyally. "It's true!" he replied to her skeptical look. "I mean, she is—you are—" he corrected himself, looking at Suliel. "You *are* very beautiful, but Aris is more lovely."

"I guess I do have bigger breasts," Aris muttered.

"That's only the smallest part about why I love you," Anton said. "As beautiful as Suliel is, there's no choice to be made."

He called me beautiful! Suliel thought, rooted to her chair. She wanted to say something, but she couldn't get past the thought that *Anton* had called her beautiful. Instead, it was Kelsey that spoke up.

"But! You don't have to make a choice. You can have both of them. Aris *and* Suliel, and a noble title to boot."

Anton gave her a glare. "I notice you don't include *yourself* in that enticing offer."

Kelsey chuckled. "You're stuck with me no matter what you choose," she pointed out. "I get that you're still upset about my little joke, but when you're snuggled up in bed with two naked beauties, you'll be thinking that just maybe, ol' Kelsey had your best interests at heart after all."

Anton didn't say anything to that, and neither did the two girls. His skin was too dark for Suliel to see him blush and she thanked the gods that her own skin was even darker. Kelsey looked around in the sudden silence.

"Wow. Talk about horny teenagers," she said. "All of you reacted to that? Even Aris? You were just in bed with him fifteen minutes ago."

Nobody said anything to her words, although Suliel did wish even harder for the rock beneath her to melt and let her escape.

"Well," Kelsey finally said, once the silence had been extended for an excruciating length of time. "I promised Suliel a chance to think about *my* offer, so unless the three of you want to jump into bed, I think it's time for her to go."

"That . . . wouldn't be appropriate," Suliel managed to say. "Even if—until it's announced—we shouldn't."

Kelsey sighed. "Once again, good manners get in the way of a good time. Oh well."

She rose from her chair and stretched. The door to the room opened on its own.

"Come on, Suliel, I'll get you back home, safe and sound. You two can keep yourselves out of trouble for a few minutes at least?"

Safely back in her father's study, Suliel sank back into his old chair, unable to stand. She was trembling from the exhausting climb up the concealed ladder. Going up had been *much harder* than going down. Trying to process all the revelations that she had been subjected to made her mind tremble just as much as her limbs. She glared at the architect of all of it.

"Why did you come up with me?" Suliel asked.

"Not *just* to make sure you made it all the way up the ladder," Kelsey said. "Wouldn't want all that investment to go to waste from one slipped foot."

She pointed at the door. "I came in here with you, remember? If I go mysteriously missing, people are going to suspect something."

"Oh. Right." Checking that the secret door was concealed again—Kelsey had done that—she indicated the door with her head. Chuckling, and managing a fair approximation of a curtsy, Kelsey went over and opened the door.

"Can you escort Mistress Kelsey to the gate," Suliel told the guards outside. "Put her on the approved list."

They both saluted, and one of them indicated to Kelsey that she should follow him.

To the other one, Suliel asked, "Has anything happened while I've been . . . busy?"

"No, my lady," he replied.

"Good. Close the door but knock if there are messages, or if someone wants to see me."

"Yes, my lady," he said, bowing as he pulled the door closed.

Suliel sighed and turned her attention to the desk in front of her. Kelsey had mentioned that there were things here that Suliel should learn. She'd been putting off filling her father's full role, concentrating on local events, but it was about time she learned what was going on in the greater world. She sighed again and went to work.

It was about three hours before a knock came from the door.

"Yes?"

"My lady, there's a ship been sighted, bearing the colors of House Kinn. It should dock shortly before sunset."

Uncle Ria Suliel thought. For the first time, thinking of her uncle's imminent arrival didn't bring unqualified joy. She *would* be glad to see him, but now she was—she had responsibilities. Instead of presents, Uncle Ria would be bringing opportunities, secrets, and dangers.

"If Mother hasn't arranged anything yet, make sure the kitchens are aware that we'll have a noble guest—make that two noble guests—for a feast." She was almost certain that Uncle Riadan would have brought someone. Maybe a marriage prospect, maybe someone else from the Circle.

I need to change, she thought. She couldn't greet guests wearing this, even if it hadn't been dusty from her subterranean adventures.

"Uh, my lady?" The guard said. "You sent Dakar away, so I can't leave my post."

She stared at him for a second. "Ah, yes, of course, Milem. Come with me then, we'll find some more guards."

She had him lead her to where Captain Oldaw was being held. At her gesture, the guards there unlocked the door.

"Captain Oldaw," she said formally. "Information has come to light that has cleared you of all suspicion. You are free to go, if that pleases you, or return to being a welcome guest."

The captain peered suspiciously out of the gloom of his cell. "Just like that? What information?"

"I'm afraid that must remain a secret for the time being," Suliel said. "But yes, just like that. You have my apologies, of course." She bowed deeply to the man.

"No . . ." Oldaw said slowly. "It looked bad, I must admit. You did what you had to. I hope you don't think I'll be leaving it there, though. I was framed, wasn't I?"

"I can't stop you from investigating further," Suliel admitted. Oldaw didn't have the right to investigate crimes or apply justice in her demesne, but she couldn't stop him from asking questions. "Lord Kinn is arriving shortly, so I hope you'll join us for dinner. There will . . . I expect circumstances will have changed after that."

"Lord Kinn . . ." Oldaw's eyes narrowed. Suliel wondered what that might mean. Oldaw reported to the King and was unlikely to be a member of the Rose Circle. Did he know that her uncle *was*?

"He's an old friend of the family," she said. "No doubt, he's here to offer condolences on the death of my father."

"But under the circumstances, other topics might be discussed."

"I'm sure it will be eventful," she agreed blandly.

Baron Riadan Kinn was as big as she remembered. He had hardly walked in the front gate before she was enveloped in a big bear hug.

"Little Su," he said. "You're more beautiful than ever."

"It's *Baroness Suliel*, now," she told him, looking up at his bushy beard. "I have to keep my dignity."

"Ho, ho, yes, your dignity, very important," he chortled, pretending to take her seriously. "But you'll always be Little Su to me."

He released her and got a more serious look on his face. "Tikin sent us word on the way—I was so sorry to hear about your father."

Her own face fell. "It's been hard," she admitted. "Father's death, right after the raid . . ."

"You seem to be doing well in that regard at least," he told her. "Coming through the town, it seemed to be recovering nicely. I was all ready to give you some advice, but it seems you have it well in hand."

"Most of that was Father, at least for the start of it," she said sadly. "I've mostly been making sure that his original orders were implemented properly."

"You'd be surprised how rare it is to find someone who doesn't break what's working," he told her. "You've done well."

He hesitated for a moment. "How is . . . your mother?" he asked.

Suliel looked away. "She's . . . better?" she said. "Tikin has been helping her, but she's still grieving. I think she'll be down for dinner; she said she would be."

"Good, good, I look forward to the chance to catch up. Hopefully, though, there will be room for one more at the table?"

"Of course, Uncle," Suliel said. A young man, richly dressed and better groomed than one would expect from having just come off a sea voyage, stepped forward.

"Let me introduce you," Uncle Riadan said. "This is Feldan Rahm, second son of Count Rahm. Feldan, this is Baroness Suliel Anat. Not my real niece, but you'll find I'm just as protective of her."

Feldan bowed. Like all Zamarran nobility, he had black skin, a shade or two darker than Suliel's own. He was clean-shaven and his short hair was oiled and bound up in tight curls. Young as he was, he looked older than Suliel.

Suliel checked *Nobility's Privilege*.

Feldan Rahm (Level 8)
Living Relatives: Brekin Rahm (father), Melva Rahm (mother), Forstan
    Rahm (brother) (5 more)
Citizenship: Zamarran
Primary Loyalty: Brekin Rahm

Nothing unexpected, Suliel thought. She wondered if the Rose Circle ever showed up on the conspirators' profiles, and looked at her uncle to check.

Riadan Kinn (Level ??)
Living Relatives: (blocked)
Citizenship: Zamarran
Primary Loyalty: (blocked)

He must have a trait to block it, she thought. Turning back to Feldan, she gave a small bow. As the hosting Baroness, it wouldn't do to curtsy to an untitled noble, no matter who his father was.

"Welcome to my home, Lord Feldan," she said.

"Thank you for allowing me," he replied. "I see that the rumors of your beauty were grossly inadequate at properly describing it."

Suliel smiled. Not because he'd told her she was beautiful, though she never did get tired of that. But because now she knew for sure why he was here.

"I hope you two will get along," Uncle Riadan said, with just a hint of smugness.

The first serious marriage candidate, Suliel thought. *I'd better hurry and level or I'll be married off by the end of the week.*

CHAPTER FORTY-THREE

Relax

MEL

Rathuan watched the monster, suspicion on his face. "What level are the other invaders hiding on?"

"There are no invaders—aside from your own group," Faerdan said placidly. "So the answer is: on no floor."

"That can't be right," Tikin interjected. "We know—"

He stopped short as Fear hissed at him, his lips drawn back to show all of his teeth.

"Nothing from you, grave robber," the revenant said. "We dealt with Wrath. Wrath will ask the questions."

"It's a good question, though," Rathuan said. "We came down here looking for infiltrators, and you're telling me that there are none?"

"Was that all you came for, I wonder?" Faerdan mused, still looking at Tikin. Then he turned back to Rathuan and cocked his head to the side.

"There were three Elitrans that arrived at the Great Dungeon after the last raid. They took foolish risks and were all slain. No other Elitrans remain."

"How do you know about the raid?" Risor asked uneasily. Faerdan looked at the man for a second and then turned back to Rathuan, who nodded.

"Answer the question."

The revenant shrugged. "I know of it because I was informed by the Great Dungeon. I do not know how the Great Dungeon came to know of it. The Great Dungeon knows many things, more than you can understand."

"What's with all the Great Dungeons?" Mel asked Kelsey.

Kelsey shrugged. "I told them not to use pronouns or give away my avatar's gender. I guess that's what they came up with. I don't hate it."

"Don't let it go to your head," Mel warned.

The conversation had actually paused while the invisible pair had been talking. Spooked by the answer, the humans had pulled back and briefly conferred amongst themselves. Mel was amused to see that they'd almost entirely dropped their guard.

"What happened to the cavalrymen that came down here?" Rathuan finally asked.

"They died," Faerdan said. "They didn't get this far, so I couldn't say how."

"There's no way," Rathuan objected. "The dungeon couldn't have killed all of them; some would have gotten away."

Fear hissed. "Do not judge what the Great Dungeon is capable of, based on what it has shown you in the past. A new age is beginning, and you'll find that the Great Dungeon is less tolerant of . . . pests than it once was."

"He's broken character," Mel noted.

"Yeah, all this is based on a bunch of new orders, so it's only to be expected," Kelsey replied. "The new age stuff bothers me, though. I didn't tell it to say that, it must have inferred it."

"Or someone else has stepped in," Mel said softly. Kelsey shot her a look, but the conversation was continuing.

"If there are no infiltrators, then who killed the Baron?" Rathuan asked.

"He's not going to know—" Risor objected, but the revenant spoke over him.

"You were all tricked by the true killer," it said. "The killer is not hidden, they walk among you."

Kelsey winced. "Okay, now that I hear him *say* it, it sounds—"

"Who murdered the Baron?" Rathuan pressed.

"I do not know. The Great Dungeon has only given me the information I have told you."

"Can we talk to the Great Dungeon?" Inutan put in. "Either directly, or through you?"

"The Great Dungeon hears you," Faerdan told her. "But I cannot receive instructions when you are on the floor."

"So we could leave to let you get more instructions . . ."

Faerdan made a rasping sound, which was probably supposed to be either a laugh or a cough. "As long as you leave our payment behind."

"But that would prevent you—" Inutan started.

"Once you've got the prisoners, there's no reason for you to answer our questions," Rathuan interrupted. "We're not giving them to you early."

The revenant smiled. "Under the terms of our agreement . . ."

"We can always go back to the original plan and ask the vampire," Rathuan said, his hand going to his sword. Inutan stopped him.

"What makes you think that reneging on a deal is going to make the dungeon want to answer our questions?" she said. "I think we're stuck with the answers we have."

"I could try reading its mind," Tikin said. Everyone looked at him, including the revenant. He flinched under the sudden attention.

"I don't know if it would *work*," he continued. "And . . . I'm not good enough to do it at range. I'd have to touch it."

"Which means *we'd* have to hold it down," Rathuan said. "Revenants are pretty strong."

"It might also be taken as an attack on the dungeon," Inutan said. "We know that it doesn't react well to anything Tikin does. I don't think it's worth the risk."

There were mutters of agreement all around, and Mel was amused to note that both Tikin and Kelsey seemed relieved at the decision.

"Were you worried about it?" she asked.

"Well, that wasn't on my contingency list, so I don't know how it would go," Kelsey said. "It'd probably count as an attack, so things would go pear-shaped very quickly."

"How *are* things going?" Mel asked. "I'm not sure exactly what you're trying to achieve here."

"Mostly I want them to *go*, and leave the courls behind. Everything else is just a distraction, mainly. The *real* negotiation is with Suliel."

"Oh," Mel said and thought about it. "Then . . . I think it's going pretty well? I don't think they have many more questions."

Sure enough, after some heated discussion, the party was running out of useful questions to ask. Everything they tried now was being answered with "I don't know."

"We're wasting time, asking questions about the dungeon's intentions," Inutan insisted. "It's only told him what it wants us to know."

"I don't want to go back and tell the Baroness that we were *told* there was nothing to find here," Tikin countered. "Shouldn't we at least look further? Or get some answers about how the Lancers were killed?"

"Not sure I want to press on that matter," Rathuan said. "We might find out, the same way they did."

"Whatever this danger is, I'm sure my magic can handle it," Tikin said. His voice betrayed some uncertainty, though.

"Let's not put that to the test," Rathuan said sourly. "We're out of here. Bring out the prisoners!" he called back into the cave.

"I don't like this," Inutan said. "Leaving people for these . . . monsters."

"If it's bothering you, ask them how many of your friends they killed," Risor snapped at her. Inutan winced but didn't say anything further. The two courls were led out, hands still shackled and hoods over their heads once more.

"Two Tier Three prisoners, as agreed," Rathuan said.

"Just leave them there, that will be fine," the revenant said, not moving. "It has been a pleasure doing business, and if you're ever back, please accept—"

"Shut it," Rathuan said. "Next time I'm back, it will be to burn your village down."

The rest of the party left. Rathuan was the last to leave, backing off slowly, never taking his eyes off the revenant. Then he was gone.

"Hmmm," the revenant said to the two remaining. "You should stay where you are; someone will be here to collect you shortly."

One of the prisoners said something, muffled by the sacks.

"Oh, I'd love to, but I'm under orders not to go near you unless you try to escape," Faerdan said.

"Whora un undead?" one of the muffled figures asked.

"Oh yes. It's a pity you can't see my teeth," Faerdan complained. "A revenant, a dead body that eats the living, if you're not familiar. Have you thought about running?"

The two prisoners stayed very, very still. It was a long time before something happened, and it felt much longer for the prisoners. They were swaying on their feet when they heard a new voice.

"Whoo! That was a run. Out of the castle, through the town and the secret passage, through my own dungeon, dodging the expedition on their way out, but finally I'm here."

"That's what you get for having a body," Mel told her. "It's really inconvenient."

"It has its advantages," the immaterial Kelsey answered. Meanwhile, the corporeal Kelsey lifted off the hoods of the prisoners.

"Boop! Welcome to the dungeon!" she said into their surprised faces.

"Who—who are you?"

"Your new boss," Kelsey said. "Turn around," she added, as a long metal tool appeared in her hand.

"I—I loyal soldier of Emperor!" Kusec protested in broken trade. He glanced uneasily at the revenant, standing silently off to one side.

"That's nice. Turn around." She hefted the tool meaningfully. Kusec looked at the way she lifted its weight easily. It clearly wasn't meant as a weapon, but it was long and heavy and made of metal. Swung by someone with enough strength . . .

He turned around. There was a loud *snick* from behind him, and his hands were free. A moment later, his companion was free as well. Kelsey did something to make the tool disappear. Kusec looked warily at the empty space where it used to be. Such Traits were generally a sign of a Tier four, or higher.

"Feeling like making a run for it?" Kelsey said. At her words, there was a rustle, and ten more revenants popped into view. The courls looked at them and then back at her. They clutched the chains hanging from their wrists as if to use them as weapons, but they shook their heads.

"I own you," Kelsey said. "Forget about your Emperor, your lives are in my hands now, and you exist solely at my pleasure. Understand?"

"Just who are—" Kusec stopped, as every one of the revenants took a step forward. "Yes! I understand."

"What about your friend?"

Kusec quickly filled Erryan in on what the woman had said. "Say you understand," he said nervously, looking at the revenants.

"I understand," Erryan said in Elitran. Kusec started to interpret, but Kelsey looked off to the side.

"Mel?"

"Oh, he said he understood," Mel said. She remembered now about the language thing.

"Good," Kelsey said, ignoring the confused look from Kusec. "You want to live?" she asked him.

"Of course," he said carefully.

"Then here is what I propose," she told him. "You will not try to escape, or attempt to harm anyone who does not attack you. You will obey any reasonable instructions from Anton, Aris or myself."

"I don't know who . . ."

"I'll introduce you. You're going to teach us Elitran as best you know, and you're going to escort us into the Elitran Empire, helping us as best you can. You will not betray us to the authorities there."

"You want me to help spy on my homeland?"

"Eh. We're looking for the slaves that were taken in that raid. I don't have any larger goals. Once we find Aris's sister, your contract ends and you'll be free to go. Or if we don't . . . let's say a year and one day."

"Those slaves are the property of the Empire now! Taking them back would be striking a blow against the Emperor!"

"It's no problem if I buy them, though, is it?" Kelsey held up her hand and made gold appear in it. Kusec felt a stab of greed at the sight. Elitran soldiers fought for coin, but they saw precious little of it, and he'd lost all of his when he was captured. By now, his savings would have been spread across the survivors of the unit.

"I suppose . . . that would be all right," he conceded.

"Explain it to your friend," she said. "Mel, make sure he gets it right."

Casting a curious glance at the empty air she seemed to be addressing, he explained her demands to Erryan. Unheard by him, Mel offered a running commentary on his efforts.

"He forgot the bit about reasonable orders!" Mel pointed out.

"All reasonable orders, remember?" Kelsey repeated so he could hear. He stared at her, but complied.

"If can understand me, then why?" he asked. Kelsey ignored the question.

"So, you do that, and you get to live. The alternative is that I torture you for a month or so for whatever language lessons you can give me, and then I feed you to the Vampire Queen." She chuckled at his blanched face. "Don't give me that look, dying of a vampire bite is one of the best ways to go."

"You're the second person to tell me that," Kusec said wonderingly.

"Well, it's a bit of a topic around here," Kelsey said. "If you want to know more, Fear here can tell you all about it. That's how he went."

Kusec looked over at the indicated revenant, who nodded enthusiastically.

"I don't want to die," Kusec said. "Neither of us do."

"Then you accept?" Kelsey said.

He talked it over briefly with Erryan. "We do," he finally said.

Kelsey smiled with a wide, predatory grin. "Then it's a deal," she said.

CHAPTER FORTY-FOUR

Guess Who's Coming to Dinner

SULIEL

Dinner was not as straightforward as Suliel had expected. Even as the first course, a thick vegetable soup, was served, Suliel felt the shadows of secrets casting a pall on the conversation.

She had her own secrets, of course, the wild revelations that had been forced on her that morning. *Some* of them she wouldn't have minded sharing with *some* of those that were at the table tonight. But the presence of Captain Oldaw and the Count's son, Feldan, gave her pause.

Oldaw himself was keeping quiet, not being keen on discussing his own recent incarceration. Suliel could feel his expectations for her to bring up what she knew about her father's murder, but she had wanted to discuss things with her uncle first.

She *knew* her uncle was here to discuss the guns, and the Rose Circle, but she also knew that he didn't want to raise those topics in front of Oldaw. Instead, he kept talking up the qualities of the man he had brought, clearly trying to suggest Feldan as a potential suitor.

Here, though, he was being discouraged by Suliel's mother. While she didn't openly disparage the man, she was quick to divert the conversation with questions about their mutual acquaintances any time he tried to bring Feldan up. Subtle signals were flashing between the pair. Lady Anat wouldn't normally have been reticent about discussing Suliel's marriage prospects in front of her, so something was going on. Suliel's best guess was that her mother and her uncle were going to have a "discussion" about Suliel's future husband, and didn't want her to see them fight.

Suliel watched the exchange nervously. Kelsey's claim—her completely unsubstantiated claim—that her mother was being influenced by Tikin, weighed heavily on her mind. It might explain why her mother didn't want Feldan's prospects promoted.

It was left to Feldan to promote himself, which he did with aplomb. He *might* be concealing his membership in the Rose Circle, but he didn't let that stop him from complimenting and engaging Suliel in conversation. Suliel let him—it would have been rude to ignore him when everyone knew why he was here, and it meant that at least one of her guests was able to talk freely.

It was also more than a little flattering. He was handsome and pleasant to talk to. Older than her, but not by more than five years, she judged. A far cry from Tikin who was in his thirties, at least. He would surely have been the front-runner . . . if a certain option hadn't been placed on the table.

After the second course was brought out, Feldan complimented her on the pastries, which *were* delicious. Succulent roast chicken, seasoned with spices and complemented with sweet raisins, wrapped in golden pastry. She couldn't really take credit for that, though; it was all the cook's work. When she demurred, Feldan switched tacks, claiming it was to her credit that she had the pantry for such a feast so soon after a terrible raid.

That was more the doing of her father, for laying in stockpiles and for managing to keep the Keep intact. But she allowed it, smiling graciously and thanking him for his concern.

Riadan waited for the exchange to finish before bringing up a new topic of his own.

"I thought that Liem would be attending," he said.

Suliel bit into a fresh pastry before answering, letting the burst of fragrance wash over her as the chicken melted in her mouth.

"Magister Tikin is unavailable at the moment," she finally said. "He's aiding in the expedition currently underway."

Her uncle raised an eyebrow. "An expedition?" he asked.

"There was a theory," Suliel said, her voice going flat, "that Father's killer was hiding in the dungeon."

Oldaw leaned forward. "You said you had information about your father's killer—but the expedition isn't back yet?"

"It isn't," Suliel confirmed with a sigh. "It made sense at the time, but it seems that sending them was a waste of resources."

"Su," her uncle said, his deep voice rumbling. "Who killed Renn?"

Suliel looked over at her mother, sitting as straight as an arrow at the other end of the table. Tikin had been treating her grief, but it seemed to be coming back now.

"Father died the same way half my ancestors have died," she said. "He was killed by the dungeon."

Oldaw was the first to break the silence. "But," he pointed out, "he was found *outside* the dungeon."

Suliel nodded. "As you are aware, the dungeon has become able to act outside of its previous limits."

Oldaw narrowed his eyes. "The zombies in town . . . that was a deliberate *act*?"

"To frame you," she explained. "The attack got your people out of their barracks and allowed . . . the dungeon to place the crates inside."

"Little Su, are you saying that the dungeon is aware of Captain Oldaw—and knows enough to try to frame him?"

"Oh yes," Suliel said bitterly. "The dungeon is aware of . . . many things. Father was . . . investigating some of its actions, which is what got him killed."

"If this is true, then aren't we—isn't the town—in danger?" Oldaw said.

"Not immediately," Suliel said. "Or, rather . . . it's a threat that's been there for some time, we just haven't been aware of it. It *could* have crushed the town, but it chose not to."

"It sounds like it has gotten out of control," Oldaw said. "We can send word back to the capital, have the King send out his elites to put it down."

"No!" Suliel exclaimed. Everyone looked at her in surprise.

"Dear, this thing killed your father and attacked the town. It needs to be destroyed," her mother said.

"No," Suliel repeated. "Father made a mistake, and it got him killed. This barony is still held by House Anat, and managing the dungeon is now *my* responsibility, as decreed by the King."

Oldaw frowned. He knew that what she said was true. Unless the King decided to get involved, she was the final arbiter on both justice for her father and the disposition of the dungeon. Her mother, however, was not dissuaded.

"But sweetie, if it could kill your father, there's nothing that you can do against it,"

"I can't fight it," she agreed. "But I can make a deal with it. There are *considerations*," she said, glancing significantly at Uncle Riadan, "that I can't go into at this time. But the decision is mine."

She looked at Uncle Riadan and Captain Oldaw. She would have leaned into her *Aura of Nobility*, but she was of a lower tier. It would have had no effect. But the law was on her side, and they both knew it. Reluctantly, they nodded. She felt experience flow through her as they acquiesced. Her mother though, *tsked* angrily.

"I'm sure you'll put these silly notions aside once you're properly married," she said. "I need to make a decision before you do something foolish."

"That is your prerogative, Mother," Suliel said calmly. Her attention was elsewhere.

You have reached Level 5.
Applying Benefits for Level 5:
Perception + 1
Willpower + 1
Charisma + 1

Please allocate 1 free Ability point.

Charisma, Suliel thought. For a noble in her position, there was no other way. Physical abilities would not save her. She quickly glanced over her status page.

Suliel Anat, Scion (Level 5)
Path: Scion
Strength: 2
Toughness: 9
Agility: 2
Dexterity: 9
Perception: 14
Willpower: 12
Charisma: 12
Traits:
Nobility's Privilege
Aura of Nobility

Tier Two was so close. *I just have to finish this level*, she thought.

Feldan coughed, reminding them of his presence. "Is anyone else ready for the main course?" he said. "And may I say, you have grown even more lovely in the last few moments."

He noticed my Charisma going up, Suliel thought, with some irritation. Riadan and Oldaw's eyes glazed briefly as they inspected her. Presumably, her mother's did as well, but she was a little too far away to see in the dim light.

"You've grown so quickly, Little Su," Uncle Riadan rumbled. He cast a sympathetic glance Feldan's way. Her value as a bride was greatly reduced if she didn't award him a titled class.

Mother knows now that she doesn't have much time. It wouldn't surprise Suliel if her mother made her decision tonight. It would take longer than a day to organize a wedding though, and Suliel had yet to take Kelsey's offer. It should be enough to put her over, she thought.

The main course was brought out, a suckling piglet roasted to perfection on a spit over an open fire. The pig was presented whole, its golden skin glistening with a mouthwatering glaze of honey and herbs. The conversation returned to inane pleasantries as the cook carved off slices of the juicy meat.

Nothing of consequence was discussed for the rest of the meal. When they were done, Riadan asked to speak privately with Suliel's mother.

"You should take Feldan up to the main tower, show him the view," Riadan told her.

Ah, a private conversation to convince me, while he tries to convince Mother, Suliel thought. It was better to play the gracious host, though, so she agreed.

Despite Riadan's words, there wasn't much to see at night. The moon wasn't bright enough through the clouds to light up much. The town was lit enough to see it, but there wasn't anything particularly unique about it.

There was one pattern of lights that meant something to Suliel. "See there?" she said. "Those lights are on the path to the dungeon. The expedition must be coming back."

"Ah," Feldan said, without any real interest. "Lord Riadan wasn't entirely accurate with the description he painted of this place. I don't want to say he *lied*, but . . ."

"He was a little out of date," Suliel said coolly. "Things changed quickly, with the raid, and Father, and . . ."

"Of course," he said. "But he was wrong about some of the basics as well. He thought you would be a shy and acquiescent level two, and here you are, at the top of your first tier."

"I've had some opportunities for growth," Suliel said.

He laughed. "You're not planning on taking *Lady* for your second tier, are you?"

"I'm not." She paused, looking at him warily. "I'm not planning on marrying my Mother's choice, either. I have someone else in mind."

He raised an eyebrow. "Who?"

"You don't know him."

"A local? A *commoner*? Really?" He laughed again. "You can't be serious. Marrying some bumpkin because of his broad shoulders?"

Anton's not a bumpkin! Suliel thought, but bit back her response. "I think you've said enough," she said aloud. "We can go back inside."

"What? I haven't even had a chance to *convince* you, yet," he said lightly and stepped forward. Suliel stepped back instinctively, but it put her back to the parapet.

"Although," he continued, "it occurs to me that if you've been seeing a man behind your mother's back, he might already have *pressed his case*, if you take my meaning. There's even less value to used goods."

He stepped forward closer, uncomfortably close. Suliel tried to step aside, but his arms were on either side of her, arms that she knew her paltry strength would be unable to move.

Where are the guards on watch? Suliel asked herself frantically. There should be a pair of guards up here—there had been when they arrived. Had they left to give the noble couple some privacy? *I should call out—*

The breath stopped in her throat as Feldan brought his hand up to caress her cheek. It looked like a romantic gesture, but his strength made his casual grip irresistible. Suliel froze in fear, as she realized that he could easily crush her throat or face.

"I didn't get to take Scion, you know?" he said, his breath warm on her cold face. "Had to take Squire, as the second son. But the physical abilities do come in handy."

Suliel didn't whimper. Her Willpower was *twelve*, more than enough to bite down on her fear.

"If you kill me, you get *nothing*," she hissed. "And if you *touch* me, I will have you *executed*."

For a long moment, he just stood there, looking into her eyes. Then he smiled and stepped back, releasing her.

"We'll see," he said. "I wonder if you'll be as defiant, once I've gotten rid of this little obstacle of a commoner."

"I look forward to him killing you," she spat, and stalked away.

CHAPTER FORTY-FIVE

Our Purpose Here

Anton woke up, and everything was perfect. The bed was comfortable and warm, Aris was in his arms, and Kelsey wasn't there. For a long moment, he just stayed where he was and appreciated it. Then Aris started to stir.

"Morning," she said sleepily. "Is it morning?"

"I don't know," he replied. It was hard to tell underground. They got up and had breakfast anyway. They were halfway through eating it before Kelsey showed up.

"Good morning!" she said brightly.

"Is it?" Anton asked.

Kelsey cocked her head and looked at him for a second. "Oh! Right. Yes, it is morning. A bit early, but the sun has risen. Remind me to get you a watch or something."

Anton shrugged, having learned to ignore the things Kelsey said that he didn't understand. "What's the plan for today then?"

"Training! And more training," Kelsey said. "Language lessons, and then I thought we'd try for some more levels in the Forest of Gloom."

"Skipping the spiders then?" Anton asked. Not that he minded.

"The spiders would be okay for you," Kelsey told him, "But Aris doesn't have *Stone Skin*, so she'd be at risk from the little ones. And I have some concerns about the safety of her guns in that environment."

"I'm fine with skipping the spiders, they sound creepy," Aris said.

"All my floors are pretty creepy, it's part of the theme," Kelsey warned. "Hunting undead wolves in the forest won't be a cakewalk."

"What's unsafe about her guns, though?" Anton asked. There was so much that he didn't know about the strange weapons.

"Mnnm, well, it's the muzzle flash really. There are a lot of flammable things on that floor that drape across you or drip down on you. . . A spark at the wrong time, in the wrong place, could go pretty badly for you. Plus, the tight quarters . . . make it easier for a stray bullet or a ricochet to hit one of you."

"I see. What are the wolves' levels like?"

"Top of Tier Two," Kelsey told him. "Between twelve and fifteen. The spiders are Tier Three, though, so you'll want to avoid them."

"I thought we were skipping the spiders?" Aris complained.

"There are spiders in the forest as well, but they're bigger. Easier to shoot," Kelsey said, grinning.

"Harder to kill, though, at Tier Three," Anton said.

"Sure, but you can deal with that when the time comes. For now . . . language lessons!"

Anton was surprised to see a courl in the dungeon. His heart beat a little faster to see one of the soldiers that had killed his family and almost killed him. It *was* one of those soldiers, he knew. His armor had been removed, and the uniform he wore was torn and dirty, but it was still recognizable.

Plus, there was always *Delver's Discernment*.

Kusec Ganarch (Level 22)
Class: Seaborn Raider (Rare)
Path: Foamrider (Common) / Marine (Fine) / Seaborn Raider (Rare)

"What is—is that a revenant?" Anton asked. He'd never *Discerned* a revenant before, but he had heard they showed up as human with some Identify traits.

"Nope! He's a real live prisoner," Kelsey said brightly. "I traded with the expedition."

"They did that? Traded another person?" Aris asked.

"Well, I suspect the *person* part of that statement is a debatable point, upstairs. This is one of the guys that attacked the town, after all."

"Oh, I suppose that's true," Aris said sadly.

"Cheer up! Those guys thought that they were selling me food, but instead, these guys get to live!"

Kelsey grinned at the courl with all her teeth. "Don't you Kusec?"

The courl's ears flattened against his skull and he went down on one knee.

"I serve," he said.

Kelsey turned back to the others. "I don't know if this dominance ritual is a racial thing or a custom of the Empire, but I love it!"

"You made a deal with him, didn't you?" Anton said with resignation.

"Yeah! Don't look at me that way; his life was mine to use however I chose."

"So what was the deal?"

"In exchange for their lives, they have to teach us as much Elitran as they can, and they'll be our guides on the trip. They have to obey any reasonable orders from any of us, and they're free after a year and a day, or when we get Cheia back."

Anton frowned. "That sounds pretty complex. Didn't you say that simple deals were the best?"

Kelsey snorted. "You think that's complex, I should show you a record contract sometime. It *is* more complex than I'd like but . . . well . . . they're just not that important."

"Not important? He's got ten levels on me, and a Rare class to boot!"

"So?" Kelsey asked. "Look, it's not about that, it's . . . this guy, even if I hadn't made a deal, he'd pretty much be stuck doing whatever I said, right? It's not like he's going to escape."

"I suppose . . ." Anton said. He looked over at the courl.

"I serve," the courl said. Anton wasn't sure how much of their conversation Kusec understood.

"He hasn't even *tried* to test the geas, because what would be the point?"

"Have you told him about it? He must have noticed something, right?"

Kelsey shrugged but otherwise ignored the question. "Now this guy, one way or the other, in a year he'll be gone. Most of that time, I'm going to be watching him so closely, it will count as his yearly colonoscopy. He's not going to have a chance to try wiggling out of the deal."

"So deals can be wiggled out of?" Anton asked.

"Not you and me, buddy, we're forever!" Kelsey said and tried to give him a hug.

"Please stop," Anton said.

Incredibly, she did. "It's possible to get out of a deal, or change what it means," she said. "When it comes down to it, a deal is just words, and they can mean lots of things. There's no way to make sure you've eliminated every extra meaning that could twist the deal out of what it was intended for."

"But isn't that why you make it more complex? To avoid ambiguity?"

"That's an approach," Kelsey agreed. "But a better one is to remember that deals are *arbitrated*. It doesn't matter what you think the words mean, or what I think they mean. Someone, or something, decides what's allowed and what's not."

"A god?"

"Maybe. I dunno. I don't *think* so, though, because the impression I get is that they're not very happy at having to do it. Who's going to tell a god what to do?"

Anton stared at her. "And this has to do with simpler deals because . . ."

"Less work for them. Makes them happier, less likely to bite the one respon-sible for the deal."

Anton covered his face with his hands. "So there's no time limit on our deal because you wanted to make the arbiter feel better?"

"Don't be silly," Kelsey said. "I didn't *want* there to be any limits on our part-nership. The fact that it helped keep the deal simple was just a bonus."

"Of course," Anton growled. "I should have known that you'd never let your-self be inconvenienced. You wanted me enslaved forever from the start."

"Hey! Not enslaved. Partners! I saved you, remember?"

"Yeah," Anton said and took a deep breath. Aris stepped up and gave him a hug from the side. "Not much point complaining about it now," he agreed and turned to the matter at hand.

"Did you say there was more than one? Where are the others?" he asked.

"Just one, and he's asleep. I had them split shifts so they could teach me twenty-four hours . . . well, more like sixteen."

"I suppose we should start catching up then."

"That's the spirit!" Kelsey said. She produced two thin booklets and some strange-looking sticks. "Here's some writing materials, I recall that helps when you don't have a perfect memory."

"Fine." He took the items, and then a seat at the stone table. Kelsey nodded at Kusec to start.

"First, start with greetings," Kusec said.

Hunting in the forest was a relief after two hours of study. He just wasn't made for it. At least he'd had some experience with book learning. He'd spent some time studying paths, traits, and monster types at the Adventurers Guild. Aris, once she'd completed the basic education provided by the Church of Tiait, had learned her trade entirely from experience. Both of them learned faster that way.

Neither of them were particularly good at stalking prey through a forest, but they were learning fast. Not fast enough to avoid the ambush from a pair of wolves, but that was why Aris was taking the lead, and he was guarding the rear.

They'd already learned that when the wolves howled, they weren't going to attack. When they attacked, they were entirely silent. Anton glimpsed movement out of the corner of his eye with barely enough time to push Aris forward, out of the way of one of the wolves.

The other, he had to block with his sword. A sword in the face would have discouraged most wolves, but the undead felt no pain. It pressed the attack, even as the first wolf turned against the person who had foiled its first attack.

Aris was already whirling around, bringing her gun to bear, but Anton knew she'd hesitate to fire with him in the middle of the fight. *Sure Shot* meant that she wouldn't *miss*, but bullets had a tendency to go right through undead flesh. He had a feeling that *Uncanny Evasion* one wolf would put him right in the path of the other, so he elected for a different option.

Leaping Attack.

There hadn't been a lot of opportunities to do this in the upper levels, but there was a high ceiling here, and *trees*. Grappling counted as an attack, so Anton's grasp of the high branch was unerring. He pulled himself up one-handed, just trying to get his feet against the bark while he waited for—

The crack of Aris's shot was much more bearable in the forest. One of the wolves jerked to the side, tumbling, its throat torn out. It wasn't dead—wolves were tougher than skeletons, and you had to decapitate them if you wanted a one-shot kill—as Anton was about to do.

Leaping Attack.

Leaping *down* from the tree put a lot of momentum behind his perfectly timed blow, against an opponent who had just turned its attention towards his girlfriend. His blade flashed, the head tumbled, and Anton did a tumble of his own to absorb the speed of his landing. Before he recovered, there was another shot. By the time he got to his feet, the second wolf had fallen.

"Nice work!" he called out, carefully scanning the woods. Wolves weren't particularly attracted to sounds, they'd learned, but it never hurt to be careful.

"Thanks. Still no level, though," Aris reported.

Anton shrugged. It would come soon enough, he knew. He looked down at the corpses, feeling the urge to process them to take back to the guild. Deathwolf skins were fairly highly valued. They weren't *pretty*, but they were one of the only local sources for Tier Two leather. Their ragged nature meant that they had to be cut into small pieces and then resewn, but it was better than rat leather.

Even if the rats were Tier Three. A patchwork style was a distinctive look of locally made armor. It didn't make the pieces any less protective, but Anton was glad his pants weren't of local manufacture.

Valuable or not, they were leaving them for Kelsey to reprocess today. They weren't short of money, and skinning the creatures was a time-consuming, disgusting process. Their time was better spent grinding for experience.

"Ready for a break?" Kelsey said, stepping out of the bushes.

"Not really?" Aris said. "I think I'm getting close to a level."

"It can wait," Kelsey told her. "Suliel just showed up at my back door, and I need to go and meet her."

"She's made her decision already?" Aris asked.

"Hopefully. How about you two?"

"I—" Anton said. He looked at Aris uncertainly. They'd discussed it, but . . .

"It's up to you," Aris repeated. "I'm pretty sure you don't hate the idea . . . and becoming a noble isn't something you want to turn down."

She frowned. "I'm not sure how my parents will take it, though. We need to make sure I've had a chance to explain before anything gets announced."

"Right," Anton agreed fervently. "You explain it. Best if I'm not in the room at the time."

"So we're ready then?" Kelsey asked.

"Yes," Anton said. "We're ready."

CHAPTER FORTY-SIX

Jump

SULIEL

I want to take the deal," Suliel said, her heart thumping.

Kelsey grinned widely. She started to say something but stopped, holding up a hand.

"Settle, Kelsey. Do this *properly*."

She took a deep breath. "The deal I'm proposing is: You protect me with all your might, and I provide you with the means to do so."

Suliel frowned. "That's so vague. You don't want something more . . . specific?"

"Making it specific gets you a contract. I want us to forge a *partnership*."

"One without an end," Anton pointed out. "There's no way for either of you to get out of it if you change your minds."

"Oh yeah, this is forever as far as I'm concerned," Kelsey said.

"That's actually the norm, with agreements between nobles," Suliel said. "Of course, those agreements *can* be broken, if one of the parties is willing to bear the consequences. What I'm worried about is that this wording doesn't address *sovereignty*."

"Ah," Kelsey said.

"What does that mean, exactly?" Aris asked.

"That was what Kelsey promised, at the start," Suliel said. "Extending my domain *into* the dungeon."

"But what does it mean? Does Kelsey have to become your servant?"

"No . . ." Suliel said slowly. "Although the Baron can issue orders for the good of the barony. You and Anton are my subjects, Aris, but you're not my servants."

"Um," Aris said. "I think I feel like . . . we'd have to do what you say? Or we'll get in trouble?"

"If I *were* to issue you orders," Suliel explained, "it would be for the sake of my barony—the community—as a whole. Like ordering Anton to fight on the wall. Fetching and carrying . . . I have servants for that, whom I pay."

She frowned. "That's not to say that some haven't . . . abused the privilege of speaking for their demesne. It can be a fine line."

"More than that, though," Kelsey said, "it's about the law. Administering justice."

"It is," Suliel said.

"I've committed a fair number of what would be crimes, if I were human," Kelsey said. "Some of them were even committed with this body."

"You have," Suliel said.

"Like your father."

"Like my father."

"So if I were to—I'd basically be submitting to your judgment on . . . that matter."

"Haven't you already?"

Kelsey smiled sadly. "We both know that was just words, right? There wasn't anything you could do to me at the time. If I grant you this, then I'll be committing to accepting whatever judgment you lay down."

"You would, legally. I'm not sure if I'd be able to *enforce* it, but—"

"I'd have to mean it," Kelsey interrupted. "For it to be what your class is waiting for, I'd have to really mean it."

"I think so," Suliel said. "I normally couldn't tell, but for this, you would. You could change your mind, of course; nobles do all the time."

"Not if it's part of the deal, I wouldn't," Kelsey said. She sighed and closed her eyes for a moment. "So the solution is . . . to just do it. Suliel, I accept you as my lord."

"Just like that?" Suliel exclaimed.

"It can't be part of a deal. I have to offer it freely . . . an act of trust." Kelsey said, looking at Anton. "I place my trust in you, my liege."

You have completed Level 5! Please select a new class to continue your progression.

"I'm . . . going to need a minute," Suliel said, shaken. She quickly, eagerly, started going through her options.

She quickly dismissed the common options that every person had available to them, looking for the ones that were suitable for her station.

Noble (Tier 2, Fine)
Requisites: Complete Scion, hold a title
Ability Improvement: 5 points per level. PWC[S|T|A|D] (1 Free)

The most basic one, that would be taken away if she married before she could take it. She kept looking

Faithless Noble (Tier 2, Rare)
Requisites: Complete Scion, hold a title, Significant Betrayal
Ability Improvement: 6 points per level. PWC[S|T|A|D] (2 Free)

She winced to see it, but she *had* decided to work with her father's killer. No one set out to get this class, but it was a straight upgrade of Noble, so more than a few that qualified took it. She knew there was something better on the way, though.

Noble Necromancer (Tier 2, Unique)
Requisites: Complete Scion, hold a title, rule the undead
Ability Improvement: 7 points per level. PWWC[ST|AD] (1 Free)

Suliel made a sound of delight and confusion. "What's a necromancer?" she said to the waiting room.

Kelsey raised her eyebrows. "A necromancer controls the undead with magic," she said. "It's what I do, though I'm not sure if my stuff counts as necromancy since it's really just standard dungeon magic with a theme."

"So I'd get traits that control the undead?" Suliel asked.

"I guess," Kelsey said thoughtfully. "Could be useful. I can't control my guys outside unless I'm looking right at them. It might only be undead that you raise yourself, though."

Suliel blanched at the idea of raising the corpse of one of her people. Had she come to this class earlier, there would have been plenty of dead bodies to practice on, but the raiders' corpses had all been disposed of.

"There's still more, I'll keep looking," she said.

Sovereign of the Crypts (Tier 2, Epic)
Requisites: Complete Scion, hold a title to a Necropolis
Ability Improvement: 8 points per level. PWCC[ST|AD] (2 Free)

Suliel made a high-pitched keening sound as she stared at the class.

"What's wrong?" Aris asked, alarmed.

"An *epic* class? At Tier Two? And it's . . . *Sovereign*. Sovereign of the Crypts."

"Nice," Kelsey said. "You're welcome, by the way."

"I can't take this," Suliel protested. "It's not a noble class, it's *royalty*."

"Good," Kelsey said smugly. "I don't want just any old nobility ruling over me."

"You can't have two kings in a country," Suliel said. "If I take this, I'll be setting myself up against the crown."

"Eh, aren't there two of them already? Adding a third doesn't seem so bad. And it was going to happen sooner or later."

Suliel glared at her. "So that *was* part of your plan."

"It's not something I wanted," Kelsey said, shrugging. "But human nature is what it is. They'll be coming after us sooner or later. We'll see them off together, *partner*."

"Gods guide me," Suliel muttered. But it wasn't as though she was going to turn down an Epic class. She made her choice.

Sovereign of the Crypts Class selected.
Applying Benefits for Level 1:
Strength + 1
Toughness + 1
Perception + 1
Willpower + 1
Charisma + 2
Assign free points:

Since her Charisma was going to be shooting up, Suliel elected to cover her weak points.

Strength and Agility Selected.

She checked her status to make sure.

Suliel Anat, Sovereign of the Crypts (Level 1)
Overall Level: 6
Path: Scion / Sovereign of the Crypts
Class: Sovereign of the Crypts
Strength: 4
Toughness: 10
Agility: 3
Dexterity: 9
Perception: 15
Willpower: 13
Charisma: 14

Traits:
Nobility's Privilege
Aura of Nobility

This is really happening, she thought.

Kelsey waited for Suliel's attention to return to her before she spoke. "Well, my lady, are you ready to make that deal now?"

Suliel sat up a little straighter. She wasn't a child, or a half-child, now. She was a lady—a *queen*. She needed to start looking like it.

"You want to get it in place before I start administering justice?" Suliel asked, amused.

"Well . . . it was worth a try?" Kelsey said. "I thought we were past all that, though."

"Father's death won't ever be past," Suliel said, with a pang of sorrow. "But . . . I can accept all the good that you're going to do for Kirido as a kind of penance. Even if you're only doing it for your own survival."

"That's . . . good? Yeah, it sounds good to me," Kelsey said.

"As well . . . protection is something I owe to my subjects. If I see your contributions as penance for your crimes, then we don't need the deal. Everything has already been covered."

"Huh," Kelsey said, looking discomfited. "But it's not *exactly* the same. I can withdraw from your rule, and you can abuse your privilege. Having the deal locks in the parts we want."

"So you would lock in the protection and the goods, while retaining the right to cancel the part that makes the deal righteous?"

"Well, when you put it like that, it sounds stupid," Kelsey said. "But yes."

"All right then, I accept the deal," Suliel said. Immediately, she felt *something* lock into place inside her. Separately, she felt her experience increasing. Not enough for a level, but some. She'd hoped for more, but as she'd said, everything in the deal was implied when Kelsey became her vassal.

Kelsey seemed to feel something similar from the way she looked distant for a moment. Dismissing the feeling, she returned her attention to Suliel.

"So, with that settled, did you want to discuss logistics, or did you want to discuss the other matter?"

All of Suliel's poise deserted her. "Um," she mumbled, looking at Anton. "If you've made a decision, I—"

She stopped herself before she could fumble asking the question. He knew what she was asking.

Anton shared a look with Aris and then stood. Walking around to her side of the table, he took Suliel's hand as she quickly scrambled to her feet.

Has he always been this tall? she wondered as she looked up at him. She was used to looking down at him from her father's dais at festivals. Even recently, she'd been seeing him in formal settings, with a certain amount of distance between them. But now he was standing right next to her, looming above her.

"Suliel," he said gently. "I'm still not sure why you want to raise up a commoner, to give yourself to me. But if you're sure, if you're willing to become a family with Aris and me . . . and well, I guess you've already committed to a life with Kelsey. If you're sure, I'll marry you."

"I'm—" Suliel squeaked, and then fought for control of her voice. "I'm sure," she said, more normally.

Anton nodded. Moving carefully, he stepped closer. As Suliel froze in confusion, he brought one arm around behind her pulling her closer. His other hand took a gentle hold of her face, raising it up as he stooped lower. He kissed her, and she felt herself melt into him.

She wasn't sure how long it lasted, but when they broke apart, all she wanted was to do it again.

"Woo! Let's celebrate the occasion with an orgy!" Kelsey called out, recalling Suliel back to reality.

"I—I—I don't think that's a good idea," she managed to say. "Until the ceremony, we should, that is we *shouldn't*, I mean, unless you want to," she babbled.

"No, it's fine, we should do this properly," Anton said. He kept holding her. His strength was at least as overwhelming as Feldan's had been but Suliel relaxed into his embrace, feeling safe.

"That's good! I should tell Mother, get her used to the idea, and she can start preparing for the ceremony. You can tell—"

Your parents, she was about to say, before remembering. The pause would have been awkward, but Anton filled it.

"I have to—well, Aris will—tell her parents. It's going to take some explaining."

"I suppose it will," she agreed.

"So you want to break here then? We can discuss logistics tomorrow, and it sounds like you've got a lot of family discussion to have," Kelsey interjected.

To Suliel's displeasure, Anton released her from his embrace. She wanted to protest, but Kelsey had a good point.

"I suppose," Suliel said, disappointed. "Can I send the Guild Master to you?"

"Have him wait alone on the first floor, and I'll come and meet with him." They discussed arrangements for a bit more, and then Suliel had to leave.

"Will you be all right on the ladder up?" Anton asked.

Suliel smiled. "I didn't slip last time, and I'm stronger now."

Suliel headed back, escorted by Kelsey until she got out of the dungeon. Her excitement built as she climbed, the thought of marrying Anton finally crystallizing into something real. The anticipation flowed through her, energizing her climb, and when she got to the top she wasn't tired at all.

She was practically skipping as she went to find her mother. She found her talking quietly with Uncle Riadan.

"Mother, I've got wonderful news!" she said brightly.

"Suliel," her mother said. "Why don't you sit down? We have to talk."

CHAPTER FORTY-SEVEN

Smooth Operator

MEL

Kelsey was in an excited mood when Suliel left.

"Let's celebrate!" she said to Anton and Aris, "with some good old-fashioned sex!"

"Um, shouldn't we get back to training?" Anton said, glancing guiltily at Aris.

"No way!" Kelsey exclaimed. "We're having a break, and it's not a break unless you *relax*." She grabbed Anton's arm and pulled herself close, pressing her body against him. Eyebrows raised, Aris promptly followed suit.

"Oh, uh, you're not talking about Aris and me, are you?" Anton said.

"Of course I am, I don't want to exclude Aris from this," Kelsey said, reaching out to touch Aris on the shoulder. "It's all about the experience, you know? Why limit yourself?"

With both his arms trapped by the beautiful girls clinging to him, Anton looked at his girlfriend.

"Help?" he asked.

She frowned slightly. "I think we've kind of already committed to this," she said thoughtfully. "You already agreed to marry Suliel, so we're definitely having *that* kind of relationship . . ."

"And your commitment to *me* is locked in," Kelsey purred.

"That deal didn't involve sex!" Anton protested.

"C'mon, it's practically inevitable," Kelsey said. "Being in each other's pockets like this. Unless you want me to take you down to the docks and have you watch me get rammed by some sailor in a back alley?"

"I don't want that," Anton said glumly.

Aris giggled, "I'd say it was a taste of your own medicine, but you'd like being watched, wouldn't you, Kelsey?"

"Oh yeah," Kelsey's avatar replied.

"I can't believe you're actually going to do this," Mel said to the *other* Kelsey as the pair of them watched the discussion. "Having sex with a mortal, it's disgusting."

"It can't come as a surprise. I've been talking about it since I got my avatar," the immaterial Kelsey said, while her avatar continued to blandish Anton. If she had any trouble maintaining both conversations, she gave no sign of it. "And come on! You've watched Anton and Aris going at it—they're both super hot."

"I don't even know what that means," Mel told her. She had watched Kelsey's current companions having sex and had been oddly disturbed at the sight.

It wasn't her first time viewing sex. It was rare for adventurers to have sex in a dungeon, but there had been a few, over the years. Those trysts hadn't had the same effect on Mel. Safe spaces or no, there had been a level of fear and desperation in those encounters that spoke to Mel's—to a *dungeon's*—purpose.

Mel remembered one couple who had realized that the only chance for *one* of them to survive was for the other to draw off the skeleton patrols. Their final goodbye had been a poignant reminder of the nature of mortality. Mel wished that Kelsey had developed that film stuff back then so she could capture it as more than a memory.

Watching Anton and Aris, Mel had felt none of that desperation. They had been *comfortable*, free to revel in pleasure, and in each other's bodies. Dungeons were supposed to bring fear and terror to mortals, not *orgasms*.

To her dismay, she saw that Kelsey had managed to convince Anton. They were already in the hospitality section, so the room that Mel had started to think of as *their* bedroom wasn't far away.

"You going to watch?" the immaterial Kelsey, the *real* Kelsey, asked.

"I suppose so," Mel said glumly. She didn't want to, but it was her duty to monitor all of the dungeon's activities. She would have preferred to talk Kelsey out of this foolishness, but Kelsey was right, before. This wasn't a surprise, and her previous efforts had failed. Her long association with Kelsey had taught them both the limits of each other's patience. Further protests would be crossing a line.

So instead, she drifted through the walls to find a very naked Kelsey sitting on Anton's lap, kissing him.

"See, I told you you'd get into it," the avatar said smugly.

"Yeah," Anton said thickly, his hands caressing her slight body.

"Am I cold to the touch?" she asked curiously.

"Cooler than Aris, but not *cold*," he replied. "Warmer than the air."

"You're like a furnace," she told him. "I can't get enough of that heat." She ran her hands across his chest as she lifted his shirt off, giving him a few kisses. Then she looked over at Aris, who was slowly undressing herself while keeping her eyes on the pair. "Let me show you how to give a guy a proper blowjob."

"How do you know this stuff?" Anton asked as she unlaced his pants. "You never had an avatar before."

"I'm filled with all manner of eldritch knowledge!" Kelsey cackled. Then she was forced to shut up as she took his member in her mouth. At first, she just licked at the tip, lubricating more of it with her tongue as Anton swelled to full hardness. Kneeling before him, she bobbed her head up and down, each time going a little deeper. Anton groaned at the sensation.

Now fully undressed, Aris came up next to him on the bed and gave him a kiss. She broke it off quickly, though, fascinated by the sight of Kelsey sucking her fiancé. She wasn't the only one.

"Something's wrong," Mel muttered. She couldn't stop looking at Anton's sex going in and out of Kelsey's mouth. Why was it so fascinating? She hadn't felt this way when she'd seen him plunging it into Aris's . . . she stopped herself, shocked, as the memory of seeing that started to exert an equal fascination.

"Mnm?" Kelsey said. She looked distracted, but that was only an affectation, Mel was pretty sure. Kelsey didn't need to *look* at you to be paying attention.

"Something . . ." Mel trailed off, not sure what to say. She felt flushed, her breathing was heavier, and . . . wait.

Mel didn't breathe.

She didn't have a physical body, she didn't need to breathe in air to fuel it. She didn't have blood to run to her face and make her feel hot. She communicated with pure *meaning*; she didn't need to blow air through her mouth to make *sounds*.

And yet, she was breathing heavily and feeling a heat in her cheeks that could only be . . .

"Help, I'm having feelings," she wailed. "I can't—"

Of course, she *could* have feelings. She could feel angry and sad, pleased and gratified. She could feel *emotions*. But she couldn't feel sensations, at least she hadn't been able to before. In the stress of whatever was happening to her right now, she wasn't able to properly express the distinction.

Kelsey understood immediately, though, her immaterial self fixing Mel with a piercing gaze. Her avatar didn't pause, climbing on top of Anton and rubbing herself on his member. Mel couldn't look away, knowing what was coming next. She wanted to . . . she wasn't supposed to . . .

"You're horny," Kelsey said. She said it with fascination, but Mel couldn't help but hear it as an accusation.

"I'm not!" she cried. "That's not possible."

"Are you being affected by my avatar? Can you feel what I feel?"

"No! I—" Mel stopped, transfixed by the sight before her. Kelsey's avatar had posed herself over Anton and was slowly lowering herself down on him. To Mel's disappointment, she didn't feel Anton entering her. But her feelings intensified, and she made a little whine of frustration. *Wait, disappointment?*

"What's happening?" she whined.

"It seems like you're being affected by my avatar's arousal," Kelsey said calmly. "How are *you* not?"

"Oh, I am. Look at me," Kelsey said, nodding at her avatar. The other Kelsey was moaning exultantly as she impaled herself again and again on Anton's throbbing member. She was kissing Aris, who had climbed up on Anton's other end to receive attention from his tongue.

"That's the part of me that's feeling this," Kelsey told the fairy. "Well, that and *you.*"

"I'm not feeling it! I just feel . . ."

"The emotions? The need?" Kelsey asked. Mel nodded miserably. "So you're feeling my need for a good pounding, but you can't have any? Must be rough."

"It's torture," Mel admitted. "I've never felt like this before."

Kelsey grinned. "Want me to help you out?"

"How?" Mel asked nervously.

Kelsey sat down, an imaginary chair appearing under her. "Come sit in Kelsey's lap," she said.

Confused, Mel drifted over. She couldn't really sit down, because she didn't have a body . . . until she *did.* Until Kelsey *imagined* one for her.

Kelsey giggled. "That's better isn't it?" she said to the small figure on her lap. "Fairies are supposed to be smaller than you are, but this is convenient."

Mel looked down at herself. She saw a small figure, about three feet high, but unlike a dwarf, her body was proportioned like a normally-sized woman. It made her limbs and hands impossibly dainty.

"Is this how you imagine me?" Mel asked, a little piqued. "As someone this small?"

"Well, I *am* much bigger than you," Kelsey said. "But I'm not sure where this image comes from. I don't think I've ever imagined you with green hair."

She pulled Mel closer, her hands reaching around to caress Mel's fully developed breasts. Mel's wings twitched at the sensation, surprising her with their existence.

"I think you're cute this way, though. You're like a doll—a little horny doll," she whispered into Mel's ear. "Shall we take care of your little problem?"

"What are you going to do?" Mel gasped. Kelsey hadn't waited for an answer. Her hands were already moving over Mel's body, teasing her with gentle touches.

"Spread your legs for Kelsey, little doll," Kelsey purred, and Mel had to comply. The need she was feeling wouldn't let her do otherwise. The feel of her buttocks moving against Kelsey's thighs was distracting for a second, but then Kelsey slipped her fingers between Mel's legs.

"You're so small, I bet just a single finger would fill you right up," Kelsey mused, as she ran a finger up and down Mel's slit. Mel didn't reply, too busy moaning as she felt a slickness developing under Kelsey's finger. Kelsey's other hand caressed Mel's breasts, holding Mel tight against her. Mel's wings were splayed to the side, pinned in a forward position by Kelsey's body. It was a little uncomfortable, but Mel had far more urgent sensations to pay attention to.

Her body shuddered as Kelsey's finger entered her. It felt just as she imagined from watching Anton, pushing her legs open and stretching her wide. She gasped and then started moaning as Kelsey started moving her digit back and forth.

"You like that, don't you? You like having my finger inside you," Kelsey said, her voice incongruously calm. Mel was almost too far gone to notice, but the other Kelsey was anything but calm as she bounced up and down. The sounds of her passion merged with those of Anton and Aris, and with Mel's own sounds.

Mel felt as if she was on fire, split in two by Kelsey's massive digit. Her burning flesh pushed against it, somehow failing to raise its temperature. It remained, cool and indifferent, pounding her into submission. She felt a strange feeling rising within her, an electric tension that built and grew, threatening to destroy her.

Kelsey seemed to feel it within her.

"You're going to come for Kelsey now, little doll," her cool voice whispered in Mel's ear, cutting through the sounds of passion that filled the room. "You're going to come, again and again."

Mel tried to protest. Just one time would be too much, she felt. She struggled weakly against Kelsey's inexorable grip.

"Sorry, little doll," Kelsey said and giggled. "You're going to be horny for as long as I'm going to be having sex—and I'm not going to be satisfied with just one time."

Mel tried to think of an answer to that, but she was out of time. The tension had reached its limit and she was about to break. Her body spasmed in Kelsey's grip and she let out a full-throated scream as her first orgasm ripped through her body. Kelsey pulled her finger out but kept stroking Mel's body as she kept twitching.

Finally, it was over, and Mel slumped in Kelsey's grip. Unconsciousness eluded Mel, but her body was completely spent, unable to do more than hang in Kelsey's arms.

"Interesting," Kelsey said. "Do you know, we came at exactly the same time?"

She looked down at the exhausted fairy. "Well, time for round two!" she announced brightly.

CHAPTER FORTY-EIGHT

I Want Her

I'm worried about Suliel."

It didn't escape Anton's notice that Kelsey had waited to announce this just after he'd managed to gain another level.

```
You have reached Level 7.
Applying Benefits for Level 7:
Strength + 1
Toughness + 1
Dexterity + 1
Perception + 1
Assign free points:
```

Dexterity, Anton thought. It was lagging behind his other physical abilities.

```
Free point assigned to Dexterity.
```

Anton glanced at Kelsey, but he checked his status before saying anything.

```
Anton Nos, Adventurer (Level 7)
Overall Level: 12
Paths: Delver/Adventurer
Class: Adventurer
```

Strength: 15
Toughness: 19
Agility: 15
Dexterity: 13
Perception: 12
Willpower: 12
Charisma: 10

Traits:
Delver's Discernment
Leaping Attack
Stone Skin
Uncanny Evasion
Sense Mana

"Worried she's going to betray you?" he said, taking a guess at Kelsey's concern.

"No way," Kelsey snorted. "If you'd seen how fast her heart beat when you were kissing her . . . she's all in, I'm pretty sure. But she was supposed to have gotten back to us by now."

"It's still morning . . . isn't it?" Aris asked.

"I just got level seven," he told her.

She pouted playfully. "I'll catch up to you at some point," she promised. She'd just gained level five two fights ago.

"It might be only a few hours late," Kelsey continued, ignoring the byplay, "but it's been long enough that my geas is twitching."

"Twitching?" Aris asked. Anton didn't need the explanation; he knew how the geas felt.

"I've got to provide her with stuff, remember? I'm not in violation yet, but I'm getting reminded to deliver . . . but I've got no one to deliver it *to*."

Kelsey paused and cocked her head in thought. "It might not be a time thing, actually. She could actually need something right now, but if I don't know about it, I'm gonna have a hard time getting it to her."

"You want to go and see what's up," Anton said.

"And since it's not safe for you to delve this deep unsupervised . . ."

Anton frowned. It wasn't as if they'd run into trouble thus far. But he knew that Kelsey was worried about them running into one of the hidden spiders in the forest. They could probably take them . . . but Anton would like them to have another level before they fought a Tier Three monster.

"That's fine," he said. "I'll come with you, and Aris—"

"I need to visit my parents," she said with a smile. "I've got a lot of explaining to do."

"Great!" Kelsey said brightly. "Let's get going then!"

"What do you mean she's unavailable? She put me on the list! Anton!"

To Anton's consternation, Kelsey tugged on his arm like he was a child.

"I just *got* on the list, and now I don't get a chance to use it!"

"I'm sorry, ma'am, but that's just how it is," the guard said. "If you want to talk with someone else, like her mother?"

"That won't be necessary," Anton put in hastily. "But can you get a message to Syon?"

"The chamberlain? We can do that, easily."

"Thanks, Ryodar," Anton said. "Just tell him to meet us at the Selkie as soon as he can."

It wasn't long before Syon showed up, but Kelsey did her best to make it *feel* like a long time.

"What's gotten into you?" Anton asked. "Is your geas giving you trouble?"

"Not yet," she said. "I'm just nervous. We were so close to getting this all set up, and she disappears into the castle? Something's wrong."

"Maybe she just got sick."

"No . . . I would have noticed if she was coming down with something." She sipped distractedly at her wine.

"Sometimes it happens fast," he said.

"You only *think* that it does, because you can't really tell what's going on with your own body," she said and took another drink. Having something to do with her hands seemed to settle her, but Anton was glad he hadn't tried to match her drinking rate. "Believe me, I'd know."

Anton didn't argue with her, but only because Syon came in at that moment. He looked nervous and gratefully grabbed at the cup of wine that Kelsey gave him.

"Thank you," he said after he'd taken a swallow. "You want to know about her ladyship."

"Yeah," Kelsey said.

"She's taken ill," Syon replied. Kelsey frowned, but Anton gestured for her to keep quiet. "Or at least that's what her mother says. The other servants have been kept away, and it is only Lady Clena that tends to her."

"Is that unusual?" Kelsey asked.

"A little?" Syon answered. "For a mother to care for her child, not so much, but to refuse all help . . . it is a little strange. And there's . . ."

"What?" Kelsey said when Syon didn't seem as if he was going to continue.

"It's Lord Kinn's men that have been tasked with guarding her door. Not our own men," he said. "This was at Lady Clena's instructions. And they've started preparations for a marriage ceremony."

"That's—wait," Kelsey said, glancing at Anton. "Just *who* is she going to marry?"

"There haven't been any announcements, but Lord Kinn brought a young noble with him. Feldan Rahm, second son of Count Rahm, I think."

"They're going to marry her off?" Anton asked, aghast.

"I thought they couldn't do that once she got her second Tier?" Kelsey asked.

"Well, no, but her ladyship is still a Scion," Syon said.

"No, she got her second class yesterday," Kelsey said. Syon looked at her curiously.

"Did you *see* her yesterday?" he asked, "I thought her whereabouts were well accounted for."

"Not as well as you think," Kelsey said smugly.

"This isn't *just* about the guns, is it?" Syon speculated. "If you've been meeting her in secret, as well as the times I know about . . . and you know her class? Did she take Lady?"

"No," Kelsey said. She paused, considering her words before speaking. "She took Sovereign of the Crypts."

"Sov—" Syon exclaimed, before clapping his hand over his own mouth. "Sovereign of the Crypts?" he repeated in a more hushed tone. "What kind of class is that?"

"An epic one," Kelsey said smugly.

"One that some people might take exception to," Anton warned.

"You don't have to tell me that!" Syon exclaimed quietly. "It's extraordinary and terrifying in equal part. If the King were to find out . . ."

He paused. "Messages have been sent," he said. "Captain Oldaw has sent word to the capital, and Magister Tikin has sent his bird out. I don't think either of them wanted the other to know."

"What about Lord Kinn?" Kelsey asked.

"If I had to guess, I would say that Tikin's message was from him," Syon said. "Lord Kinn, Master Tikin, and the old Baron would often have private meetings."

"This is looking more and more like a coup," Kelsey said. "Can they pull it off? Suliel has her class, after all."

"I'm not sure," Syon said. "With a class like that, if she married Feldan, I don't think he'd be able to qualify for a normal noble class. Maybe something like *Prince Consort* or something."

"Wouldn't that be better than *Noble*?" Anton asked.

"It would be *Rare*, or maybe even Unique, if there were a variant like *Prince*

Consort of the Crypts. But politically . . . the King wouldn't like there being another Prince that wasn't his son."

"So what would he do?" Kelsey asked.

"It depends . . . it would depend on the relationship that he has with the person with the title. He doesn't have any relationship with Lady Suliel, of course, and I don't know how close the Rahm family is to the crown. People have been executed for having the wrong classes."

"Do you think that's Oldaw's play?" Kelsey wondered. "Alert the King, and get awarded the title once Suliel's been executed?"

"It *might* work out that way," Syon said, his face screwed up with distaste. "Or with Lady Suliel . . . out of the way, the title might go to her mother or one of the cousins."

"That seems a little random to be part of a plot," Kelsey mused.

"If I were Lady Clena . . . the class is the problem. If Lady Suliel could be persuaded to renounce it . . ."

"You can *do* that?" Kelsey asked in surprise.

"Of course. It's not *often* done. If she were to break her path at this point, she'd lose all her progress so far on the first level of Sovereign and become a level zero Lady."

"Level *zero,*" Kelsey said, skeptically.

"Yes, she would get no benefits, but she could gain experience from fulfilling a Lady's duties, and eventually qualify for level one."

"And what are those?"

"Getting married would probably get her there," Syon replied, looking a little uncomfortable. "Managing the household . . . attending to her husband . . ."

Kelsey grimaced. "*That* sounds more like a plausible plan. What's the likelihood of Suliel caving in?"

"Lady Suliel has always been strong-willed," Syon said proudly. He glanced at Anton and quickly looked away. "And she has a strong incentive to stand firm. But ..."

He looked worried. "I presume the pair of you had a *plan* to ensure that this class wasn't a death sentence."

"You could say that," Kelsey said coolly.

"What is the *likelihood* of enacting that plan with Lady Suliel imprisoned in her room?"

"Ah. Not great."

"So. Lady Clena can put a great deal of pressure on her daughter already. If keeping the title means Lady Suliel's execution . . ."

"Got it. There was supposed to be a judge or someone coming in a few days . . ."

"Yes, that would probably be the deadline. I doubt they could keep her class from him."

"Okay, then I guess the next question is where do *you* stand, Mr. Chamberlain?"

Syon looked startled. "I?" he asked.

"Now that it's come to a clash between the mother and the daughter, whose side are you going to take?"

Syon looked pained. "If it's as you say," he said, "my loyalty would have to lie with Lady Suliel. I can't take your word for it, though. I've known Lady Clena for years; I have trouble believing that she'd sacrifice her daughter like that."

"You'd be amazed at what people will sacrifice when their lives are on the line," Kelsey told him. "Of course, it goes the other way, too. I'm beyond being surprised at what people will do when push comes to shove. Do you have an identification trait?"

"I do," Syon said slowly. "A Chamberlain needs to know the classes of the people in the house he keeps."

"Then all you need to do is get a look at Suliel, right? Then you'll know if we're telling the truth. What about the rest of the staff?"

"Most of the staff feel the way I do, I think," Syon said. "We would back Lady Clena against just about anyone, but not against Lady Suliel. The guards . . . many of them look up to Lord Kinn or Captain Oldaw. That might make the difference in whom they support."

"And they'll believe *you*, right? If you see Suliel's class, you can tell them what's going on. Even if you can only get half the guards, I don't think the coup can last long after that."

"Perhaps, but they must have thought of that, and that's why Suliel is not allowed to see anyone. Lord Kinn brought only a few men, but he has enough to mount a twenty-four-hour guard."

"You'll need an opportunity . . . and maybe some help," Kelsey said, staring off into space. "Anton and I can provide that. Do you know Aris?"

"The baker's daughter? Not well . . ."

"She's a lot more than that now." Kelsey cocked her head, thinking. "I'm still formulating a plan, but look out for her. I might be sending her to you to help.

"I'm not sure that's a good idea . . ."

Kelsey waved off his objections. "We'll get you a chance at Suliel," she said. "Once you've talked to her, it's all going to be clear, right?"

"I suppose, but what are you going to do?"

"Better you don't know," Kelsey said with a grin. "Plausible deniability and all. If we fail, you want to be able to say to the judge that you had no idea what we were trying to do."

"What *are* we going to do?" Anton asked. "It had better not involve monsters pouring out of the cellars again."

"Anton, Anton, Anton," Kelsey said, shaking her head. "Don't you know, I'm a changed woman? A law-abiding member of this small community?"

"I must have missed the proclamation," Anton said wryly.

"Well pay attention! We're going to do nothing more or less than our civic duty. We're going to participate in civil discourse." She winked at him. "It's people like us wot cause unrest."

CHAPTER FORTY-NINE

Fight for Your Right to Party

Y ou've got a lot of nerve, coming back here," Belan growled.
Anton looked nervously at Aris. "You were going to explain it to them!"
he said. Both her parents were looking at him with unfriendly expressions. He
hadn't seen them looking at him like that since he and Aris had gotten caught
outside after dark when they were kids.

"I *did* explain," Aris said, rolling her eyes. "They're just being stubborn."

"Stubborn is it? To be upset that this ungrateful brat is abandoning my
daughter—"

"I'm not abandoning her!" Anton interrupted. "It's just—Aris explained—"

"We're still getting married, Dad!" Aris exclaimed. "He just needs to become
a noble first. We're going to become nobles, Dad!"

"Bah! I never heard of such a degenerate custom! Nobles! Isn't being a baker's
daughter enough for you?"

"There's nothing wrong with it, but being a noble is better. It means status
and money. I'll be able to live in the castle—and you will too!"

Belan scoffed. "And how would we manage the bakery, if we were living up
in the castle like degenerates?"

"You wouldn't have to," Aris said. "You could retire, and spend all day drinking tea and crumpets with Lady Clena. Let Cheia run the bakery, after we rescue
her, or hire someone."

"As if that is a way to live," Belan complained. "Lazing about while someone
slaves away making you rich. Why would you want to be such a parasite on
society?"

"For starters," Aris said grimly, "*Everyone* wants to be a noble, and wear pretty dr—wear nice clothes, and you know it. If you weren't trying to find fault with Anton, you'd admit it. And *secondly*, it's about shoring up support for Suliel, so she can back Kelsey's plan."

Both parents glared at Kelsey, who hadn't taken part in the discussion but was sitting at one of the bakery's tables, avidly listening to the conversation. Under their scorching glares, she affected a scared and guilty look, before shedding it with a grin. She gave them a little wave.

"Wait a minute," Belan said. "This feast that's been ordered in three days . . . is that Suliel's wedding feast? I'm to bake for the one who stole from my daughter? I'll poison them!"

"Don't . . . do that," Aris said, sighing. "And . . . I'm not sure that it is. We haven't been able to speak with Suliel since we made the deal, and we're worried."

Belan sighed, and let some of his anger leave him. "You're serious about this," he said. "I thought your plan was to leave, to rescue Cheia. How does this help with that?"

"It . . . helps," Aris said, looking over to Kelsey.

"For a proper expedition, we'll need support," Kelsey explained. "There's already five of us going, and we'll need transport, equipment, and supplies. That's a lot easier when it's the Baron"—she pointed at Anton—"giving the orders."

"But there's a problem," Anton put in. "Suliel—Baroness Suliel—has got her second Tier, but we think her mother might be pressuring her to renounce it and marry the noble that her mother has picked out."

"Really?" Belan frowned. "That doesn't sound—"

"She's being held prisoner in her own bedroom," Kelsey interjected. "Are you really fine with your barony being handed over for some stranger to rule?"

"Well, no, but . . ." Belan sighed and looked back to his daughter. "Are you really fine with this plan?"

Aris smiled. "I really am. Anton asked me before he even considered it."

"Then . . . I suppose it is true that I don't want the barony going to some stranger from outside the town. But what of it? I have no say in the matter."

"That's true," Kelsey agreed. "But what these guys are planning, it's not legal. They're trying to get it accomplished when no one is looking and then bully their way to acceptance."

"That will probably work," Belan said sourly. "It has worked many times before in other towns. They have the guards, so we can only accept the ruling that comes down."

"Well sure, if they get it done," Kelsey said with a conspiratorial grin. "But *right now*, Suliel is still the Baroness. The guards will obey *her*, *if* they know that she is being imprisoned. This whole plan depends on secrecy."

"So you want to break that . . ." Belan said thoughtfully.

"More than that," Kelsey told him. "I want to get all the people out in front of the castle, demanding to see their Baroness."

"Not an uprising?" Belan asked, "Not that one of those would work anyway . . ."

"Exactly. The town is loyal to the Baroness. All we want to do is get the guards to show that *they* are loyal. Demand to see that Suliel isn't being held captive."

"They could hardly object to that," Belan admitted. "But what if they just refuse?"

"They could, but doing that in front of everyone will have the guards wondering why. Once rumors start there, it won't be long before we can win over enough of them for an actual uprising. If they do allow her out, then anyone with an identification trait will be able to see that she has her second Tier. They won't be able to keep up the facade."

"I see. So you want us to . . ."

"We're spreading the word," Kelsey said. "Anton and I, and anyone else we can convince. Tomorrow morning, show up at the front gates and demand to see the Baroness."

"Is it really wise, to have everyone identify Suliel?" Anton asked as they went on to the next house. Aris's family would notify their neighbors, so Anton and Kelsey had a bit of a walk to the next target.

"Why?" Kelsey asked absently. Anton didn't know where she had gotten it from, but she was consulting a map of the town.

"Her new class . . . it's pretty scary. If the townsfolk see it, they might think that Lady Anat is right to be suppressing her."

"Maybe, but I'm not really worried about it. There's no way that Suliel's mother is going to let her be seen."

"Then they'll let the rumors spread?"

"Nah . . . well, a certain amount of rumor will spread regardless. They'll try to nip it in the bud."

"How?" Anton asked.

Kelsey shrugged. "You know, I don't really want to be one of those sorts that predicts every little thing and then goes 'Bwahahaha, everything is going according to plan.'"

"That's a lie, you want to do exactly that."

"While holding my hands on my hips and standing on some sort of tower," Kelsey admitted. "But the first step is *acknowledging* that you have a *problem*."

"I have a problem," Anton said. "I'm starting to think that you haven't told me your plan."

"The plan hasn't changed," Kelsey demurred. "We create a distraction out front, while Aris sneaks in the back way and rescues Suliel."

"I still think we should be the ones sneaking in."

"Aris can't be as distracting as we can."

"She can be very distracting . . ." Anton trailed off, thinking about last night. Kelsey hit him, gently, breaking off his train of thought.

"Mind out of the gutter, partner. Look, by now this Riadan character will have figured out that I'm the one behind the rifles. Also, I'm very noticeable."

"You do stand out from the crowd," Anton admitted.

"Right. And there's a good chance that Suliel has told her mother that she's going to marry you. So she's going to want to keep an eye on you."

"So with us out front, all of the leaders are going to be watching us—a distraction. But Aris is only level ten . . . is she going to be able to handle it?"

"She'll be fine," Kelsey said. "She'll meet up with Syon, and he'll lead her through to Suliel. Any problems, she should be able to take care of by shooting."

Anton nodded, but he was still doubtful. The guns were a great equalizer, especially when you weren't expecting them. Anton's *Uncanny Evasion might* be able to defend against bullets, but they were so *fast*. Still, he was worried.

"The important thing," Kelsey said, "is to make sure that we get as many soldiers to the walls as possible. That means drawing the biggest crowd that we can."

"Right," Anton said. He squared his shoulders as they entered the next building.

After a few more houses, Kelsey felt the need to point out something.

"You really do know everyone in this town, don't you?" she asked.

"That's not unusual," Anton said defensively. "It's a small town, everyone knows everyone."

"Everyone knows everyone *to look at*," Kelsey pressed. "With you, it's different. It seems like everyone we meet, you've helped them out with their groceries, or fixed their roof—"

"Or stolen apples from their backyard," Anton admitted. "I suppose I might have gotten around and met more people than most."

"It's been useful, and I love it, don't get me wrong. But where did it come from? You started with low Charisma, didn't you?"

"Well . . ." Anton stared out at nothing for a second, remembering. "My parents were the heroes for this town, you know? Dad was a Stalwart Hero, Mum was a Wandering Hero . . . they did a lot for this town, defending it, and dealing with beasts in the countryside. There wasn't a person in town who didn't know who they were, and my brother and I . . . just sort of tagged along on that."

"Ah. Sorry to bring that up, then."

"No, it's fine," Anton said slowly. "I like . . . remembering them like that. People were always coming up to them with thanks and small gifts."

"Pretty soon, they'll be coming up to you," Kelsey said. "After you come back with Cheia, they'll be lining the streets cheering for you."

"I doubt that," Anton scoffed. "Maybe if we find *all* of the others, but . . ." he stopped, not wanting to admit to how low their chances of success were.

"Don't worry about it, just solve the problem in front of you," Kelsey told him. "First we rescue the Baroness, then we work our way up to a Princess."

Anton snorted. "Cheia isn't exactly a princess," he said.

"Sure, but she *does* count as a damsel in distress," Kelsey said. "That's just as good."

The next morning dawned bright and clear, the early sun shining down on the crowd that made its way up to the gate of the castle. At Kelsey's insistence, none of the crowd was armed, not even Anton. Kelsey had told them all that violence was absolutely off the table.

"We want to keep the moral high ground," she'd said, again and again in front of innumerable households. "Get the soldiers to see *us* as the righteous party."

Promising a peaceful demonstration had helped attract townsfolk to the cause. No one wanted to take part in an uprising. But now, in the shadow of the gates, people were feeling nervous at how helpless they were in the face of trained soldiery.

As the crowd approached the gates, they swung open. Evidently, they'd been expected. A squad of soldiers, armed with halberds, was waiting behind them. The sergeant stepped forward. There was a murmur in the crowd as they worked up the courage to speak, but the sergeant spoke first.

"Arrest the ringleaders," he said, pointing right at Kelsey and Anton.

Anton started to move, but Kelsey gripped his arm tightly. "Don't resist," she muttered softly. Anton stiffened, made as if to protest, but he realized that she was right. Not all of the guard squad out-leveled him, but enough did. He might be able to put up a fight, but he'd lose, and some of the townsfolk might get hurt. Kelsey on the other hand out-leveled the soldiers handily. She could—but she wasn't resisting either. The soldiers bulled their way through the crowd, taking hold of both of them and forcing their arms back.

Anton's heart sank as he noticed what was missing from Kelsey's face—surprise.

Manacles were applied. Anton got a look at the ones that they were applying to Kelsey.

Steel Manacles: Tier Three
Quality: Magical

His heart sank further. He was pretty strong; he could probably break ordinary crafted manacles. The fact that the guard had brought out such valuable artifacts meant that Kelsey was being taken extremely seriously.

The crowd had barely had a chance to protest before the guards had manhandled Kelsey and Anton out of the crowd and behind the gates. Soldiers held the crowd back, and the gates swung shut. The crowd wasn't dispersed by any means, and Anton thought that there was a good chance that they'd stay outside and make their demands.

But that wasn't going to help him, inside. Dragged into the middle of the courtyard, he was forced onto his knees next to Kelsey. Then the guards backed away, giving them some space. He took the opportunity to glare at Kelsey.

"This was your plan all along!" he hissed. "You knew they were going to capture us!"

Kelsey shrugged. "Maybe," she admitted. She indicated a direction with her head. Anton looked that way to see three nobles approaching. "You've got to admit, though . . . This is a hell of a distraction."

CHAPTER FIFTY

Let's Dance

D o you take us for fools?" Lady Anat sneered down at Anton. "*Of course* your rabble-rousing was reported. *Of course* we had a response ready."

Anton shrugged. He had pointed out that the guards were watching them last night, but Kelsey had dismissed the possibility of them being a danger. *Now* he knew that the guards had been a part of her plan all along. There wasn't much he could do, though, aside from hope that Kelsey knew what she was doing.

"And why would you need a response, when all that these loyal subjects are asking is to see their liege?" Without shouting, Kelsey's voice was just a little louder than it needed to be, ringing across the courtyard. Anton thought that even the guards on the walls might be able to hear her.

Lady Anat's eyes narrowed. "It doesn't matter what their *demands* are. We are their *betters*, and I will not be questioned by rabble!"

"It's too bad, then, that *you're not in charge*. Suliel is. You don't have the authority to do anything to us."

Kelsey's words, stated loudly and with confidence, took Lady Anat aback for a second, and spawned a sliver of doubt in the guards. Anton could see it in their faces. They'd taken for granted that Lady Anat was in charge, but if she wasn't . . .

"Suliel is *ill*," Lady Anat stated, her eyes flashing with distaste. "As her mother, I obviously take over as Regent for as long as she is unavailable." Her Charisma pushed against Anton, making him want to believe her. How could he doubt that what she said was true? Kelsey, though, was entirely unbowed.

"Is she? Or did you just lock her in her room? Or worse?" Kelsey challenged, her simple statement blowing through the lady's words.

"You dare?" Lady Anat shouted, her voice raising a pitch.

"Uh, ma'am?" One of the guards spoke. Not just any guard, Anton realized. It was Draer Rynmos, the captain in charge of the barony's men. "There's a judge coming in a few days; perhaps it would be better to wait . . ."

"No need to wait, Captain, I believe we can deal with this." It was the younger nobleman that spoke up, stepping forward with an arrogant look on his face. Anton didn't know his name but under the circumstances . . .

Feldan Rahm (Level 8)
Path: Squire/Knight

A quick *Discernment* might be called for.

"You have even less authority here," Kelsey said scornfully. "You don't have a title or claim. You're just some noble's brat."

Feldan flinched, and his face went a little red. "That may be," he said. "But I still have some privileges, as a noble. Namely, the right to answer an affront to my honor."

He sneered at Anton. "Perhaps Suliel will change her mind, once I present her with your head on a spike," he said. "By infringing on—"

"Don't be a fool, boy," the older noble interrupted. "If it's a duel, you don't get to kill him in chains and on his knees."

Anton decided that he might as well see who this person was.

Riadan Kinn (Level 23)
Path: Scion/(Knight)/Noble

Much more serious, he thought. *Scion* also qualified a person for *Knight*, so *Scion/Knight* wasn't, strictly speaking, a *broken* path. It was a detour, though, meaning that Lord Kinn was still only Tier Two, despite being level twenty-three. It meant his physical prowess would be much higher than a regular noble. None of the nobles were wearing magic gear, which surprised Anton, but he supposed that they felt safe within the castle.

"I know that!" Feldan protested. "I was going to free him and get him a sword."

"You do that, and he'll kill you, boy," Riadan growled. "He's level twelve."

"How? At his age? He's a peasant!"

"He's an *adventurer*," Riadan replied, keeping his eyes on Anton. "Still, it's not a bad idea. Anton Nos, you have offended *my* honor by putting your grubby hands on my niece."

"I never touched her," Anton said. "And am I really forced to take part in a farce like this? I'm not a noble, I don't have any honor."

"If you want to marry Suliel, then you seek to become one," Riadan told him. "You wouldn't want to start with a black mark next to your name. If you don't want to . . . well, we'll see. Maybe I'll just cut you down where you stand."

"Anton," Kelsey said. "Do it."

He looked over at her and saw that she was grinning. "He's twice my level!" he said.

"You can take him," she said confidently. "I *believe* in you—Aris does too!"

Anton glared at her, realizing what she meant when she mentioned Aris. This was all in the cause of being a good distraction. Lady Anat and the two interloping nobles were here. Looking around, he could see that the other people Kelsey had been worried about were here as well. Captain Oldaw was standing back but had a good view of the proceedings. The person he was talking to was probably his lieutenant. Even Magister Tikin was looking on.

"Fine, I'll fight you," Anton spat. The two guards who had been holding him down pulled him up so that he could face Lord Riadan. Lord Riadan was distracted, however.

"Why can't I see your—" he said, looking at Kelsey. "Guard! Has this woman been searched for magical items?"

"Yes, sir!" replied one of the guards holding her.

"Search her again," Riadan commanded. The guards hesitated but jumped to work as *something* flickered around Lord Riadan.

Aura of Authority, Anton thought, a common noble trait. It only worked on people that thought you had authority over them. Kelsey and himself would be mostly immune.

"Mmn, yes," Kelsey said. "Search me harder . . . search me right there!"

"My lord," Tikin said, stepping forward. "I've already scanned the prisoners for magic. The boy's clothes are Tier Two, enchanted for additional protection. The woman . . . though she has an air of magic around her, the likes of which I've not seen, doesn't have any magical items on her."

"An air of magic?" Riadan asked. "Could that indicate a higher Tier?"

"I've had the privilege of observing multiple Tier Fours in the capital, my lord," Tikin said. "They didn't look anything like her."

"Very well," Riadan said. He turned back to Anton. "A few pieces of armor won't make a difference, and we'll deal with the woman afterwards. Get him a sword."

Anton's arms were freed, and a sword was placed in his hand. He took a few practice swings to feel the balance. Tier One, but well crafted. He'd heard guards complain in taverns about being issued cleaned-up skeleton weapons, but this wasn't one of those.

"Begin when you're ready," Lord Riadan said. "I'll allow you the first blow."

Anton didn't say anything but shifted into a combat stance. Normally, he would close the distance with *Leaping Attack,* but he felt that against this opponent, he shouldn't give away his traits so early. He moved forward cautiously, preparing for a probing attack.

The first few blows were tentative, both sides feeling each other out. As Anton had expected, he was outclassed. Lord Riadan was stronger, faster, and more agile than Anton. It was hard to tell who was tougher, but between Anton's *Stone Skin* and armor, he thought he might have the edge there. Like the noble had said, though, it didn't make a difference.

What *did* make a difference was the disparity in skill. Anton was *better* than this noble. It was, Anton supposed, only natural. Nobles didn't fight every day, after all. Anton had been trained by two masters of the blade since he was five. Lord Riadan had years on him, but few of those years had been spent at war.

Anton had seen skills beat abilities. The Lazybones had shown him how. *If you pay attention to leverage when you parry, you don't need to be stronger. If the distance you move the blade is shorter, you don't need to be faster.* He started pressing his opponent, moving in, striking with more commitment.

He felt the difference the first time Riadan used a trait. The noble's sword blurred, moving into position to block. *He's going to follow that up with*—Anton leapt back quickly. The return blow followed him, but the extra distance let him catch his opponent's blade close to the tip and turn it away. *Leverage.*

Lord Riadan's eyes widened as his blow was stopped, and not by a trait. That had been *Mighty Blow*, if Anton was any judge. As strong as Anton's attacking trait, without the need for a leap for added power. But it wasn't Riadan's best attack. The most popular of the Knight class's capstone traits was an attack trait.

Done with subtlety, Lord Riadan started swinging. Not wildly, but dangerously, letting off *Mighty Blows* with every second or third swing. Anton backed away, letting the man tire himself out.

"Don't you get tired of missing?" he taunted, trying his hand at the combat repartee that Kelsey said was so important. Riadan sneered and raised his sword again.

Then a shot rang out from the castle, muffled by the stone walls. Not everyone recognized the sound, but even Riadan was distracted by the loud *crack.*

"What was that?" he asked, looking over to where the sound had come from. Anton knew that this was his chance.

Leaping Attack.

Lord Riadan's sword was out of position as Anton suddenly closed the distance. Compounding the difficulty of defense was the fact that Anton was leaping *past* the man, away from where the blade was. The attack was more of a swipe as he moved past. If Lord Riadan had been wearing armor, it would surely have glanced off. But he wasn't, and nobles weren't renowned for their defensive traits.

"First blood," Anton said. It wasn't actually the first *blow.* Anton had been knocked around just by parrying the noble's extra strength. But his *Stone Skin* prevented minor cuts and scrapes just by existing.

"Just a scratch," Lord Riadan snarled. The rules of the fight hadn't been gone over, but Anton was pretty sure that this fight wouldn't be over as easily as that. Riadan was glowering, tired, and now wounded. He'd be looking to end the fight, and waiting for Anton's next *Leaping Attack*.

Not that Anton was going to be so predictable. Even skeletons could figure that trick out. Instead, he moved in again, cautiously, as if he was expecting another flurry of *Mighty Blows*. Leverage and distance wouldn't save him from what was coming next, though.

He triggered *Uncanny Evasion* as soon as he saw Lord Riadan move. It was barely enough. The noble blurred in Anton's vision, *Irresistible Blow* moving Lord Riadan's entire body behind a blow that was . . . irresistible.

Anton didn't try. He let his trait bend him out of the way . . . almost far enough. The blow that would have split him in half just struck his left arm, already tucked in as far as it would go. The blow glanced off his enchanted protection, but it added to his sideways motion, sending him tumbling.

Anton leaned into the roll, doing an extra spin before coming to a stop on his feet. He had flown a fair distance, but that was actually to his advantage. His left arm was numb, but his sword was in his right hand.

Leaping Attack.

Riadan was still shocked that his attack had missed. His arm was extended and he hadn't even looked around to see where Anton had gone. Anton hadn't gone anywhere. With a scream, he let his strike land with all his weight and momentum behind it.

Lord Riadan's sword went clattering to the ground, his hand still holding it.

"My lord!" Tikin cried, moving forward. He stopped at Anton's gesture. Anton's sword was pointed at Riadan's throat.

"Do you yield?" Anton asked, hoping that this was the right etiquette.

Lord Riadan glared, but even holding onto his wrist with the other hand, he was losing a lot of blood. "I do," he growled sullenly.

Anton stepped back and let Tikin approach to tend to the man's wound.

"Look out!" came a cry from one of the guards. Anton's head whipped around, but he was too late. Feldan had found a sword and was charging him from behind.

With the warning, Anton could have dodged out of the way. But he was still too late, because even as he took in the sight of the charging noble, another shot rang out. This one was clearer, not as muffled. And in the instant that it rang out, Feldan's head exploded.

CHAPTER FIFTY-ONE

Mad Over Me

SULIEL

Suliel was mad. No, she was *furious*. After all her arguments, all her explanations, her mother had elected to just ignore her as if she was a child.

"You can't do this!" she had exclaimed. Yet Lord Riadan Kinn—*Uncle* Riadan, whom she'd known all her life, just bundled her up effortlessly and deposited her in her bedroom.

"You'll come around," her mother told her. "This is just a phase that you will grow out of."

"Have you been listening?" Suliel had protested. "The dungeon—"

"Has become a problem, yes, that much I understand," Lady Anat said firmly. "It has been a boon all these many years, but if it thinks it can suborn my daughter, it will learn differently."

"But the benefits—" Suliel tried.

"We will send for a party from the capital," her mother said, ignoring her. "Tier Fours. If this dungeon can communicate, then perhaps we can allow it to live, once it has capitulated. Then these benefits, if they truly exist, can be allowed to flow."

"But you don't need to! I've already secured—"

"Secured! More like *surrendered*, to the *thing* that killed your father. No, we will *deal* with it from a position of strength. If it refuses to submit, then some would-be mage can pay handsomely for a new core."

"You don't have the authority! I'm—"

"You," her mother stated frostily, "will stay here and reconsider what a mess you've made of things. Renounce that cursed class and take up Lady. Then you can marry Feldan and start putting this whole affair behind you."

"I—" Suliel tried, but her mother wasn't waiting for an answer. With a final glare, she swept out of the room. Lord Riadan followed, with a more apologetic glance.

Her door only locked from the inside, but there were two guards—Riadan's guards—outside. If they had been hers, she might have ordered them out of the way, but these two just barred her exit and refused to speak to her. They just stared at her until she closed the door.

Could she scream out of the window for help? It would be embarrassing, but what stopped Suliel was the fact that she didn't know how it would go. Would her people be able to make out what she was saying? Would they respond? Or would it just lead to her room being invaded and her being tied and gagged until she agreed to lose her class?

Renounce her class. The idea of it filled her with a burning outrage. Renounce an *epic* class. Who could imagine it? Admittedly, the name of the class was . . . somewhat problematic. It was going to be challenging, but wasn't that the norm for epic classes? No one was awarded such a class for farming in an ordinary field.

Suliel had wanted to rise to the challenge. But now, at the very first step, she had been stymied. Locked in her room until she surrendered. There wasn't anything she could do, except . . . trust her friends. Her *partners*, as Kelsey would say. They had to realize something was up. They would help her.

The thought of what Kelsey might do to get her back almost broke her resolve. Zombies attacking the castle from the inside was the least of it. But . . . Anton wouldn't let her do that. Suliel was fairly sure.

Time passed, and Suliel waited for word. She prepared herself to hear that Anton or the others were dead. She wouldn't put it past her mother to give her a false report to destroy her hope, but at the same time, she suspected that her friends were going to take some risks.

The first thing to break the monotony was a loud crack, just outside of her door. Suliel jumped in surprise, but she had heard such a sound before, when Kelsey was demonstrating her rifles to Suliel's father.

She raced over and pulled the door open. The two guards were still there, but one of them was slouched against the wall, clutching his bleeding stomach. Aris was there, pointing something at the remaining guard, who was drawn back in fear.

"Unless you want to share his fate, lie face down on the floor," Aris said. Her other hand was occupied by another of Kelsey's strange weapons. This one was smoking slightly. "Oh! Hi, Suliel," she said as the door opened.

Suliel stared at her rescuer in shock. She noticed that Syon was there as well, but for the moment her attention was fixed on Anton's fiancée. The weapons she was carrying had been mentioned by Kelsey and the others, but this was the first time Suliel had seen them in use.

Suliel *did* recognize the longer rifle slung over the girl's back. These were the weapons that Kelsey had offered her, saying that they were more suitable for defending walls. The . . . pistols that Aris was carrying were much smaller, but seemed no less powerful for it.

"My lady," Syon said, attracting her attention. He was staring at her with a wide-eyed look. "It is true then?" he asked.

"My class, you mean?" Suliel replied. She couldn't keep the pride out of her voice. "Yes. An epic class."

"Are you sure, though?" he asked. "The name . . . it's ill-omened and will cause problems with the capital besides."

"I'm sure," she told him. "It will be a challenge, but I will rise to meet it."

"Then . . ." Syon paused, swallowing. "Then I am with you, my lady, and the rest of your staff as well."

"Good," Suliel said. She felt the first trickle of experience going into her class. Looking over at Aris, she asked, "Where is Anton?"

Aris busied herself securing the uninjured guard with a pair of familiar-looking manacles as she replied. "He's doing the more dangerous part—being a distraction out front."

"Out front?" Suliel asked uncertainly. She looked across the corridor. *That* room—her father's bedroom—had windows that overlooked the courtyard. Without thinking further, she opened the door and entered.

The windows had originally been arrow slits, but they had been glassed over when the outer keep was built. The glass was clear—alchemically treated. Nothing but the best would do for Father, who liked to look down on his men while they trained. She could see Anton clearly as he brought his sword down on Lord—never Uncle again—Riadan's arm.

She saw Feldan, hidden behind Anton, raise his sword.

"No," Suliel whispered. Then, "No!" shouted at the men below. But she couldn't be heard behind the glass.

Beside her, at the other window, Aris cursed and smashed out the glass with the wooden end of her rifle. Moving swiftly and surely, she reversed the rifle and pointed it out the window.

"*Sure Shot,*" she snarled as she fired.

This time, the crack was *much* louder. But Aris didn't even flinch, manipulating the weapon to cause a shiny brass object to pop out of it. Suliel's attention, though, was down in the courtyard.

Feldan was dead.

So easily, she thought. *These weapons can deal death from so far, so easily.*

Everyone in the courtyard had frozen at the sudden intervention. Suliel took advantage of the pause. Her ears still ringing, she shoved Aris out of the way and called out the window.

"Everyone stand down! On my authority as Baroness, Anton is not to be harmed!"

It wasn't immediately clear to Suliel if her order was being obeyed, or was even heard. Everyone was already standing still and looking at where the shot had been fired from.

"We've got to get down there," she told Aris.

"You sure you don't want me to stay up here and pick off any troublemakers?" she asked.

"No, it's too far, you won't be able to tell what's going on, and I won't be able to tell you," Suliel said. She turned to see Syon, who was standing behind them nervously.

"Syon, get a healer for that guard and take the other one into custody. I don't want any *needless* deaths today."

Syon bowed. "Your will, my lady," he said.

The three of them left the room and started heading downstairs. Aris paused just long enough to smirk at the guard, face down with his hands manacled behind him.

"Thanks for the experience," she said.

Syon split off from them when they reached the lower levels, looking for the servants. Suliel and Aris headed for the front doors.

"Do you have a plan?" Aris asked Suliel as they approached it.

"Not really," Suliel confessed. "Try not to kill my mother, if you can help it. Does *Kelsey* have a plan?"

"She did, but we're pretty much at the end of it," Aris said. "They make a big distraction, I go in and find you. I think you're supposed to figure out how it ends."

"I will," Suliel promised her. They were at the front entrance, a pair of imposing doors. Normally, they were kept open, but Suliel supposed that whatever was going on out there counted as an emergency. She and Aris each took hold of one door and tugged. The doors slowly opened, and they stepped outside.

Standing on the steps leading up to her front door, Suliel had a good vantage to view the entire courtyard. She took the opportunity to grasp the scope of her battlefield.

Half of the soldiers standing here were not hers, but members of the Glimmered Lancers, now on foot. Oldaw and his lieutenant were here, not part of the main action, but standing close. Her mage was tending to Lord Riadan's injury. Suliel wouldn't normally have minded that, but Tikin had already given enough reasons for her to suspect his allegiance. Her mother had drawn near the pair, making a knot of people that drew the focus of her ire.

Anton and Kelsey were here too, of course. Kelsey appeared to have her arms shackled behind her. A sudden realization struck Suliel at the sight, and she realized where the shackles Aris had been carrying had come from. At least she'd gotten them back.

It didn't seem as if anything had happened since the shot. They had been all looking at the window where it came from, and now they were all looking at her. Or possibly Aris, Suliel supposed. Of the two of them, the gunslinger was the more dangerous.

"I am in command here!" she called out, pushing her *Aura of Nobility* to the maximum. Now that she had her second tier, there were some here it would actually affect. It didn't control them, it wouldn't even dissuade someone who had decided to participate in a coup. But they would feel it. They would *know* who was the rightful ruler here.

"My mother has overstepped her bounds," she continued. "She tried to imprison me, tried to make me give up my class. Arrest her."

There was a moment, a pause. It probably lasted for less than a second, but to Suliel it seemed to last forever. It felt as though she could see the thoughts on the faces of every one of her soldiers as they processed her command.

Never give a command you're not sure will be obeyed was her father's advice from not so long ago. Suliel now felt the wisdom of it in her bones. Every one of her soldiers had taken orders from her mother, or from Lord Kinn. Her soldiers respected her mother. They might think that she would be a better ruler.

They *knew* she was the rightful ruler. But they could take actions right now that would change that truth. And they also knew that if they made the wrong decision, if too many people chose a different side, they would die as traitors.

As the silence extended into another eternity, Suliel knew that her mother was going to protest, was going to say that Suliel had gone insane. Her soldiers were going to look at each other, trying to gauge which way the wind was blowing. She was going to have to kill . . . someone. She was going to have to ask Aris to execute—

Then another voice spoke into the silence.

"Now, now, little Baroness. You can't arrest your own Regent, that's just not how things are done."

Time started again, and Suliel was able to whip her head around to look at the one who had spoken.

Captain Oldaw.

CHAPTER FIFTY-TWO

Push Comes to Shove

When the shot rang out, everybody froze looking at Feldan's dead body. Not everybody knew about guns, but those who did started looking for where the shot had come from. It didn't take long, as there was someone shouting from the window.

Is that . . . Suliel? he thought. *Aris must be with her. Suliel couldn't make that shot.* He was surprised that *Aris* could make it, but Kelsey had said that the rifle was more accurate at long range.

"Stand down! . . . Anton . . . not to be harmed," was all he could make out. She was shouting from the topmost floor of the main tower. Then she disappeared, pulling herself back inside.

"Looks like we succeeded," Kelsey said, having wandered up next to him. No one was paying attention to them anymore. The only person still occupied with a task was Magister Tikin, still working on reattaching Lord Riadan's hand. Everyone else was either looking at the front door, where Suliel would presumably appear, or speculating about what was going on to the person next to them. Anton noted that Lady Anat moved up next to Lord Riadan, and started whispering to him urgently.

"Why haven't you done anything?" he asked Kelsey accusingly.

"Huh? I'm still a prisoner, remember?" she said, rattling her shackles.

"Don't try and make me laugh, this is serious."

"Fine," Kelsey sighed. "I don't get any experience for anything that happens outside of myself. Your duel, Suliel winning back her castle, you're all gonna get *beaucoup* experience for it. No need to thank me."

Anton took a deep breath but stopped to consider before yelling at her. He had forgone a large chunk of experience from sparing Lord Riadan, but his rewards had still been considerable. Not enough for another level, but still.

"I could have died," was all he said.

"Nah, you had that," Kelsey replied. Looking over to where Lord Riadan was standing, she grinned. "I didn't expect you to spare him, but other than that, everything has been proceeding as I have foreseen."

"I thought you weren't going to be that kind of person," Anton said sourly.

"And I *said*, that I have a problem!" Kelsey exclaimed. "Weren't you listening? Wait, is that—"

She broke off as everyone's attention was drawn to the front door. Suliel was striding out, Aris at her side.

"I am in command here!" Suliel shouted. "My mother has overstepped her bounds. She tried to imprison me, tried to make me give up my class. Arrest her."

It was impressive how . . . impressive Suliel was. She was slightly shorter than Aris, but she projected a presence entirely at odds with her physical size. Anton realized that there must be a trait at play. It *felt* like she was in charge.

But her opponents had their own noble traits and were a higher level besides. Anton felt the conflict brewing around the courtyard. He wasn't a target of it, but he felt the power in the air as if a storm was brewing.

Kelsey narrowed her eyes. Stepping closer to him, and a little ahead, she made her manacles disappear. "This might—" she started, but she was interrupted.

"Now, now, little Baroness. You can't arrest your own Regent, that's just not how things are done."

Captain Oldaw spoke up, louder than he needed to. He was playing for an audience. The tension changed, as a third player announced himself. There were, Anton noted, more than enough Lancers in the square to win against a divided town guard.

Suliel shot Oldaw an angry look. "I need no Regent, Captain. I have reached my second Tier, as you can plainly see."

"I do see. Sovereign of the Crypts. Do you imagine that the King will not take issue with it?"

"He may do, that is his privilege," Suliel admitted. "It's of *the crypts*, though, not of Zamarra. I'm sure we could come to an understanding."

As they spoke, Anton felt the mood in the courtyard change. Being *acknowledged* by Oldaw had elevated her standing in the eyes of her men. At the same time, the threat of Oldaw's men reminded the town guard that they were only strong if they fought *together*.

Oldaw scoffed, meanwhile, at Suliel's words. "You must be even younger than you look if you think that," he said.

"And will you claim his privilege?" Suleil challenged. "Will you claim offense on his behalf and strike me down as a rebel?"

Aris stepped closer to Suliel. One hand went on the girl's shoulder, the other firmly held the grip of her holstered pistol.

There was a hushed silence as Oldaw looked around the courtyard. He paused as his glance fell on Kelsey, frowning as he saw that she had freed herself. Then he moved on.

"No," he finally said. "I will not break guest-right on this matter. I *will* take it to the King, though."

Suliel grimaced. "I have no right to stop you," she admitted. "You should leave, then, if that is your plan."

"I agree," Captain Oldaw said. He turned to his lieutenant. "Get my things," he told her. She left, and he gestured at the stables. Another one of his men went running there.

Turning back to Suliel, he announced, "I'll collect my gear and horses, and join up with the rest of my men at the barracks. We'll be out of town before sundown."

"That's fine," Suliel said, nodding. "Open the gates!" she called out. The guards jumped to obey.

As the gates swung open, Anton was surprised to see that the protesting townsfolk were still there. They'd gotten quiet since the first shot was fired, no doubt trying to hear what had been going on. As the gates opened and they got to see inside, there were cries of "My lady!" and "Baroness!"

Suliel was even more taken aback.

"What are you all doing here?" she asked.

After a hurried colloquy, Menton Burr, the harbormaster, stepped (or was pushed) forward.

"My lady, we heard that you had been imprisoned, that they were going to take your title away."

Suliel shot Kelsey a look that Anton couldn't interpret. "And you came to protest this?" she asked the crowd.

There was a murmur and Menton spoke up again. "Yes, my lady."

"I see," Suliel said. Then she spoke more loudly. "Thank you for your concern! It was well founded, but thanks in part to your help, I have been released!"

There was a cheer from the crowd.

"Huh," Kelsey said. "I guess that resolution was enough for her to get her first level."

"You Identified her?" Anton asked awkwardly. Identifying people still didn't sit right with him.

"Nah, she got a trait that lets her talk to me," Kelsey said. "Dunno what it's called, but I think she was expecting it to give her a sense of her land."

There *was* a sour look that passed across Suliel's face, Anton noted, but she quickly wiped it away and addressed the crowd once more.

"Now that things have been resolved," Suliel shouted over them, "You may return to your homes. You can also stay—there will be an announcement some-time later today. Please clear a path for the Glimmered Lancers, as they will be heading back to their barracks."

She paused to let them settle down. "Thank you for your support," she said. Then she turned back to Captain Oldaw.

He was standing there waiting for her, holding on to the bridle of his horse, which had been hastily loaded up with saddlebags. Military folk travelled light and packed fast, Anton supposed.

"Thank you for *your* help, Captain Oldaw," Suliel said. "Please pass on to his Majesty that I remain his loyal servant, and I stand ready for his summons."

Captain Oldaw cocked his head. "I think I shall," he announced. "It will do you little good, and me even less, I think, but you deserve that much."

"Thank you," Suliel said wryly. "Clear the way for the Glimmered Lancers!" she called out to her men and the crowd. Then there came another cry.

"Wait!" Lady Anat called out to Captain Oldaw. She had been silent all this time, standing next to Lord Riadan, but now she spoke out. "Do you mean to leave me at the mercy of my mad daughter?"

Oldaw, about to get on his horse, froze for a second. Then he turned around, very slowly.

"I'm not averse to taking you back to the capital," he said carefully. "If that's what you want."

"It is!" Lady Anat exclaimed. "Please save me!"

"No," Suliel said, her voice icy. "You are a subject of the barony, *Mother*, and you will face justice."

"*I'm* not your subject," Lord Riadan spoke up. "I'm leaving, and I'm taking your mother with me. Unless you want to violate the sanctity of the guest-right."

"*You attacked me in my own home!*" Suliel yelled. "*Uncle*," she added sarcasti-cally. "You violated guest-right of your own free will."

"It was for your own good!" Lady Anat protested. She called out to Oldaw, entreating him. "Please sir, my daughter has been . . . corrupted or seduced by the dungeon somehow. She's not in her right mind."

"You have no proof of that," the captain said awkwardly. "A class is just a class, however it is named. I have no right to decide for the King on this."

He turned back to Suliel. "That said, I can't ignore a plea from a noble in fear for her life."

"I spoke of justice, not revenge," Suliel said coldly. "It *is* my right as Baroness."

"Maybe," Oldaw agreed. "I'd question your impartiality, though."

"*Would* you," Suliel said sarcastically. "Not that it matters, it *is* a noble's privi-lege to give answer to insults against their person. But there is a judge who is supposed to be arriving in a day or two. Will his judgment be impartial enough for you?"

"We won't live that long!" Lady Anat called out. "Captain, you're not dealing with a noble here. She'll feed us to her master!"

"Ooh, that sounds nice," Kelsey whispered to Anton. "Be honest, would now be a good time to suggest it to Suliel?"

"No," Anton said without thinking. "Definitely, no," he repeated after a moment's thought. Despite keeping his gaze on Suliel, he somehow knew that Kelsey was pouting.

Oldaw was still speaking to Suliel. "It's a valid concern," he said. "I could take them with me, meet up with the judge along the way, and hand them over to him."

Suliel narrowed her eyes. "I will swear that these two shall remain unharmed until the judge arrives to give them their due. Can *you* swear that they will be returned to me for a trial?"

"You know that I can't," Oldaw admitted, embarrassment showing on his face. "I can't order the judge, nor can he keep them in custody without my men."

"Then which of us can meet the other's demands?" Suliel said. She started raising her voice, playing to the crowd. "If you don't trust my word as a noble, as a *sovereign*, then what trust do we have?"

At Suliel's words, the remains of the crowd of townsfolk perked up their interest. A murmur started to arise from them. Anton couldn't make out much, but the word "sovereign" was repeated numerous times. Oldaw and Suliel, meanwhile, simply stared at each other in frustration, neither willing to give in to the other.

It was Tikin that broke the stalemate. "Head for the gate, my lady!" he yelled, calling on his magic. Fire burst into existence all around him. A pair of walls of bright flame sprung up, separating himself and the two threatened nobles from just about everyone else. A narrow lane was left, pointing towards the gates. At Tikin's urging, all three of them started to run that way.

"Make for the gates!" Captain Oldaw called out, an order to his men. Rather than follow his own order, though, he drew a dagger and headed in Suliel's direction.

"Forgive me, my lady, but this will end when you've been captured," he said, only to be stopped by Aris interposing herself.

"Don't move, Captain, unless you want to die," she said.

The confidence in her bearing halted him for a moment, even though he didn't recognize the gun she was pointing at him as a weapon. Puzzled, he focused on it.

"What *is* that?"

CHAPTER FIFTY-THREE

Let's Go Crazy

O h, this isn't good," Kelsey said pensively, staring at the wall of fire.

"Aris!" Anton yelled, dismayed. The walls of fire had cut him off from Aris and Suliel, and they were facing off against Captain Oldaw, the highest level soldier in the castle. "I have to get to her."

He looked around widely. The walls didn't extend across the entire courtyard; if he went around, he could—

"Hold up there, lover boy. Suliel wants us to stop her mother," Kelsey said. She stepped up to the wall and held up her hands, close enough to feel the head.

"Zombie summoning powers, activate!" she called out. At her words, two zombies appeared and stumbled forward into the flames. There was barely a pause before two more appeared and pushed the first two forward. There was an immediate sizzling sound, and a cloud of black smoke as they started to burn.

The calls of alarm at the zombies' appearance were barely distinguishable from the yelling about the walls of fire. Kelsey ignored them.

"Come on!" she shouted, pulling Anton forward. The zombies had moved forward together but had then spread out. In the gap between them, the fire had been extinguished. Anton held his breath and tried to ignore the heat, and the sickly sweet smell of roasting rotted human flesh.

The nobles had shied away from the flaming zombie incursion into their lane and now stepped back farther as Anton and Kelsey blocked their way.

"You!" Lady Anat exclaimed. "Demon!" she yelled, pointing at Kelsey. Standing next to her, Lord Riadan looked fairly displeased to see them. His hand was back on, but he was holding his sword in his left hand, which suggested to Anton that he might not be as much of a threat the second time around.

Magister Tikin was a far greater threat. With a snarl and a gesture, he slammed two spears of fire into the closest zombies. They staggered back under the impact, but continued to shamble forward.

"Yeah, you just walked through the beginner levels, didn't you?" Kelsey said. "Let the grunts do all the work. If you hadn't, you'd know that fire isn't great for zombies. Oh, it will kill them, sure, but slowly. And until it does, they're even more dangerous."

She watched as the trio backed away from the approaching corpses.

"Oh, and Clena? It's Dungeon, not Demon." She spawned another two zombies, just in time to intercept two fire spears thrown at her and Anton.

"Don't refer to me so familiarly, you monster," Lady Anat spat. "You'll be a bauble for a mage soon enough!"

"Someone's going to wear my corpse, but I'm—" Kelsey started, but she was interrupted by a shot.

Then two more, in quick succession.

"There are more of those accursed weapons?" Lady Anat complained.

"Kelsey!" Anton said urgently. There was still a wall of fire between him and Aris.

"Yeah, yeah," Kelsey said. "Don't worry, I've got this."

Two more zombies appeared and hurled themselves at the wall. Knowing what to do now, Anton quickly followed. He took a last look back. Tikin had switched spells to something that turned the approaching zombies into dust. Then he was through.

I'm not separated from Kelsey, he thought to himself, as a twinge of fear ran through him. *She's right there, it's not a real wall, I can walk through it any time I feel like burning to death.*

He focused on what was in front of him. Aris was standing between Oldaw and Suliel, her gun raised. Oldaw was still standing, but three shots had been fired. Who had been shot then?

Anton's gaze was drawn to a shield lying on the ground in front of Oldaw. He tried identifying it.

Flying Shield: Bonded Item, Damaged, Tier 3

Of course, he thought. Unlike the nobles, Oldaw had been garbed for war. And that meant . . .

Glimmering Sword: Bonded Weapon, Magical, Tier 3
Wyvernscale Mail: Armor, Magical, Tier 2

As expected, for a captain. Aris must have fired at the man, and his shield had interposed itself. Anton had heard stories of such equipment. Aris's shots had damaged the shield to the point that it could no longer fly. No wonder Oldaw was standing there shocked.

Anton quickly glanced around at the rest of the courtyard. A large group of Lancers was boxed in by a much smaller number of Suliel's men. They were all waving their swords at one another, but neither side seemed willing to start something. Oldaw's men didn't seem eager to leave him, and the wall of fire was blocking off the exit anyway.

"You've already thrown away your honor, Captain," Suliel called out from behind Aris. "Do you want to throw your life away as well?"

"She's level *ten*," Oldaw growled.

"Then I'm sure your death would make a sizeable contribution to her experience," Suliel stated grimly. "It would cause considerable problems for *me*, though. There would be no way for me to explain it to the King."

"Forgive me if I'm more concerned about how many shots that thing can fire than about your troubles, my lady," Oldaw said sarcastically.

"Take a step and find out," Aris said. Her voice sounded nervous, but her hand was steady.

Anton realized that he was badly positioned and moved to the side. Backstabbing wasn't his style, and he didn't want to be in Aris's line of fire. Oldaw shifted slightly. He probably had a situational awareness trait that told him that Anton was behind him. Just what he was going to do with that information, though . . .

Oldaw tensed, looking as if he was going to make a lunge. Anton drew breath for a warning but at that moment a shot rang out. Not from Aris, but *behind* Anton.

Anton took another step to the side, turning as he went. He felt the heat from the wall die down. Oldaw gave a half turn as well, trying to keep watch in both directions at once.

The walls of flame guttered and extinguished themselves. Kelsey and the nobles were revealed again to the rest of the courtyard. Kelsey had another one of her revolvers in her hand, pointed at the pair of nobles.

"Clumsy old thing," she complained. "I prefer the semi. Hey Suliel! I captured your mother for you!"

Suliel didn't respond directly, though Anton thought she looked relieved. Instead, she turned to Oldaw.

"Well, Captain? Do you still want to make a fight of this?" she asked.

Oldaw looked around the courtyard, evaluating the situation.

"You'll still allow us to leave?" he asked.

"You and your men only," Suliel told him. "Leave in peace. I don't think there have been any serious injuries so far, among your men at least."

"Aw, Tikin can put his knee together again, no worries," Kelsey called out. "Don't worry about the corpses, they weren't anybody you knew."

Oldaw shot an irritated glance at Kelsey but didn't say anything to her. He kept on addressing Suliel.

"You'll still warrant their case will be heard by a judge?"

Suliel grimaced. "Much as it irks me, that will help my case before the King. I'll agree to it."

Oldaw looked over to Lady Anat. "I'm sorry, my lady, but it seems that this is the best I could do."

Lady Anat looked as if she was going to speak, but Kelsey silenced her with a casual wave of her gun.

"Uh-uh! No talking from the prisoners. Speaking of which, can I get someone to take these two into custody?"

A few of Suliel's guards stepped forward nervously. Kelsey made her manacles appear again and tossed them to the guards to use.

"So that's it?" Aris asked. "You're just going to let him walk after that?"

"I can't kill him," Suliel told her. "I'd never come to terms with his Majesty if I did such a thing. Still . . ."

She stepped forward, coming out from behind her protector. She stayed on the steps, so she wasn't looking *up* at the captain, but came as close to him as she could.

"You raised your sword against me, against the laws of hospitality and the laws that govern your station. Do you deny it?"

"I suppose not," Oldaw admitted, frowning.

"There should be a price . . ." Suliel said. Then she pointed. "Your sword."

Oldaw looked down, surprised to see he was still holding it.

"What?" he asked.

"A knight's honor is his sword, is it not?" Suliel asked rhetorically. "You forfeited one, you should lose the other."

"I—" Oldaw opened his mouth to argue. Then he stopped and shrugged. "I can't lose it," he said.

Dropping the sword to the ground, he put his hands behind his back.

"It's bonded to me until I die," he explained. "If I drop it, then . . ." as he spoke, the sword flew up and slid neatly into his scabbard. "It returns. Either to my hand or my scabbard, whichever suits."

Suliel frowned. "Then—"

"Don't worry! I gotcha!" Kelsey said, bounding up. Her gun had disappeared, and she now deftly withdrew the sword out of Oldaw's scabbard.

"Hey!" he said, but it had already disappeared. Kelsey winked at him.

"Not being entirely honest, were we? Sure, it'll *fly* back to your hand, but lock it up, or put it far enough away, and it's stuck. Can't teleport, that's too much for a mere Tier Three."

"What are you doing—" Oldaw said, but Kelsey just kept talking.

"Now I *could* rework it, but that would cost more than I want to spend. Plus it would be a shame to lose the history on it. This thing is older than I am. But a few cosmetic changes . . . there!"

The sword appeared again. She held it out, not to Oldaw, but to Anton, who had walked up to them.

"That's mine!" Oldaw said, but Kelsey continued to ignore him. Wary of a surprise, Anton Identified the sword again.

Chainbreaker: Bonded Weapon (free), Magical, Tier Three

"Go on, take it," Kelsey said. "Bond with it."

Anton reached out. With an effort of will, he felt the sword join with him as he took it in his hand. Wonderingly, he gave it a toss.

Before it had even struck the ground, the sword flew up and returned to his hand.

"What have you done?" Oldaw said despairingly. "That sword was part of my unit's history!"

"Ours now," Kelsey said smugly. "Or rather, it belongs to my partner."

Captain Oldaw didn't leave happy, but he left, taking his men with him. Lady Anat and Lord Riadan were taken away, to be locked up in their old rooms or a cell, Anton wasn't sure. Suliel gave a speech to the gathered townsfolk, telling them everything was resolved and to look forward to big changes and an era of new prosperity. The number of guards in the courtyard went back to the normal level, as Suliel's men returned to their regularly scheduled duties.

The four of them were left in the courtyard with one other.

"Did all that really happen?" Aris asked. "It feels like a dream, only I've never dreamt of being part of such important events."

"Get used to it, girlfriend," Kelsey said smugly. "You're going to be shifting the fate of nations soon enough."

"I never wanted that, though," Aris said. "I just wanted to rescue my sister. Also, I'm not your girlfriend."

"Ouch! But that's just the sort of quest that can change a nation, though. You'll see."

Feeling that Aris didn't want to respond to that, Anton changed the subject. "So why is *he* still out here, Suliel?"

Suliel shrugged, looking over at Magister Tikin. He had been manacled, but with his arms in front, allowing him to continue working on his injured knee.

Suliel shrugged. "Kelsey asked me to leave him out for a bit," she said. "Over the link," she added when the others looked at her curiously.

"Ah," Kelsey said. "You've all become my partner in ways unique to each of you. I love it."

"Excuse me, we've all become part of Anton's harem, not yours," Aris said firmly. Kelsey raised an eyebrow.

"First time I've heard you use that term."

"Well—I—" Aris stuttered. "After that . . . time, it seems silly to deny it."

"What time?" Suliel asked curiously.

"Um! Well, I'll tell you about it later. After we're married."

"Sounds like a fun time," Kelsey agreed. "But it's probably time we finished this other bit."

She walked over to Magister Tikin, still on the ground, still focusing on his knee.

"Knees are tricky, aren't they?" she said with a conversational tone.

Tikin grimaced but didn't look up from his work.

"Now, I know you've got no earth magic, so you're not going to get those manacles off," Kelsey said. "You could try and burn us up, but that's a quick way to get a bullet in your head. You've got enough human magic to destroy a corpse, but not enough to kill a person. Not quickly enough, anyway."

Tikin finally looked up. "Monster," he said. "You won't get away with this."

Kelsey shrugged. "Maybe. I figure your plan was to finish the knee, and then make us forget about you. Then you could just walk out of here. Wouldn't work on me, though. Out of range."

She grinned and reached out to the chain hanging around his neck.

"I let you finish your knee because I am a kind and generous soul," she said. "But it looks pretty much done to me."

With one hand, she crushed the soft gold links between her fingers. With the chain broken, she could just lift the necklace away, leaving her other hand to fend off his manacled hands as they tried to grab for the stone that she was stealing.

"No! You can't! It won't do you any good! You can't break my bond that easily!"

"Maybe not," Kelsey said easily. She held the orb up so it caught the light. it was a milky translucent sphere, about two inches across. Everyone's eyes were drawn to it, feeling as though they were looking into hidden depths. Then Kelsey made it disappear. "Maybe I don't have a use for it. I just didn't want you to have her."

CHAPTER FIFTY-FOUR

Down on Bended Knee

SULIEL

Suliel would never admit it, but she was still giddy over the new level.

I just doubled my Agility! she thought, not for the first, or tenth, time. That wasn't something that happened very often, a combination of a low Agility score and the incredible luxury of two free points to spend.

Suliel had always cursed her clumsiness. An inordinate amount of her childhood had been spent learning to walk gracefully, in the manner of a proper noble. Without the innate ability, she had been forced to practice just walking. Again and again, until she had gotten it right.

Now, in one step, she'd gone from clumsy to . . . well, average. But a *high* average, at least for someone who didn't have any levels. Both Aris and Anton moved with an unconscious ease that she could only envy.

She brought up her status again, just to look at it.

Suliel Anat, Sovereign of the Crypts (Level 2)
Overall Level: 7
Paths: Scion / Sovereign of the Crypts
Class: Sovereign of the Crypts
Strength: 4
Toughness: 10
Agility: 6
Dexterity: 10
Perception: 16
Willpower: 14

Charisma: 16
Traits:
Nobility's Privilege
Aura of Nobility
Bonded to the Domain

Her eye twitched. She was . . . *less* giddy about her new trait. *Bonded to the Land* was a trait highly regarded amongst the nobility. Granted by the rarer noble classes, it allowed a ruler to just *know* everything she needed to about her territory. It was a rare Tier Three trait. Suliel had thought—hoped—that *Bonded to the Domain* was a lesser version of that. From one way of looking at it, it *was*. She wasn't bound to the *entirety* of her territory, just the part of it that happened to be sapient.

So it made a certain inexorable sense that the sapience would serve as a middleman.

> <I'm not actually distracted by supervising your men mixing liquid rock, you know. I'm still available for fashion advice.>
> <I've seen your idea of fashion,> Suliel sent back. <I can do without any more of your input.>

The link wasn't fully present at all times, a gift for which Suliel thanked all the gods. She could focus on it to bring it to the fore or suppress it until only the awareness of the link itself was there. It didn't just carry her words, either. Either Kelsey or herself could send thoughts, emotions or even sensory impressions. More than a fraction of Kelsey's senses was enough to overwhelm Suliel, though. The way she saw a room from *every* direction . . .

To placate the obviously curious (and curiously human) dungeon, Suliel allowed her to see what they were doing. She added a feeling that commentary, particularly lewd commentary, would be unwelcome.

Right now, what she was allowing Kelsey to see was Aris being fitted for a dress. She was going to serve as a handmaiden for Suliel's wedding, and Suliel was going to return the favor the next day. All of them would have preferred to hold the weddings simultaneously, but the loophole that they were relying on required that Suliel marry first.

Normally, one of Suliel's cousins would have served as handmaiden, but given the circumstances, they weren't inviting family. Suliel's family, at any rate. Aris's family would be attending, along with most of the town.

Noble weddings were normally an affair for nobles, with attendance of the lower classes strictly forbidden. A generous lord, or even a moderately sensible one, would put on a feast for his people so that they might celebrate with him.

Once the special circumstances of this wedding had been explained to the priest of Tiait, who would be conducting the ceremony, he had suggested that it be opened to the common folk, so that they could see one of their own promoted.

Having Aris as a handmaiden would show that she was acceding to the marriage. There was a surprising number of townsfolk who thought that Anton should be marrying Aris instead of Suliel. They wouldn't be fully mollified until the second wedding announcement was made, but her presence would help. For her to participate, though, she needed a dress, and none of her common clothes would do.

Suliel, of course, already had dresses that would be suitable for the ceremony. There was no need for the ideas that Kelsey had expressed, ideas that bordered on a lunacy of excess. Suliel couldn't imagine a dress that was *only* for a wedding. Though if she'd somehow managed to assemble a garment out of *that much* silk—*white* silk, at that—it wouldn't have stayed clean after more than one use. The thought of being so wealthy that she could spend that many resources on a dress for one event boggled the mind. Not even the King was so wealthy. Maybe in the faraway empires that were a constant threat to the Kingdom, there was someone so rich that they could do that.

No, Suliel would wear her existing clothes. And Aris would wear . . . something of Lady Anat's. Aris was closer to Suliel's mother in size, and Suliel found that she felt no guilt at all going through her mother's clothes to find something to gift her soon-to-be co-wife.

"Are you sure about this, though?" Aris asked her. "You're going to reconcile with your mother, aren't you?"

"I don't know," Suliel confessed. In the heat of the courtyard confrontation, she'd been absolutely ready to sentence her mother to death, but now . . . she wasn't so sure. "She'd need to . . . accept what I'm doing. Maybe after enough time has passed, she'll accept that she can't unburn the candle."

Aris shook her head sadly. "I can't imagine it, being that position," she said.

<You're probably going to talk to her, at some point,> Kelsey put in. <My avatar has a few perception advantages that might help determine if she's telling the truth to you . . . but to be sure, you'd want to interview her inside me.>

"I'll keep that in mind," Suliel said aloud so that both Kelsey and Aris could hear.

Aris looked confused for a second, and then said, "Kelsey?"

Suliel nodded.

"Has she convinced you to give her your prisoners yet?" Aris asked.

"Not yet," Suliel said, "Though, for some . . . I'm having trouble arguing against her. She says she gets a benefit from keeping prisoners alive, but she admits she gets more from killing them."

"I'm glad I don't have to make those decisions," Aris said, then frowned. "I *won't* have to make those decisions, right?"

"No," Suliel assured her. "You'll be a Lady, the same as my mother was—is. You won't have any title, so your duties will be limited to maintaining your Lord's household."

Aris giggled. "It feels so weird to think of Anton being a lord," she said. "Let alone *my* lord."

Suliel smiled uncertainly. Weird certainly described what she felt at the thought of Anton being her lord. Of him ordering her, controlling her . . . dominating her. She put those feelings aside, though, making absolutely sure that they didn't flow down the link, and changed the subject.

"How are the preparations for your trip coming along?" she asked.

"Good! All the supplies are being assembled by Kusec and Erryan down at the warehouse," Aris replied. "We just need to find the right boat to hire."

Suliel frowned. She wasn't happy with the fact that the two courl prisoners would be free to return home.

<You—or rather your men—traded me for them fair and square,> Kelsey reminded her. <What I do with them is my business. Think of it as proving that I don't have to kill everyone I capture.>

<You just want to,> Suliel sent back, sourly. A sense of amusement came back down the link.

<Humans get the same experience from killing each other as I do, and you manage to avoid slaughtering each other. Most days. Speaking of slaughter, do you want to restart delving?>

Suliel stepped back from watching Aris and sat on a nearby chair, the better to focus on the telepathic conversation. <I would have thought you wanted me to forbid it. Didn't you make all those complaints about people pillaging you?>

<Well . . . a little light pillaging wouldn't go amiss. Having people inside is disruptive, but you've got all those delvers wandering around not being able to make a living. Unless you wanted to recruit them into your army?>

Suliel snorted silently. <Delvers are the sort of people who don't do well in any kind of organized fighting unit,> she sent.

<I suppose that's true,> Kelsey replied. <Anyway, my mana budget sort of assumes a certain amount of delving. Too little is as bad as too much, at least from your point of view.>

<Are you talking about a dungeon break?> Suliel asked nervously. There hadn't been one of those since the town was founded, but there were stories.

<There's no danger of that,> Kelsey assured her. <But the reason there's no

danger of that is because I keep an eye on the mana and take steps before it becomes a problem.>

<We're in your debt, for keeping such a thing from happening,> Suliel sent, with only a hint of insincerity.

Kelsey sent back an image of a tongue sticking out. *<It would help if there was a predictable level of delving.>*

<Talk to the Guild Master about it. If he shows me a schedule, I'll authorize it.>

<Thanks,> Kelsey sent, along with the feeling of uncertainty. *<Scheduled dungeon delves, who'd have thunk it? Next thing, I'll be doing tours.>*

Suliel carefully didn't say that most of her time in the dungeon could be considered a guided tour, not to mention what Aris and Anton had been experiencing.

<Speaking of delvers,> she sent instead, *<there have been a number of them sniffing about the warehouse.>*

<Probably the ones with mana senses. Some leakage is unavoidable. It should be greatly reduced once everything is in place.>

The warehouse that Kelsey had leased had been repurposed as a distribution center for Kelsey's gifts. It wasn't operational yet. It had been sealed off from the outside but Kelsey had extended herself up through the floor of the building. Taking over the building itself would have exposed her to sunlight, which was undesirable, apparently. Instead, she was constructing something called a goods elevator.

This elevator could be operated remotely, so once it was constructed, Kelsey could withdraw to the safety of the underground, and the warehouse could be opened. Kelsey was confident that the elevator would allow her to transport goods to the town, without intruding on it.

In the meantime, though, the warehouse was a third entrance. One guarded by men, not monsters.

<The guards are handling it?> Kelsey asked. *<There's not actually a passageway down, but . . . delvers have a way of getting past obstacles.>*

<It's fine. They're not having any problems.>

<Then I guess everything is going well?>

<Mostly. The judge hasn't arrived yet. I suspect he must have been intercepted by Captain Oldaw, and has stopped to get instructions from the King.>

<That will increase the speed of the response, but the judge was always going to consult with his boss before making a call.>

<That's what worries me. We're not ready for a response that comes quickly.>

Suliel knew that the training of the unit that Kelsey had insisted on calling "the Minutemen" was proceeding well. The men could load and fire their muskets reasonably well. What they lacked was experience.

It didn't take a class to shoot a gun, or wield a sword for that matter, but the correct class made a significant difference. The majority of her small squad were Tier Ones. Children who had been too young to fight in the raid but now wanted to take up arms. A smaller part were older soldiers, somewhere in the middle of Tier Two, who were willing to break their class once they qualified for a better one. And just two officers at the top of Tier Two, ready to find out what new Tier Three class they might qualify for.

All of them needed experience, though. Drills and duty manning the walls provided *some*, but only a trickle. Kelsey was confident that killing ten men, or monsters, with a gun would qualify them for Musketeer, or something similar. One lucky fool would probably get Original Musketeer, and set themselves up for a charmed life.

The obvious solution would be to send them into the dungeon, but as things stood right now, they would refuse to go. The Tier Ones weren't soldiers yet, and the Tier Twos were already leery of giving up their existing progression. They had guns, but they had all been raised on tales of the dangers to be found in the dungeon. Deadly poisons, sneaky spiders, and terrifying ghosts. Guns wouldn't help against any of those.

<I might have an idea to help with that,> Kelsey sent. <I'll wait until after the wedding to tell you, though.>

<Why then?>

<You're probably not going to like it, and it is going to cost you,> Kelsey replied. <I'm gonna wait until you're in the best possible mood to hit you with it.>

CHAPTER FIFTY-FIVE

White Wedding

Anton wasn't frightened. He'd *been* frightened before, felt true fear. On the night of the raid, he'd run to the very limit of his endurance and had still been chased down like a dog. The fear he'd felt then had lodged itself deep within him. Every time that he was separated from Kelsey, he felt its icy touch again, courtesy of the geas she'd placed on him. Risking his life in the dungeon, or fighting a man twice his level, didn't compare to *that*.

So he wasn't frightened, but he *was* nervous. Ask him to disable a trap while hanging upside down from the ceiling and having skeletons shoot him with arrows, and he could . . . well, he'd probably take a few arrows. Maybe he'd die, but he'd probably be fine with a healing potion. He wished, now, that some sort of similar feat had been an option instead of . . . making a speech.

As he stared out across a sea of faces, Anton was *slightly* comforted by the fact that he knew all of these people. Some of them he'd grown up with, others had fed him treats, or yelled at him for one misbehavior or another. He'd helped some of them over the years, when they needed it, and they had all been behind him when he and Kelsey had marched on the castle to demand Suliel be freed.

Now he was going to be their lord, and he had to make a speech. He swallowed.

"You'll be fine," Suliel had told him when he asked her to write his speech for him. What would have been a blithe dismissal coming from Kelsey sounded like real reassurance coming from Suliel. "Your Charisma has come up so fast, you're not yet used to it. The words will come, if you let them flow from your heart."

Anton had been doubtful, but Aris had confirmed that, lately, he'd been finding the right words at difficult times. Now, Anton reflected, at least in terms of finding the right words, the times had never been quite this difficult.

"People of Kirido," he called out. That was what Suliel had started her speeches with. It didn't sound right, though. *From the heart.*

"My friends," he said. "We've been through some hard times recently. There's not one of us who hasn't felt the loss of someone they loved."

He looked out over the crowd again, and this time saw not just a sea of faces, or even a crowd of people he knew. He saw the faces of his friends and the expressions they were wearing. He saw their eyes glaze over as each of them thought about the ones that *they* had lost, dead or stolen.

He saw the effect his words were having as he called out some of them, named the dead. Suliel had assembled a list of the dead and missing, but he didn't need it. There were too many names on it to name them all, so he just called out a few.

Anton didn't mention his family. He knew he didn't have to. Everyone knew how they had died.

"And it didn't stop with the raid," he continued. "The Baron was lost right after . . . killed by the dungeon."

That started a murmur. Few of the crowd had heard that story, but most people had heard that the Baron had been killed *outside* of the dungeon. Anton glanced over at Kelsey, on the stage with him and the others, as far off to the side as he could manage. She was shifting nervously, but not protesting. That particular secret had been blown already, even if it had not been widely spread.

"Yes, the dungeon is changing," Anton spoke over the murmurs. "The Baron tried to control it . . . and failed."

Now the murmuring became more fearful, people putting together the Baron's death and the zombie attack. Anton kept talking. He didn't know what he was doing, but it *felt* right.

"That left us with Lady Suliel in charge," he said, remembering at the last second to use her title. "She's young, but I don't think anyone has complaints about her ability."

Anton would have been embarrassed if someone had called him out like that, getting everyone to look at him suddenly. However, Anton was fairly sure that Suliel would just stand behind him, in full view of the crowd, standing proud and looking . . . regal.

"She's kept this town going," Anton said. "More than filled in her father's footsteps and . . . she succeeded where he failed. She made an alliance with the dungeon."

Now there was a shocked silence, as everyone tried to process what that would mean.

"Not control," Anton insisted. "A partnership. The dungeon was acting in self-defense, but it *is* sorry for what it has done and has offered reparations. It can grow crops faster than we can, so that means more food. It can give us raw materials and tools, far more easily than it did before. You know of some of the changes that have happened. More are on their way. The dungeon can show us how, help us to live better lives."

The murmurs started again, more confused than anything else, but Anton kept talking.

"The dungeon has acknowledged Lady Suliel, not as its master, but as the rightful ruler of this territory," he announced. "The same as she is for us. And that has granted her a new class! The epic class, Sovereign of the Crypts."

Anton paused to let that sink in.

"And Suliel said . . . she wanted me to stand by her side. Not because she wanted my help, but because she wanted *me*. She wanted to make a choice that wasn't arranged by her mother for the benefit of the family."

Anton beckoned Aris over. She came up to him and hugged him from the side, facing the crowd.

"Now you all know that Aris has always been the one for me," Anton said proudly. A few in the crowd chuckled, but Anton felt a pang as he realized that a number of the girls that Aris had fought with were missing, taken by the slavers.

"But it's *Suliel*," Anton said, and the chuckles got louder. Suliel had always been the beautiful, untouchable princess for most of the men and boys in the crowd. Famed for her beauty, she had been a safe target for their dreams, as everyone knew that she was, and would forever be, out of reach.

Until she wasn't, for Anton at least.

"When she asked me like that, how could I say no?" Anton asked the crowd. "Fortunately, it turns out that when you're lord, you don't have to choose."

"It's good to be the lord!" Myron, owner of the *second* best tavern in Kirido called out.

"Yeah," Anton acknowledged. He gestured to Suliel and she stepped up to his side, taking his arm much more demurely. Seeing this, Aris quickly copied her stance, causing another laugh from the crowd.

"Today," Anton called out over the laughter, "one of your own will become your lord!"

About half the room cheered at that. Part of him had expected that, had known that the line might rate a cheer. Most of him was surprised, though.

"Don't worry!" he addressed the largest group of the ones that didn't cheer. "I'm not going to start overruling Suliel. She's the one who knows what she's doing, not me!"

That got another laugh, and a belated cheer from some once they'd stopped chortling at him.

"Tomorrow!" Anton continued. "One of your own becomes a lady!"

This time the cheer was more unified. People were ready for it now.

"And my first duty as lord . . . will be to get our people back!"

This time the cheer started strong but petered out quickly as people processed what he said. They stared at him, concerned, but it was Chamberlain Osvor, as a leading town figure, who spoke up.

"You can't, you're still too young," he said.

"I'm not Tier Three yet, but I will be soon," Anton said. "My parents were just starting out as Tier Threes when they rescued as many captured townsfolk as they could. Everyone's told me that story."

Osvor nodded slowly. "My sister . . ." he said.

"This time, we'll have support from the dungeon," Anton said. "We have captured soldiers to serve as guides, and we have supplies and weapons and Aris's Unique martial class."

"But the Elitran soldiers, they're all level twenty or more," Osvor protested.

"Lord Riadan was level twenty-four, and you saw me beat him," Anton countered. Not everyone here had seen that fight, but the chamberlain had been there.

"That's . . . true," Osvor admitted, and a lot of the faces in the crowd changed from uncertain to hopeful.

"Can you really do it?" Lyman, the blacksmith, called out. His young son, only twelve, had been taken.

"We can," Anton stated confidently. Part of him wanted to equivocate, to admit that the future was uncertain. The part that was speaking, though, knew that his people needed hope, and having that would help them accept all the change that was coming their way.

"If you can do that, if you can get Fasir back," Lyman said, "then I'm your man, no matter who you marry."

A few shouts of approval came from throughout the crowd.

"That's great," Anton said with a smile, "but I think I might marry Suliel anyway."

That got a laugh. A little bit of tension, which Anton hadn't even realized was there, flowed out of everyone, and out of Anton himself.

"Friends," he called out again. "I've kept you from tonight's feast long enough. It's time to get this ceremony started."

This time the cheer was sustained and started to include his name. "Lord Anton!" was chanted three times before he waved them to silence and turned to face the priest who had been waiting patiently.

His women rearranged themselves. Suliel stayed by his side, but Aris moved to be beside and a little behind her, as Suliel's handmaiden. Aris's dad, Belan, stood beside Anton as a stand-in for his parents. As an adult, Anton didn't strictly need a parental presence—Suliel would be doing without. But Anton had wanted the support, and after a bit of chivvying from Aris, Belan had agreed.

"It's too bad you don't have a Noble class," Suliel whispered. "That speech would have been worth quite a bit of experience."

Anton shrugged. He knew where his experience came from.

The priest waited for everyone to settle before starting to speak.

"There have been too many funerals of late. Every death of a human is a tragedy for us all, and a loss for the God of Humanity. Tiait mourns with us, but she also takes joy from our gains. A wedding is a reminder that life is always renewed and that no matter how many may fall, the race goes on."

The priest looked at the pair of them. "I have before me two young humans in the prime of their life, who have decided to become partners, to become family. One of them will be elevated to noble status. From now until the end of time, they will be equals. Face each other."

Anton and Suliel turned to face each other. They held up both their hands and clasped them, palms touching. Aris and Belan stood on either side of the couple. Aris held a wreath of flowers; Belan held a thin gold chain.

"You stand in the eyes of the god," the priest intoned. "He sees into your heart and will know if your words are true. Do you take each other as partners, to stand against the world as one?"

"I do," they both said, looking into each other's eyes. Anton felt something quite profound. It wasn't the same as Kelsey's geas had felt, locking itself into place, but it was *something*.

"Then let the couple be bound together," the priest said. Aris and Belan wrapped the wreath and the chain around the clasped hands that were closest to them.

"Forever one," the priest said. "The world will try and tear you apart, but you will only grow together." At his words, Belan and Aris each took hold of the couple's clasped arms and gently pulled them to the side. As their arms were drawn out to the side, Suliel and Anton were pulled closer together. Bending slightly, Anton kissed Suliel for only the second time.

"It is done," the priest said. "Lord Anton and Lady Suliel, face your people and share your joy."

The strange feeling that Anton had felt had indeed changed into joy. Smiling at Suliel, he knew she felt the same. Tucking his arm around his wife's waist, he turned back to the waiting crowd.

"Why aren't we feasting already?"

CHAPTER FIFTY-SIX

Gimme All Your Lovin'

SULIEL

Suliel wasn't frightened, but she was a little nervous. Part of it was being back in the dungeon. Kelsey might have acknowledged her, but she had been the first to warn Suliel that there were still dangers down here for her. Clambering down through tunnels and through the deserted city of the dead was not how she had dreamed of her wedding night starting.

Part of it had started with the knowing look Kelsey had given her. Aris's sisterly hug, warm as it was, hadn't helped calm her. Now that she was alone in this room with Anton, her nervousness had swelled to its peak.

"My—my lord, I hope that this pure body is pleasing to you," she said. His hands went slowly to the fastenings on her dress, undoing them.

Anton looked up from taking off his shoes. "Is that . . . what noble ladies say when they get married?"

"Y-yes, there's a traditional . . . response . . ." Suliel trailed off as Anton padded over towards her, barefoot. He was slightly sweaty from the celebration they had just come from, as well as his exertions in getting them here. Kelsey had insisted that he carry Suliel over one of the thresholds that they'd crossed.

"Sorry, no one explained that bit to me," he said, smiling. He'd drunken quite a bit at the party, but his adventurer's constitution seemed to have absorbed it without issue, leaving him with just a warm glow.

Suliel hadn't dared touch any. She couldn't bear the thought of any loss of self-control. Back when her mother was still giving advice about marriage, she had said that drinking yourself into a stupor was an accepted method of getting through the first night. It helped a woman submit to the desires of her new husband.

Anton wasn't unwanted, undesirable, or even cruel. She had dreamed of this; she wasn't going to need artificial acquiescence. She was just a little nervous.

"Oh! Of course, you wouldn't have . . ." she said. Anton had been prepared for the ceremony by her servants, but they weren't noble, so they wouldn't have thought to say anything. The only one who could have said anything was herself, and she would have been far too embarrassed to mention it, even if she had thought to.

"Let's skip it then, and just say we did," Anton said.

"That is . . . fine," she said, looking up at him. It wasn't that he was tall, though he was, a bit. She was so much shorter, though. Looking down at him from the stage, she'd focused on his broad shoulders, and not how overwhelming he was up close.

He bent down, and Suliel gave a little yelp as she felt her feet lift off the ground. He lifted her easily. She wasn't crushed against his chest so much as cradled in his arms. One of his hands was supporting her b—above her thigh, while the other one was behind her back.

Then he kissed her, and Suliel forgot . . . things. Forgot everything except the warmth of his lips and the taste of the spiced wine he'd been drinking. When they broke for air, she found that she was clinging to him, pressing herself against him as much as she could.

She suddenly became aware of just how restrictive her dress was. His hands were on her, but not *touching* her, not like she wanted.

"Please . . . help me out of this dress," she asked. Smiling, he set her down and obliged.

Suliel had been dressed and undressed by maids, but it was an entirely different experience being undressed by Anton. His fingers were clumsy on the fastenings, clumsy enough to get a maid reassigned duties. But where the maids had been clinical and professional, this undressing was passionate. Suliel writhed with impatience, making it harder for him.

Finally, it was almost done, Suliel's nakedness concealed only by a thin silk shift. When the dress hit the ground, Suliel had been facing away from Anton. Now he drew her close, kissing her neck. He ran his hands up her body, cupping her small breasts. She made a small gasp of pleasure, delighting in the feel of the silk between his hands and her skin.

His own clothes were off much more quickly. Suliel barely had time to turn around before they were tossed aside. She looked down at his manhood and gulped. She'd been told, but it was so . . .

"Don't worry," Anton said. "I'll take care of you."

Suliel nodded, and drew the shift up over her head, exposing herself to her husband.

Anton made an appreciative noise, and she flushed at his rapt attention, unable to take her eyes off the part of him that was standing even taller.

She knew her looks were something to be proud of. Aris may have had bigger breasts, but Suliel's skin was darker, a trait prized by the nobility. The curls of her hair were looser, letting her wear it long, cascading to her shoulders. Her smaller breasts stood high and proud. On her smaller frame, they looked . . . still smaller than Aris's.

Anton didn't seem to have any complaints. He stepped closer.

"That pure body thing . . ." he murmured.

"It—it refers to my virginity," she replied before he bent down to kiss her again. He pressed forward, leaning her back until her feet left the ground again. This time, instead of lifting her up, he took a few steps more and gently laid her on the bed.

"Nobles care about that?" he asked. She looked into his eyes, only a handsbreadth away from hers. His body was on top of hers; she could feel his warmth, but not his full weight.

"The value . . . ah! . . . of a noblewoman is . . . what are you doing?"

Seemingly uninterested in her reply, Anton had moved down her body, leaving a trail of kisses, until he found her breasts. Suliel gasped at the sensation as he teased her nipples, running his tongue around them.

This isn't right, Suliel thought, *I'm supposed to be servicing him!*

She tried to struggle out of his hold, but he held her effortlessly in place.

"You don't like it?" he asked between kisses.

"Ah! Yes! But I'm not supposed to . . ." Suliel babbled.

"Not supposed to enjoy it?" Anton asked, amused. It only took one of his hands to hold her in place. The other drifted down her stomach, to her sex. "Just relax."

As his fingers touched the wetness between her legs, Suliel could do anything but relax. His touch sent a fiery pulse running through her. She arched her back, pushing her breast back into her lover's mouth. He chuckled appreciatively and started exploring her folds with his fingers. Every movement of his now-slick fingers sent another pulse through her body, making her gasp in mortification and delight.

This wasn't becoming of a lady. She shouldn't be moaning like a whore, but she couldn't stop herself. Anton was in control, and he was determined to make her embarrass herself. Worse than that, she wanted him to. The thought crossed her mind that Kelsey was fully aware of her state right now. She had suppressed the link as much as she could before starting, but she was in Kelsey's halls right now. Kelsey was watching as she spread her legs with total abandon.

Somehow, the thought that there was a witness to her humiliation turned her on more, bringing her close to . . . something.

"I think you're ready now," Anton said, bringing her back to the here and now. He'd shifted his position. Still leaning over her, now he was kneeling between her spread legs, every inch of her exposed to him.

Suliel couldn't disagree; her body was crying out for more stimulation. She couldn't seem to find words, though, so she just frantically nodded.

"Don't worry, I'll be gentle," Anton said. He leaned forward, and Suliel felt the heat of him at her entrance. She moaned, caught between fear, longing, and delight. He moved further forward, his heat pushing her folds aside, stretching her flesh to its limit.

His face was close to hers again, close enough to kiss her on the neck and nibble on her ear. "The next bit has to be quick," he murmured and shoved his whole length in.

Suliel screamed. *Something* gave way within her, and then her whole body was pain and pleasure as the full length of him lodged itself in her body.

Everything went white for a moment. When she came back to herself, Anton was murmuring reassurances to her. He seemed to notice something change with her.

"Are you all right?" he asked. "Are you ready for me to start moving?"

"Yes . . ." she managed to gasp. The pain had faded somewhat, and the heat within her *needed* to move. She wanted it to drive further in, until it came out of her mouth.

Instead, it withdrew. Suliel felt disappointed for the briefest of moments, before it slammed back into her, driving another scream from her mouth.

Oh, of course, she thought. *This is how it works, this sensation, again and again until . . .*

Until *what*, was a thought that was beyond her. There was only the present moment, the ecstatic fire coming from her groin, and her husband's weight pressing down on her. She wanted to ask him what came next, how this ended. She wanted to ask him to make sure that it *never* ended. She wanted to ask him what was happening.

Words were beyond her, though. She found that she could move her hips to match his thrusts. She found that her legs had wrapped around him of their own accord. She found that her arms could pull him closer, increasing the feeling of his skin against hers that she craved. But these were things of the body, not words.

And her body was speaking now, to her. Something was coming. She tried to express it to Anton, to warn him, but all she could do was gasp and moan and then it was upon her.

Like a wave, it crashed through her body, every part of her spasming with

delight. The last thing she felt before the wave took her away was a different kind
of fire in her belly. A liquid warmth.

"You're back with us?" Anton asked.

He was lying on his back, and she was draped over him like a blanket. She
hadn't been asleep, not exactly. Some part of her had been conscious, but all she
had been concerned about was keeping as much of her skin in contact with his.
And kisses.

"I . . . apologize for my shameful display, my lord."

Anton made a surprised noise. "A lot of things are wrong with that," he said.
"First, there wasn't anything shameful about what we just did. That's just sex, and
that's what married couples are supposed to do."

Suliel buried her face in his chest. She was surprised the heat of her embarrassment wasn't burning him, but adventurers were made of sterner stuff.

"I was taught . . . about it," she muttered. "It wasn't anything like what . . . I
lost control of myself."

Anton chuckled. "That just means I was doing a good job. But I haven't finished with what you said before. This 'my lord' stuff . . . maybe you need to do it
when there are other nobles around, but I won't stand for it when we're in bed."

Suliel started to say something, but Anton cut her off with a kiss.

"You're in charge," he continued. "Here in the dungeon, and up top too. I
don't know anything about running a barony, and I'll be off on a trip first thing.
So don't turn into a dutiful, useless wife."

"All right," Suliel said. "But . . . I like calling you 'my lord' in bed. I'm not
sure why, but it . . . excites me."

"Sounds like you can't wait to make another one of those shameful displays,"
Anton teased. "Well, we can talk about that, as long as you stay yourself, Suliel."

"I will," she agreed. "So . . . what do we do now?"

"Well . . . I don't know if you've noticed, but we're absolutely covered with
sweat and . . . fluids," Anton said.

"Ah . . ." Suliel realized that Anton was right. She was *filthy*.

"So," Anton continued. "How about I show you how Kelsey does baths. You
might be used to this, being a noble, but I'll wager there are a few surprises there.
And then . . . we can get dirty all over again."

CHAPTER FIFTY-SEVEN

Forever and Ever, Amen

When Anton kissed Aris, it felt as if his life was finally back on track. From the moment the raiders had come over the wall, it had felt as though everything that happened was pushing the future he'd dreamed of further and further away. The loss of his family, the terror of being hunted down like a dog. The anguish when it looked as if Kelsey was going to keep Aris and himself apart. Every crazy thing that Kelsey had done, or had *him* do.

Somehow it had worked its way back to what he'd always wanted. Aris in his arms, as his wife. Anton wasn't sure, yet, what to think of all the other things that had happened, good and bad. But this, he knew, was right.

He made his way down off the stage, one wife on each arm, to accept the congratulations of the townsfolk. Not his peers anymore, which was an odd thought. Happily, few of them were treating him like a lord. It might have been because of the festive nature of the night, or because they hadn't gotten used to the idea, but Anton was glad of whatever it was. He wasn't ready to have "my lord" tacked on to everything that everybody said to him from now on.

"Is it my imagination, or are they congratulating you more fervently this time?" Suliel said when the trio had a moment to themselves.

"I think that last night, they still weren't sure what to think," Anton said diplomatically. "Aris is one of their own, and some of them thought I was abandoning her, even with what I said."

"He's living the dream!" Kelsey said, bursting into their quiet circle, a goblet of wine in each hand. "Two lovely wives doting on him! They all wish they could be where he is."

She winked at them. "They haven't thought about how much work it is keeping multiple women satisfied," she said. "Better start putting those free points in Toughness, Anton."

"I'll be fine," Anton muttered. Kelsey raised an eyebrow, and the other two women looked at him speculatively. "Really! Toughness is already my highest ability."

"It only gets better from here," Aris said smugly, pulling him towards her.

"Ease off there, girl," Kelsey said. "You've got a lot more training to do before you leave."

"I get my wedding night," Aris said firmly. "Suliel got hers."

"Don't think I'm not aware of how much you two have been wedding it up the last couple of days," Kelsey said with a leer.

Aris started to protest, but they were interrupted by one of Suliel's guards. From the fact that he was in uniform, Anton guessed that he was still on duty.

"Uh, my lord . . . my ladies . . ." he said, unsure of whom to report to.

"Do you want to take this, Suliel?" Anton asked. There wasn't much point in having everyone report to him when he'd be gone soon.

"Of course, my lord," Suliel said, slipping into formal speech in front of the guardsman. She looked at the man inquiringly.

"Yes ma'am," the guard said nervously. "There's been a report from the castle. The prisoners—some of the prisoners—have escaped."

They made quite a procession, going to the cells. Suliel had to go, of course, and Anton felt that he should accompany her, even if there wasn't anything for him to contribute. That meant Kelsey had to go as well, and finally Aris tagged along, insisting that she wasn't going to let Anton get distracted.

"Cells" was perhaps a misnomer. Due to their status, Lord Riadan and Lady Anat were being held in the guest rooms. Someone who'd seen how quickly and efficiently the locks on the rooms could be removed and replaced by outside locks might have been concerned about accepting a stay in one of those rooms for the night.

Tikin—Anton wasn't sure if he still rated the Magister title or not—had also been confined here. Lord Riadan's men had been given much more cramped quarters, lower down in the castle.

"They've gone, ma'am," the sergeant reported. "We only had one man here, on account of the feast. He's still out unconscious, we only found out when the guards changed."

Suliel eyed the empty rooms. "Are we getting a healer for . . ."

"Bristo, ma'am. Yes, a priest has been sent for. It's just a knock on the head, shouldn't need a potion."

"What about the other captives?"

"Still secure, ma'am."

"They wouldn't have stood for leaving me behind." The words came from behind the third cell, still closed. "Which, while laudable, would have gotten them caught."

Suliel gestured for the door to be opened. Not to identify who was speaking, but so she could look him in the eye. Behind the door was Lord Riadan, sitting on his bed, his hands still manacled behind his back.

"Little Suliel," he said when the door opened.

"Lord Riadan," Suliel said coldly. "Is there anything about this that you want to share?"

He shrugged. "I was most grateful for the extra serving of wine served in honor of your wedding. Two days of feasting is a bit excessive, though, don't you think?"

"How did my mother get free?" Suliel demanded.

"There's no trace of magic," Kelsey put in. "Not that I thought there would be, but it doesn't hurt to check." She was addressing Suliel, but she approached closely and stuck her head around the doorframe, making a face at Riadan.

"They had help," Riadan sighed. "I didn't see who, but they either had a key or got it off the guards. They *didn't* have a key to my shackles, which was why I was left."

"Where are they!"

"I have no idea," Riadan said. "They didn't tell me anything. They left about an hour ago, so they're probably out of the castle by now."

Suliel groaned. "I should have known that Mother would have a few people loyal to her."

"I guess you should count the servants," Kelsey said thoughtfully. "If no one is missing, you still have a traitor around. If some are missing, you *might* still have one."

Suliel shot Kelsey an irritated look but turned to the guards instead. "Start the search," she ordered. "Seal the gates and search the castle. Notify the guards on the wall as well.

"Yes, my lady," the guards said. Most of them left, leaving just one behind. He looked uncertainly at Suliel, and she nodded at the door. Leaving him to secure the cell again, Suliel led the wedding party down the corridor.

"I'm not going to say I told you so," Kelsey said. "Because, let's face it, the concerns you had about me eating them were valid."

"Do you think they're still in the castle?" Aris asked.

"I have trouble imagining Mother leaving," Suliel admitted. "But her best move is to flee the town. We have relatives with estates near the surrounding villages; she might seek safety there."

"Do you want Anton and me to track them down?" Kelsey offered. "My deathwolves don't all have noses, but they can still track pretty well."

"No, thank you," Suliel said with a shudder. "We're easing people into knowledge of you; let's not have them see you leading undead abominations about the place."

"What, then?" Anton asked.

"There aren't many horses here, but there are some," Suliel said thoughtfully. "Assuming they didn't manage to steal some, we'll have a speed advantage during the day. I can send riders to the outlying villages, perhaps intercept her before she finds sanctuary."

"These villages . . . do you think she's going to try and muster a rebellion?" Kelsey asked. Suliel shook her head.

"Even if she raised the whole countryside, they wouldn't have the men to breach the walls. Most of them took shelter here during the raid and helped guard the walls. They took as many losses as we did."

"Then what's her next move?" Anton asked.

"Probably . . . get to the judge and try to sway him, or get word to the King directly."

"That's no big deal if she does that," Kelsey said. "You already promised to give her access to him when he comes."

"I doubt *she* sees it that way," Suliel said wryly. "But I suppose you're right. I don't like that she has first access to him, but Captain Oldaw will have met with him already. So . . . you should go back to the feast."

"What?" Aris asked.

"The guards will do their work, but I don't think they'll find anything," Suliel explained. "There's not much to be done here until morning. We—our new Lord, that is—should show the townsfolk our strength. Show them that we're unconcerned."

"But not you," Kelsey pointed out.

"I should stay here, to coordinate the search," Suliel insisted. "It's not my wedding night, I won't be missed. And . . ." She trailed off, not saying anything further.

"If you're sure," Aris said, putting her hand on Suliel's arm. "I'm not sure we should leave you like this."

"It'll be fine," Kelsey said. "After all, she can call me up if she has any problems."

"That's right," Suliel agreed. "And showing our confidence is just as important as the search."

"All right," Anton said slowly. "We'll see you later tonight, then."

Suliel nodded and they headed back into town.

The party had been only slightly impeded by the departure of the guests of honor. The wine still flowed freely after all. A few of the less-drunk guards had been called away, and many of those that remained had started drinking water. Tomorrow promised to be a busy day for some.

There was also an undercurrent of nervousness that Anton did his best to dispel. Yes, the old Baroness had escaped, but she probably wouldn't get far. She'd surely speak ill of Suliel and her choices, but Anton had nothing to hide from the King. The judge would come and everything would be sorted out.

Somehow, Anton found the words to calm nervous crafters and merchants. As he spoke to more people, he felt their attitudes change. People who had known him all his life as an annoying kid had flipped briefly to fearing him and his new status. Now he saw that fear easing, and as it did, they looked at him with a newfound respect.

"I admire your optimism," Kelsey said when he rejoined Aris and herself in a quiet corner. "Or is that glibness?"

"I believe in Suliel," he said shortly. "You must too if you gave her your allegiance."

"I suppose I do," she admitted. She was drinking wine, and Aris was drinking water. Both of them were looking at him with a little more intensity than he was used to. "Things are proceeding . . . a little ahead of schedule, though. I was hoping for a little more time before we faced higher-level scrutiny."

"Never mind that," Aris said, leaning into him. "Isn't it about time we headed back to the dungeon?"

"Slow your roll there, girl," Kelsey said laughing. "I'm glad my hospitality is appreciated, but the Baron had a pretty big bed. Why don't we use that?"

Aris glared at Kelsey. "It's my *wedding* night. I get Anton all to myself," she growled possessively. "If we're not in the dungeon, you have to be there."

"That's fair," Kelsey said holding her hands up placatingly. "But . . . you've had plenty of alone time with Anton and you're about to go on a trip with him. Suliel just got one night, and that's all she'll get until you get back."

Aris's glare softened, and she looked more doubtful. Kelsey wasn't done yet, though.

"And, she's just had an emotional blow from this whole escape thing. Do you really want to leave her alone tonight?"

"I don't think that sex is—" Anton started to protest, but Kelsey interrupted.

"You're right. As awesome as a foursome would—will—be, what she needs right now is hugs. A night spent bonding with her *new* family"

"Damn it, that's not fair," Aris muttered. "I *like* Suliel."

Anton looked at Aris. It seemed that the decision had been made. "Should we send word ahead to let her know?" he asked.

"It's already arranged," Kelsey said smugly.

It took a while for them to all get to sleep. There had been tears, talking, giggles, and discussion about the temperatures of various body parts. Human weaknesses being what they were, though, a combination of tiredness and not insignificant amounts of alcohol had brought them down.

Lacking any such weakness, Kelsey was still awake. Moving slowly and gently, she untangled herself from the huddle and got out of the bed. With a thought, her strange clothes appeared once more on her naked body. Carefully, she adjusted the bedspread to cover them all once again.

She looked down at the trio, and a smile quirked her lips.

"Don't worry, my liege," she said softly. "I'll keep watch so you can sleep. You've got a big day tomorrow."

Glossary

Abilities: The basic stats possessed by people and monsters. They are Strength, Toughness, Agility, Dexterity, Perception, Willpower and Charisma. They are sometimes abbreviated by their first letter.

Example: STADPWC

Alchemy: Alchemy stores a spell, not in an object, but in a potion, powder or ointment. It also uses the power from a monster core, but it is less efficient, using up the power after only one use. The advantage of Alchemy is that Alchemists can create effects equal to their Tier, while Enchanters need to be one Tier above the effect they wish to create.

Class: A temporary profession or role that a person can have. Classes confer benefits. As a person progresses through their Class, they gain bonuses to their Abilities and additional Traits. Classes generally have some requirements that must be met before they can be taken. One cannot take a Class of a certain Tier without having *completed* a Class of the Tier below. Classes are described by both their Tier and their Grade.

Enchantment: Magical items can be created that essentially store a spell as described above into a physical object. They can be created by wizards (if they take the appropriate traits) and many crafting-type Classes also have traits that allow for the creation of items. In the latter case, the enchantment must be powered by a monster core that contains the appropriate mana. Dungeons can also create enchanted items through a similar process.

Grade: The Grades commonly known are: Common, Fine, Rare, Unique, Epic and Legendary. The better the Grade, the better the Class, both in terms of the number of Ability points granted each level and the quality of the Traits provided.

Level: The Tiers of people, monsters and dungeons have levels. Tier One has five levels, Tier Two has ten levels, Tier Three has fifteen, and so on. A person's level is the sum of all the levels they have gained in all the Classes they have taken.

Magic: Many traits have magic-like aspects. Some of them may even seem like spells. For example, one of Kelsey's Liches has a *Cast Fireball* trait, which does just that. True magic, though, can only be done by someone with a wizard-type Class, and then only when they are in possession of a dungeon core.

Mana: There are fifteen types of mana. Five action types: Create, Destroy, Change, Perceive, Control. Ten verb types: Fire, Water, Air, Earth, Human, Animal, Plant, Mind, Magic and Illusion. A mage combines a verb with an action to derive their desired effect. Sometimes a third type is required.

Example: to change a human into a pig, one would want Change/Human/Animal.

Different ores provide differing amounts of each type of mana. If the core cannot produce enough mana to power a spell of that power, then the mage cannot cast the spell.

Path: Sometimes used to refer to the list of Classes that a person has taken, but it has a more specific meaning. Every Class, when completed, qualifies the holder for at least one other Class of a higher Tier.

Example: Scullion (Tier 1) -> Baker (Tier 2) -> Patissier (Tier 3)

This is a Path. There is no requirement to take the next Class, but those that do not, or who change their Class before completing the existing one, are said to have broken their Path.

Tier: Most things in this world have Tiers: Classes, Monsters, Equipment, Traits and Dungeons. Tier represents a qualitative difference between something with a higher Tier and something with a lower Tier. That difference grows as the Tier increases. People do not have a Tier, but they are considered to be in the Tier of their highest Class.

Spells: Wizards get traits that allow them to cast spells of a certain power level. The type of spell they can cast is determined by the core they possess. They are not limited to set spells but can cast anything they can conceive of, as long as it is within their ability.

About the Author

Christopher Hall, also known as Maxlex, is the author of the Dungeons Just Wanna Have Fun and Phantasm series. Hall started writing his first novel while sailing the Tyrrhenian Sea one summer, the salty night air flavoring and enriching his worldbuilding. Since then, he has continued to hone his craft while holding down diverse jobs in metalworking, marketing, perfume sales, and briefly, modeling. In addition to writing, Hall's interests include illuminated lettering and artisanal brewing. He endeavors to convey a sense of l'esprit in all his creative pursuits.

DISCOVER
STORIES UNBOUND

PodiumAudio.com

Printed in the USA
CPSIA information can be obtained
at www.ICGtesting.com
JSHW022129060524
62644JS00004B/308